I0662364

Other books in this Series by Julia Caesar
(arima Publishing)

THE TAPESTRY OF TTEN

3. ANOTHER SHADE OF MYSTERY

BY JULIA CÆSAR

Published 2011 by arima publishing

www.arimapublishing.com

ISBN 978 1 84549 493 3

© Julia Caesar 2011
Book Jacket design (based on original artwork by Hillz Dunsdon),
Chris Howard of Blondesign.
Blondesign@gmail.com

Printed and bound in the United Kingdom

Typeset in Garamond 11pt

Swirl is an imprint of arima publishing.

arima publishing
ASK House, Northgate Avenue
Bury St Edmunds, Suffolk IP32 6BB
t: (+44) 01284 700321

www.arimapublishing.com

<u>Dedication</u>

In memory of my dear friend,

DAVID GRANGE

who was always to me

"The Sailor with the Navy Blue Eyes"

With thanks for the continued friendship of his wife

ROSEMARIE GRANGE

and their family including

"The Sorrel Hounds", past and present,

"Bella, Donna, Polo, & Sky,

including my own

"Members of the Clan Sorrel"

George & Misty.

Author's Note.
If you want to meet a real live Sorrel Hound, look for a Hungarian Vizsla, but be prepared to lose your heart as I did, thanks to Rosemarie and David.

CONTENTS

Pronunciations

Note: Emphasis or stress should be placed on the underlined syllables. Characters shown **bold** should be hard, e.g. **g** as in **g**o, rather than g as in gesture. Syllables in brackets are soft. e.g. (g) as in gesture. Characters separated by an underline follow the previous syllable with no change of emphasis.

Word	Pronunciation	Description
Ahnell	Are <u>nell</u>	Daro's foster brother
Adruna	A <u>droon</u> a	Sorceress Elect (Amethyst)
Anempor	Ann em <u>paw</u>	Capital of the Azure Sands
Arriera	Arry erra	Daro's birth mother
Ashgenar	<u>Ash</u> **genn** are	Wilderness
Beddick	Bed ic	IIkella's brother
Beneva	<u>Ben</u> evver	Guardian of Knowledge
Buerchan	<u>Booer</u> Chann	Capital of the Amethyst Sands
Caranchar	<u>Caran</u> Char	The Town above the Low Pass
Carolus	<u>Carol</u> us	A wandering Apothecary
Czerezin	<u>Cherra</u> Zin	Clan of the Cynabarr Sands
Colonth	Cuh <u>Lonth</u>	Large town
Cynabarr	Sinna Barr	4th Sand of Pelshar
Dinajh	Dinnar(g)e	Invisible water tracts in the Sands
Diras	<u>Deera</u>ss	Daro's bodyguard
Djellim	Jellim	Library established in Selesh
Dolcan	Doll_kan	Small monkey-like creature
Drecon	Dreckun	Dragon (legendary animal)
Errish	Ehrrish	The Master Builder of Selesh
Feydora	Faydrah	Mysterious Sandsinger from the past
Fronish	Froe Nishe	Small Cavern Healer Hold.
Gresshe	Gresh	Clan of the Malachite Sands
Greenfruit	Green fruit	Grean peaches
Greeeyn	Gree <u>yain</u>	Academic caste, city dwellers
Guaradeign	**G**arra<u>dane</u>	Governor
Hukvah	Huck va	Headdress like an Arab Keffiya
Ikella	<u>Eye</u> kella	Sorceress Ruler of the Opal Sands
Inahana	inner harna	Member of the Council of Nine
Inesh	In <u>Nesh</u>	Second Clan of the Opal Sands
Iscatan	Iz Cat Tan	Ruined Gattarene Temple
Irix	<u>Eye</u> rix	Antelope like creature
Ivinish	<u>Eye</u> vinnish	Beast Master

Jentaroth	Jenn ta roth	Winter Rite of Passage
Jhirelle	Jirrelle	Clan of the Amber Sands
Kora-Mai	Corra My	Clan of the Onyx Sands
Koth	Koth (as in moth)	High Priest of Gatta
Lushens	Blush ens	Mango like fruit
Malos	May loze	Capital of the Malachite Sands
Maraken	Marra ken	Trail stop where the story starts
Mihort	My Hort	Bear like creature addicted to berries
Miokinish	My ock innish	Boy killed at Tearchan
Myst Cat	Mist Cat	Puma sized feline which can disappear
Nahamida	Nuh Hamm idda	Sorceress of the Onyx Sands
Nishanawa	nih SHANN awa	Mysterious sect of the Ashgenar
Nishan	Nishun	Dedicated to the Guardians as warriors
Othervoice	Other voice	Magically empowered voice
Olneth	Oll_neth	Sybillsce Guard Commander
Opalwear	Opal wear	Traditional garb of the Shalhanhi
Patris	Pattriss	Felmin Wagon Master
Pelaquins	Pell ackwins	Pineapple sized cactus fruit
Pretulish	Pr'_Toolish	Small Prickly Melon
Ruanneth	Ruin_arth	Ikella's brother
Sandsinger	Sand Singer	Extinct class of mage
Seobra	See oh bra	Wolverine like animal
Skythe	Sky_th	Flowering herb which promotes fertility
Shadushantesh	Shaddu Shanntesh	Ritual mask of a Sorceress
Shalhanhi	Shallarni	Ruling clan of the Opal Sands
Shenamai	Shenna my	Caverns with strange crystal roof
Shjaratel	Sharra Tell	Ancient city in the crater of Scartel
Shiarjha	She ara	Sorceress Elect of the Opal Sands
Skyrrh	Skirr	Cavern system, Temple of Gatta
Soloria	Soll orya	Late Sorceress of the Amethyst
Suraya	Surr rah yah	Baby Sorceress born empowered
Sybillsce	Sibillsh	Clan of the Amethyst Sands
Tearchan	Tier shann	Hospice at the crossing below Maraken.
Tirjhinar	Tier rinn are	Fabled lost city of the Sandsingers
Tuennis	Tue enniss	Inesh woman Guaradeign of Caranchar
Usticus	Us_tick_us	Daro's pet Dolcan
Vetali	Vitt arly	Trifoliate plant with magical properties
Zeglurs	Zegglures	Donkeylike Pack animal
Zenitheon	Zenith_ee yon	Summer Solstice
Zephryn	Zefrin	Legendary single horned storm horses
Zurias	Zurry ass	Clan of the Azure Sands

Terms of Reference	Definition

Planetary System

Seleus	Solar Body
Pelshar	The world of this series
Jenta	Primary moon
Gatta	Secondary Moon

Special Characteristics of Pelshar

The Source	A universal field of energy which empowers magic users

Sands (In order of precedence)

Opal	Predominately white, iridescent
Azure	Grey blue, shade ranges pale to very dark.
Malachite	Deep green with seams of silver
Cynabarr	Luminescent burnt orange to yellow
Onyx	Dark grey to black
Carnelian	Vibrant red
Tourmaline	Pale translucent green
Amethyst	Translucent shades pale to dark purple

Named Wilderness

The Ashgenar	Rough scrub, mineral deposits & mining spoil

Castes

Greeeyn	City dwelling technologists & artisans
Felmin	Traders, farmers, landsmen
Clansmen	Sand Dwellers, (also known (inaccurately) as Sandsworn)

Time

Sector of the Sand-Glass	15 minutes earth time
Turn of the Sand Glass	Hour
Day	Day
Dawn	Dawn or Breakday

Height of Sun	Noon
Evening	Sunfall
Night	Night
Week	Ninenight (referring to the number of nights)
Journight	Two ninenights
Journey of Jenta	Lunar Month
Rotation	Year

Clans (In order of precedence)	**Location**
Shalhanhi	Opal Sands
Zurias	Azure Sands
Greshe	Malachite Sands
Czerezin	Cynabarr Sands
Kora-Mai	Onyx Sands
Jedrun	Carnelian
Quexoni	Tourmaline
Sybillsce	Amethyst

Minor Clans or Sub Sets

Inesh	Opal Sands
Nishanawa	The Ashgenar
Rangers	Northern Hemisphere

Centre of High Magic	**Location**
Sanctuary	The Heights of Surrandel
Selesh	Mount Torrenesh, Opal Sands

Legendary Locations

Tirjhinar (City of the Sandsingers)	Behind the Cavern of Daro's Birth

Animals	**Nearest Earth Comparison**
Irix	Antelope
Coatan	Goat
Dolcan	Spider Monkey
Zeglur	Donkey
Mihort	Black Bear

Biron	Bison
Sandrigal	Snake
Cuirax	Giant Snow Raven
Dorrowen	Cattle
Mystcat	Puma like feline
Seeobra	Wolverine

Mythical Beasts (Depicted in ancient artwork)

Drecon	Dragon
Zephryn	Single horned Storm horse

Classes of Character

Star-Weavers	Unknown class of Mage mentors for Sandsingers
Sandsingers	Previously legendary Mages of both sexes
Guardians	Tutors of all things Historic, Magical or Mysterious
Sorceress	Magically empowered Female Rulers of the Nine Sands
Healers	Women who can use the Source to heal
Apothecary	Pharmacist, herbalist. Practitioner of practical medicine
Guaradeign	Town or regional Governor
Servitors	Domestic Servants
Drudges	Menials

Guild Occupations

Blacksmith	Highest Rank Master Smith
Builders	Highest Rank Master Builder
Brewers	Highest Rank Brew-Master
Carpenters	Master Wood-Smith
Dyers	Highest Rank Master Dyer
Glassmakers	Highest Rank Master Glass-Smith
Tanner	Master Skinner
Wagoneer	Highest Rank Wagon Master
Weaver	Highest Rank Master Weaver

The Opal Sands South. © Peter Jenn 2010

Legend:

- – – - Trade route
C - Caranchar
M - Maraken
Q - Quinnox
O - Omnel
S - Selesh
Sm - Selesh Minora
T - Tsarchan
? - Tirjhinar
Cs - Cavern of the storm

Map labels: North Opal, Mount Toranesh, Great Divide, Slingh Divide, Silent Sands, Low Pass, Azure Sands, Sherrol Pass, Amethyst Sands

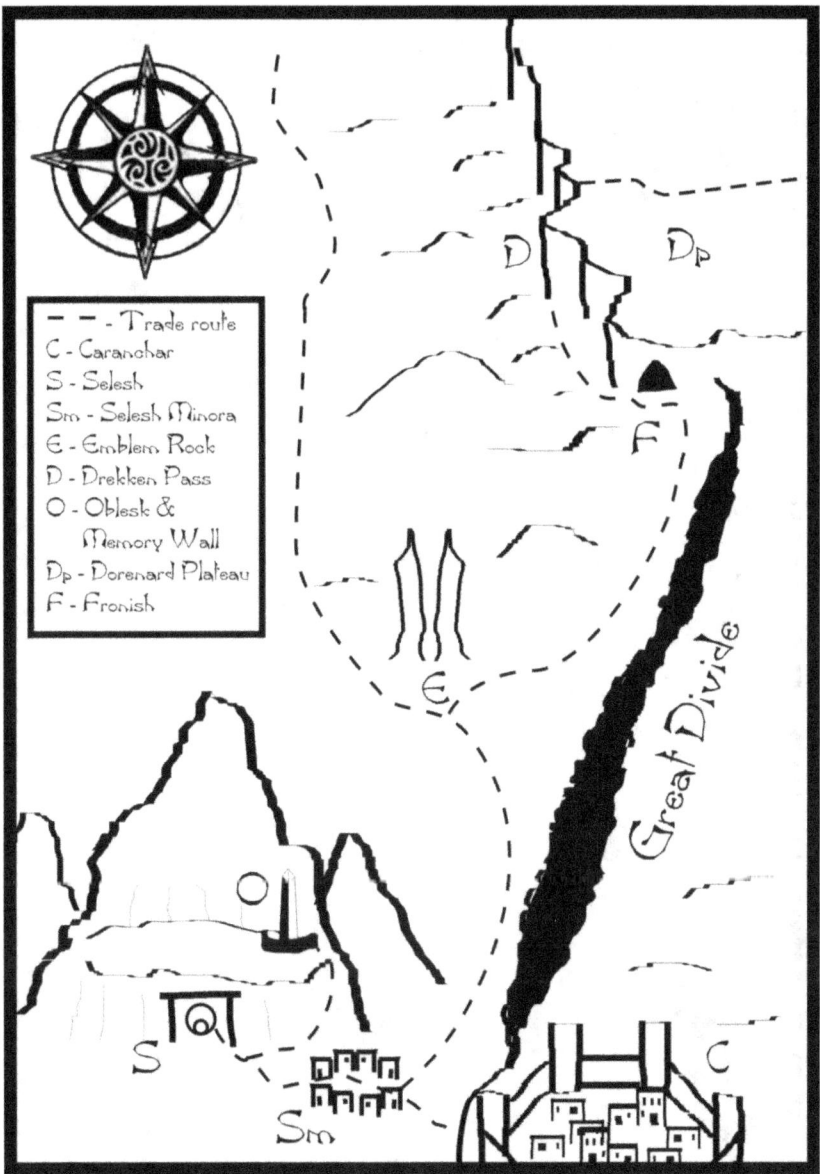

The Opal Sands. (Central Eastern Borderlands) © Peter Jenn 2010

The Azure Sands North © Peter Jenn & L. J. Caesar 2011

Along its Northern border the grey blue Azure Sands are dominated by the rugged highlands of the Drekken Heights. This inhospitable range is home to isolated pockets of Felmin settlers who farm the valleys and lower slopes of the Drekkens. Dense low thorny scrub and unpredictable terrain forms an impenetrable wilderness to the north-east beyond the Temple of the Winds. Historically, the Dorenard Trail provided access to the Opal Sands, via the Dorenard Plateau, but this pass (unused in Rotations by anything other than foot traffic), has fallen into disrepair. Only the trail east from Cathlea to the small settlement built in the extinct volcano of Scartel is regularly travelled by traders brave (or foolish) enough to ignore the legends surrounding the mysterious city, whose ruins cover the crater floor. With dangerous Sinking Sands and terrain too hostile to cross on foot, the northern areas of the Azure have remained largely untouched, except for the rebuilding of a new capital at Darnesh, where a catacomb strangely like Selesh has been discovered.

Key to Map opposite.

A - Ashgenar
TW - Temple of the Winds
S - Scartel
DP - Dorenard Plateau
Do - Dovodan
SG - Sholtan's Gap
An - Anempor
Sh - Shorronal
F - Fronish
Ca - Cathlea
J - Jerritol
C - Caranchar
D - Darnesh
⌨ - Trail Stops
– – – - Trade Routes
············· - Jalni & Darro's Route

PART 1 - TEST OF TALENTS

Prologue

Written in the twentieth Rotation following Partition, by the hand of Carolus - long unpractised in this art.

"Not being in the Opal Sands at the time, I have collected the reminiscences, rumours and reports of those who were. Yet, even from such cobbled and patched writings, I perceive the beginning of understanding, if not of my own place in the weave of time, that of another's. However, I beg my readers indulgence, for I must attempt to convey events I did not see and emotions I did not feel as I tell this tale."

If events could herald a Second Age of Mystery, those that took place at Selesh, during the First Rite of Spring this Rotation, would certainly qualify. Born in a Storm so apocalyptic as to defy description[1], Daro (an orphan adopted by our Sorceress), has eventually been exiled (in his seventeenth Rotation of life), for reasons I cannot divulge here[2].

In the three Rotations since, an uneasy peace descended on the Healer Hall and the School of Sorcery, for nothing was so provoking as Daro's presence. However, on the night of his return, (in my own absence), another Storm struck at the heart of our Sands, threatening Selesh, where everyone sheltered behind barred gates, hiding from the force of nature that was my Songchild in all his anger.

It seems that determined to understand the High Magic of the past, Daro has fallen headlong into the trap from which mortal man has been protected, by obedience to the Way and to the rule of the Guardians. Now, he has unleashed the power, there is no other like the boy whose life entwines inextricably with mine. I am told on the night of his return, the rocks of the desert rang. In the cities of the Greeeyn, men spoke fearfully, as their women found the quiet depths of the city shelters and built defences for their children. In the Fringe settlements, Felmin traders, farmers and builders, huddled into cellars, or underground caverns.

Even the heights of the Central Plateau seemed to draw in, as dim echoes of a forgotten Age, raged across the Opal Sands towards our settlement. The Healers, the Sorceress and the Guardians all tell me that they felt a change in the magical field from which they derive their power. As "The Source" blossomed from gentle flow to raging torrent, a witness travelling our borders, saw a dim glow, as if the memory of the lost city of the Sandsingers was sketched on the horizon, where it once stood.

Tirjhinar, created a thousand Rotations ago, by mages using the magical power of their *othervoice*, has been a closed subject even in the Mother House of Sorcery. Now, in a society which barely survived the Storm in which he was

---

[1] See Dawn of Darkness © Julia Cæsar 2010
[2] See Curse of Night © Julia Cæsar 2010

born, Daro has returned to confound conventional wisdom and set the House of Sorcery on its ears.

Witnesses report a man running, fire in his eyes, whirlwinds at his heels, lightening at his fingertips. Frightened inhabitants fled to hide, even Mount Torrenesh shrank from this vision, or so the outposts report and still he ran on.

A growl of thunder greeted him as he came to the Gate in the Rock, finding it locked and barred against him, then he was surrounded by an eerie flickering light. A silvery blue sheen masked his features and as if irritated beyond control, he raised a hand and struck out angrily. My witness tells me that his hand only encountered air, for in some despair, he had turned away from the Gate, but out of his hand came a ball of lightening. It streamed, hissing from his hand in a terrifying arc of power, roaring toward the Gate, where momentarily, the incandescence lit up the smouldering fury etched on Daro's face. I have no doubt that it was my Songchild and no other that committed the unthinkable, for from his hand, a lightening bolt struck and with an awesome groan the iron clad Gate, leapt in its housing, toppled and fell, to a thunderous roar which rang round the Gathering Square below.

As my witness fled to raise the alarm, Daro strode forward, lightening flickering in his eyes.

Approaching the doors to the Healer Hall in a trance, he apparently stopped outside, ear pressed against the door, listening for a familiar voice. Even as my witness gathered her Command and disposed them to protect those within, Daro lifted his head and smiled, a smile born of some intent other than joy. I am told that he felt for the metal hasps of the doors, pausing only a fraction, before crying out:

"Ikella, come forth Sorceress! I am returned. Now let us see who really wields the power in Selesh?".

Nothing other was said, nothing other was done to forewarn those who watched from the shadows. He simply tapped the door with his fingertips, once, twice and...

Chapter 1 - Sun Song

Inside the Hall, everyone paled as the massive Torrenwood doors groaned. Guards eyed the huge black metal crossbars apprehensively, as they jumped uneasily in their brackets. Outside these doors, long ago, the cavern roof had fallen, leaving the Gathering Square, a courtyard open to the skies, but the winds had never prowled so ominously before. Now they rattled the doors, keening and moaning like lost souls in torment.

In banked ceremonial seats, Clan and Guild leaders shifted fretfully, for according to tradition, this night's weather, predicted that of the following Rotation.

The villagers of Selesh Minoria, greeted the Novice Healers with reassuring whispers, as they took their seats, noting how some glanced around to locate visiting parents while others held hands anxiously. As the violence outside increased, the sight of Guild members stoically ignoring the turmoil calmed the congregation, although visiting Clansmen wondered if they would still have homes to return to as the elements screamed. Many here, still remembered another Storm and trembled.

Then, in stark contrast to the chaos outside, the Council of Healers stood, ceremonial robes shimmering in the shades of their homesands. Serenely processing to fill the Sacred Circle shoulder-to-shoulder, they radiated calm control behind those who protected their Holy Book of Rule. Shiarjha, Guardian Designate of Power and Ikella, Guardian of the Way, waiting for the first sign of Spring as the Storm raged.

As lightening struck nearby, the incandescence lit up shocked faces. The cavernous Hall shuddered, dust motes danced and a peal of thunder broke overhead, then, into a sullen suspension of sound, Ikella stepped forward.

Sandals slapping softly, she walked down into the Way of Challenge. Her Staff gleamed palely, her aura a pulsation of Opal. Pausing to allow the winds to die away, she, (along with her visibly frightened guests) felt the Hall shudder. There was a soft sigh, then a screeching, grinding crash and an ashen faced woman dropped at Ikella's feet, struggling to verbalise a concept too great to grasp.

"The Gate, my Deshun! The Gate in the Rock has gone!".

Jashell's voice, so used to being raised to a bellow, dropped to a fractured whisper, as an ominous vibration shook the mighty doors behind her. With a terse nod, Ikella set a well rehearsed plan into action. Bracing herself, Staff planted firmly in a Sand bearing channel set in the tiled floor, she drew power from the Sands of her Rule, as she stood at bay. The Opal Staff blazed, her aura cracked and sparkled as an eerie silence dropped over the terrified community. A low confused muttering sound began outside. Then two mighty blows shook the doors. A phalanx of guards knelt, spears braced as despite their mass, the third blow splintered the doors apart. To a triumphant shriek from the wind and a low growl of thunder, a young man came stumbling through the entrance.

The gathering gasped, holding on to each other, fearfully peering from behind a screen of standing Healers. Several Chapters of Guardswomen poured past the Sorceress, encircling the intruder at spear point, whilst others secured the doors again. Then the Sorceress spoke, icy outrage evident in her voice:

"Daro? However you came here in such a state, I command you to withdraw immediately!".

Heads raised to catch a glimpse of the stranger, then a low buzz of speculation ran through the mass, (none of which escaped the enhanced hearing of Daro's mother).

Where had the slender boy they remembered gone, they asked each other, as Ikella thought wearily, "Indeed, it takes a mother's eye to see the delicate limbs of his youth in this broad shouldered man.".

Ikella's eyes narrowed as she examined her prisoner closely. Dressed defiantly in the ragged remnants of Clan Colours, he knelt under Jashell's spear without a trace of submission in his body. Hair long and unkempt, framed a face that drew the eye and stopped the breath of more than one woman. In the last four Rotations he had achieved a potent masculinity that even a Sorceress could recognise, embodied in scowl, lowered eyelids, even the lustrous sweep of eyelashes, that hid his eyes. Gazing thoughtfully at his finely moulded mouth, the stubborn tilt of his chin and the shadow of unshaven stubble, she winced, recognizing trouble when she saw it. Her command was brusque.

"Stand up!".

He gleamed with sweat, yet his eyelids remained obstinately closed, as if against the low lighting traditional to this evening's ritual. With the instinct of a born Healer, Ikella recognised pain, but ignored it, as staggering, he regained his feet.

Fenced in by the Inesh, he stood, face averted, as she began to speak.

"So. You dare to bring your disgrace before the people! Were my instructions not clear, or do you choose to defy me? Where is Ahnell? I sent you forth together, telling you to return together, or not at all. Yet you return alone, and in public. Am I to suppose you not only failed me, but that you failed each other? Abandoned him to the storm did you?".

The warriors supporting him felt a ripple of reaction, but allowed him to stretch to his full six spans in height and face her. He was bathed in a soft light, which glimmered on his skin and haloed his hair, as he spoke in a low voice shaking with fury.

"I left Ahnell app Minidrahl lying with his love amongst the ranks of the Honoured Dead. We neither failed this Clan, nor each other. Because of his faith in me, because he believed what you would not, I live to return and testify. To his faith, to his courage, to his devotion to the duty you imposed on him.".

A low chorus of grief was wrung from the congregation, as Daro's voice lashed out remorselessly.

"My friend gave up his life in obedience to your command. I left my milk brother, my soul and quite possibly, my sanity in Tirjhinar. I only return (as I promised him), to tell those he loved, what we found. That included you, Mother!".

He spat out the last word, as though it was a curse, then continued, his voice soft, yet carrying.

"Because of your pride in your power, you placed a terrible burden on us. Because you could not, would not listen, you condemned him to death and me to a fate far worse. You accuse me of obsession, but I bring you the proof you say does not exist. I didn't abandon Ahnell to the Storm Mother! I **am** the Storm!".

Wearily, Ikella faced him in silent contemplation and came to a decision. Her aura flared into life, her Staff blazing in her hand, as she spoke evenly:

"Whatever stands between us, I truly sorrow for the loss of Ahnell. I excuse you his absence. Wherever you left him will be a place blessed by his sacrifice, his care for you. However, Tirjhinar is but a myth, those you seek are but legends Daro. Your obsession does your friend no honour and you try my patience sorely. I will accept your apology when you have recovered your wits. Now, get out of my presence before I forget you are my child. Clean yourself up and wait in my quarters.".

As her personal Guards surrounded him, she saw the rebellion in his body and spoke, her voice laced with sweet sarcasm, as if to a recalcitrant child:

"Oh, if you encounter a Sandsinger on the way, for the sake of the One, get them to do something useful! Like singing back the Sun, so we can grow food and travel safely.".

Daro drew himself up silently and at a touch from Indeera and Jashell prepared to leave with dignity, turning on his heel, to be swiftly escorted from the Hall.

Similarly, Ikella, resumed her place in the Sacred Circle, calling her bemused congregation to prayer, as the winds dropped. Obediently the faithful bowed their heads and had hardly done so, when a deep sonorous groan came from the cavern walls and startled people sat up fearfully. As the Hall trembled, a novice cried out.

"Look! Look up!".

Some seven hundred pairs of eyes, peered up into the dim recess of a vaulted roof, where midway along a semicircular gallery, there was a shield shaped rock. This had always been vaguely associated with the Smith's Guild, originally founded in Selesh and no-one had given it more than a passing thought, for the immense tongue of stone was beyond reach, eighty spans or more above the Sacred Circle.

Now it was moving. Pivoting, to the accompaniment of the low creaking groan of an affronted mechanism and the frightened cries of those below. Slowly, it tilted, jutting up into the vault, at an angle, until its pinnacle was suspended directly above the Book of Rule.

Stunned, they watched glows in the vast vault light themselves. Piercings which had never been noticed sprang into life, pouring brilliant light onto the pivoting rock, illuminating a hip high rail that ran around the tip, as it stopped moving and locked into place.

Power was building. Even the general population could feel it flickering on their skins. It crackled around them, flushing the walls with colours ranging from pale bronze through blues, greens, lilacs, into delicately pulsating creams. Dazzled, they didn't know where to look next, until Daro walked straight out to the pinnacle, clad in the glow of magic. Without a pause, without a single glance, streaming power from the beating heart of Selesh, the Opal Sandsinger raised his *othervoice* and sang.

That voice brought them to their knees. From all the outer parts of the complex, others came running, as if summoned. The aisles filled with cooks and drudges, sleepy children, guards and patients, who abandoned their stations to hear that pure tenor voice. He stood, apparently oblivious of their awed presence and sang as no man in a thousand Rotations had sung on Pelshar and somehow, in that melody, the long absence of High Magic, was explained, the wounds repaired and Selesh blazed its love for the Opal Sandsinger.

The notes poured like a cadence of liquid gold and the colours on the walls danced and flickered, shifted and flared, as head thrown back, eyes closed, he contrived to cause such a disturbance in the Source that the walls rang, an accompaniment entwining with his Song.

Later, someone remembered the light shining at the doorway, the dim lights in the roof dazzling in their intensity. Time itself obeyed his will, as hanging in thrall to his spell-song, every Guardian, Sorceress, Healer or novice sang as they never had before. Everyone of them contributing their own essence to the torrent of power that rose in dizzying waves from the Hall at the heart of Selesh, spreading outwards in a healing wave to the desert and its affronted skies. His *othervoice* swept and soared, shimmered before them as though tangible and throughout it all, the people raised their faces to the Sandsinger, as if to their long hidden Sun, until, a deafening peal of thunder rang out inside the Hall itself. Dust motes swirled sparkling in a beam of light and then as the colours in the walls faded, Ikella slowly, with deliberate ceremony, knelt.

Her voice was unwavering, her capitulation complete, as she made obeisance to him saying:

"Welcome Ichspeller. Sandsinger of the Opal Sands. With abject apologies, I welcome you home.".

There was a thunderous roar of approval from the floor of the Hall. All eyes turned to the solitary figure poised above them, as without a sound, the Sandsinger collapsed.

Chapter 2 - Sunrise at Selesh

The Sandsinger sprawled unconscious of the furore below, as Spring Rites abandoned, the congregation was dismissed under a vow of silence. While would-be rescuers gathered, unable to approach his precarious position directly, a Healer climbed to a level from which she could relay visual observations.

There was (she said), an unusual glow around the tongue of rock. A whisper ran through those near the Sorceress, who raised a hand, commanding sharply,

"No power! That platform is warded. We could do more harm than good.".
Turning to Patris, she murmured wistfully,

"If only Carolus, Olneth or Somner were here. Ivinish ran for ropes.",

Patris said thoughtfully, "Yes, Rowbet took our hounds to help Jashell find that gallery. Would that be warded too?", and Ikella stared at him mutely, her throat closed on the memory of that last dreadful confrontation, she whispered painfully:

"I don't know. We know nothing of Sandsingers, save that they are as far removed in power from Sorcery, as a Sorceress is from you. I can't even engage my power to protect him for fear of dislodging him.", she was wringing her hands helplessly.

The large trader listened gravely, his hands clasped around his workbelt and then he said softly:

"None shall ever know that from me, but I understand your caution.".

He tilted his head, silently surveying the situation, until a half Chapter of Guards appeared, carrying the precious ropes, Diras in the lead. Saluting, she spoke softly:

"Master Ivinish is behind us. We have everything we need, including experienced climbers. We can use a sling to lower him. Please Lady? It must be eighty spans to where he lies! Were he to fall...", she gulped and Ikella paled at the unspoken thought.

"Clear the Hall,", she ordered. Then in a low murmured aside to Patris, "I would preserve the dignity of his rank at least, though what has left him thus I cannot imagine".

Patris nodded in agreement, then visibly brightened as the Commander of the Day Watch appeared,

"Ah, here comes Sorrill bearing news. Good news I think.".

The warrior walked briskly towards them, acknowledging Ikella and her companions as she approached, her hands flickering coded enquiries to Diras, already organising the rescue party. She saluted Ikella, saying huskily:

"Lady, I believe I know why our Sandsinger collapsed. Will you go into the Square to see for yourself?".

Her voice was so strangely modulated, that Ikella glanced at her sharply and saw that Sorrill had lowered the secondary membranes that protected the eyes of all Sand dwellers from the Sands. From...the Sun?".

Even framing that question left the Sorceress reeling, unaccountably light-headed. Numbly, she cast an agonised glance into the vaulted roof where Diras climbed towards the son of her heart and exclaimed, (as mothers do):

"O Daro! What have you done you dreadful boy!", then more softly, "Forgive me, I didn't know it was possible!". She wavered, struggling to contain her emotions.

Sorrill stood her ground, saying gruffly to Patris:

"I will keep the watch here, until my child rescues hers.".

She turned to watch Diras rope herself to the gallery, before adding firmly,

"Go with her Master Songfather! Reassure her, but keep her away until I send word that her boy is safe.".

That Patris never questioned how he was to achieve such a thing, stood him high in Sorrill's approbation for Rotations. He simply gathered the faltering Sorceress on one arm and led her into the blessed light of Seleus, reminding her (just in time), to protect her eyes, shading his own with his hat, as he took her out to the people.

It seemed to the Sorceress that all Selesh had crowded into the Gathering Square. For all born in the last twenty Rotations, this brilliant light was a new experience, this surge of heat was a miracle. The sullen roil of cloud had gone and anxiously she pivoted, glad to see Healers passing among the crowd, reminding them to shade their eyes and skins. Slowly, she made her way to the dais under the Summoning Bell and joined Indeera, Second in Command of the Inner Guard and reached up to the Bell, imposing silence before she spoke.

"Upon this House, its Schools, Guilds and communities, upon the Clan Shalhanhi and all in its Gather and upon the Clan Inesh and all obedient to the Way, I have placed a solemn vow of silence regarding the events of this night.". A rueful smile touched her mouth, as she commented gently. "It seems that our Sandsinger has other ideas.", and she raised her face to the sun, but held up her hand as a shocked congregation finally saw the joke.

"However until we have established the health and well-being of our Sandsinger, it is not necessary to announce the means by which this happened. For now, he is exhausted and will require time to recover.".

She looked at the bright expectant faces and said fiercely:

"We must protect him. I don't know what price he paid to meet my foolish demands, but Mothers sometimes expect too much of their children.".

There, it was said, she had admitted her fault and thrown herself on the mercy of the Clan, she closed her eyes and prayed, opening them at a light touch from Sorrill, who had come to fetch her back. Around her, the entire Gathering knelt, in the traditional pose of supplicants and she relaxed, letting Indeera touch the Bell, announcing her departure and withdrew to the Hall.

Amidst shouted instructions and the earnest exhortations of the Infirmarian, Daro had been secured, then lowered in one of Ivinish's cattle slings. Patris, recognizing the bass rumble of the Herd Master's voice maintained a serene expression, although amusement quivered at the corners of his mouth as he recalled the indignant bellowing of the last herdling that had been snatched to safety in it. He rather suspected that the current incumbent would have been as vociferous, had he been awake or aware of his undignified descent from Pivot Rock. However, he watched as Ikella forced herself to say personal thanks to the rescuers before turning to supervise the Sandsinger's removal on a litter.

As limp and unresisting, he was tenderly covered with the Guard's own cloak, Ikella lifted an eyebrow enquiringly, to which Diras responded fiercely:

"From a babe, I carried him to ceremonies wrapped in my cloak, to keep him warm and steel his nerve. We made him a cut down version, admitted him as a member of our Chapter and he marched with us, wearing his uniform with pride, as did Ahnell ap Minidrahl of blessed memory. Can I not carry one of my Chapter to the Healers, wrapped in my cloak? Especially if it be for the last time Lady?".

Suddenly Ikella saw how it was. The Inesh had known more about her child than she had. They had understood his sudden tearful silences, seen how overawed he was by the high ceremony of her ritual life and had boosted his courage with little acts of kindness. She saw in her mind's eye, two bored little boys, parading to the shouted instructions of their Commanders and with a strangely submissive gesture, she permitted the intimacy, a cloak, gently draped and tucked in around his bare feet.

Six of the Chapter lifted the litter and he was borne away. Diras in the lead, Sorrill behind. The remainder forming a rearguard, ready to die in her son's service. Out of her gaze they bore him, into the Inner Sanctum of the Healers and beyond the main Infirmary, into a suite of rooms reserved for her own use.

Thoughtfully, returning to the doors, she stood gazing rapturously at the waking sky. People thronged the Square, drunk with wonder, but the cause of all their joy, lay in a black void between life and death, only a hairsbreadth between the two conditions. She wandered in a dream towards his sickroom, passing many who she should have acknowledged, deep in thought.

"How could I have known?", she asked herself, hearing the reply in the voice of her absent Apothecary.

"How could you not have known?", he demanded sternly, as she sat rocking in the old nursing chair that had mysteriously appeared beside Daro's bed. Considering the many small incidents that had peppered Daro's life, she was forced to admit, that her position had left her singularly unprepared for motherhood of any kind. However harsh this self-examination was, one truth stood. She had been too afraid to try and understand. Too jealous of her own position to probe so many mysteries. Was this why she had feared the word "Sandsinger" so instinctively? Would this change her love for him? Steadily as the day wore on, she watched him with a mixture of awe and pity, for if she thought her own position lonely, how much worse was his? Deep in thought she barely noticed the door quietly opening, until Mina entered, followed by their only fourth Rotation novice, prepared to begin treatment.

"My Deshun.", Her Senior Healer acknowledged her, standing aside, observing the girl as she placed a tray laden with salves and bandages on a low table opposite the Sorceress.

Ikella was surprised to see Jalni accompanying her foster-mother, for the novice was in disgrace and needed strict supervision. However, considering the nature of her own relationship with a fosterling, she made no comment, turning back, to look at Daro as she thought of him. She froze, for his eyes were, at long last open. Eyes like none she had seen in her unnaturally extended life.

Where they had blazed turquoise shot with gold, now an incredible change had occurred. There was a swirl of fire opal in the dark depths. A shimmer of gold-rose, turquoise, flickers of flame, drew her spinning senses down, down into the cold bitterness of his total exclusion from love, life, or the company of friends. She broke free with an inarticulate moan that drew the attention of both Mina and Jalni.

Mina, averting her own gaze, bent over the bed.

"Can you hear me?", the Healer questioned gently, but although his lips moved, he was far from conscious. As his eyes closed again, both Sorceress and Healer returned to their seats, while Jalni trotted backwards and forwards to the small preparation scullery, creating a palette of treatments for the cuts, weals and bruises that they had found on their patient's feet.

Ikella examined the medication tray cautiously questioning as the girl named each preparation, subconsciously comparing what she knew about this girl, with the undoubted talent that she was exhibiting .

"This my Deshun.", said the immaculately polite voice, "is bloodbane.", The spatula indicated a greenish compound and Ikella bent to sniff the air above it. "We Zurians, were once a warlike people and we found that even large wounds packed with this compound dry, didn't fester. Though my mother told me that the resulting scars were an unusual colour. Now we use the powdered root to make a salve, which seems to counter blood poisoning from infected wounds and I thought to use that on the soles of his feet.", She indicated a particularly large injury on Daro's heel and Mina winced, more in alarm at Jalni's temerity, than at the sight of the wound. Ikella smiled and said softly,

"Ah yes. Viness would have known about treating wounds. How would you tackle dressing this then.?"

The novice didn't hesitate.

"Wash with tincture of woundwort for cleaning, dress the wound and keep the patient in bed!", she eyed the recumbent figure curiously and unaware of the sensation she was about to cause, asked curiously:

"Who is that? Whatever happened to him?", and Mina's jaw dropped in surprise.

"Jalni!", she exclaimed in mortified tones,. "Wherever have you been since Sunfall last? I know everything is on its head right now, but for the sake of the One girl! Did you not hear our Sandsinger arrive? Were you not in Hall when he sang?", but it was Ikella who saw the blank incomprehension in the child's eyes, along with the mutinous scowl she directed at her foster-mother.

"No. I am still excluded from Hall by my obligation to the Infirmarian.", the tight, rebellious voice responded. "While everyone else was celebrating, I was freezing in the lower storerooms, searching for more powdered Merishwhen to counter eye pain. My party returned just as Sorrill came looking for a Healer to bathe her daughters hands, so I took them to Andria, but before I could get a drink, you dragged me here.". , There was a hectic flush on her face and Ikella sighed as Mina corrected her fosterling automatically.

"the correct form of address should be either, "Healer", "Mina'", or "Mother", not "you". Do I have to tell you every time we speak?".

Jalni's face was white, her eyes blazed and her lips hardly moved as she hissed:

"Healer Mina! My mother's name (May she rest in the arms of the One), was Viness.", and before Ikella could stop her, the novice strode to the head of the bed, staring down at their patient.

"What's a Sandsinger?", she asked conversationally and lifted his hand in hers.

As they touched, skin to skin, the remaining colour left Jalni's face. Even her lips drained and a sweat stood on her brow. Daro's eyes had opened again and now Ikella realised why she had thought them so strange. There was no white to them. They swam glittering glints of Opal, then Jalni's lips parted and from her mouth Daro's voice pleaded huskily.

"Help me, oh help me home.". Then there was the shaft of a spear, reversed in the hands of an expert as Sorrill threw herself between them, breaking the grip Daro had exerted on the novices hand and Jalni was weeping in Ikella's arms.

"O my Deshun.", she sobbed, "He is so alone, he is so frightened and Lady, forgive me, but he is blind!"

Chapter 3 - Son of Seleus

Supporting the shattered novice, the Healers moved away from the bed, leaving the unconscious man, restlessly seeking human contact. Sorrill withdrew , stepping over Diras, who slept across the threshold, while Ikella helped Mina administer a sedative intended for Daro.

Sinking into the nursery chair, she watched Mina stroking Jalni's hair, thinking cynically,

"Isn't it astonishing how we forget the sins of our children, once they're in trouble?",

She continued her vigil, as Mina tenderly tucked a rug over her truculent fosterling's pallet and came to Ikella's side, saying in a pain filled voice:

"Deshun? He is beyond exhaustion and she is beyond my reach. Is there anything we can do?".

Ikella leant forward, saying gently. "The wounds we seek to heal are not visible. It may be a long slow task. Watch them closely Mina. We must know more before we act.", she sat back in her chair, grumbling under her breath.

"Daro was always secretive and may have felt "different", from the start. However, secrets hold dangers, particularly now.", she shook her head sorrowfully, "He trusted Ahnell implicitly, but I doubt he will ever let anyone else get close to him.".

She sighed.

"It is so frustrating, I would the One took all my powers, in exchange for the knowledge to help him. Just why Beneva took herself into retreat I don't know and if Carolus ever returns, I will pin him by the ears for deserting me, just when I need his practical help!". She lapsed into silence, staring at this stranger who inhabited her son's body and if Mina saw the glitter of tears in her eyes, she made no comment as she continued her observations.

Ikella placed a hand on Daro's throat, feeling the muted beat of his pulse, as he and his power slept. Mina curled up in the Healers chair, nodding drowsily as night fell over Selesh.

At the start of Third Watch, the Sorceress oversaw the changing of Daro's sweat soaked sheets and Hanna appeared to assist in washing him. Afterwards, the Infirmarian silently slathered his feet with a disinfectant, before renewing his bandages. She paused in the middle of binding one foot, to comment quietly:

"He is traumatised by his experiences no doubt, but a normal healthy adult should recover from the minor injuries he displays.". She patted Ikella's shoulder reassuringly, breaking her stern resolve to bear the pain alone. Her voice was harsh, self-accusing, as the words tumbled out.

"Experiences Hanna? Don't you mean twenty Rotations of neglect? All those times he tried to reach out to me and I failed him. Refused to see what others found obvious! When he could bear no more and sought his power, I banished him. I, who once heard a voice call me "Honoured Mother!", she drew breath, adding bleakly, "How honoured I was, still am while he lives, but what if he dies? He has suffered four Rotations Sand walking. The death of his friends and has found power beyond my capacity to imagine…" and the tears flowed, silencing her briefly. Eventually she gathered strength, whispering reluctantly,

"That's not all Hanna. That's not all. My boy, my courageous boy is totally blind and I don't know if, due to my foolish challenge, I bear the blame for that condition."

She sat, quite suddenly looking frail, as old as the legends of her life rumoured her to be and burying her face in her hands, muttered, as if to herself.

"I blame myself! For refusing to recognise that Daro was so much more than an orphan of the Storm. For indulging in stupid prideful challenges, when if I think back, he was "in magic" as he arrived. If we lose him, it will be my fault.".

Hanna, unable to console her, clasped Ikella's upper arm in mute sympathy, leaving the Sorceress brooding over Daro until eventually even her legendary stamina gave way and she slept in the nursing chair beside her son's bed.

When she woke, she stretched and sat forward, disgusted with herself for sleeping, just when Daro needed her. She turned her head to look for Mina, who kept the vigil, watching not only Daro, but her own foster child. Jalni still slept and Ikella was faintly amused to hear gentle snoring coming from the child.

Mina whispered: "Dorra came to find her a while back, but I didn't have the heart to wake her, though I think she stirs now. Shall I send her back to her room?", but Ikella shook her head, whispering,

"There is no point now.", using the infallible internal clock developed by all Healers, to confirm that dawn was but three turns of the sand-glass away. So they sat, quietly keeping watch on their respective foster children and wondered what the new day would bring.

Near the end of Fourth Watch, Jalni woke, aware of Ikella and instantly on the move. Freeing herself from the blankets, she sat up, adjusting her clothing for modesty as she stood. Mutely, looking at the door, her hands requested permission to leave. Ikella's hands danced in reply and Jalni fled. A door closed along the passage and Ikella smiled, thinking sympathetically.

"Poor child. Let her go. This is no ordinary patient. No place for a novice undertaking punishment duties, she has enough problems without frightening her further!".

She rose to her feet stiffly and moving deftly, tidied Daro's bed, until a breeze warned her that the door had opened again. Quietly, Jalni re-entered bearing a tray, with hot stemmis in delicate ceramic bowls. She blushed whispering. "I borrowed these from Hanna. You both need some warmth and refreshment. I thought you wouldn't mind.".

Ikella stared at her pensively, thinking that there were qualities in this odd, awkward girl that had been overlooked. Jalni served them and she found even the scent of the infusion reviving and watched as Mina drank with relish. Jalni moved towards the bed, as Ikella rose to intervene, but the young Healer was observing Daro, fearlessly.

"Can I try something Deshun?", she asked abruptly, "It is only a baby thing, but it might help him settle. He is far too restless.",

She waited while Ikella steeled herself to refuse, until she realised that Daro had ceased to pluck at the blankets as Jalni approached. She set down her drink and drew closer, warning Jalni.

"Don't try power unless he invites it. You know from touching him earlier that he is a troubled soul and I don't want to lose you to his demons!"

Fighting increased tension, Ikella watched Jalni sit by the bed, taking Daro's hand loosely in her own, maintaining just enough contact to gain his confidence, Jalni began to chant. Without engaging *othervoice*, the young Healer coaxed an odd, syncopated rhythm into a low, sweet melody, slowly dripping power into the beat she had established, until Daro relaxed. Ikella listening intently, thought with wry amusement, "Had I tried that, he would have fought me to the death!", and watched a half trained rebel from the Azure Sands, provide what she could not, without a tinge of resentment. Astonished but thankful, the Sorceress saw Daro's other hand moving gently to the rhythm of the chant.

"Whoever would have thought of that?", and instinctively knew, that no-one but this strange awkward novice would have done.

For the rest of that Watch, Jalni sang on, anchoring his attention in the unusual rhythm of the weave. It was so subtle, the pattern repeating endlessly, but the inflection, the persuasion deftly syncopated, so that the rhythm seemed to wax and wane, like the shifting of their twin moons. Just as Ikella wondered if she was seeing some reflection of Daro's own power, quite suddenly, he was awake and very much aware, although incredibly weak.

As the Sorceress felt his emergence from the blessed cocoon of unconsciousness, Jalni felt a sunny cinnamon scented glow emanating from him and just the faintest touch of something beyond. She smiled and continued to sing, reaching delicately for the well of loneliness she had felt earlier, but as his pain and misery were revealed, the breath caught in her throat, as Daro covered it. Astonished, her hand withdrew from his, as she questioned what she had seen. Her voice died away and she moistened her lips, suggesting cautiously,

"As I know less than I should, I beg your indulgence, so that I might report more exactly?".

Ikella nodded and Mina moved to stand next to Jalni, as the novice searched for the words, the diplomacy to express herself accurately.

"I think he is able to raise an inner shield, much as we do before engaging the Source or touching a patient. I don't understand how a man, denied access to power, can do such a thing. but I sense something there, however ineffectual.", totally oblivious to the expressions on the faces of her audience, she added,

"I thought that if he felt alone and in the dark, I should try and lead him outward to meet the spell-song and I remembered how to approach a frightened animal, which is a thing that Master Ivinish does. He always whistles and taps his hands on his legs when he attends his herd, so I thought of tempo as a distraction. When I probed a little deeper, I felt very strange. As if I walked a path, with a deep precipice on one side and a high wall on the other. He is deeply distressed, barely aware of me and I was frightened by his own fear I think.".

Paying no regard to the reception of this long, rambling speech, she took Daro's hand again and returned to her syncopated chant. In that last turn of the sand-glass, Ikella watched, mind racing as dawn drew near.

"Now!", Her Healer knowledge told her. "Now we are at the battleground, for he has to want to live, whatever the difficulties, whatever the distress.".

Absently she engaged her power, immediately aware of Daro's terror. She anchored herself to the Sands, touching her song-beads to do so and saw Jalni's jaw tilt pugnaciously. She simply refused to let a perfectly useful man die without a fight. The novice clasped his hand more firmly allowing Mina to take the other and join their efforts together.

So the remnants of night passed and at dawn came the crisis. With a tremendous sweep of sound the room was filled with the cold pure notes of crystals warming to the sun. Mina and Jalni, wearied through chanting were suddenly repelled, swept away from their patient by a surge of power.

The sound, brought room servants, Healers and novices running to the gallery outside the door, as a startled Sorceress leapt to her feet laughing. They all stared at her, but she couldn't contain it for all of her famous self-discipline. It bubbled in her throat, until she nearly wept with the strain of holding it back and her companions eyed her doubtfully, as she embraced Mina and hugged Jalni.

"Oh, I had forgotten.", The Sorceress cried to the throng at the door. "I forgot that this happens everyday. It is the sound of the desert welcoming the day, as the light of the sun returns.".

Only Jalni saw Daro's hand fumbling for something and acting purely on impulse, she carefully placed him in contact with the wall, feeling as she did so, the instant connection with the Source, the Sands and something beyond.

Only she felt the connection form, as Daro chosen Son of Seleus, opened himself to the Source. Jalni would never have admitted it, not even to herself, but in that moment, she slammed down a barrier between herself and that knowledge.

Unafraid of anything she understood, she ran from something that called to her, coaxing and wheedling, beguiling and bewildering. She would not, couldn't listen, or she would be lost. The door beckoned and without waiting for Ikella to dismiss her, she fled.

Allowing nothing and no-one to penetrate the shield she had erected, she simply put as much distance as she could between herself and the sickroom.

Immune to the curiosity of others, she went first to her dormitory, washed, changed and went out into the Gathering Square to stare at the sky. All about her, knots of people gathered gossiping, warming themselves in the unaccustomed glow of the sun. She listened quietly to the rumours. All of Selesh was humming with the news that Daro was possessed of great power, but Jalni, secure in the knowledge that men couldn't use magic, simply nodded and privately scoffed at the idea.

None of what she heard made sense. "Did nobody know that Daro was blind?". She moved silently amongst the crowd, wondering at the lack of disciplined order. Hearing a tall dark bitter sounding Sybillsce, who had just arrived at the door of the forge, she paused, listening as, lamenting the absence of the Apothecary Carolus, he unpacked a weary Zeglur. He was saying that he had come direct from Malos and appeared to think, that the absence of the old man, added to the tragedy of the three young companions, whom he apparently knew well. She heard the men that gathered about him agree and turned away in disgust. All this talk of Sandsingers confused her. No-one she questioned knew what a Sandsinger was and feeling that it was all too much to take in, she retired into the shadows of the Hall of the Healers.

Here, she listened with amazement to the rumours in the settlement. Daro was responsible for the lowering of Pivot Rock.

"Whatever a Pivot Rock is!", said the young Healer to herself testily, but apparently he had done that in front of everyone who had attended First Rite of Spring.

"To which I was not invited!", said Jalni to herself grouchily concluding that she had preferred to stay searching the undercroft for the remedies that Hanna needed. That should have produced some credits to her account, but it seemed that the events in Hall, had quite systematically removed all interest in her exploits and refocused the attention of the populace on Daro.

"Its not fair!", wailed the novice to herself. "I was being so good, so helpful and no-body noticed. I hope his ears blister in this sun!".

She left the Gathering Square, happy to seek the shade in the Great Hall. Grumbling to herself,

she went and looked at the vault above the Sacred Circle and stood, frozen to the place in shock, just staring at the huge platform.

"That's just ridiculous.", Said the novice to herself. "No man alive could do anything with that rock alone!".

She stood in the Way of Challenge, arms folded, head on one side looking up at the great pinnacle, teetering at an angle, protruding from the wall, dominating the Sacred Circle.

"Stupid!", muttered the girl aggressively, under her breath. "Stupid, stupid lot! Don't know why I even bother to listen to any of them. These Sands are mad and their Sandsworn, including their Sorceress are even madder. I can't wait to get out of here!", and then she sighed, for she had not been there to see it.

One of the workmen, currently tidying away extra seating, approached her, bowing respectfully.

"Were you here Mistress, When the Sandsinger sang?", he asked her hesitantly.

Jalni shook her head, suddenly and inexplicably saddened that she had not been

part of the event.

He was plainly bursting to tell her what he had seen, but Jalni barely listened, busy

with her own thoughts. Abruptly her attention refocused, as she heard him say something, so astonishing that she could hardly believe what she heard.

"That's when he sang back the sun! I know it for I saw it happen Mistress. After twenty Rotations of this cloud, that lad brought Seleus back, clear and shining, that is how great his power is Mistress."!

He seemed to gulp on the words as he turned away and Jalni saw the depths of the emotion that gripped him and not sure whether to laugh at the man's gullibility, or cry because she had not witnessed it herself, the novice retraced her steps and went wearily to her bed and dreamt of a warm hand and Opal eyes.

She kept to herself for the next day or two, thinking about her life to date and wondering

what her part was in all of this, for she had a feeling she was already caught up in events beyond her control. In the sickroom, Daro continued to sleep for much of the day, but gradually it became obvious that he would survive. Ikella began to determine how to rehabilitate him before revealing his presence and Mina considered the question of Jalni, whose future as a Healer hung very much in the balance while she refused to conform.

Chapter 4 - Another Shade of Mystery.

Mina watched the sleeping Sandsinger. Used to long hours of observation, she used the time to consider her own fosterling's intervention in Daro's case, privately wondering if he would survive Jalni's disruptive influence. Smiling to herself, the Senior Healer's mind went back to the day Ikella had taken Jalni in.

The child (then known as Jalani del Orto), had arrived alone and in haste, flinging herself at Ikella's feet, as she left the Hall of Healers. Simple compassion stopped Ikella in her tracks, but as others ran to help, it was the untamed power driven by terror that caught her attention and before Height of Sun, the Sorceress began to investigate her distraught supplicant.

Identifiable by tattoo's, dress and hair as a child of the Azure. Jalani finally sobbed her story out, as Ikella, grim faced with outrage, listened. Then, leaving the child to sleep, she went to the Council Chamber and summoned the full Session of Elders, to consider her case.

Silenced by the expression on Ikella's face, they sat, as she cut across the usual chatter, with a question aimed at Dorra, Novice Mistress of the Guild School.

"Have we any foster spaces?", she demanded seriously.

"I need a home and long term stability for the daughter of Viness and Rowin del Orto!"

If she had thrown a bucket of iced water on the Elders, it could scarcely have had more effect and into a shocked silence, the Sorceress continued in a voice that held both ice and fire in its depths.

"I have trebled the Guard, even turned out the Night Watch to gather in Selesh Minoria, for at some time during this consultation, I expect visitors. One of which I shall personally welcome, for he has questions to answer!", and a ripple of static touched her hair and the Elders shivered at the promise in that "dangerous" voice.

Mina spoke abruptly.

"I beg your pardon Deshun, surely that child and her father died Rotations ago? I remember hearing that Viness herself died of grief not long afterwards.", she glanced up, paled before the fury glittering in Ikella's eyes and subsided. An oppressive silence fell, beyond which the steady tramp of patrolling guards could be heard in the corridor beyond. Finally the Sorceress roused from contemplation and said:

"You will forgive me if I depart from the usual pattern of these discussions. I will reveal the facts before I call Jalani to testify.".

There was a stir around the table, until Ikella held up a silencing hand.

"I took the memories and dreaming images of the child to show you the story. (The One defend all children from such memories!)". Her voice dropped, as though she could hardly believe what she was saying.

"I have not yet heard all of it, but I used my scrying skills to read her Source beads. She is in truth Viness and Rowin's child. Her Grandparents have conspired to report her dead, attempted to steal her inheritance and hunted her, in order to silence any complaint.".

Ikella's brows drew together and her eyes flashed brilliantly as she continued.

"Only the need to survive Winter drove her here. All she asks is somewhere to sleep out of the cold, but I felt power in her and won't surrender her to more abuse.".

The Elders gathered closer, as Ikella went on slowly.

"Rowin wove the material for our uniforms, while Viness underwent fertility treatment with Sanra, conceiving Jalani as a result. Despite the fact that we could never repeat that treatment, Rowin tithed every Rotation, in thanksgiving for the help we provided that once. Knowing that there was no obligation, he used his goods and money to provide for others, saying that he just wanted to share his joy.".

The Sorceress's hands sketched a vision of a man, devoted to wife and baby daughter, whose only thought was to help others, but as that image collapsed, another grimmer one formed in its place, full of horrific significance. The Elders blenched, watching the tragedy unfold as Ikella's inexorable voice continued.

"On the face of it, Rowin's death was one of those stupid, fair day accidents that I have worked so long to eradicate. A hurly-burly of marketeers, stalls, carts and beasts. However, there seems to be more to it than the child knows, but maybe that's just my nasty suspicious mind!".

The hanging images reflected her words and the Elders grew visibly older as they watched the young mother, father and child on the wall-side of a parked cart. The tired beasts fretting in the shafts, a drunken driver snoring unaware of an unattended oven. Then, the inevitable result.

Around the table the tension grew and the image changed relentlessly until the story was told, in the Sorceresses grave voice.

"However!", Her voice bristled with anger as she declared, "Serba and Sowdin lied about the accident, declaring the child dead as well. Sowdin del Orto has even claimed her sand-rights, contested Rowin's rights to the Weaver's Halt, and launched a vicious campaign against his daughter by marriage, which I have no doubt contributed to her death.".

The circle of bleak faces mirrored her mood as she stood, pacing as she spoke.

"The child tells me that they took over, keeping mother and child prisoner. When Viness pointed out that she, not they, owned the trade rooms, they persuaded the Headwoman to pronounce her incompetent through injury. That much I managed to verify before I called you here.".

Her voice trailed away momentarily, as she rubbed her back, resuming her seat and folding her legs under her. Mina knew the signs, they were in for a long discussion and she rose discreetly dispatching a guard to fetch drinks, as Ikella lapsed into a brooding silence. Eventually, the Sorceress sighed, roused herself and the session resumed as she remarked darkly, "It gets worse!".

"There was no help for the crippled widow. They took over her living quarters, confining her and her child to one store room, with nothing other than discarded furniture, leaving the child to sleep on the floor. Sowdin restricted their movements to an outside necessary and sight of her husbands grave. Food was minimal, comforts were none.".

Failing to keep the anger out of her voice she remarked, "They tried to force Viness to return to the dyeing rooms to work for food, but she was far too ill.".

She stood abruptly, thumping her Staff on the floor to emphasise her words.

"Sowdin returned to Jerritol after a long and problematic period of service in the South Azure. His excesses there were noted, but have not recurred since. He is known to have a rapacious character, admitting to no rights but his own. If he seeks to steal that child's inheritance, she is in danger of her life, as she very obviously fears.".

The Sorceress continued to pace the Council Chamber as she mused over what the child had told her about her mother.

"Viness was interested in dyeing cloth, discovering a method of dyeing which allows several shades to appear in the same material. Her daughter believes that Sowdin will go to any length to steal the secret that her mother died to protect, so she smuggled a piece of cloth out to show me. I feel certain that there is something in that theory, but there may be more. Much more.".

Like the traditional Jentaroth conjurer, she produced a small bolt of material, saying softly.

"Don't ask me how to dye like this, for I don't know. I only wish that the knowledge hadn't gone to the Sands with Viness. However, I wonder if Sowdin seeks possession of that knowledge and this swatch, rather than his granddaughter, whose inheritance this is!".

She flung the swatch on to the table, where it unrolled silkily shimmering in the light, shades shifting subtly. As one body, all the women reached out to touch the fabric, exclaiming over its velvety texture, the heaviness, the depth of the vibrant blue colour.

They soon discovered that if turned to the light, it brightened, apparently shot with gold. Turn it to the shadows and it danced with shades ranging from lilac to turquoise, turn again and the colour was just plain blue! There was no understanding it.

Ikella, as absorbed as the others, didn't immediately respond to the gentle tapping at the door, but before she could roll the cloth once more, she became aware of a hesitant voice. She looked up and there on the threshold, not daring to enter, was the subject of their discussion. She held out a hand to her..

"Come child. Tell us about your mother's wonderful cloth.", she said invitingly and the girl came to stand opposite the Sorceress, her eyes fixed on the material between them.

Like a wild animal poised for flight, she withstood their inspection. She was slender, tall for her age, with a delicate creamy skin and the most amazing lilac-blue eyes. Her hair, curling on to the nape of her neck, was cropped so raggedly that it could hardly be termed her crowning glory, although it cradled her head in a corona of copper flame. Standing stiffly, very aware of the open door at her back, her hands gentling her mother's fabric, she spoke quietly struggling to control her emotions.

"I'm Jalani.", She muttered, adding defiantly.

"My parents are dead, and my grandparents wish me so!".

There was no doubt that she believed that stark statement and the council held their breath as she continued more confidently.

"I come from Jerritol in the Azure, not daring to appeal to my own Clan for assistance. My grandfather told me that I have no rights without parents and that I was already dead to the Clan.".

She undoubtedly heard the hiss of indrawn breath as the Elders reacted to this statement, but doggedly continued, in what was plainly a rehearsed speech.

"They used me a slave, caring for my crippled mother, but I ran away when she died leaving me alone.", she gulped, then stifling sobs, went on.

"I think he'd told everyone I was dead. My mother said... my mother...", she finally broke, tears streaming. Somewhat incoherently the child muttered.

"The cart was so big you see. It crushed them against the wall. The poor Biron were screaming, no-one could get to them. No-one tried to get to them.", she whimpered in agonised remembrance of the horror, as Ikella's hand forbade intervention.

"The driver was drunk and the beast was burnt so badly it died. Like my Poppa...it died.".

The tense, bewildered little voice recounted that event, in the frozen snatches of a child's memory. Then the cacophony, the confusion, smell and fear was theirs to experience, along with Ikella's imagery as the child invoked reality. They were hearing , smelling, sensing the terror-filled agony of the burnt beast, the crippled woman and the child, as Ikella leapt to her feet, rounding the table at the same time as Dorra the Novice Mistress.

The Sorceress grasped the child's heaving shoulders firmly, looking deep into those lilac eyes and chanted.

"Lanachthii, tonachthii, lanachthii, tonachthii....", soothing the tremors of a mingled grief and anger, before the naked emotion did them all harm. The Elders chanted with her, eyes closed, until Jalani relaxed in Ikella's control. Gradually as her throat and airways relaxed, Jalani raised a hand and brushed away her tears crossly. Ikella waited for her to regain her poise and then seated herself again, her eyes never leaving the child's face in the process. She leaned forward, resting her chin on one hand.

"Continue.", she commanded and Jalani began again, anger building in her voice as she recalled the events of her seventh Zenitheon.

"When they lifted the wagon, my father was dead, my mother unconscious. They took her to the healers, but Serba wouldn't pay for medication. She said my mother would die anyway, so what was the point in wasting exchange trying to keep her alive.".

Silenced by the knowledge that no payment or exchange was ever asked for healing, Ikella wondered where this was going, aware that even the air in the Chamber shivered at the bleakness in Jalani's statement.

"Grandfather didn't want to bring her home, but she quietened when I sat with her, so they brought her home, and left me to manage.".

The Elders looked at each other knowingly. If it was hard for trained Healers to manage a paralysed patient, how much worse had it been for a child? Before anyone could ask her, Jalani took up her story once more.

"I sang to let her know I was there when she didn't wake. I wanted to make her better, so I thought about her citrine tree and the smell of citrines. I knew she could hear me.", she paused until Ikella motioned her to continue.

"One day, when it was very hot, my mother was suffering. I thought of citrines and their scent, mixed with Winter snow. How cooling that would be. I heard a tune in my head, so I sang the mixture against her legs and back where they were crushed and she woke up.".

Ikella leant forward, utterly absorbed.

"The child was a natural Healer then.", she thought. Very rare, hard to train, but immensely powerful! The story continued.

"I don't think they wanted her to wake up.", she said thoughtfully. "Sowdin came to our room every evening after work. He always said, "No change then?", in a hopeful sort of way. ".

At this, the Elders glanced at each other, having seen similar behaviours themselves. The clear voice continued condemningly.

"On the night she woke all they could say was, " Oh you're back with us again!", The girl added,

"I think they were really disappointed.", but Ikella was sure of it.

"What happened next Jalani?", The Sorceress asked softly.

"I sang to her, making songs about the flybys when she got sad. I sang flowers for her when the clouds were thick and the day dark. I tried to help her see father again, when she cried. Citrines and snow for her pain, crushed pine and petals took the fluid from her legs and then I sang the colour, to help her dye the cloth.".

On that intriguing statement the child wavered and it was clear that fatigue was overtaking her. Ikella called for a chair and refreshment, opening the questions again, with a swift glance that told the Elders, that time was shortening.

"Jalani, who looked after your mother's needs ? Washed her, clothed her, fed her?",

She already knew the answer, for the child looked up, pain etched in the lines of her mouth.

"I did it all Deshun Ikella, even though Grandfather told me, it was a waste of his hard earned money. Grandmother beat me, saying the room wasn't kept to her standards, but it was our room, our house!", She declared, tears starting in her eyes. She shook her head, ignoring the tracks on her face and continued bitterly.

"I washed her, cleaned up when she couldn't manage the necessary, kept the room sweet and she got better, she really did.", she stated defiantly. "I made her exercise, got her legs to stop shaking and she managed to sit on a chair. I saw one with wheels once, but Grandfather said I shouldn't encourage her, for she was bound to fail.", The child's voice grew tight with resentment.

"She really tried for me, she really did and her last summer was good.".

A faint smile quirked the corner of her mouth, as she gestured to the cloth.

"She wanted to give me something to remember her by, although I needed nothing! We found the material. My father intended it for some purpose that was never fulfilled before his death. It had been discarded, overlooked, so, reasoning that it was part of her inheritance, Mother took it and made me a skirt. She sewed it with her own hands, using only thread from her own spinning, so that Grandfather wouldn't find out. We washed the size out of it, but there was something in the barrel that we used. Something that came from the barrel itself, which softened the material and made the dye different somehow. Mother remembered using it when she lived in the Ashgenar. It was some trick of the mix between the raw makings of a new barrel and some of the compounds used by dyers.".

Ikella concentrated, a frown on her face as the story continued.

"Mother got very excited, when she saw bubbles rising from the cloth.", The child continued slowly. "She made a list of things that she needed to make my skirt pretty and I gathered them. Some roots that grew in the garden, some other "sowcers", you know, the kind of things like salt and the fixer that stops dyes from working too long. I got those from the dyeing room, then soot from the fireplace. Each dry part had to be added in its own order, vegetable, mineral, active and passive and then she made me keep what came to liquid in the necessary.",

Her face flushed in embarrassment as she stammered.

"Just hers and mine and all fresh and clean.", She hurriedly explained.

"Then?", Ikella prompted gently.

"Oh. She took my skirt and made a steeping. We hid it in the dyeing room for three nights and

when she took it out, it was just like this.", She pointed to the material on the table.

"We dyed the rest later that week. Mother exchanged some of it to get bread when Grandfather refused us food.".

She braced herself against the table edge, before the threatening babble of questions broke out, begging, "Can I continue Deshun?".

The Sorceress nodded and the weary child stumbled on.

"Grandfather found out about the material. Everybody wanted some. He was furious and came into our room shouting, calling us thieves and robbers. He called my mother Nishanawa whore, and asked when she would put me to work.".

Her face tautened with remembered fear, as the adults absorbed this last statement in outraged silence.

"He threatened to beat me until she handed over the recipe for that dye, along with any other that she knew. Everything my father owned passed to Sowdin on my father's death, (including me), according to Sowdin. I didn't understand what he meant, when he told Mother he would put me to work with some of his friends, and she couldn't do anything about it.".

Seemingly unaware of the others in the room, she held Ikella's gaze with her own as she said.

"He said my father never loved her, while he held her by the throat and shook her until her teeth chattered. He said Father only wanted her to get children, at which she was a miserable failure..".

Shocked silence fell, as those that remembered Viness as a tall, lithe, Nishan warrior realised how terrible her injuries must have been as the young voice dropped into a hopeless monotone.

"He said, that father wanted rid of her, that the accident was no accident, but planned in such a way that no-one would suspect him of murder.", The Session of Elders shrank back in their chairs as though they heard that venomous suggestion in its originator's voice.

"He accused my mother of witchcraft,. He said, she had made his son lose his senses, stolen his love and his life, turned him against his own family and that he would personally torture her to death for her evil influence.".

The room grew still, as the bright, brittle voice tallied the sins of her Grandfather and in her chair, Ikella drew her shawl about her and shivered as an arctic chill grew in her heart.

"He took the chair that Father made her and broke it on his knee. He threw the pieces on her bed and told her he could break her like that, but that he had no need to do so, because my father paid you to curse my Mother.".

An accusing finger pointed unswervingly at Ikella's face.

"Was that why she never conceived another child? Was that why she never recovered from the accident? Tell me! Did you curse my mother?".

She broke down suddenly, clutching the material as she slid to the floor, cradling the last thing her mother had touched, as she rocked in a paroxysm of grief, anger and despair.

Ikella sat, as though turned to stone, then the room erupted in outrage around her. She closed her eyes thinking, "Clever, cruel, manipulative man.", and as she sat trying to absorb the implications, the child spoke from the floor.

"My mother never recovered from that. She took to her bed and I nursed her until the flybys went away and the garden song stopped. Then she died and winter came.".

Her voice dropped to a whisper and the Elders heard her out silently. She knelt, raising her face to the level of the table surface and peered at Ikella as she told them.

"Grandfather came everyday after that. He stopped pretending to work at Darnesh, sent the weavers and dyers home without pay. He made my life a misery, searching our room for tablets, scrolls, notes of any kind. He wrecked her bed, tearing up sheets and clothes. He took our drinking vessels, crushed things Father had made with his own hands, but Mother wouldn't tell him the secret of the dye. She said she had dreamt the colour and made it but the once and then she died.".

She looked at Ikella challenge written all over her face, no scrap of fear visible, despite the fact that she knew of the Sorceress's power.

"Did you curse my mother?", She demanded. "Was my Grandfather right?".

Ikella stood, reaching for her Staff and at her touch, the Opal flared into life. She held out a hand to Jalani, staring at the child unwaveringly across the Council table, as all around the table the Elders also stood. Slowly, reluctantly, Jalani placed her hand into Ikella's.

"Look child.", Ikella's voice hovered at the edge of power and in the centre of the table

reflected in the light of the glowing Opal, was the golden seal of Sanctuary. The child blinked in

wonder, for it had not been there a moment before.

Ikella held her hand fast for a moment and then quite simply she placed it firmly into the heart of the glowing Seal. Jalani gasped in wonder for her hand was held fast in the light, as if caught there by some attraction. Ikella placed her hand beside the child's and spoke solemnly.

"This is the Seal of Sanctuary, binding us to that place of Blessed memory. Know that the most holy, the most binding Vow of any Guardian is to honour truth. Here, in front of witnesses, with my hand and with my heart I deny any malicious intention, by word, thought or deed against Viness or Rowin del Orto.".

Across the table the child stared transfixed at the Sorceress, cloaked in power. Ikella's body glowed "in Opal", her aura standing away from her, left a silvered silhouette around her, but as the glow faded, so did the Seal, leaving only the child's hand. Ikella lifted it, but feeling Jalani flinch away, she maintained her grip, albeit gently, saying,

"I am sorry child, but if you want my help, I must ask more questions. Time is short and I need to know much more.".

The girl shook her head mutely, plainly listening to something else and terror flared in her eyes. In the background, in the corridor outside the Djellim, there was shouting, arguing, running feet and one of the Inesh guards slipped out of the Council Chamber to investigate.

Ikella persisted, more aware than she, that certain questions had to be answered quickly, correctly, or she might not be able to protect her.

"Would you like to remain here with us and train as a Healer?", She asked, adding urgently.

"You plainly can't go home!".

Jalani thought for a moment and then said softly, thoughtfully:

"I could be a Healer? Without a dowry?", and in displaying that knowledge, Ikella knew that her suspicions were correct.

"Isn't that what Viness made the dye for Jalani?", she asked and the child jumped to her feet panic in her eyes. Quickly sketching a symbol in the air, the Sorceress succeeded in calming the girl, who stood poised on the edge of flight.

Ikella continued:

"Don't be frightened child, I will protect you, I promise.".

The child's surprised eyes blinked just once and she whispered:

"He must never know that Mother planned this. He tried to claim my Sand-rights when Father died. Tirjella never knew the truth, but she refused him while Mother lived. I have been hunted from Jerritol to Scartel and back towards the Great Divide. I was lucky to get help into the Opal and my friends paid heavily for their assistance. He is using cross-bred hounds to scent my tracks.".

Astounded and outraged Ikella said angrily. "In my Sands? How dare he!".

The sound outside the door increased and Jalani whispered frantically:

"Hide me, oh, hide me. He shan't take me, I will die sooner.".

She ran to Ikella's chair, placing both hands in those of the Sorceress, pleading, "Help me Lady, hide me with your magic.".

Ikella glanced down at the hands laid so trustingly in hers and stiffened. she knew little of the customs of the Nishanawa but she saw the skilled execution of symbols representing plants and crystals as the girl caught the direction of her gaze, even as Ikella heard running feet outside the Djellim.

Hurling herself weeping into Ikella's unprepared arms, the girl's rising terror was audible.

Don't let him take me... don't let him hurt me!".

This last was uttered on a shriek of fear, as the door to the Djellim was thrust open abruptly. Loud footsteps approached the Council Chamber and only a discreet motion of an empowered hand prevented the door sealing itself against the intrusion of an angry man. Shrugging off the Guards, he forced his way round the table to Ikella's chair in a second.

Before thought had time to coalesce into action, he had hold of Jalani. Wrenching an arm behind her back and grasping her hair, he thrust her to the ground, subduing all protest with a knee in her back. Supremely confident, with an arrogance born of contempt for all things female, he addressed the Sorceress mockingly.

"Thank you Lady!", as he picked up the material from the floor. "You nearly gave solace to this thief without knowing the truth.".

He shook the cloth in their faces.

"This is mine by inheritance. I was not sure until recently, but now I know she murdered her own mother to get that cloth and the magical dye. My poor daughter by marriage was foolish to trust her child, but I will return her to the Azure Sands, where true justice can be done.".

He sketched a quick bow to the company and retreated, dragging Jalani with him to the accompaniment of a low muttering sound which echoed around the Djellim, before bursting forth in a terrorised litany from the frantic girl.

"No. No! No. No!", her voice shot up an octave as she resisted him. "No! No! No! Grandfather, no!".

As that last shriek cut the air, everyone felt the power. Wild, untamed, born of sheer desperation it lashed out, lacerating nerves, capable of searing sinews. In the space of one heartbeat, the cloth was wrested from Sowdin's grasp as he was hurled against the solid wall of the chamber, dropping in a crumpled heap at Mina's feet. Even before Ikella's magically enhanced reactions could take over, Jalani hurled herself towards the table, falling to her knees as she thrust both hands (tattoos glowing), into the heart of the Seal of Sanctuary which had materialised in response to the child's distress.

"He lies. I swear it.", as a chime of acceptance rang out.

As the man on the floor convulsed, she cried out urgently:

"Mother, protect your child!", and Ikella who in all her many Rotations had never before been begged for Sanctuary touched her gently, saying,

"The Guardians of Sanctuary hold you safe.", and the child looked up doubtfully.

"Is he…?", her voice dropped, but Ikella, who had already ascertained Sowdin's condition, shook her head.

"Dying? No, although he will wish he had for a ninenight. We will Heal him and when he leaves, he won't remember why he came. I will send word to Tirjella. He will find himself barred from the Weaver's Halt. Another thing child. He never held your Sand-rights, nor could he claim his son's possessions. Your mother was legally bonded to Rowin, which means everything came to her, and from her to you at her death. You are past Nine Rotations old so you can claim them yourself.".

She stared down at the child gravely.

"Tirjella will send a journeyman Weaver to your hold in Jerritol. They will set things to rights. I shall see to that, as your mother would have wished. Tirjella will know how she was deceived and that your mother's remains are to be sought. I will suggest that she deals with Sowdin and Serba on that matter. I have no doubt that he won't be comfortable in the Azure for a long,. long time.".

Dorra, the novice mistress held out her hand to Jalani, who was shivering with reaction, weepy and exhausted.

"You'd best come and sleep with the other novices for tonight at least.", She offered, but Ikella had Jalani's other hand and studied it thoughtfully.

"Jalani, you said that you guessed what this is and now I am sure.", She continued, "It is your dowry child. This," She pointed to the symbols, patiently tattooed on the girl's left hand.

"This is the recipe.", She lifted the other hand from Dorra's grasp.

"This is the method.", she paused.

"I think your Grandfather knew your mother would have placed it somewhere safe. Perhaps he didn't recognise that it was hidden in plain sight, until you ran away.".

The child lifted her eyes to Ikella's.

"Can I be a novice?", she asked breathlessly. "If this is my dowry?".

Ikella answered whole heartedly:

"A scribe will copy these symbols precisely. Your own dyers can make the colour, which we can sell to pay for your keep and training.".

Room servants were carrying the unconscious man to the Infirmary and the room was clearing when Ikella asked curiously:

"How did you "sing" a colour to your mother?", and the child blushed as she answered.

"Dyers and weavers can talk in colour Deshun. I dreamt it, then I made a tune in my head and sang it to my Mother.".

Ikella watched her pick up the bolt of cloth, shimmering in an intensity of blue, shot with lilac, turquoise, gold.

"It will be difficult to name that colour!", Ikella remarked thoughtfully and Jalani smiled at some far off memory, as she replied, softly, her voice drifting around the Council Chamber, stirring strange harmonics from its ancient trappings:

"I think its the colour of love, but my mother said it was another shade of mystery, from which came the Tapestry of life.", and departed sleepily, with Dorra, leaving Ikella musing, eyes narrowed contemplatively.

Chapter 5 - A Most Unruly Novice

In the following days, Sowdin was silently nursed back to health. Examining his injuries meticulously, Ikella found numerous contusions, but nothing to explain the state of abject terror that she found in him. He had recovered consciousness, trembling from head to foot, becoming agitated and tearful every time a door opened.

Ikella, (not naturally vindictive), nevertheless recognised a certain justice in this situation. However, she knew that whatever young Jalani had done, would have to be undone, if only for her own sake. Taking advantage of the paralysing dread that kept this most aggressive man passive, the Sorceress initiated a soothing chant, as she tidied his bedclothes and sorted through tinctures on the shelf beside the bed. Rousing no apprehension in her patient, she persisted, but avoided touching him, preferring to use gentle indirect magic to fill Sowdin's mind with images of a minor accident. Eventually he slept and while she influenced his memory, she examined his dreams and had to force herself to subdue her own sense of loathing.

Sowdin dreamt of cruelty, wanton destruction and death. As though drunk on the despair of others, he was motivated by practices too abhorrent to observe, at which she recoiled, thankful that he slept. She modulated the chant, side-stepping issues beyond her control and found besides fear, greed, superstition and jealousy, a nature too stunted and twisted to recall. She sighed and sat thinking that even if Sowdin had asked for Healing, there was no likelihood of it succeeding, for he clutched his depravity to him like a cloak. She shuddered, thinking inconsequentially of another and the perversion that had seen her exiled. Over her own mental image of Adruna's eyes, swam those from Sowdin's dream. Huge, lilac blue, full of recrimination, stirring the remnants of his conscience.

"If an after image remains to haunt him, he might continue to seek her.", she decided, retiring to her study to spell-cast.

She had taken the Healers oath, never to knowingly harm a patient, so she decided that as Sowdin's mind was as many layered with hatred as the pungently flavoured bulbs that cooks added to stews, she would use that analogy to add a layer of false memories. She had prepared for this eventuality, collecting together Sowdin's gloves, a hair from his pillow and a few pebbles found in a pocket. She set out her spell-plan to create a dream for Sowdin, matching the desire of his black heart in every way.

She was exhausted when she finished planting in Sowdin's mind, the image of the girl imprisoned deep in the underground chambers of Selesh. She depicted herself as unreasonable, the implacable man-hater of Sowdin's imagination. Allowing the possibility that she had refused to give Jalani up to surface, she embellished the truth, with a vision of her Inesh warriors, trickling a deep dread of torture into his sleeping mind. Before implanting the idea of embarking on a journey which would ensure Jalani the chance to mature in power, she prayed earnestly that never again would this unnatural Grandparent get an opportunity to interact with her.

Sending an advanced Healer to sit with their unwanted guest, she continued to monitor his recovery. He responded to rest, but reacted suspiciously to having his minor wounds healed, making it plain, that he feared and distrusted Healers. He refused the food offered and would only drink water provided by one of his men, who came looking for him. Mina reported that he spoke little, preferring his own company and on the third day a concerted sigh of relief went through the Infirmary, when he insisted on leaving the Healer Hall, to return to the Azure Desert.

His comments on leaving did little to endear him to any inhabitant of Selesh, for he strutted aggressively past the morning watch of the Inesh Guard, announcing his intention of returning to the Azure Sands and the company of "normal folks", as he put it.

Jalani however, had disappeared into the anonymity of the Novice Hall and with her future to discuss, Ikella called on Dorra (the Novice Mistress), who had so far, taken care of the refugee.

They were in the clothing store, where Dorra, patiently laid out plain robes, ready for yet another new girl to enter the noviate. The Novice Mistress eyed the pile of tan clothing sourly, remarking, almost to herself:

"Let us pray that this one doesn't outgrow her first Rotation clothes in a single journey of the moons, or wear it out like young Jalani, or we will need to send for more material. We really need our own weaver again Deshun!".

The Sorceress studied the steadily growing pile of clothing and thought about the near Rotation that Rowin and Viness had spent weaving and dyeing tan material, before conceiving Jalani. She wondering if the girl knew that the many bolts from which her clothes were made, had been woven by her father and dyed by her mother, deciding that if for nothing other than economic sense, she would tell the girl, before she abused another uniform.

Walking around the well stocked room, as Dorra baled day wear, work wear, travel cloak, night clothes, underwear and ritual robes, in a set of bed sheets, Ikella considered Guild policy. Students wore identical garments from first intake. Light tan (like the robe of a qualified Healer) in the first Rotation, bonded them into an exclusive group, membership of which was hard won and in which no previous social status had a bearing. Ikella had hopes that Jalani would feel the benefit of such a bond, finding for herself friendship amongst peers, a family of sorts and asked Dorra directly, how Jalani was settling in.

Dorra's answering scowl was not the answer Ikella wanted, for if they were to resettle Jalani, she had to 'conform. However (the Sorceress reasoned), she'd only been with them a ninenight, so it was entirely too early to despair, although Dorra was bursting to confide her own misgivings. She settled herself down and prepared to listen.

"Out with it, tell me the worst.", She demanded and Dorra, folding the last cloak away settled herself to talk.

"The girl is not precisely Healer material.", Dorra started slowly, "She has great potential, but there is an untamed elemental in there somewhere!", she sank down on a great basket and gnawed on one thumb, an irritating habit she effected when uncertain.

Ikella nodded.

"Go on.", She urged and Dorra frowned, fumbling for words.

"She is secretive, suspicious and quite aggressive.", she offered.

"Already some of the others have felt her temper and she now sleeps alone.".

This was as Ikella had guessed the child would react, but she was saddened that Jalani was

finding it so hard to settle.

"What about classes?", She asked and was relieved to hear that in that setting, Jalani responded well, coming top of her group with an ease that seemed only to set her further apart from her fellows.

"Do you think that the aggression is triggered by fear?", she asked Dorra, as the Novice

Mistress began folding sheets once more, Dorra swung round,

"No, I don't think that young woman has an ounce of fear left. Her Grandfather beat all that out of her, but I think it has been replaced by something that won't sit well on Healer shoulders.", she said firmly.

"She is not bad, just angry with everything and everyone. She has obviously made up her mind that someone is going to suffer for what happened to her parents and she is not particular whom that person is. It is nothing to do with fear, it is simple frustrated anger and unless we control her, or teach her to control herself, she will not do as a Healer!".

Ikella's eyes narrowed, it was unlike Dorra to be so emphatic, she would definitely have to take an interest in Jalani, try and follow her throughout the first Rotation of her training and monitor her progress.

Towards the end of that Rotation, she sat again with Dorra and tallied the incidents which to do Dorra justice bore out her earlier pessimism. Dorra solemnly sorted the dark Tan clothing given to second Rotation students and made piles ready to hand out as that Rotation's intake moved onward into more detailed studies. Soon each girl would be addressed as Healer Soniya, or Healer Jalani, they would be able to gather wild herbs, mix and dispense minor medications. Mindful of this, Ikella probed for further information on her unusual novice.

Dorra snorted at the naïveté of her initial question.

"Forgotten her grudge against her Grandfather?",

Dorra's eyebrows disappeared into her hairline with surprise.

"Never!. She can remember every little incident, just as easily as she remembers herbs,

ingredients and quantities. She seems to prefer medicinery to magic incidentally.".

She commented as an aside. Ikella frowned at that.

"You surprise me!", She returned,

"She seemed to have happy memories of singing to her mother, I would have thought that her

othervoice would have developed here.".

Dorra paused for a moment, thoughtfully.

"Could she be afraid of using power Deshun?", She questioned.

"Could she be blaming herself for not saving her mother? I thought that might lie behind her anger.".

Ikella nodded, reluctant to hear the latest catastrophe, for the very fact that Dorra had summoned her to this quiet session of garment packing, meant that the Novice Mistress wished to have the ear of the Sorceress in private. She already knew that Jalani had been given the boring task of rolling bandages in the Infirmary, so had assumed her to be in disgrace again.

"Tell me what has she done now?", She commanded.

"We can analyse it later.", She sounded and looked weary and disappointed, so Dorra began the story quietly.

"My class was about pessin oil, its uses and properties. I had already covered its calming qualities and had just touched on its ability to relieve tension and ease womanly humours,

When Tjerri, the new girl from Jandan, made a comment that I didn't hear. I invited her to enlighten the class and although naturally embarrassed, Tjerri suggested that Jalani should have been given an infusion of pessin oil with her mother's milk!".

Dorra flushed, saying hastily, "It seems Tjerri had been trying to befriend Jalani and having been ignored and finally rebuffed used my class to get her own back, but it backfired on her.". She paused until Ikella prompted,

"Go on then. I can't help if I only know half the story!", and Dorra continued in a low embarrassed voice:

"Jalani, as usual, over-reacted suspending Tjerri upside down over the waste pits.".

Dorra, not given to joking, must have been mistaken, Ikella thought. A child of thirteen, couldn't have been wielding the kind of power that took decades to develop. Dorra gave an apologetic shrug.

"Tjerri was a little unkind, but Jalani demonstrated real malice, which worries me. It took four tutors in harmony to recover Tjerri, who was left hanging twenty spans high. You do see what I mean Deshun?", She asked anxiously, then made a swift but significant list, ticking off points on her fingers.

"She conceals her abilities, although there is no lack of control. She uses power instinctively, like a weapon, but finds the use of the controlled *othervoice* difficult. Under stress, she exhibits tendencies that set her apart. Although I am certain she is unaware of how different she is, she use the mood of the moment and she is a bundle of conflicting emotions! How will we ever control her?".

Dorra hazarded a peep at the Sorceress, but she sat, deep in thought, drumming her fingers in the manner that she adopted when absorbed. The

Novice Mistress picked up another sheet and carried on folding, waiting for Ikella's response. Somewhere, not far away a door banged shut and young voices were heard, laughing, as novices made their way to the robing rooms. Bobbing an apology to Ikella, Dorra exclaimed,

"Is it time already?", and casting a glance at the sand glass, swiftly lifted a bale of clothing and headed for the door, excusing herself hastily.

"Forgive me Deshun, duty calls.", sandal's clacking as she departed.

Ikella rose silently and turning in the opposite direction made her way to the Djellim, where she spent the rest of the day seeking guidance for this most unruly of novices.

As the Rotations of Jalani's training passed, with no contact from Sowdin, she slipped into a new way of life. Days were filled with classes, practice, exercises and more classes. She continued to flourish, but kept to herself. Never joining social activities and perhaps as she wished, eventually never being invited to do so. She hid on visiting days, stubbornly refusing overtures of friendship, suffering inevitable isolation, which eventually saved her life.

In the last Rotation of training, just a ninenight before Zenitheon, a frantic novice sped towards Dorra's room in the early hours. The Novice Mistress was fast asleep when the first knock came, but roused as the tapping became more insistent. She slid out of bed, hastily throwing a wrap around her thin shoulders and opened the door to Jalani. The girl was shuddering, whether from cold or fear she couldn't tell, but reaching out a hand, she drew a steadying symbol on the girls forehead, demanding, "Whatever is wrong child.?", drawing her in and bundling her into a shawl before Jalani could answer.

"Tell me while I dress then.", Dorra commanded, but Jalani was clutching her stomach with both hands. Her eyes glazed as Dorra hastily checked her temperature with the back of a hand. Turning away abruptly, the novice caught up a wash bowl and vomited, waving away assistance as the nausea seized her again.

"Sorry.", she gasped, struggling to keep her composure, tears welling as Dorra supported her. When finally she managed to catch her breath, she protested fiercely.

"No. Its not me. Bo to the others, they need you Dorra..".

Diagnosing shock, Dorra swiftly placed a steadying palm against Jalani's back and sang a long low note. It pulsed, once, twice and Jalani gulped as the nausea died away. The Healer caught up a scrip, opening the door and sped swiftly to the landing above the stairwell. Reaching up, she caught a rope and pulled hard, sounding the alarm. Urgent, clamorous in the night a bell rang out as Dorra returned to Jalani.

"That will summon everyone I need.", she explained, thrusting her scrip into the student's hands and scooping up another, as she ordered.

"You carry this, it will give you something useful to occupy your mind! Where are we going? Who is ill?".

Staring uncomprehendingly, Jalani stopped dead in front of her. "Dorra! I told you.", and the child's voice shook, "The others. All of the others!".

Dorra never quite forgot that moment. She remembered pausing in mid-stride, staring incredulously at Jalani, stammering,

"All the others?".

Jalani nodded sombrely.

"The children anyway. I can hear them and some of the villagers as well.".

"I was studying an old treatise on sympathetic resonance, when I fell asleep. I woke up cold, feeling pain and nausea and thought I was still dreaming. When I peeped into the dormitory, my Rotation were doubled up. I doused for other sufferers, thinking of food poisoning, but there are too many!", gathering the duty Healers, they went out into the night to investigate.

That was the beginning of the agony. However it came, the epidemic spread through the school and village beyond, until the cries of bereaved parents rang out over the Desert itself. The youth of Selesh Minoria burnt up in fever and died with the dawn of each day. As the students fell sick, Healers sang themselves hoarse in a vain attempt to save the youngest novices. For a very short while, there was a break in the pattern of the illness, then it returned, to crush all their hopes.

Amongst them untouched, walked Jalani. Growing colder, more remote, more withdrawn with each death. She sat with the children, singing strange little melodies for each one, holding a hand here, stroking a brow there, every inch a Healer, but Ikella and Dorra noted the dark rings under her eyes, the wistful twist of the mouth, as she straightened young

limbs, closed young eyes in death.

Wearily Dorra pulled the exhausted Sorceress to one side, saying urgently, "We have to do something for that child.", and Ikella nodded, her eyes following Jalani as she walked steadily to the room in which the last of her classmates lay dying.

"I know.", she patted Dorra's hand.

"We have to do something for all of us. If I only knew what!". They followed Jalani to the last room, to the last death and stopped speechless at what lay within.

On the bed lay Tjerri, hair carefully braided in the manner of the Gresshe whose child she was. Her clothing(all the shades of Malachite), was carefully draped, the sights and sounds of her home surrounded her. Vision scenes of the great sands of Tijamin glowed brilliantly. A lush oasis appeared to a pulsing beat, as a sweet melody, sung in a low, steady voice filled the air. Struck with the poignancy of those scenes, the Sorceress and the Healer stood silently, wondering as Jalani sang her only friend to sleep.

Burnt to the socket by fever, Tjerri's hands fluttered as a swarm of brilliantly hued flybys filled the room. Her face full of wonder lifted towards Ikella, as she whispered, "O, Jalani! Thank you!".

As the dying girl caught a glimpse of Ikella, she struggled to rise saying, "Look Deshun. Jalani has taken me home.", but the effort was too much. Voice failing on the last word, smiling sleepily, she nestled into her pillows. Her chest rose and fell once more, then as if she couldn't bear to look away from the vision scenes, her eyes half closed as Tjerri slipped from life into that longest of sleeps.

The Sorceress was stunned.

"How in the Nine Sands…?", She began to ask, but Jalani had fallen silent, her head bowed, her shoulders shaking with suppressed sobs. The chant and the vision scenes were fading and then Jalani herself collapsed into Dorra's arms, mercifully unconscious, leaving the Healers to steel themselves for another hopeless battle.

It was not to be however, for it transpired that their sole surviving student was simply exhausted, and after complete bed rest, she made a full recovery.

Ikella observed her over the next few ninenights, drifting around the Healer Hall like some novice ghost, as things started to return to normal. From all over Pelshar, parents came to visit the graves of their young ones, promising to return when a sibling grew old enough to be enrolled. Others came simply to offer help, money and moral support. The villagers mourned the students as their own and then set about the huge task of cleaning, disinfecting and preparing to start again. Amongst all of this, the sole survivor flitted like some forgotten soul, nothing to do, no-one to talk to, no-one to care.

One morning, Ikella noticed her, staring intently at Mina – who was packaging remedies in

the herb store, despite the tears of sorrow that lined her cheeks. Mina, who having given up her cherished position to marry Ikella's Master Builder, had, of all of them, suffered the most, losing both husband and child in the epidemic.

Ikella lacking any remedy for her sorrow, had simply dropped in to see how she was managing and suddenly seeing the two of them together, an idea crossed her mind.

She glanced at Jalani, who sat on a bag stuffed with leaves of some herb and wondered if

she could bring these two together. Narrowing her eyes thoughtfully, she sketched a symbol in the air and was immediately repelled by a blaze of lilac blue eyes and an expression that she could have read from the neighbouring Sands.

"No!", it fairly screamed at her, but Mina turned bewildered and in that moment, Ikella thought triumphantly that at least one of the parties interest was engaged. She locked gazes with Jalani.

"We'll see.", she thought, "We'll see.".

Chapter 6 – Preparations

That Rotation turned inexorably forward and Ikella talked to Jalani regularly, gauging her moods, bringing nothing but gentle advice to the table as she observed her closely. She was both enchanted and amused by the girls choice of studies, one moment applauding her determination, the next plunged into despair by her volatile temperament. However, she made a regular point of teaching their lone student, in the hope that when the school re-opened, she could be persuaded to finish her training.

However, before Zenitheon, the Sorceress summoned the novice to break the news that her grandparents were dead.

"Are you sure Deshun?", Jalani asked suspiciously. "What if this is some trick? It is the sort of thing they might do. I mean, encourage me to go home, half trained and unprepared!".

Restraining the impulse to tell Jalani that this was precisely what she had suspected, Ikella reassured her.

"We are as sure as we can be my dear. Shiarjha and Beneva are travelling the Azure searching for new students. They were just a settlement away when a sand slip buried a trail stop. They took half a Chapter of Guard to assist in the rescue, but recognising Serba amongst the victims, sent word immediately. It so happened that Benith, who was present when Sowdin came for you, inspected the bodies. She reports that you need have no fear, they are quite dead.".

She watched as the weight fell off the girl's shoulders, then came the hesitancy, the bewilderment that she had expected.

"What shall I do now?", the novice muttered. "How shall I manage? Am I truly free,?", then in a worried tone, "Can't I stay here? Can't I be a Healer now?".

For the first time, Ikella felt Jalani wavering. A long suppressed uncertainty showing as she considered her future. The Sorceress intervened quickly but firmly.

"That's far too many questions in one sentence my dear! First things first.", she lifted a hand enumerating her prime considerations.

"For the moment, you are safe amongst friends. After the revelations attached to your arrival here, the Weavers Halt is now fully supported by the Guild on your behalf. They have plenty of orders, Deshun Tirjella having interceded to arrange full employment for your father's weavers and dyers.". Ikella's voice betrayed her deep satisfaction.

"The Clan used the terms of your Great Grandfather's will to exclude Sowdin and Serba.".

She smiled gravely at Jalani's surprise, "It seems that even amongst his own family, Sowdin was ostracised. They never returned to Jerritol after Sowdin left here. I think he knew that I could pursue him there. The Headwoman told Tirjella that their own house has become uninhabitable, but that your family home has been restored ready for you to claim your inheritance. It is currently let to the journeyman.".

The girl hung her head and whispered.

"I am grateful for my own Lady's intervention, but with such a heritage what am I to do? I feel his anger in me and it frightens me so!".

Deliberately deciding to ignore this comment, Ikella continued with her current train of thought, in an attempt to divert Jalani. The student rubbed her hands over her face wearily and sighed as Ikella commented.

"Your continuance in the craft is certainly not a decision to be made today. Your keep here is more than covered by the work of Madiv, now Master Weaver at your father's Halt. In fact my girl, you have the foundation of real wealth building up, a fine home and business to inherit should that be your choice.".

Jalni's eyes flashed dark blue with anger.

"I don't want it! I would choose never to see Jerritol again but for my father's grave. Sowdin stole everything, my parents, my childhood, my faith! He even stole his death from me, for I planned to find my mother's last resting place, return her to lie with my father, then burn the Halt about his ears. "

She smiled with bitter mirth, her voice low, an implacable hatred in its depths, and eyeing her volatile student askance, the Sorceress said gently.

"You're like a prickly pretulish some days," and smiled to take the sting out of her words. Jalni scowled ferociously, then pleased with the analogy, nodded in agreement.

"What you do with the Weavers Halt is up to you child.", Ikella suggested slyly. "Perhaps there is another member of your father's family who would benefit from a home and work if you really don't want to return. Do you know of anyone?".

She watched as Jalani frowned in concentration.

"He had an older brother who died in some epidemic when father was only a baby. I once wondered, if that old grief had anything to do with Sowdin and Serba's attitude, but I can't think how it could. I don't know of any others, my Grandfather discouraged any outside contacts, calling Clan and Kin, wastrels and hangers on.".

Oblivious of the look on Ikella's face she asked suddenly, "Can I take time to think what I want to do? There is no-one to share classes with now and I missed so much this term. Can I stay my Song Walk until next Rotation? I'll study really hard!".

This wistful promise made the hair stand up on Ikella's neck, for it echoed the promises from Daro and Ahnell. They had vowed to submit to training. They too would stay out of mischief if she only gave then leave to stay. Ruefully calculating that Jalani, possessor of a fine intellect, a strong connection to the Source and an unpredictable temper, would still be here when the wanderers returned, she forced herself not to react too hastily.

"Take your time child.", she advised guardedly, "You have a Rotation in hand.", and Jalani left ignorant of the apprehension that gripped Ikella as she meditated on that subject.

The Summoning Bell chimed, the hour glass turned and aware of impending duties, the Sorceress rose and dismissing all thought of Jalani, went to consult with Beven, who awaited her in the workrooms behind his old forge. He and Errish, (her late Master Builder), had turned this into a combination of design shop and miniature forge, with a detailed layout area in which to conduct construction experiments. She hadn't been there since Errish died and it was a very sombre Sorceress that followed her Guard through the heavy door, to stop dead in astonishment.

On the layout floor was a representation of the Gate in the Rock. Ropes and thin threads ran everywhere, odd panels were open and the bemused Sorceress stepped forward peering at it, just as a man she hadn't noticed rose to his feet. He wore a long tunic of deep burgundy, offset by a glittering embroidered badge on his chest. However, it was his hair that caught the breath in Ikella's throat, for it was short, curling and blonde. His skin was light, his eyes speedwell blue. In one hand he held an instrument and in the other a notebook. He straightened with a low mutter to Beven who crouched at his feet and then Ikella found her tongue.

"I give you good morrow Citizen.", she remarked as though she met Greeeyn scientist's everyday and her Forge Master turned inn-keeper grinned amiably at the stranger.

"Told you she wouldn't eat you!", announced that worthy from the floor and Ikella stepped forward, holding out a hand in greeting and added sweetly,

"Oh no! I only eat small children and never this close to Zenitheon!", as they were introduced. Her visitor eyed her strangely and then seeing the silver wristlet flare as they touched, said in a gentle melodic voice.

"I am sure the Lady Guardian exaggerates. A whole child? Even I can only manage half, provided I take it with brandy!", and a jovial voice from the floor remarked,

"Don't trust him, he takes everything with brandy, including brandy!", and Beven got to his feet grinning amiably and presented Master Glass-Smith Doloran.

The tension dispelled, Ikella listened as Beven explained the late Master Builders obsession with the Gate in the Rock and Ikella listened, one hip perched on the work table as he explained.

"My Guild and others, believe something is happening.", he announced gravely. "The city of Omnel is in shut-down, but I extracted permission to leave Quinnox to carry a message to the Guardians. Master Errish visited us often, but we only knew of his passing after a traveller told us. I came because he had given me drawings to interpret and because I hold writings that may protect both you and us against further infections. I discover Master Beven has continued my friends work and hoped to remain while my contribution is tested.".

Ikella (now thinking herself impervious to any surprise) found herself taking the notebook from Doloran's hand and stared in amazement at the familiar notations of her ancestress, Adaria te Syrene. The sheets were ancient, penned on vellum, but stitched together in a way that she knew Beneva would envy greatly. A sketch caught her eye and involuntarily she exclaimed.

"Sympathetic resonance? Is that what this is about? How can we extend such a principle without an army of Healers to provide the constant tone?", and watched as Doloran held up the strange instrument and grinned.

Ikella nearly shrieked as he struck it on the table. A tone rang out surrounding her, causing the bones in her skull to resonate, until he inserted it (still vibrating) into an odd shaped slot in a panel on the model "Gate". There was a muffled clatter, which seemed to go on for a long time and both men looked hugely pleased with themselves, as Beven pulled on a rope and the clatter started again. Ikella rolled her eyes.

"May the One preserve us!", she muttered to herself and watched in amazement as Doloran touched finger tips to head, lips and heart.

"So, this man is a believer.", she thought numbly, following as Doloran began installing what he called a "diagnostic field", at the Gate in the Rock. Wrapped in a warm cloak, she walked out across the icily chill Gathering Square to the entrance through which every inhabitant entered this great fortress.

She stood watching as some last minute instructions were given and the Guard at the gate solemnly shut the huge black metal door. She saw that the men had skilfully inserted a long thin row of glass plates into a chiselled channel on the inside and that now, with the door closed, a narrow band of light showed not only where these were, but also lit up the interior of the door.

Jashell stepped out of the guardroom and made a signal to her guards, who lined up to either side of Ikella, then the Gate in the Rock was opened, the guard who had worked the bolts stepped back and Beven stood in the entrance smiling at her.

"I will demonstrate the new arrangements.".

He walked forward a pace and the guard touched a metal plate, set into the wall so cunningly that Ikella hadn't noticed it. A slight buzz followed the low tone that it emitted and the air around Beven quivered and then he was striding towards the Sorceress.

"What happened?", Ikella demanded. "I saw no barrier like the one on the council Chamber!".

"No.", the retired Master Smith agreed equably. "We want to welcome visitors, not frighten them to death. We also have a long way to go in the understanding of resonance, before we can achieve all that Lady Adaria knew. It must be approached cautiously, for we don't want to cause any harm to visitors either.".

This sober warning caused Ikella to pause, but then she questioned abruptly.

"How would I know that someone was carrying illness? What happens then?".

Doloran grinned amiably. "We thought of that my Deshun. What this field does is to give a low buzz if the body passing through the field is of normal temperature. If it is significantly higher as in fever, the corresponding sound will be high pitched. If the person has a dangerously low temperature it will sound lower, but louder to attract attention.".

Ikella nodded then asked thoughtfully, "Won't it slow down the passage of people enormously?", at which Doloran chuckled.

"We have pressed the Guard into service to provide an example.", he said cheerfully and made a hand signal which sent the imposing Inesh warriors scampering through the Gate in the Rock, like a gaggle of unruly children. They were gone but a moment and when they returned, the Sorceress saw that one carried a warming brick wrapped in cloth. As they proceeded in an untidy chattering group, much as pilgrims and workers tended to enter, a bright white light lit up the woman who carried the brick and simultaneously a high pitched buzz was heard.

Somewhere there was a click and a shutter descended, barring the entrance, a number of Healers appeared and well pleased with the experiment, Ikella sat back on the chair provided. Only it wasn't quite over. Even as the guard congratulated each other, the Gate opened again and a number of their fellows entered to join them. In the same instant, a high buzz followed by the same light, picked out Sorrill's tall figure and everyone froze, as Sorrill sneezed!

Ikella smiled with deep satisfaction, as her Healers surrounded a protesting Guard Commander.

"If all it does is to prevent Winter chill from decimating my Guard, it will work well Master Doloran.", she remarked to the Glass Smith and smiled, thinking privately.

"Not to mention establishing friends in unusual places!", as they retraced their steps down to the Gathering Square, where she questioned the Glass Smith cautiously.

"Will it take long to establish the procedures for the Guards, the Healers? More importantly, how soon can we implement the permanent use of the one we have?".

Doloran smiled seraphically at her.

"We only need to establish the procedures for traders bringing goods and wagons through my Deshun and this field will be permanent. I have made replacement plates in plenty and we are in the process of establishing something like this for the underground pastures as well. I saw the Infirmary tent in the far pasture and realised the potential for a segregated nursing area. I also thought that if we could make a portable field we could perhaps eventually use this in the care of our animals.".

Ikella stared at him, delight in his ingenuity written all over her face.

"Well.", she said. "I am so delighted that at last we seem to be returning to an Age in which past theories can be married to current skills and used without fear or favour for the benefit of all.", and so saying she retired, feeling that her preparations for re-opening the School of Healers were complete.

Chapter 7 - Schontish!

Occasionally during that Harvest term, the Session of Elders met to discuss the progress of the New Hall of Novices. On such an occasion, still bothered by niggling doubts about the wisdom of persisting with Jalani's training, Ikella rested her elbows on the Council table, cupping her face in her hand as she said thoughtfully. "We still have an odd number. Micherryan in the second Rotation is not too difficult to deal with. However, Rowena and her twin in the Third and Jalani in the Fourth, present a problem. Who gets accelerated training and who do we hold back? Surely not Jalani, although she is somewhat behind hand, despite our best efforts.".

Dorra frowned, as Mina said softly.

"Of course, she has completely missed the opportunity to undertake special nursing duties. She has not yet set up an emergency nursing station in the field, nor has she undertaken personal care to a permanently disabled patient, or one that has a terminal illness.".

To which Dorra muttered, "With her experiences in the last journeys of Jenta, I think we can spare her attendance on another death-bed. Her diagnostic skills are not in doubt, though her impatience needs tempering.".

She paused for a moment and then went on briskly, "We can't do anything about balancing numbers now. Should others fall by the wayside we can examine class structures again, but it's a shame we can't continue to tutor Jalani privately. If she was fostered by a tutor, who had time to devote to her training, she wouldn't feel so "different", but I can't take her myself, because of other duties. Satra is currently setting up a permanent sickbay in the barracks and Hanna's in charge of Selesh Infirmary, which precludes her also. Would anyone else care to try?".

Ikella said firmly, "Don't look at me Dorra. I am expecting Daro and Ahnell to saunter in during the First Rites. Short of visiting Sundreth's revenge on myself, I can imagine nothing worse!".

Hidden by the table, her hand made a gently encouraging gesture, which only the odd shifting humours of the ancient room disguised.

There was silence as the impossibility of that situation dawned on the Elders, who, undoubtedly intimidated by the thought, recoiled visibly. Ikella concentrated, augmenting her will without changing expression or position and as she did so, Mina spoke hesitantly:

"I don't teach the first Rotation students.", She said mildly. "If I take Jalani over the areas we need to strengthen and provide one to one training until Jentaroth, we should catch up. I could foster Jalani until she leaves. Now she is free of her problems, perhaps she'll find her own place once she qualifies.?", Another thought struck her and she turned, throwing out a hand in a pleading gesture, speaking in an unusually impassioned tone.

"Selesh owes her a great deal.", She rose to her feet, her expression begging the Sorceress to indulge her and Ikella bent forward to listen.

"While she bears the del Orto name, any posthumous retribution can be applied by Sowdin's followers. We know he had a pack, for they hunted her with him. ", Mina said slowly, voicing her theory even as she thought of it:

"If the Guild were to adopt her, she would have the protection of a name that goes a long way in these, or any other Sands.".

Ikella added her own thoughts.

"If we confer a different name on her, get her out of Hall, before anyone knows her, she will just be another anonymous student when she leaves.", She said thoughtfully.

"She richly deserves our help, for her courage during the epidemic. Perhaps, her prickly personality will provide the cloak she needs, so that she is able to meet what life throws as her, without the seeds of anger and guilt that her Grandfather planted in her mind.".

She glanced round the table. What say all of you?", and with delighted approbation, a unanimous vote was given.

High in a long forgotten Gallery, Jalani caught every word. She listened scowling until Ikella spoke, when she found a lump in her throat. For a moment, her eyes lost focus, as she searched her memory, then she quietly came to a decision.

"I shall be Jalni", she said, remembering the baby contraction of her name. "Yes. I shall be Jalni, meaning "Little Weaver", but let those who wait to do my grandfather's bidding beware, for I have woven a strand of power into my plans. I will hunt as those who once hunted me...", and the promise in her eyes was not merciful.

A full journey of Jenta brought them into the start of Winter term. During that time, the lower school filled with busying students and intent teachers and Jalni moved yet again, to live in Mina's quarters.

All about her, new first Rotation students gathered around the corridors and dormitories and she passed amongst them in solitary silence, arms full of clothes and books.

"They're just a swarm of excited fly-bys.", she thought, as she moved through the multi-coloured throng. "Youngsters, dressed in Clan colours for Induction Day.",

She considered (with an ironic grin), the fact that only three Rotations separated them, then gasped and almost giggled aloud, as one nervous novice (parading in her uniform for the first time), spotted her and hastily bobbed a curtsey.

Crossing the Hall to the Senior Healer's landing, she paused to watch, refusing the impulse to look at their faces, for she knew that amongst the living, she would see her dead friends, forever racing the corridors, Tjerri in the lead, Zambro of the Onyx following and in their wake? Herself?.

She shook her head in exasperation, scolding herself.

"What mood of morbid introspection is this?", she argued. "You can't have premonitions when nothing more momentous than a move of quarters lies in store for you!", and the landing door closed behind her, leaving her truly excluded, neither part of their world, nor really part of the world she had agreed to live in.

"Will I ever find my true place?",

She wondered ruefully, as she made her way to Mina's

quarters and knocked on the door. It opened with a rush, Mina swooped on her seizing the bundle in her arms and dragging her in.

"Come in, come in, no need to knock. This is your home now.", The garrulous little healer hugged her impulsively, exclaiming. "This is wonderful, I am so happy I could burst.".

Unable to emulate Mina's enthusiasm, Jalni nevertheless managed to smile, for the Healer had spared no effort to make her welcome.

She allowed herself to be ushered into a comfortably equipped room, furnished with wall hangings dyed with her mother's recipe. Mina opened the clothing cupboard.

"Don't worry, the original material is here for your use when you are ready.".

Mina indicated the bolt lying on a shelf.

"I thought it would be something to make you feel more at home, so I spoke to Madiv when he delivered last. He supplied the cloth, wove and dyed it himself, then agreed to "forget" it.".

She chuckled adding, "I don't think he had any idea that's what I really meant, but xaniton tea works wonders when you know how to use it!".

She winked conspiratorially at Jalni's expression, but Jalni was overwhelmed and somehow repelled by this much kindness, Though she tried to express her thanks, she couldn't find the words and divining her strange lost mood, Mina smiled at her and simply said.

"We will eat later and perhaps talk, but homework comes first.".

She departed, closing the door behind her, leaving Jalni to her own devices. So began a strange time for the solitary member of the fourth Rotation. Busy with her studies during the day and trying to comply with Mina's wishes during her free time.

She tried, really hard, but Mina was unable to comprehend her need for absolute privacy, total solitude. She took to spending her free time roaming the High Plateau, studying plants with curative properties, or in the peace of the Djellim, researching minerals and some strange salt deposits that she found in the natural soakaways on the Plateau itself. As Winter tightened its grip on Selesh, she took to roaming the ancient recesses of the fortress. Wandering through the corridors, examining cupboards and bookshelves that remained in rooms abandoned by their mysterious predecessors so long ago.

The days rushed into ninenights and she flew through the tests that Ikella set her and all too soon found herself departing formal classes to be tutored privately by Mina daily. She learned avidly, as Mina stretched her abilities relentlessly, but disappeared into the depths of Selesh, rather than endure a social life in the company of her bewildered foster mother, who saw less and less of her worrisome charge outside the classroom.

She avoided all attempts to strengthen their relationship, until Ikella took her to one side, warning her that dangers lurked in the ancient fortress, but Jalni said calmly.

"With respect Deshun, I am not in as much danger as Mina is. Her ceaseless chattering follows me, day in, day out, night in, night out. I know she misses her husband, her baby... but I am not them and she is killing me with kindness. I only look for peace in which to study. In order to hear my own thoughts, I need to be alone!".

Looking into her fearless eyes and seeing her steely resolve, even Ikella relented and did not exactly forbid her explorations.

Jalni's time at Selesh was coming to a close as Jentaroth passed. In three journeys of the moons, First Spring Rites opened the last quarter of her training. Then she would leave Selesh for four Rotations, to roam the Sands of the New Union, learning the song spells to bring back to Ikella. She was not actively looking forward to this part of her training, finding the connection of *othervoice* to the Source, acutely restrictive. She described this sensation to the Sorceress, as a "tightness in her chest", but receiving only that enigmatically raised eyebrow, had never referred to it again. She struggled on with the training, enjoying the applied medication course, hating the *othervoice* training and resenting Mina's attempts to bond with her, until the night she found the spell charts.

She finally rowed with Mina that night, setting off into the lower galleries in a high temper, with Mina panting along behind, trying to apologise. She escaped into the unmarked lower depths of old Selesh, breaking into a run that caused the torch she was carrying to bob and weave, casting huge bewildering shadows about her. Turning through an unfamiliar doorway, she found herself in a small, but lavishly furnished room and ignoring the crazy canting of the floor, raised the torch to investigate.

An elaborately carved comb, made in a rich blue oily stone, lay abandoned on a worktable. She tucked it into her hair and pulled a drawer open, glimpsing scrolls before it jammed. Then the floor beneath her, creaked ominously.

Planting the torch in a sconce, she lay full length on the floor and gritting her teeth, pulled steadily on the drawer, until it opened in a rush, as the floor tilted and slid. Seeing rugs sliding past her into a yawning chasm, Jalni hooked one foot into the bed frame that stood on the door side of the room and using it as a launching pad somersaulted through the doorway and into the corridor beyond. Praying frantically for the grating sounds to stop, she realised that she was clutching the drawer, pinning its contents to her bosom and lay laughing weakly at her close call with death. After the vibrations ceased, she slid backwards, reversing, until she could thrust herself up the wall, into a sitting position, staring through the door into a floorless room.

Only a footspan from her feet yawned nothingness, even the bed had gone and by the light of the abandoned torch on the inside, she sought another to light the corridor. She sang a long, high note as if by habit and above her, well out of reach, one kindled and flared into life. Frowning over this unexpected ability, she crouched, examining the spoils of her adventure. The drawer was crammed with parchment, but she couldn't examine it here, so providing herself with a customary door wedge, she closed, then rendered the door safe, before retiring to a storeroom to examine her finds.

The book she had glimpsed was small, boards bound together with narrow leathery ties, in a beautiful shade of blue. She opened it, glimpsed a fine spidery script and decided to keep it until later. She knew from the vellum that it was very old and hoping it might hold something useful, she slid it into her pocket.

Turning her attention to the scrolls, she discovered that they resembled the spell charts under lock and key in the Djellim. All the students had been allowed to use the great library under Guardian Beneva's supervision and, at the start of the last Rotation, they had all been shown the rare texts and delicate pictograms, encased in a magical field to prevent damage. Now Jalni leant against an underground wall with a highly decorated scroll across her knee, trying to remember what Ikella had told them.

Spell Charts were ancient. Written before Cataclysm, by the long dead Sandsingers. No one knew what they meant and Jalni recalled Beneva saying, that studying these Charts had been banned, to prevent the accidental unleashing of arcane powers that none could control. Jalni (of course), immediately redoubled her efforts. She carefully spread the scroll across a bench, scrutinising it closely. The heavy vellum seemed to come alive under her hand, revealing pictures and ornately framed symbols which she took for words and then, as she turned the scroll rod, one of these leapt up at her, a word that she knew, "Merishwhen!", she whispered and found a link to a picture of the rare fungus. The astounded novice bent closer, but even under the flickering torchlight, she saw beyond a shadow of a doubt, that this scroll might help her read others. The next picture was of a group of houses, centred in a distinctive crater, this, in turn was linked to a block of symbols that she didn't understand. However, the particular juxtaposition of depictions and symbols was compelling evidence that the two subjects were linked in some way. She stared pensively down at the scroll and could resist temptation no longer.

"Merishwhen.", The novice muttered, then. "Merishwhen in Scartel?", then decided that the scrolls merited further attention. Gathering them carefully, she transferred them to a wider drawer in a worktable embellished with carvings of vetali and left. Retaining the book and the odd shaped piece of pottery that had jammed it, she disposed of the original drawer in a pile of furniture and chalked a distinctive yellow cross on the door of the collapsed chamber. She surveyed her handiwork critically, checked the door was wedged and went to bed.

Sliding the book under her pillow, she slept and dreamt.

She stood on a high precipice, singing in a voice she didn't recognise as her own. As she sang, she swooped through the air like a fly-by, landing in the midst of Azure sands, she began to sing again. A strange word came into her mind. "Schontish.", she said and woke.

"What in the Nine Sands does that mean?", she asked herself falling back to sleep.

When she woke, the first thing she remembered was the strange word of her dream. She puzzled over it while she bathed, considering that dream over breakfast, taken alone in the empty refectory, overlooking the Gathering Square.

She was not the only one up and about, for she spotted Ikella leaning on her Staff, coming down the path from the Gate in the Rock. Jalni (naturally curious), looked for visitors, but Ikella was alone.

Tearing herself away from speculation, the novice looked around to see if anyone was close, then pulled the small book out of her tunic pocket and pored over it.

She had to admit to disappointment. Either the light was not good enough and the One only knew that she had chosen the best lit table in the room, or the writing was too badly faded to read, every page filled with closely packed script. She yawned, struggling to keep her eyes on the words, which seemed to jump about as she ran a finger along the line.

"I can't follow this!", she thought crossly, shutting the book with a snap. As she did so, a small piece of parchment fell out, fluttering under the table.

With a muttered curse, she bent to pick it up, as a word leapt out from the scribble written on the scrap. This time, the words really did jump about, the letters twisting and turning as she stared at them and this was not a script that she had ever seen before. Bold and black the word on the parchment nearly burnt her finger as her tongue laboured to form it.

"Schontish.", She breathed the word gently. It sounded strange chimes in her head and she eyed it nervously.

"This could be an incantation of some kind.", She thought, wondering what other words went with it.

She sensed no glamour when she tried the word, tasting it as she spoke it under her breath. Varying the pronunciation, until it came to her lips easily, she worked down the parchment scrap, looking at what seemed to be a list, but as no translation surfaced, she gave up and sat staring at it blankly, tapping her teeth with an impatient finger.

When a drudge eyed her curiously, Jalni carefully folded the scrap inside the book tucking it away safely, and went to a class with Dorra.

One full turn of the sand-glass before Height of Sun, Jalni returned to her quarters, wandering from room to room trying her new word. She sang it cautiously up and down the scale, until the Summoning Bell rang, and Mina reappeared, fluttering around the novice, asking endless questions.

"I missed you last night, where did you go?", (Jalni had learned to ignore that one.)

"Did you sleep well, where did you break your fast?", Jalni told her quite truthfully that she had slept, but had suffered a strange dream, (adding that she had, as usual, taken her dawn meal in the students refectory). This was only the beginning of the ritual interrogation however, and Jalni sighed, determined not to respond.

"Was Jalni well, or was she suffering her difficult times… what had caused her to be so out of humour with everyone, should she tell Ikella that Jalni was ill…".

Jalni rolled her eyes in exasperation.

"Couldn't Mina see that if she just didn't try so hard, they could rub along together tolerably well?".

Eventually, she made her escape to the study rooms allocated to fourth Rotation students, which standing empty somehow underlined her sense of isolation. Collapsing into a chair, she let the temptation of the book enfold her, and leaning against a deep window embrasure, overlooking a herbarium, she leafed through it once more. With growing impatience, she flicked through the pages, looking for the loose scrap, but had reached the last section before becoming aware that the spidery lines were straightening under her tracing finger and she could understand the words on the last page.

They read, "Schontish, a method for silencing a rattling tongue!".

Thinking that she could hear a voice she looked around, but there was no-one there, so she bent her head to read on.

"Take two cups of salt ash leaves gathered when dry. Pound them to a fine powder and add five ling berries, making sure that all seeds are crushed and included.".

She could hear a voice. It sounded in her head, but still the excited girl went on, taking note of each ingredient. Most of them were easily available, and the thought of binding Mina's rattling tongue was a lure she could not ignore.

"Add to the mix four hairs from the head of the one whose tongue you bind. Cover and steep with tange, or citron spirits. Now use nine spoons of grated tastis to create a mix, this will moisten and lighten the flavour. Blend well, into a paste, with ground cerle grains and butter,

shape into a small cake and bake for one run of the sand glass. Cool and cut in four parts, and give to the intended subject only…".

Next came a part that Jalni couldn't read, finishing on the exhortation, "Do not exceed the recommended dose.".

Jalni found herself smiling as she thought.

"How much nicer Mina would be, if only she wasn't so determined to please. More particularly, if she didn't talk so much!".

She spent Sunfall gathering, mixing, grinding and baking industriously. Some of the ingredients were not so easy to find, (such as Mina's hair), but a cautious visit back to their apartment yielded a hairbrush. She was confused by the question uppermost in her mind, which was how to employ the word.

"Do I engage *othervoice* and sing it while mixing the ingredients? Do I make a tune and sing it as a chant while the cake bakes? Or, do I assume "Schontish" is single word command, to be pronounced as the cake is eaten?".

She avoided thinking about the last suggestion in her mind. That sounded too strongly of magic, the sole province of Sorcery to which she definitely didn't have aspirations. Hardly daring to think she could make this strange combination work, she decided to cover all eventualities, chanting softly as the cake baked in a common kitchen area.

No cook, she stared at the result doubtfully thinking it passable, if smaller than expected.

"Now comes the hard part.", she thought, schooling her features to bland innocence. Wrapping the cake in a clean cloth, the precious book in her pocket, she returned to her quarters once more.

Mina was absent and Jalni to her horror realised that she had been so absorbed that she was late for evening refectory, and scowled defiantly at the mirror in the hall as she fled to catch up on her day.

She apologised to Satra, saying (not entirely untruthfully), "I'm sorry I had a very bad night and I came back from classes feeling sick. I'm not hungry.".

Satra, used to adolescents, looked into her eyes, checked her pulses then said placidly, "Your eyes are very dark. Go home, get some sleep and if you are still indisposed tomorrow, tell Mina.", Jalni fled, returning to the silent apartment, where she put the cake on a platter in their day room and went to bed.

In the morning. she rose early, having thought better of her plan and went to retrieve the cake. However, the empty platter sat on the table, silently accusing her. There was no sign of Mina and the Healers door remained closed. Jalni drew a long steadying breath.

"Perhaps the experiment was so disgusting Mina had discarded it?", she looked at the plate and saw crumbs. "Perhaps it hasn't worked?", she thought, "After all, I still don't know how many cakes to employ!", Then another thought struck her and horrified she realised that Mina could be lying dead, or dying, unable to call for help!

Sickened, she retrieved the book, flicking to the back of it and the scrap of parchment fluttered on to the bed. She absently gathered it, turning pages, but no matter how hard she looked, she couldn't find the recipe.

She was almost in tears when a sound made her look up. Framed in the doorway Mina stood looking absolutely dreadful. Normally a plump, cheery little woman, today she looked old, haggard and she had wrapped her throat in a scarf.

Jalni's heart lurched painfully, as the Healer looked at her searchingly, then tapped her hands together indicating the use of hand code. Her fingers flickered with a single question,.

"Why?", she begged silently.

When Jalni followed her to their day-room, she sat rocking desolately in her husband's favourite chair, and Jalni saw (with horror) that she had cut Mina's connection to the Source by silencing her *othervoice* as well. A single tear trickled down Mina's face as Jalni signed urgently:

"Ikella…?".

Mina, nodded once, rose unsteadily and went back to her room, closing the door, on her distraught fosterling as Jalni fled.

Satra was crossing the Gathering Square when she caught sight of Jalni headed in her direction. The look on the girls face stopped her in her tracks.

"What is it?".

Jalni was gabbling something at her, pressing objects into her hands. Satra grasped a piece of parchment then

a plate on which a few crumbs remained. She barely understood what the child was saying, but caught the sense, if not the actual words.

"Mina. I poisoned Mina. I didn't mean to hurt her. Help her Satra. Give this to Ikella!".

Then Jalni passed her in two strides, racing up the tunnel to the Gate in the Rock.

Once outside the complex, Jalni didn't know where to turn, or what to do. Walking slowly up the track to the plateau above Selesh, she sought solitude. She plucked a leaf here and there, adding ingredients to the scrip she carried, hoping something she found would help Mina. She wandered aimlessly, waiting for the inevitable summons, the heat boiling under the lowering roll of cloud. A voice called, commandingly.

"Jalni return!"

She ignored it for as long as she could, sat on a rock, in a shallow depression, well away from the usual paths taken by herb gatherers, but the voice continued, coming closer and closer, louder and more insistent. Sighing, she got to her feet and resigned to her fate, turned her feet back to Selesh and the punishment waiting below.

Jalni, tired and dusty, handed her scrip to Hanna at the Gate, noting that her usual companions were conspicuous by their absence. Alone, ignoring the guards (who shadowed her every move), she walked head bowed, through a deserted Gathering Square, oblivious of the oppressive atmosphere in the corridors beyond and went to bathe.

Leaving her clothes where they fell, she entered a plunge pool, washed swiftly and returned to her cubicle to change. Fresh robes had appeared and she was nearly dressed when she abruptly remembered the book secreted in her tunic pocket. She froze, eyes searching frantically, but both her grubby work wear and book had vanished!

Stunned, she drew the curtain and an armed escort surrounded her. Silently, they

marched her through guarded doors to an inner sanctum, where bracketed by the restraining hands of her captors, she was forced to kneel at the pleading stand, facing the Sorceress.

Only now, did the prisoner glance at her escort. Driss and Jashell, Joint Commanders of the Inner Guard, behind them, Sorrill and Diras, Captains of the Watch. Briefly, something perverse in Jalni was entertained.

"At least they're taking real notice of me now!", was the thought that crossed her mind, tempered by the realisation that an appearance in Ikella's small Judgment Hall, might end in her death...

"Or worse.", agreed an icily silken voice in her head, as Jalni staring into those lambent green eyes, became totally convinced that Ikella could read her mind.

The Sorceress opened the proceedings gravely.

"Jalani del Orto, now known as Jalni bin Selesh, you have admitted causing dire injury to one Mina bin Attwa. You are not on trial for attempted murder. Having sensibly admitted your fault, you are here to explain your reasoning in this matter and submit yourself to your fellow Healers, who must decide your future in the craft.".

As the Session of Elders gathered to judge her, Jalni's mind raced.

"What defence could she offer? They knew everything about her, perhaps more than she realised.", and she subsided miserably convinced that she wouldn't get a fair hearing, because Mina was one of their number. Her thoughts were hardly allayed by Indeera, prowling stealthily behind her. It was unnerving! Jalni could feel the speculative gaze of the High Priestess. From her scalp, a thin needle of ice traced a terrifying trail behind her left ear and the razor sharp blade of Indeera's ceremonial spear glittered thirstily, intent on drinking her attention, if not her blood. The novice shuddered.

Ikella stood tall and imperious, the runes worked into her robes glittering with power. Thankfully she wasted no time on protocol, demanding gravely:

"Who speaks for the Healer, Mina bin Attwa?".

Hanna rose to her feet.

"I speak for Mina", she responded with dignity and as a scribe wrote hastily, Ikella nodded, asking, "Who speaks for this novice?".

To an overstretched imagination, her dry tones proclaimed, that Ikella wouldn't willingly entertain Jalni's name in her mouth and belatedly, the novice remembered their long term friendship. Satra stood, her voice reassuring if not friendly.

"I will speak in defence of Jalani del Orto.", she said calmly, to which Ikella raised an eyebrow, before appointing Andria to speak for the Guild, stating in an undertone that she would take no part in the proceedings as a Guardian, but would retain her interest as Sorceress, head of the Clan whose hospitality Jalni had abused.

The sand-glass turned four times as the court examined her. They listened carefully, hearing in her own words how estranged from society she felt. Childhood memories (long suppressed) surfaced. Evenings spent weaving on a wooden frame with Rowin, her needle board carved by Viness. Happy days washing out dyes, testing colours, then the dark days under the influence of her grandparents. In the middle of describing Serba's regular confrontations with Viness, she hesitated, retreating once more into reticence, until Ikella said in a carefully neutral tone.

"Jalni, you have this one chance to redeem yourself. No-one here understands why you are as you are. If you don't tell us everything, we can't help you find a better Way to conduct your life.", and Jalni forced herself to consider her fate as the Session of Elders sat in uncompromising silence.

Eventually she told them about her escape. A half Rotation of hiding, running, sleeping through the days to travel at night and lastly her arrival at Selesh, only to be ostracised by the other students. They were made to see a lonely, orphaned child, so used to starvation she couldn't bear to eat with others. They saw her inability to trust, her fearful refusal of friendship, her sorrow and needless guilt over the lost students of the epidemic. In mid-sentence Jalni herself suddenly understood that she was angry. Not with everyone else, but with herself and that happy garrulous Mina was the last straw.

She closed her eyes, whispering desperately. "I can't understand her. She is always so happy and yet her life is full of sorrow. She nursed many of my friends and they died. She lost her own man and their child, but she still smiles, still sings! She says she would be proud to call me daughter, but why? I'm no good, I killed my own mother! If she hadn't made the blue dye for me, Sowdin would have left her alone. I probably brought the epidemic, poking around, studying things from the past".

She was frantically clutching at the pleading stand, her knuckles white. She mentally clutched at stray thoughts linking them to her sorrows, in a voice choked and hoarse with unwept tears.

"I kept away from everyone, because Sowdin told me that I was death. That everyone I loved and cared for would die and they did. Father, Mother, Tjerri...".

Sobbing convulsively, she collapsed, only a fragment of speech audible, she wailed:

"I couldn't save the children. They all died, Sowdin was right and it is my fault, my fault, mine. I am death, I am death.".

Horrified Healers looked helplessly at each other, then Satra spoke for them all .

"How could such pain walk amongst us unseen? How could an untrained Talent conceal it so well?", She asked, dropping into her seat, resignation in every line of her body.

Dorra answered awkwardly. "Deshun, we overlooked one point. A party of Wanderers disguised her presence in their midst, sneaking her past Sowdin's huntsmen, from Caranchar to our village. Could her erratic grasp of power have attracted their interest? Could something have contributed to the antipathy of her grandparents in an equal and opposite reaction?",

Ikella looked at the Novice Mistress sombrely. "It never occurred to me until now.", she said reluctantly, "However, everything needs to be considered very seriously. Viness was Nishanawa and the One only knows how little we know of her people! Raised in the Ashgenar Wilderness, she served at the Temple of the Winds, then went to Sanctuary as a warrior, returning at its Fall, in the Rotation preceding Partition.". Eyeing Jalni sombrely she explained.

"She took your father two Rotations later, but they lost their first child before it quickened. Service at Sanctuary normally prevents conception, but after Sanra's Skythe treatment, you were born. Did your mother's history have any bearing on your erratic grasp of power? Or was it your Father's death and your Grandparents influence that distorted your temperament?.". She sighed, suddenly very humanly aware of the consequences for the novice and answered her own question.

"The One help me, I just don't know! However, the combination of the two is dangerous. To yourself, to others, including us. Now, we have to decide what to do about you.".

She faced the judges and said slowly, "I ask you all to search your minds and hearts. Take time, for we cannot afford mistakes.".

A bell chimed and The Elders folded their hands in contemplative silence. Jalni recovering her composure, adopted a more comfortable position and thought about the question herself.

"Was she really dangerous?", and devoutly prayed not to be, as Ikella's eyes rested on her thoughtfully.

At the turn of the sand-glass, the Sorceress spoke to her gravely.

"The first principle of Healing is trust. Trust in each other, permits the sisters of the craft to share their skills. Trusting the Rule, keeps us safe in dangerous places. Trusting our Elders with our troubles, allows us to find solutions.

Trusting experience allows us to teach, so that we, who have built our lives on mutual trust and responsibility, can pass on that training to the next generation of our kind. This trial is about trust. In particular, the trust Mina placed in one who failed to return it.". The Sorceress paused and in that moment Jalni understood that judgment swift and inevitable was about to be delivered, as four pairs of hands secured her.

All she could see of the room was Ikella, glowing in terrible power as she asked the judges:

"Trust or still?", to which Hanna said sadly, "Still!". Dorra spoke apologetically. "Still, I think."

Followed by Satra's emphatic "Trust.". Tisanna, herself an exile, since Partition, gave a considered answer:

"With great power comes even greater responsibility, Jalni. I have seen what power in the hands of one unfitted to wield it means. My vote is for the safety of yourself and for the others you encounter in your life. I vote to Still!".

She looked up at the terrified novice and an expression of great pain crossed her homely features. Andria said with great conviction. "Trust.", then Jalni realised that someone still had to vote. Ikella was looking directly over Jalni's head at Indeera and too late, Jalni remembered that as High Priestess of the Inesh, she also had voting rights where the safety of the Inesh was at risk.

She flinched as the warrior took a deep breath and nearly fainted when a calm, still voice said, "Trust, one last time.".

"So. I have the casting vote!", Ikella said softly, giving Jalni no hint of what was to come. Hardly had the dazed girl realised that her life hung by the thread in Ikella's hand, when that same hand lifted and a narrow beam of light shot from her fingers. It caressed Jalni's throat, danced along her shoulders and chest, transforming breath, paralysing speech, immobilising movement. Pinioned by power, Jalni's perception blurred, replaced by a whirl of wall, tapestry and lights. She struggled to stand, thoroughly disorientated, clinging to consciousness, to the fierce grasp of Jashell, who said softly, "Courage sister.".

Then, as the world began to fade away, Jalni heard Ikella's voice declare solemnly,

"As holder of the casting vote, I choose "Trial by Trust."

Jalni, caught in Ikella's controlling web, slipped into blessed darkness and slept.

Ikella sighed as she released the limp form of the novice and allowed her to slip to the floor gently. Driss and Jashell stooped quickly and lifted her unresisting form between them and carried her from the room and as they did so, Ikella sat in her state chair, as the magic died down in her. The scribe made tiny scratching sounds as he noted the events industriously, the Elders sat quietly and a while later the guards returned alone and a small high bell chimed. The Sorceress, raised her head and spoke.

"It is my intention to retire while the prisoner sleeps.", she began. "Every movement she makes is under scrutiny and Indeera is on call. When she wakes, I will take my watch also and we will see if we chose rightly."

She clapped her hands together and looking round the table announced.

"She has two choices. Obey the Rule, sing true and live, or, breach our Trust, be Stilled and die!"

She smiled faintly at the murmurs of shock around the table and said harshly:

"She is too unpredictable. To keep such a power imprisoned is impossible. Letting her go to seek revenge is inconceivable. No, this was always a life or death decision and I, the only one who could make it.".

She saw the reluctant comprehension in their eyes and continued briskly, rising to her feet:

"Enough, for tonight at least. She must endure her own conscience and her own company, caged in the Cavern of the Singers, if she can.".

The other women whispered together until Dorra spoke for them.

"She will have access to the greatest written treasures of Sorcery.", she objected.

"She has already used one ancient incantation for her own ends without thinking of the consequence to others.".

Ikella nodded agreement.

"This is why she will be imprisoned in the Cavern of the Singers",

She responded grimly.

"At least there, she cannot harm anyone but herself and I will make sure, that if she investigates just one parchment, just one book, she will know my power!".

She raised her hand against the babble of protest.

"A Trial of Trust can have no significance if we show no trust, give the one on trial no chance to betray that trust. Imprisoned in the Cavern of the Singers, she will have access to many texts that even we Guardians cannot read. If she can use these we had better know about it.".

With that she rose and imperiously swept out of the room.

A bare ten sectors of a sand glass saw her standing outside the bars of a great, circular cage, which occupied the centre of an enormous cavern, one whole wall of which was lined with book shelves and scroll-bags of obvious antiquity. Ignoring these, the Sorceress observed the cage dispassionately. Capable of holding up to ten prisoners in comfort, tonight, it held only one and she still lay dazed, on a solid metalwork floor.

The cage was supplied with a simple mattress covered with a rough blanket. A single pillow and a second blanket lay on the floor and the Sorceress deduced from their position, that one of her guards had attempted some rough comfort for the prisoner. An uncompromising bucket stood on one side, on the other, a washed out wineskin hung, giving the prisoner access to water. On the mattress, unwrapped, lay a piece of bread and a greenfruit.

The Sorceress closed her eyes and the air around her hummed with a tense wire thin ringing sound. Jalni stirred into consciousness, as the sound increased in volume, irritating her ears, gnawing at her brain like a buzz fly in mid symphony. She slapped out at it, coming to her senses, as she found herself facing the Sorceress, cloaked in the veil of power.

The prisoner stood and spoke defiantly.

"So, you have decided to silence me have you?", adding bitterly, "You don't have to torture me as well. I know I did wrong. I know it should never have gone that far. I freely admit my guilt, my shame and offer my sorrow. Why don't you Still me and leave me here to die? It is what you intend to do isn't it?"

Ikella eyed her curiously.

"What do you know of the Stilled?", She asked and Jalni hung her head, whispering.

"That they are shunned, punished, sent away because they cannot control the power. That

they live the life of exiles, existing in the villages on the Fringe, only employed as guides to travellers.".

Ikella looked at the girl steadily as she spoke.

"Jalni, those we Still, are as unpredictable as a Myst Cat. Often those who should succeed easily. I believe that in this night we will discover if you are of their number. Will you control not only your power, but your temper or will you allow it to control you?".

Her stern voice grew very gentle as she said deliberately: "I won't lie to you child. It is not your power that has brought you here. It is your simple disobedience to the Rule.".

At Jalni's obvious confusion, she stated in ringing tones:

"Firstly, do no harm, by action or inaction. Did you not understand that because you deliberately administered a substance that you had no chance to research, you nearly killed Mina? If you do not understand the betrayal of that action, how can I trust you with the lives of all those in Selesh?".

She held up a scrap of parchment and Jalni stared at it in horrid fascination, as Ikella continued, "I do not need this to persuade the Elders that you are too erratic to trust at this stage" and the fragment flared into flame in her hands. Jalni trembled waiting for the pain, as the power was ripped from her memory, the *othervoice* stilled in her throat, but Ikella was speaking again.

"We won't Still you at the close of the day.", She explained. "Here, you will spend this night alone, for this is the Cavern of the Singers, where no magic can escape, where for centuries before Cataclysm, we believe the ancient mages of our world, practised High Magic of an order that I pray you never see. Here, you can sing if you want to, start to feel comfortable with your othervoice, it could be for the last time.".

She lowered her voice warningly.

"You will pray most earnestly to understand what you have done and call on whatever powers you care to use to steel yourself for tomorrow, but, know that you won't again use ancient writings to which you have no right, to gain advantage or power over another.".

Her own tightly controlled power was revealed, tiny bell like notes sounding as she walked away. Standing some thirty paces from Jalni, she raised her arms to spell cast.

"By the binding of air and sight, by the binding of earth and sound, by the binding of fire and feeling, by the binding of water and wisdom.", Her voice deepened, transforming to *othervoice*, ringing with odd harmonics, as the rapid chant swelled and grew.

"I bind you by the Nine Sands of Pelshar. To the circle. To the time. To this place. Ish Voreyhhi".

A bubble of light appeared above the Sorceress. Hissing and fizzing like lightening unleashed, it leapt towards the cowering novice and circled the cage three times, before the bars of the cage shimmered and shook ominously.

As Jalni crouched, her hands over her ears, the Sorceress observed her impassively, then with a nod of satisfaction, she turned on her heel and left. A door closed softly and the novice knelt, alone in the dark and sobbed.

Chapter 9 - The Cavern of the Singers

On a secret stairway to her study, the Sorceress leant against the wall reviewing her decisions. then she wearily took another few treads, before she stopped to consider what options were open to Jalni if she passed this Trial of Trust.

"With a background and temperament as dangerous as those who may stalk her, that girl will need full social rehabilitation, (or some influence infinitely greater than mine) if she is to survive her youth.", she observed grimly, frowning over her impossible novice.

After the epidemic, Ikella had planned on extending Jalni's training, but in the light of this escapade, she doubted the wisdom of attaching Jalni to Hanna when her Song Walk was done. She considered Carolus, with his wide knowledge of medicine, but the deceptively innocent twinkle in the Apothecary's eye concealed the identity of Sanctuary's Master Spy. Even after his recruitment of Olneth in his stead, she viewed his mysterious comings and goings with the suspicion that he was playing some "long game" of his own. At the thought of combining his duplicity with Jalni's erratic command of power, she shuddered delicately, abandoning the idea instantly.

Wrapped in such thoughts the Sorceress made her way to her study, considering the questions raised by Indeera.

"We found words on her Deshun. What else has she discovered or used?".

Ikella forced herself to examine the wisdom of leaving Jalni alone with the Book of Rule, and inevitably her thoughts embraced Daro and his fascination with the Sandsingers of their far and forbidden past.

They had not yet returned, which was fortunate under the circumstances. If she knew her son, or his companion in crime, she also knew that they would be championing Jalni if they were here. It was precisely the same kind of wilful curiosity that led to their exile. She brought herself up short, thinking.

"Is it nearly four Rotations since I sent those scamps away? Nearly four Rotations since I last saw Daro?".

Knowing that the boys she had exiled, would return grown men, she wondered if she would recognise them, glancing involuntarily to the place where she remembered Daro leaning against the window embrasure. Tall and getting taller, darkly impressive good looks, deep turquoise eyes with an odd golden fleck in their depths, bronzed skin, determined jaw and sensual mouth. Then the memories turned to Daro sulking, Daro in a temper and she shivered apprehensively. Less than a quarter to First Rite of Spring and the return of the wanderers, at which thought she froze, thinking wildly.

"Is that it? Was Daro the child of a Wanderer? His mother apparently from the Amber Sands, was wandering the Opal Sands at the time of his birth? Was his heritage to blame for his strange obsession with power, and who or what was his father?".

She finally took herself to task as the watch bell chimed the Guard change. Disrobing, she lay on her bed, thinking about her twin problems.

In a way she hoped that Jalni would just sob herself to sleep. in another quite perverse sense, she hoped that the novice would take up the challenge set for her. That would prove her prowess with magic and her ability to resist temptation. If only she understood that she wouldn't be in this situation had she not meddled with a...", she yawned prodigiously as the word "medicantric" popped into her weary mind, falling asleep before she could challenge its origin..

At third watch she rose, pulling on a warmer robe and cloaked against the chill, made her way back into the secret passages that only she and Beneva knew. Cautiously tiptoeing to a small wall hanging that concealed a spy-hole, she lifted a corner and peered at her prisoner.

Only a miserable sob told the Sorceress that the novice still breathed. She had made no attempt to cover herself against the deepening chill of the night. Whilst approving the totality of Jalni's submission, Ikella viewed such uncharacteristic capitulation with suspicion. Eventually, with reluctance the Sorceress admitted that this was as much a trial of endurance for her, as it was to the now soundly sleeping prisoner. An empowered hand lifted as a comfortably padded chair materialised. Her fingers brushed a tall metal rod and it glowed to warm her. She gestured and there was just enough light to see what Jalni was doing, as Ikella settled to her self-appointed vigil.

The novice slept like one dead for three or four hours... waking with a start just before the weak light of dawn penetrated the cavern. She lay still for a moment, getting her bearings and then with a lithe movement she gained her feet and stretched deliberately. Ignoring her surroundings, she went through an exercise program until she had warmed every group of muscles, limbering up in much the same way that the Inesh did. Ikella frowned, wondering if Jalni had learned this from Viness (the last of the Nishan warriors).

After her exercise Jalni sat on the mattress and waited patiently for the grey light to grow. It came so gradually, that she didn't notice the moment at which she could see (albeit dimly), through an open door to the Syndarial. This robing room stood behind the Sacred Circle and apart from an ornately pierced screen, nothing stood between the prisoner and the Hall of the Healers. Jalni's brow furrowed as she contemplated the open door. It had been firmly shut and she believed locked when the Sorceress visited her last night. She turned around on her bed and looked thoughtfully at the door of the cage, examined the thick iron bars that surrounded her and then turned again to peer at the open door beyond.

She could see no evidence of a guard, so she prowled the perimeter of the cage, hands loosely clasped behind her back. She appeared to be relaxed, but the Sorceress, from her hidden vantage point could see the tension in her shoulders, in the tic of a muscle beside a set jaw. She waited, this was a decision for Jalni to make alone. She followed the novice's mind easily, seeing Jalni lie full length on her mattress again, staring up, running the geography of the Hall through her head. In the passageway, the Sorceress caught the thread of her thoughts, swirling them in a scrying glass, seeing through Jalni's eyes the Way of Challenge, the doors, the short walk to the Gate in the Rock and freedom.

Quite dispassionately, Jalni was comparing her options. Weighing the chance of making a successful escape, against that of surrendering her powers. Although she could hardly believe it, Ikella could see that Jalni was not particular which way the winds blew. She was tired of a life where she didn't belong, happy to lose the *othervoice* she didn't trust, which would excuse her solitary nature. A picture of a solitary cat appeared in Ikella's scrying glass.

Contemplating separation from the Source, Ikella shivered, then remembered Mina and strengthened her resolve.. Her mouth thinned and turned downward as she turned the sand-glass once more.

Jalni sat up, crossed her legs and ate the food provided. She thought about life if she was stilled, gloomily. The process changed women irrevocably, leaving them unable to live in Healer communities, so great was the anguish of separation from the Source. Many left the deserts completely, living in the Fringe, working as guides for traders. Some went mad, others died, many never spoke again (rather than remind themselves of what they had lost), but it was all the same to Jalni, who thought about Mina, cut off from everything that had been her life. She wept, burning with shame.

This much was revealed in Ikella's scrying glass and then the image wavered, the voice the Sorceress heard faded and she looked up to see Jalni caught in a wave of self-loathing.

The light stole greyly through the chambers leading from the Great Hall itself as Ikella, roused by the watch spell she had cast, waited patiently, for although the child didn't yet know it, her true test was about to begin.

Eventually roused from her introspective reverie, Jalni used the bucket provided for her comfort. She found a small bowl, poured a little water into it and damping the linen that had wrapped her food, washed her face and hands, drying them on the spare blanket. She drank only one mouthful of water, and high above at the Watchers post Ikella approved her student's frugality. Creating a serape against the pre-dawn breeze, Jalni sat playing finger games, until the light was precisely right for her final act of defiance.

Gradually, the shelved books and scroll-bags became visible. Soon the kitchen drudges would rise, soon Jalni would be made to face her future. To the Watcher above, she seemed just to be sitting still, perhaps contemplating her fate, but Ikella had learned not to trust her eyes, but always to keep her finger on the pulse of the Source. Here, she could detect subtle changes. Although she could see nothing overt and the prisoner remained on her bed, something was afoot. She heard a faint "click", leaning forward as it sounded again, but this time, she was able to detect a change in the integrity of the cage.

"Whatever is that child doing?", she wondered as the door of the cage swung gently open.

Leaning closer to the spy hole in her anxiety, the Sorceress could see that Jalni still hadn't moved and now the cage door swung shut, the lock engaged once more. Ikella moved herself into a better position and as she did so, the cage door swung open and Jalni was out of it in one bound.

So swift was the action that the Sorceress nearly missed it. One moment Jalni was perched on the mattress, the next, she was up and running. It seemed to Ikella that some force was in play as the girl blazed through the Syndarial, negotiating the narrow entrance at the rear of the Sacred Circle, to leap past the Book of Rule. Her long limbs blurred as she sped down the Way of Challenge, running like an Irix and Ikella held her breath, for if the novice left the safety of the Hall, she would surely die at the hands of the Inesh.

However, as Jalni came to the doors, she leapt into the air, somersaulting at the top of the leap, then bounded back to the metalled edge of the Circle, with a series of flick flacks, ending with another astonishingly high somersault, landing stock-still on her feet, facing the Symbol of Sanctuary, to which she made a low and reverent bow.

Ikella's mouth quivered, curved for a fraction and then she swiftly controlled the urge to smile and frowned.

"Sacrilege", she snorted, but settled to watch the novice finish her floor exercises. They came to an end at the edge of the Sacred Circle, and the Sorceress had to steel her own nerves, as Jalni approached the Book of Rule.

"If she opens it, the matter is out of my hands!", Ikella told herself, feeling as if she should shout a warning. Instead of which she gripped the table and firmly applied herself to the spy hole, thinking.

"None but an empowered Sorceress can lift the cover anyway.", clinging to the belief that their sacred Book had been provided by the last Sandsinger, for the next to follow. She continued to muse.

"Of course, they didn't know that none ever had, or that none ever would, but the Way dictates that she shall die if she tries.". She shook herself crossly.

"What am I thinking! Sandsingers indeed! They've been gone since Cataclysm, if they ever existed before. I should be grateful we don't suffer those more given to self indulgence than sense of responsibility!".

Then as she turned away, intent on returning to the Hall before disaster struck, she wondered how she had known that, blinking tired eyes at the next spy hole level with the Sacred Circle.

Jalni was sitting on the floor like a child, studying the stone stand on which the Book of Rule was chained. By the time the Sorceress had her back in her sights, The girl was running her fingers over the intricate patterns on the stand and her lips were moving as if she rehearsed a speech or a vow to herself. Ikella sensing no change in the Source relaxed as Jalni stood. Placing a hand on the Book, she closed her eyes momentarily, before turning to walk back to the cage. She swung the door shut, then sat on the bed awaiting judgment.

Ikella, leant against the wall, listening to her own heart pounding with relief. Somehow, Jalni had recognised her danger and reached the correct decision. All Ikella had to do was to steer the course of events in the right direction.

"Maybe, just maybe this night has had its purpose.", she thought as she straightened and went to begin what was to be a long, trying day.

Since Partition, mornings had been a time for reports, repairs, or replacement of supplies. Lists would be compiled, to go before Committees for approval in the cool, after Height of Sun. Only the Session of Elders or the High Council met early in the day, when punishments were to be carried out. Ikella had never seen the point in prolonging the agony. After all, if you were waiting to die, better to go to the Sands when they were warm and welcoming and the darkness of the night couldn't steal your soul.

She wasted no time calling the Elders to the Inner Sanctum, dispatching the Inesh to bring Jalni from the cage as she paced restlessly. She had dressed with care, lifted her Staff, kissing the Opal at its head in the daily ritual of obeisance to the Sands she served, but now, she couldn't remember a time when she felt less eager to greet the day.

An air of expectation filled the room, faces turned towards her and conversations ceased as she approached her chair and as one they stood as she sat. She placed empowered hands on the table, the glow of the hidden emblem blazed forth at her touch, as she convened the Session, praying that she was not about to make a terrible mistake. She cleared her throat, then began without preamble.

"One of the most disturbing thoughts I have entertained regarding Jalani del Orto, is that given the right conditions, she could become more powerful than I. We therefore must endeavour to influence those growing powers for good.".

She paused, speaking slowly and in a low voice.

"I consider that if treated carefully she could mature into a redoubtable Healer, if she has no aspirations to Sorcery. What she lacks, as a result of her life's experience, is judgement and self-control."

The other women were nodding in agreement, so she continued.

"If I still her now....", As those words left her mouth, the door crashed open and Mina strode through a press of Guards, a Healer hovering anxiously at her heels.

"You will still Jalni over my dead body.", said the invalid, albeit in a rasping whisper, her voice still affected by the medicantric, but nevertheless she spoke and stood alone, unaided.

Another door to the Inner Sanctum opened, allowing the prisoner escort to enter with Jalni between them, her face pale but determined, her back straight. Mina held out her arms to her and it was plain from Jalni's face that she longed to go to her foster-mother, but in a new sense of restraint, she looked to Ikella for permission first. Ikella nodded and wordlessly Jalni dropped to her knees in front of Mina, who simply patted her shoulder and made murmuring noises of encouragement. Ikella looked round the table, she could see the pleasure and relief on the faces of the Elders and knowing her decision to be the right one, she indicated that Mina should sit in her usual place at her own right hand, assisting her to do so gently.

Jashell pressed Jalni firmly on the shoulder so that the novice, who had regained her feet, was propelled forward to stand at the table opposite Ikella. The Sorceress looked deep into unflinching eyes, noting the quiver of her throat, the tautening of lips above the determined tilt of the child's chin, and thought...

"At last. She is fearful, but accepts her punishment without anger. She doesn't appear resentful of Mina, or me, not even with her situation. Perhaps we shall see her change yet.".

Her decision made, Ikella raised her Staff. Jalni (watching apprehensively), saw the glow start at the Staff and envelop the Sorceress, until the brilliance was almost too much to bear, until Ikella's voice rang out commandingly.

"Today, Jalani del Orto must pass into memory, never to be revived, for I believe that to take advantage of a new beginning, you must bury the past along with that name. To take that step, you must become a new person. One that expects to make mistakes and gain forgiveness, one that recognises without hatred that others also make mistakes. When you can forgive your parents for dying, when you can forgive your grandparents their ignorance and prejudice, when you can forgive yourself for fear, anger and resentment then you may become a Healer.". Ikella stared soberly across the great symbol glowing on the table and into Jalni's wide, unbelieving eyes.

"Jalni bin Selesh, If it is your intention to submit wholly to my judgement, place your hands on the Seal.", She commanded and stretched a hand to touch the magical emblem herself. As Jalni complied, she was held, pinioned by a touch of power that swept from the table to her hands and upwards enveloping her in a mist of colour, like dancing motes of dust around her.

She bowed her head, waiting for the pain that would seize her throat, severing her link to the Source. She couldn't believe she was forgiven, but incredibly she heard Ikella proclaim.

"Jalni bin Selesh, justice and judgement have been determined. Your sentence is to be bound in duty to the Infirmary of Selesh as a probationer. You are bound to the confines of settlement, village and grazing areas. You are bound to live in harmony with all inhabitants alike. When you can do that, I will judge you mature enough to complete your training in Hall. You are further bound not to make use of any records open or sealed, without the aid of a trained Healer. Furthermore, you are forbidden to use *othervoice* unless supervised.".

The light from the Seal faded and Jalni stood facing the Sorceress. Ikella leaned forward.

"Jalni, you have been given another chance, another life awaits you. This is due entirely to the way that you have conducted yourself during your Trial of Trust.".

"If you conduct yourself properly, you will return to training, but this is your last chance.".

The Opal Staff was grounded in dismissal as Jalni was led away to collect her pitiful collection of belongings. Numbly, she followed Jashell to a lowly dormitory where she unpacked.

A Healer swept her with a scornful glance remarking, "Put your belt on girl, there is work to do and mind I don't catch you trying to poison my patients!".

Then, dismissing the guards with a flap of the hand, she marched Jalni off to begin her probationary sentence.

Chapter 10 - Scroll of Prophecy

As the moons waxed and waned, an uneasy peace was achieved. Jalni settled down in the Infirmary, but failed to enrol for classes, creating the impression that her vocation was questionable. The novice nevertheless proved both industrious and obedient. Surprised, Ikella became cautiously optimistic about the girl and returned to her previous pre-occupation with the deteriorating weather.

"Perhaps,", she admitted reluctantly to herself, "The true cause of my agitation will soon be on his way home. Although I could have done with Olneth to watch for him, or Carolus to intervene if things turn difficult.".

Tensions had grown in Selesh, as previously self sufficient communities (gathered before Jentaroth), remained to over-winter in the ancient settlement

"Which would be all well and good, if only they would go home after End of Rotation.", Satra, the Guild provisioner cried in despair at which Ikella nodded.

"They seem particularly reluctant to depart before Spring Rites this Rotation.", the Sorceress agreed, "More and more of Selesh has been opened to accommodate them, despite my still not having a Master Builder to make repairs. Its all very irregular.". She sighed deeply, remembering Errish with a pang.

She ought to look forward to the return of Daro and Ahnell, but having left under less than desirable circumstances, she was curiously apprehensive. Dealing with highly charged emotions was never Ikella's favourite occupation, and she could have done without that situation within the unbearably overcrowded confines of Selesh where tensions were already running high.

The Apothecary and his spy-master friend Olneth, had departed for Malos during the previous ninenight and she chuckled ruefully, as she wished they had stayed.

"What am I thinking of? The place is full to overflowing and here I am wishing for two more to feed. I am bewitched as well as befuddled!". She shifted uncomfortably, rubbing her tired eyes. For ninenights now, she had hardly slept. The previous night, determined to find some answer to reassure the people, she had sat at her new worktable examining one of a number of scrolls that had lain in its drawers. Tonight while others rested, she laboured over it again, summoning immense concentration and drawing on enhanced powers. Absently sparking the lamp overhead with a gesture, she considered consulting Beneva, dismissing that idea as she thought of it. The elaborate preparations for First Rites of Spring, were laid out on the floor of the Library right now, captivating Beneva's attention, which was all to the good, for her own abilities eluded her.

Cold and unusually depressed, she turned her mind to a pile of Infirmary reports, worrying about numerous blind patients suffering from unrelieved pain. She re-read the reports, making mental notes and soft comments, "Odd.", she said gruffly, followed by, "Too many to ignore!", and sent a runner to find Hanna.

Leaving the scroll where it lay, weighted beneath an obsidian shard elaborately carved in the form of a mythical creature. She stood, hand gentling the scroll-weight as she often did when particularly troubled. Her fingers traced the poised head, arched neck, its flowing mane and tail. It warmed to her touch as she ran her hands over its slender legs, delicate feet and gently touched the small single horn that sprang from the creatures brow, as she waited for the slap of Healer sandals to approach her door.

Thoughtfully she stretched her back, it ached abominably and she diverted herself, with the recollection of Carolus telling her that her scroll-weight was a representation of a Zephryn, the legendary storm-horse of the past. She smiled as she thought of the ungainly beast that he had named for this elegant creature. Sighing wistfully, she abandoned the scroll-weight to consider what to advise Hanna in the matter of pain relief.

"I have to do something.", she thought dully, "but what?". Her eyes strayed back to the scroll, as she thought fiercely, "If only I could sleep, perhaps I would feel more able to cope.".

Her mind leapt to her own impossible workload. The Healers were worked off their feet, dispensing herbal remedies which were not as effective as they had hoped. Selesh Minoria had sustained substantial damage from a prolonged lightening storm and besides the damage reports from there, she must also read the recommendations of the High Council regarding an emergency unfolding in the Azure Sands.

The weary woman shifted, arching her back as the details ran through her mind. Her Sister in Sorcery, Tirjella, was now quarantined at Darnesh, another of the ancient underground settlements. Tirjella had appealed for help, staring from the scrying table in the Council Chamber, where Beneva had been working.

"Guardian, I just received a runner from Scartel.", The Sorceress of the Azure Sands blurted.

"It comes from Solana, who says that an epidemic has wiped out the entire adult population of the township. As the first crossing point on our northern border to the Malachite and the nearest large settlement to the Opal, I thought to warn you.".

The elegant redhead was pale and Beneva wasted no time, touching her wristlet to alert Ikella so that even as the Sorceress answered the summons, she heard every word as she came to the Djellim.

"Except for our dear sister Solana and her servant Orto, the children are alone. Solana has taken the children in and warded the village, before sending Orto with her message. He is in our Infirmary, recovering from exhaustion. We are keeping him isolated, but he seems well enough. However, I now have six settlements within range of Scartel, quarantined, all travel is banned in or out of the Sands, with the exception of Healers, but Solana needs help urgently. She has managed single handed to save the children. She already runs an orphanage of sorts, but she is overwhelmed and running out of food. We cannot break quarantine to help our own and they need temporary foster homes. May I send them to Selesh?".

Scartel was a sizeable settlement, comparatively close to the Opal borders, just on the other side of the Drekken Pass. Provided that an overnight stop in Fronish was taken, she thought the journey from here would take less than three days and could quite easily be accomplished in a ninenight in both directions. She wondered how many children were involved, casually speculating that if the elderly Solana was managing alone, there couldn't be that many of them.

"If only Daro and Ahnell were here, I could offer two young men to help Healers fetch the orphans, but if these conditions continue, travel will become impossible ".

Gloomily, she surveyed her options. Sending the Guard might be misinterpreted and might frighten the children. She considered using Jocasta's door, but abandoned the idea, too unsure of the portal's effect on a child and returned to her studies, still vaguely wondering who to send, when there was a gentle tap on the door.

"Enter..", she called, expecting Hanna, but it was Jalni. Neatly dressed, hair bound tidily, head held high, the Sorceress could hardly believe the change in the girl.

"No longer trying to slip around unseen.", she thought wryly, as the novice dipped her head respectfully.

"Excuse me Deshun. Healer Hanna, has just set another batch of texin bark to distil. She expects to be no longer than a turn of the sand-glass and begs your indulgence. I also have an errand to you from Bettina at Selesh Minoria.".

The surprised Sorceress straightened, crying out involuntarily, as she did so.

"Oh my aching back!",

She flapped a hand testily at the novice, who had started to come to her assistance.

"No Jalni, there is nothing to be done. I have just sat here in the cold for too long, looking through some old scrolls I found in this workbench. I hoped that something I could understand might leap out at me, though what I really hoped to find was a more effective cure for pain. The One only knows how my back needs it now!". She arched backwards in an attempt to ease the discomfort.

"Go on, child, go on, aarrhh", she cried out, grimacing in agony, and Jalni instantly crossed to her side, forgetting that this was Ikella, who knew more about Healing than she was ever likely to learn. She supported the agonised woman carefully and allowed her to straighten her tortured back

Slowly, a hand found the source of pain, a muscle in spasm. The novice frowned, drawing her brows together in a ferocious scowl. She could help, but she had given her word not to use her *othervoice*.

"Deshun.", she began carefully, "You need a Healer.", and waited, for Ikella's temper was legendary and she was in so much pain.

Ikella drew her breath in with a hiss and whispered:

"Go on then child, I can't forbid you while I am like this!", and Jalni sighed softly, then opened herself to the Source, delicately launching her *othervoice*, unleashing the power to heal with song.

She found the note, running up and down a trial scale to modulate the harmonics to the need of her patient. A gentle soothing melody suggested itself and she sang it softly, drawing in her minds eye a visible band of light from the Source to Ikella's back. She studied the glow that cloaked her hand in azure blue, extended it into a 'pad', pressing it firmly against Ikella's spine, blending vibration, warmth and pain relief in a wave of power.

The Sorceress groaned with relief as the magic took hold, and her own aura blossomed around them both. She stretched gently, as an audible 'click' told Jalni her work was done and a beatific smile crossed Ikella's face.

"Deo!", The Sorceress invoked the name of the One in gratitude.

"Jalni, you saved my life, I should have been stuck there for eternity, thank you child. You may return to using *othervoice* to third level without supervision from now on. I shall let it be known that you are a fine fixer of backs.".

She remembered Jalni's second reason for visiting her, enquiring

"What does Bettina want this time?".

Jalni, retreating from the Sorceress respectfully, met Ikella's eyes.

"Last night, there was a fire in their animal feed store after a lightening strike. As it is Eve of First Rites tomorrow and knowing that her people have little water left after fire-fighting, Bettina begs permission to bring them into shelter.".

The Sorceress saw the girl's eyes flicker as she looked at the scroll, followed by a "stillness", of intense interest, however, she returned to the other side of the worktable, saying swiftly.

"Deshun, Bettina said nothing more of their difficulties, but I have information that I should bring to your notice.", The novice swallowed hard.

"Bettina only begged night shelter for families with children.", she said softly. "They're terrified. However, what she didn't say is that all travel into the Azure has been stopped. The weather has halted travel to and from Caranchar, so that Selesh Minoria, has no cattle feed and can't get anymore until travel is possible. They also have no building materials with which to repair damage, despite their aggrea. I heard that directly from Master Woodsmith Arkneth.".

Ikella only had to pause for a moment, then aware of the undisguised interest Jalni had in the scroll, she said briskly: "Send Diras to tell Bettina that she is to bring them all in. Get Sorrill to tell Ivinish to gather all the beasts with whatever help he needs and drive them into the underground pastures. The people can camp there tonight, but I want to speak to them after Height of Sun tomorrow.". She passed a hand over her tired face, glancing at Jalni, who hovered, looking down at the scroll, frowning.

The Sorceress followed the line of Jalni's gaze, where there was a pictogram of a man, receiving treatment. Jalni seemed entranced, so Ikella, recognizing serendipity, beckoned her forward, observing as the girl traced a word from the scroll.

"Merishwhen.", she barely breathed the word, but it came clear to Ikella's augmented hearing. She looked searchingly at her.

"Can you read this Jalni?", she asked thoughtfully, her eyes firmly fixed on the girl's face. Jalni looked up.

"Only a word or two Deshun.", she admitted reluctantly. "This word, the one in the box means Merishwhen which as you know is a fungus which grows in dark cool places. We have it in the Azure. My mother collected some and dried it for a remedy which the Healer made for burns. She showed me the word and how to write it. I remembered that from Jerritol.".

She glanced up into Ikella's interested face. "I don't remember exactly what it referred to, but look!", she held out her ornately tattooed hands and Ikella saw the faint blue glow. Several symbols stood out brightly and the one that Jalni indicated matched the Merishwhen symbol on the scroll.

Next to the word, a pictogram showed a Healer bathing the eyes of a man, who was lying prone. Together, Sorceress and novice Healer bent over the scroll and Jalni pointed out several pictograms that contained words that she recognised and Ikella made notes.

Her brisk copying of symbols impressed the novice who knew how incredibly old these scrolls were and how long the Sorceress had been studying them. She listened to Ikella, who was trying out ideas and looking at the central pictogram avidly. Jalni followed Ikella's pointing finger.

"Selesh.", The novice breathed and the Sorceress nodded, for she too had recognised the Gate in the Rock. Their fingers traced the image, flowed down the parchment from pictogram to word. The scroll rod turned revealing an image of the doors to the Healer Hall, hanging askew and Ikella's energy drained away, with a groan of disappointment.

She covered her reaction, saying lightly, "Oh dear, I had hoped for a scroll of prophecy, but this would seem to be a record of the damage to Selesh caused at Cataclysm. Those doors were rehung in Adaria's time, but never since! Still, we might find something else.".

Their fingers traced a path to an image of the interior itself.

"Less than accurate,", snorted the Sorceress, puzzling over the image of the Sacred Circle, above which a great tongue of rock jutted. She stared down at a depiction of the Book of Rule which was unmistakeable, a puzzled frown on her face, before turning the scroll rod again.

There was something shining on the parchment and Jalni leaned forward to examine it, For a moment she doubted the evidence of her own eyes and then she pointed –

"Deshun, is that supposed to be the sun?", she asked curiously and Ikella studied the symbol sombrely.

"Yes, Jalni, that is indeed our sun. I forget that so many have never seen Seleus in all his glory.".

The novice looked up, seeing the disappointment on Ikella's face.

"That proves this is a scroll of Record.", she said sadly and Jalni found herself feeling sorry for the weight of responsibility that Ikella bore. Totally unaware of Jalni's silent sympathy, Ikella carried on examining the scroll, talking as she transferred rolled vellum from one rod to the other.

"With the weather so bad lately, I hoped this would be a scroll of Prophecy. Even with all my Rotations, I still need help to protect the people, and still don't know how to conduct First Rites in a lightening storm.". Ikella's turn of self-disparaging humour did far more to warm Jalni's stony little heart than the Sorceress would have believed, and so they went on.

A turn on the scroll rod brought the area that Ikella was following into view and a long finger tapped the parchment as she showed her reasoning to the student.

"After the Great Storm, the Gate in the Rock was intact. The doors to the Healer Hall didn't need re-hanging and there has been no gallery like that since Adaria's time.".

She tapped her nail irritably on the depiction of the Sacred Circle overhung by the huge pinnacle of rock.

"I have never seen that in all my time here!", said the Sorceress firmly, adding for bitter emphasis, "and that is well over one hundred Rotations.", the novice blinked just once at that, but Ikella noticed it as she leant forward, studying the scroll once more.

"See, how bright the sun is shining? I am sure young Jalni, that this is a picture of what was, not what will come, which is a huge disappointment to me.". Jalni's eyes were drawn to the picture of the Healer bathing a patients eyes.

"However, my Deshun.", Jalni spoke clearly, respectfully and touched the scroll gently, "we might use the information here to heal a man of this time, might we not?".

As she spoke the picture glinted. It seemed that a layer of pure Opal surrounded the prone figure depicted, and Ikella snorted impatiently.

"That confirms my theory..", she said crossly. "I'm sure this depicts a Sandsinger. There is no other reason for all this Opal around him. This must show the result of Cataclysm on Selesh, for we certainly know that there have been no Sandsingers since.". the Sorceress continued.

"You must be aware that we have avoided looking too deeply into our past. This is because the damage to our world during Cataclysm was so immense that few survived it. We don't even know if these records are accurate, whether these so called Sandsingers really had the power that some rumours ascribe to them. Far better to concentrate on the future, on what we can achieve ourselves rather than wait for the impossible. Jalni, the Sandsingers are in the past, they are never going to return, so we must go on alone!".

Jalni's eyes were huge as she looked at the Sorceress solemnly. Somehow, in the moments that she had taken to ease Ikella's physical pain, a narrow bridge of trust had formed and here, in this place and time, a Sorceress was telling her things which no novice had ever learned. Jalni held her breath and Ikella continued her musing.

"All that is left is mist and smoke, a trace here and there. Nothing certain but the many warnings of dangerous knowledge. This is why the Guardians exist, to prevent the unwise or unwary falling into dangerous practices. No real proof of their existence survives.", Ikella pronounced solemnly, ignoring the complex around her. "Apart from a few old scrolls, some books and the Great book of Rule, which is bound with a magic far beyond my understanding. The Guardians believe it waits here as a reminder that some things are beyond mortal understanding, not (as rumour would have it), for the next Sandsinger!".

Abruptly, Ikella began to roll up the scroll once more, snorting under her breath as she did so,

"Men using magic indeed! It makes the power in me curdle, just thinking about it.", but there was something wistful in her sigh.

"Ah well, back to today. I think we could try Merishwhen on our men and see if it helps their pain.", she seemed to come to a decision quickly, telling the novice, "Jalni, convey my message to Bettina immediately. Then go to Shiarjha and ask her to convene a Council meeting, we have urgent business to discuss.".

As Jalni sped off obediently, Ikella tightened the scroll, staring after her speculatively. Her constant finger on the pulse of the Source told her of change.

"Something is happening.", she thought prophetically. "Something that you are part of young woman, but never forget that I am watching you, waiting for your first and last mistake!".

Chapter 11 - The First Wind of Change

The following day, although gloomy, there were perceptible changes in the temperature. Spring was coming and amongst even the most morose, spirits lifted, with the exception of Jalni's. To her, the day seemed oppressive. Detailed to select a group of students to prepare the unused lower levels for occupation, she was suffering. Since the previous day, she had been running to and fro, trying to get everything done so that there were rooms for their villagers, supplies for the beasts and storage places for their own needs, without displacing the many Clansmen already sheltering the Winter out. It was only the thought that once the weather settled, all these additional people would go, that kept the solitude seeking student sane.

In the deep dim recesses of Selesh, her elicit explorations were finally put to good use. Time and time again, she produced rough plans and gradually a small village took shape in the lower reaches of Selesh. From the open door to this "undercroft", she watched Ivinish confidently driving herd beasts into the covered pastures across the Gathering Square from her. She laughed when Diras told her (in passing), that the new fever field was working too well, it having detected that the drudges were slipping hot pies out to the Guardroom.

Ivinish reported to Jalni that the village herders had taken their wives and families to the roomy barns of the underground pastures, which freed rooms in the undercroft. Crossing to make her own report to the Infirmary, after Council began, she noticed that a steady wind had sprung up. Hoping that the Council wouldn't be long about its business, she was relieved to see Hanna sweeping towards her, deep in thought. She dipped respectfully to the Infirmarian, as Hanna stopped, eyeing her cautiously.

"Jalni, I was looking for you.", she said and Jalni saw the normally cool, calm Herbalist was very flustered. Lowering her voice Hanna demanded urgently, "What is our Deshun's idea of treating the blind with an ointment or salve containing Merishwhen? Is that a Zurian treatment?", she queried, adding in a worried tone of voice.

"I know that we have some, but it is at least ten Rotations since I last used it and…" Her voice dropped to a guilty whisper, "I don't have any idea where I stored it!".

Blushing furiously, she consulted a long, narrow list scribed on to vellum, which hung on her workbelt, as Jalni realised how much poor Hanna had to remember, cures traditional, cures under revision, the ingredients needed for thousands of remedies and where they were stored. Knowing that this confidence had to be handled sensitively, Jalni wrinkled her nose as if in deep thought, before venturing an answer.

"Merishwhen are Zurian, but I don't know where the treatment came from. They're usually dried, then stored in a cold dry place. I once saw it stored in stone bins sealed with wax if that is any help.".

Hanna consulted her list, turning the vellum strip over to read the underside thoughtfully.

Jalni waited patiently and at last, Hanna made up her mind.

"Could you take a work detail into the cooling caves below the kitchens for me? Search all of the bins in the alcoves that have blue slashes on the doors. I'm afraid it may take a while, but I can't narrow the area any further.".

Embarrassed, she added gruffly, "Thank you for your help Jalni.", admitting helplessly, "I don't think I have encountered ointments using fungi anywhere. Deshun Ikella wants one made by tonight if possible, do you have any ideas to offer?".

For once, Jalni viewed a direct appeal without suspicion. It was nice to feel needed. So instead of bristling, she spoke openly, sharing her information with a sister Healer, instead of clinging to her privileged knowledge jealously.

"Did Deshun Ikella tell you that I saw the scroll and recognised the symbol for Merishwhen? I know the properties of the fungi and can help you if you wish it, but I may have to miss First Rite of Spring!".

Hanna sighed with relief and patted the novice on the shoulder, saying with authority,

"Then you are excused from attending, Deshun Ikella is determined to find a cure for this terrible pain and that has to take priority.".

Jalni looking her in the eyes, said respectfully,

"Hanna, I don't think it was an ointment that the scroll indicated, but an infusion, a sort of wash for the eyes. If the cooling properties of Merishwhen can be increased by distillation, we may achieve two strengths of application, but I saw the record and the Healer depicted was using a gouche rather than a pot which would indicate an ointment.".

The Infirmarian looked oddly at the novice and Jalni explained what she and Ikella had seen, remarking:

"The treatment was shown clearly. In the first symbol a Healer holds a cloth and pours from a gouche on to the material. The second symbol shows a Healer laying the cloth over a patient's eyes.".

She sketched out the pictograms as she remembered them, on Hanna's wax tablet and the Infirmarian nodded agreement, saying:

"I will take this theory back to the Council Chamber straight away. Beneva has the scroll now and both Ikella and Mina must agree with the proposal before I get started, but an infusion will be much faster and easier to make and less wasteful to apply.".

Jalni watched the busy Infirmarian retreat back into her normal state, totally absorbed with her work as she walked away, muttering medication tables to herself happily.

In the event, Council business kept Ikella longer than she had hoped and it was late in the day when the bell announced that the session was at an end. The doors to the Healer Hall were opened and the Elders swept out into the Gathering Square. Ikella stood on a small dais and raised her Staff for silence.

Immediately the Summoning Bell sounded, everyone in the confines of the cavern system ignored that, at their peril.

"There is a matter to discuss.", the clear voice rang out and a buzz went round the gathering. Somewhere a baby cried and a mother hushed it gently. The Sorceress continued, her voice softening as she looked at the massed faces turned to hers.

"We have lost so many precious young lives in our community recently and because of that grief, I wondered if there is the will to help another Sand in desperate circumstances?".

There was a murmur of interest from the crowd, so Ikella drew her cloak around her shoulders against the stiffening breeze and said firmly. "Deshun Tirjella has requested our assistance to evacuate Scartel.".

Her voice tinged with pain, was raised to carry to the farthest quarter of the gathering.

"At present, the Azure Sands North are quarantined. From Anempor to Darnesh, from Scartel to the Great Divide, all settlements wait for the arrival of some pestilence that has carried away the adults, leaving children untouched.".

A moan went round the crowd, who huddled together nervously, as flashes of lightening stroked the horizon, and Ikella continued the story.

"This epidemic, seems to be centred in Scartel, where every adult died. No-one knows the numbers involved, but the orphans (now living in the care of one Healer) need homes.".

A murmur of sympathy swept round the crowd as Ikella said hopefully.

"We must get our own into shelter right now, but if you could be the mother, or father that those children need come forward in the next few days. Just as soon as these storms stop, we will send help to Scartel.".

No sooner had she spoken, when a crack of thunder roared overhead. The people dashed for safety, running down the sandy floor of a well-lit passage, to the rooms that Jalni, Bettina and the students had prepared. The doors were closed and in the deep recesses of Selesh the new residents were hardly aware of the storm, as it took hold of the Opal desert and shook it until it shuddered and rang like a bell.

The sand-glass turned relentlessly, but the storm seemed fiercer. In the Inner Sanctum, Healers gathered ready for the evening's ceremony. Almost at surface level, they could hear creaks and groans, feel the winds buffeting around the ancient settlement.. As lightening seared Mount Torrenesh above them, pale faces questioned each other, and in the Syndarial,(where the Guardians and senior celebrants robed, even Ikella invoked the name of the One, in a prayer for their safety.

Still the entire Clan prepared to celebrate First Rite of Spring and eventually the students crept in to their places in Hall, the High Council lined the Way of Challenge and the visitors and other inhabitants, huddled together in the body of the Hall and waited.

Oblivious of the dramatic events unfolding above, Jalni was leading a group of enthusiastic students into the deep cool storage caverns below the kitchens. They had readily agreed to help hunt Merishwhen, and, (to be quite honest), Jalni was enjoying her newfound popularity despite the storm. She knew that many of the students would have sought any means to get further underground and away from the forces of nature that were ravaging the desert, but she didn't care what the reasoning was, she quite liked to organise people and the search was proving more than fruitful, for Jalni had already found two tubs full of the precious fungi, with several other things that Hanna required.

They were working together in a calm and orderly fashion when there was a sudden and distinct difference in the sound of the wind. Jalni had not expected that outside noises would penetrate so deeply, but there was a succession of violent crashes, then a shift in pressure, so noticeable, that when the younger novices started shivering in fright, Jalni decided to return. Holding up the glow she carried to make a swift head count, keeping her voice light and a smile on her face, she said, simply.

"I think that we have enough for now girls. Tarsi, Mari, if you can carry the Merishwhen between you, take it straight to Hanna. Whatever is going on out there, make for the next level, but no running. Not all the villagers will have gone to Hall and we mustn't make a bad impression, besides running down here is dangerous. We must tell Hanna what we have located before we do anything else.".

She turned and led the way up the corridor until the passageway abruptly started to rise, where she allowed Tarsi and Mari to rest, organising a few others to assist with the lifting of the stone tubs of powdered fungi. She had expected those not in that party, to go on ahead, as she reached the top of the ramp, but they were still gathered in the corridor as she arrived at the top. The reason for this was soon obvious, for there was a large crack running down one wall, the roof was damaged and debris lay all around them, although there was no overt danger provided they took care and negotiated their way quietly. There was light up ahead and as Jalni walked her group carefully forward she could see that a man stood at the entrance to the undercroft. He held up a flaming torch as they approached, giving them all light to see their way into the junction of a passage, that led up into the Infirmary to the right and down to the undercroft on their left. However, he held his head tilted to one side, listening intently and Jalni recognised Duvell, the blind shoemaker. She addressed him using the lingua Zurian, for he too was of her own Sand and far from home.

"Ho Duvell! How goes it with you and your sons?", she enquired, and he grinned as she led her small foraging party forward.

"Mistress Jalni. Does the One keep you all safe?". He held the torch out for one of the other girls to take, but he was still stoically listening out for rock falls in the passageways as he did so. His concern for those who had sight did him much honour, Jalni decided, but noticing him wince as the light fell on his face, she carefully lowered her torch and asked him curiously,

"Have you had a lot of pain in your eyes lately Duvell?", and he grimaced as he answered her.

"Yes Mistress, that I have and in my head and these storms make it worse day by day.".

Jalni studied him, he was paler than usual and around his eyes there were great dark rings. Her companions came closer and gathered around as she asked quietly, "Your pardon for these unorthodox questions Duvell, but I am helping our Deshun and Healer Hanna to find some ingredients for a wash to help others suffering in the same way. Perhaps your answers will help us.".

"Can you tell me if you are sleeping, or does the pain wake you?".

"No Mistress, I am not sleeping, but it is not the pain that wakes me. It is dreams. I dream of eyes Mistress, Opal eyes!".

He seemed so bothered by this that Jalni said gently:

"I have odd dreams too sometimes Duvell, but they generally mean nothing. Perhaps you should report to the Infirmary in the morning and tell Hanna what you have told me. She may want to try the new treatment on you. Getting rid of the pain should help you sleep.".

She had barely turned away to climb to the next level, when there was a great gust of wind and a rolling peal of thunder sounded overhead. There was an indescribable sound, a combination of grating and grinding and then silence.

Mari looked at Jalni for leadership and she carefully indicated the youngsters, compressing her lips until Mari nodded, tacitly agreeing to say nothing to raise the alarm, as Jalni took a pace forward. Almost at the same moment a vibration shook the walls around them. It was slow, deep and unutterably tortured, a sound that created the urge to grind their teeth in sympathy, as though the ground had cried out, shaking the very foundations of Selesh. It went on and on and Jalni, along with the others retreated to the lower levels, taking Duvell with them, holding hands in the dark as a chill wind sighed and roared through all of Selesh.

A deep groan rang from the walls around them and Jalni was suddenly infused with the most inexplicable feeling of joy. She felt a sudden desire to sing and sing and gently touched the Source with her mind's eye, wondering whether she and her companions were about to die. Several of the other students were looking at each other and she realised that they were all feeling the same. She gritted her teeth and even as she did so she heard a muffled peal of thunder and the tension lifted. Raising her eyes she saw that Duvell was still holding his head, but smiling, as if in relief. He turned towards her, saying happily:

"Mistress, it has gone. The pain in my head has gone and my eyes feel better.".

Nothing would have it, but he lifted the tubs of Merishwhen, one under each powerful arm and allowing Tarsi and Mari to guide him, made his way, slowly but certainly up the ramp towards the Infirmary. Jalni , curious to find out what had happened outside, waited until every novice passed her in a relieved gaggle, before heading towards the Gathering Square. Caught in a crush of excited villagers, she responded slowly as a familiar voice accosted her.

Mina, stood in the corridor to the undercroft, still in her ceremonial robes. Beckoning urgently, her face pale, her voice shaking.

"Oh, there you are. Thank the One that you are safe. Now, no time to spare, every hand is

needed in the Infirmary.".

She turned to hurry away on her own errands, then looked back at Jalni.

"Please don't dawdle. Whether or not you like it, every Healer must report to the Infirmary and next ninenight will be too late. If you want to redeem yourself in Ikella's eyes, get a treatment tray from Hanna. Load it with remedies for small injuries, plenty of pain medication and follow me.".

A flare of irritation crossed Jalni's mind. She wasn't a Healer, she'd been excluded from their confidence, yet she was still being ordered around. Mouth mutinous and skin prickling with a strange energy, she gathered herself, ready to engage in battle. Then her foster-mother said the most insane thing.

"Come along child. Don't you want to treat a real, living Sandsinger?".

She turned away abruptly, as both baffled and intrigued Jalni followed her, into the most bewildering adventure of her life.

Chapter 12 - Sandsinger rebuked!

"Once the damage of that Spring Storm was catalogued, it became obvious that until a new Master Builder was appointed, they would rely on running repairs. In deference to Mina's grief, Ikella hadn't considered applications before Jentaroth, but now, with the return of daylight and warmth, the planting of crops dominated their lives. Therefore, in the twentieth Spring since Partition, for purely practical reasons the villagers of Selesh Minoria remained in the cavern complex. Spreading out from traditional Winter quarters, they began to fill levels vacated as visiting Clansmen returned to their home settlements.".

While all these changes went on without their involvement, both Guardians decided that they needed to impress upon the Clan, the need for silence regarding "the Sandsinger". Both Beneva and Ikella were mildly scandalised (and amused), by the unusual possessiveness demonstrated at last Gather. The departing Shalhanhi seemed to regard Daro's astonishing feat, as "only natural, him being the son of our Sorceress!". Discretion was also assured, "It being no business of anyone other than the Opal born, what happens in our Sands!". The inhabitants of Selesh, including the villagers seemed singularly unimpressed by Sandsingers however and as comparative normality returned, it emerged that Ikella had been given another title, to add to the many that she already bore.

She had become, "Tiraj di Schpeller", (literally translated as Scourge of Sandsingers). Women already told their girl children how she had fearlessly defended them. Jashell and Indeera smiled secretively as they heard the birth of a legend and watched the love and awe grow for the Sorceress, as they emerged from the darkness, into the long sunny days of Spring. Into another time where the word Sandsinger echoed through Selesh, although of the man himself there was still no sight.

The rumours and speculation grew. One wing of the Infirmary was restricted to a chosen few, "so the Sandsinger was sick, maybe dying". They muttered amongst themselves, those who had seen and those who had not, until Mina was forced to tell Ikella, that unless they did something, stories would go off sands.

She reported with tolerant amusement, what was being said.

"They seem to have forgotten that Daro is simply the boy who carried their firewood, rocked their babies cradle, or stole fruit from their market stalls. Now, it seems he is ten foot tall, has eyes like fire and breathes smoke out of his ears.".

She folded her arms across her bosom and ignored the derisive snort from her Sorceress, declaring stoutly, "According to Diras (who nearly laughed herself sick telling me this), Daro apparently struck the Gate with a lightening bolt. He only used the fingers of one hand to shatter the doors to the Hall, then he simply breathed them off their hinges.".

She paused nonplussed, seeing the sudden rush of tears on Ikella's face.

"No...", she waved Mina away, "No... I'm alright. Its just my age and Daro.".

Ikella's beliefs had held her apart from Daro as he grew strong and rebellious. Perhaps she had always chosen to believe that he was only hers for a while, in case his father traced him. Now, Mina saw the truth. Ikella loved her son, possibly all the more for being the son of her heart rather than the fruit of her body. Yet she was struggling to come to terms with so many revelations, without once letting Daro see how much she cared.

Perhaps if her own relationship with Jalni had been more peaceable, Mina wouldn't have been so aware of Ikella's turmoil, but having seen her pain, the little Healer stopped to consider the future of mothering such a son in helpless sympathy.

On the night of Mina's marriage, Ikella had sent Daro journeying. She knew nothing of the transgression that had resulted in his exile, but she had been aware of the pain and confusion Ikella had suffered. For those who followed the strict code of the Way as long as they had, to question its teachings was unthinkable. She knew from the manner of his return, that some deep grievance still kept mother and son apart, but convinced that the Sorceress could overcome the barrier, she gently enquired.

"Shall we go and see how Daro is?", but her friend bowed her head again and sighed, saying gravely:

"I don't think so Mina. He doesn't want anyone right now. He is in denial of course. Refusing to wash, dress, eat, (although drinking water), allows him to control the situation temporarily. He is sleepless, seldom speaks, unless refusing medication. Quite honestly, I doubt my ability to reach him.".

She rose, standing over her worktable, trying to distract her thoughts by examining a scroll. Mina saw something attracted Ikella's attention as she bent closer, excitement dawning in her eyes.

"O Deo me! Its changed.", the Sorceress exclaimed, grasping Mina's arm to draw her forward. Rapidly rolling the scroll back on its rods with shaking hands, she revealed the first image. Here, the very damage inflicted on Selesh during Spring Rites had been inked on parchment a millennium ago. Soberly sparking a lamp with a click of empowered fingers, Ikella waited for Mina's reaction.

Tracing the image of the Gate in the Rock, Ikella declared, "This can't be coincidence.".

She pointed to each image in turn and Mina's brow creased as she followed the progression of a night she had lived through, predicted on parchment.

Surmounting the entire scroll, (half depicted on the enamelled rod), was a Storm. The whole image seemed to have life, to move ominously under Ikella's hand. Conjured from a darkened background were billowing clouds, deeply pierced with gilded strokes representing flashes of lightening. Below, the silver edged outlines of high mountains lashed with rain. There was a profound silence as empowered hands ran down the scroll, Ikella gently twisting the scroll rod to allow more of the parchment to show. Now the Sands showed, inked in some fluorescing dye, so that they glinted from pure white to vivid turquoise, in all the shades of Opal.

Ikella spoke emphatically.

"Jalni and I examined this scroll before Daro returned. I swear by the Book of Rule that it wasn't this elaborately decorated. It was barely readable then! I had hopes of finding a Scroll of Prophecy, but this only appears to give up its secrets after the event! Of what possible use is that?".

She sounded so disgusted that Mina couldn't restrain a smile. The Sorceress (frowning), unrolled a little more of the parchment, revealing the progress of the night in question and their humour evaporated as the next image was revealed.

A Healer, treated a prone figure surrounded by darkly inked parchment. Mina observing this unusual technique, surprised both herself and Ikella by saying softly.

"Does that darkness represent a recommendation for night time treatment? Or, does it mean that the patient is unconscious? The use of the contrasting inks seem to show that the patient concerned is Opal born .".

However, she was quelled into silence by her companions interpretation, delivered in a sober voice that brooked no further question.

"No. I think Mina mine, that the Sandsinger depicted is blind and that this is what I hoped for, a true and ancient Scroll of Prophecy. However, bearing in mind what it has already revealed, I am rather uncertain as to how much more I should attempt to interpret.".

Her tracing finger worked its way down the parchment and where it passed, the faded colours came to life, glowing brilliantly from an immaculate surface. Totally absorbed, although bemused by these changes, both women concluded that this Scroll would reveal nothing before the appropriate time. Ikella found herself almost reluctant to turn the scroll rod far enough to reveal the Merishwhen treatment, but relaxed when she saw the image blaze from the page on which was now inscribed in plain Healer script, a recipe for an eyewash, so similar to that devised by Hanna and Jalni, it defied description.

To a man, all of their patients had benefitted from the trials, so Mina swiftly noted the exact recipe on the tablet she habitually wore, while Ikella held the scroll steady.

"Is Daro getting this treatment?", she asked without thinking, then at Ikella's silent shake of the head she exploded irritably.

"For the sake of the One.", she invoked the deity. "He must be persuaded to co-operate, accepting cleanliness, water, food and rest, as the four paths to recovery. You can't just let him die because life hasn't turned out the way he planned. He is probably in too much pain to think straight, but we may have the answer to that in our hands.".

She stared at the face of the Sorceress, darkly brooding over the scroll and said sharply.

"Does magic, rank, or even the Way matter right now Deshun? He is your son and he is suffering. Whatever else can come later, now we have to persuade him to live!".

Sighing, Ikella rolled the precious chart and placed it back in its drawer. Then turning to the Healer, she caught her arm.

"There will be protest, but treating Daro's physical pain may help. He has to be diverted somehow, for he is every bit as temperamental as Jalni! So, while I am in the mood to challenge his right to destroy himself, we'd better go and face him.".

The two women caught up their medicine scrips and left the serenity of Ikella's study once more.

However, when they arrived in the normally calm and cool surroundings of the Infirmary, they found it anything but an oasis of peace. From the doorway, at the beginning of a long and winding ramp, they could hear a man's voice protesting volubly. As they turned the corner into the corridor, Ikella was scandalised by the number of drudges and Healers, crowding around a closed door.

As they approached, the on-lookers melted away, discreetly withdrawing to attend their proper duties, leaving only Hanna, Dorra and Satra stood on the landing outside Daro's private suite.

Hanna came towards them, smiling gently. Raising a silencing finger to her lips, she beckoned them towards the door. Closing the gap, Ikella recognise her son's voice raised in querulous protest against Jalni's voice. Calmly, if somewhat disdainfully, she remonstrated with her difficult patient.

"You will eat, if not for yourself, for your mother and for all the Healers who have fought you back from the brink of death. Now, open your mouth and take this soup, or by the One I will force feed you!".

Immediately there was a choking sound, but when Daro recovered Jalni's voice continued severely.

"Argue with me and you will come off worse. If you would prefer to eat soup, rather than breathe it, I suggest that you try and feed yourself. You are a big boy now and even Sandsingers can't expect a slave to feed them every meal of their lives.".

By now, the experienced Healers were holding in their amusement with difficulty. Ikella herself, nearly missed the moment that the mood changed. Daro, murmuring something weakly, roused Jalni to scorn and her young voice carried clearly to the listeners at the door.

"How dare you!", she exclaimed, roused to anger. Ikella listened thoughtfully, picturing Jalni flushed with temper, great lilac- blue eyes sparkling with rage.

"How dare you feel sorry for yourself! Yes, I know that your friends died and I am sorry for your loss and theirs. Yes, I know you're blind, but if you had bothered to take notice, so are many others. They have never enjoyed your privileged life, or the love of a dedicated mother. Something, dare I say that you turned your back on. Are you here just to punish her? Cause her more grief? Because if you are, there are many who would stand against you, including me.".

There was a muffled reply, but neither Mina or Ikella heard it. They were fascinated by the icy clarity that filled Jalni's voice as she continued,

"Do you know that during the storms, a blind man in severe pain was walking the corridors of Selesh, listening for rock-falls, trying in a strange place to look out for us sighted ones. He helped to carry the Merishwhen to treat our blind and all he cared about was our safety. He, my Sandsinger friend, was more of a man than you will ever give yourself a chance to be!".

Hanna looked at Ikella nonplussed, at a loss to apologise for her novices' outburst. However, Ikella was holding up her hand, signalling the others to stand still and listen. From within the room came the sound of altercation. First a crash, then a distinct hard slap.

The door opened abruptly and Jalni stalked out, fury in every line of her body. She dripped soup, but strode out, face expressionless, mouth tight lipped. Mechanically bobbing a curtsey to the Sorceress, she went directly to Hanna. Mina and Ikella stared at her in amazement, as she acknowledged the Infirmarian.

"You were right Sister.". Her voice must have carried clearly to the angry man who had somehow followed her to the doorway, where he stood teetering on the brink.

"Is there no-one more deserving than that spoilt child?", her eyes narrowed as she saw her patient wince. her sweetly venomous voice lashed out.

"No? Dorra, I can't possibly waste my time serving where I am not appreciated. Perhaps when another more deserving case materialises, I will continue my training then.".

Ikella observed the flush on the girls cheeks and the ominous sparkle in her eyes and reaching out, caught the novice's hand in hers.

"Thank you Jalni.".

She spoke clearly and the onlookers were quietly amused to see the look on Daro's face, as he realised that his mother was a witness to this scene.

"I apologise for my son. His manners always were atrocious. I don't blame you for leaving, but why don't you bathe and change, then come to my study, say in about two turns of the sand-glass? We can discuss this matter then.", her voice was gentle, but the words were an absolute command, and Jalni's shoulders drooped as she hurried to obey.

Ikella never looked in Daro's direction once as she cracked out her orders.

"Satra, can you arrange a cleaner? Hanna, get some help to bathe this patient. I want him dressed and presentable. Mina, come with me and I will prepare a new infusion for his eyes and we will have an end to all this nonsense.".

She stalked away, about five paces from the door and then she turned and focussed on her

Son. Her voice rang out.

"Daro, I will be back here in one sector of the sand-glass. Oblige me by allowing my Healers to bathe and dress you, or I will do it myself.".

For a moment, although she didn't have her Staff with her, the other Healers could picture it flaring into life and then Ikella slowly dipped her own obeisance to the silent man, who stood just inside the room.

"By your leave Ichspeller?".

She deliberately acknowledged his rank, before turning on her heel and walking away.

It took slightly longer for the Healers to achieve the desired result, while Mina and Ikella worked together in companiable silence. Mina glanced at the Sorceress as she ground the powdered Merishwhen to a finer consistency.

"I wonder if all children have their difficult times, just to loosen the bond between themselves and their parents, before they leave home?".

The Sorceress stared at her, one eyebrow lifted in amused speculation.

"I imagine that for every child, as many parents grind their teeth in frustration, or...", she glanced wryly at her own hands gripping the mortar and pestle as she completed the sentence, "their herbs and spices to a finer consistency than strictly necessary.",

She consciously relaxed her grip, nodded at Mina and the boiling water was added slowly and much more safely to the infusion. A voice from the doorway announced politely,

"Deshun, we are ready for you.", and carefully, carrying a tray bearing squares of fine material, pads for Daro's eyes and a bowl of clean boiled water and the precious Merishwhen infusion,

they returned to Daro's room, where order now prevailed.

Daro sat, utterly withdrawn, locked in a world into which their greetings hardly penetrated. He jumped as Ikella touched him on the shoulder, but steadied himself as she turned his face towards her. He was trembling as she prepared to examine him, so to ease the tension, Ikella remarked conversationally, "Your hair could do with a trim.", and took his head in both hands. Tilting his face towards a suspended glowstone lamp, she allowed the light to fall on his strangely altered eyes, noting sadly his lack of reaction. In a low, steady voice she murmured.

"Daro, I would spare you this if I could, but as a Healer, I must see if your eyes are infected. Left untreated they will only get worse. May I see if we can help you?".

He winced, his eyelids flinching away from her lightest touch and sweat beaded his forehead. Ikella was acutely aware that he was restraining himself from pushing her away and said as a matter of fact.

"That hurts.", and reached for a pad soaked in the clean water. With Mina handing her the items she needed one by one, Daro's eyes were carefully bathed. Ikella, expertly altering the direction of the lamp, encouraged Daro to talk, but he was unresponsive and she suddenly realised that he was simply terrified of her diagnosis. He lay on his bed, at her behest, with his head tipped back into her lap and stoically endured what she must do. Reminded of a childhood accident which had nearly killed him, she was suddenly overcome by the urge to sweep him up in her arms and protect him, if only from himself.

Mina noticed the weary compliance privately, thinking.

"Whatever he invited on himself, this is a terrible price to pay.", and in her mind she recalled the laughing face of the boy she had known and saw it fading, totally obscured by the darkness surrounding the man he had become. Finally she understood the image in the Scroll of Prophecy.

Ikella mutely held out a hand and Mina carefully soaked a cloth in the Merishwhen infusion, handing it equally silently to her companion, who nodded as she carefully wiped along the edge of one eyelid, before disposing of the soiled swab. Raising the lid gently, supporting it with a thumb, she examined Daro's eye carefully. It glowed dully, hiding the secret of his magical othergaze from her as she gently lowered the lid and turned her attention to the other eye. A spasm of pain touched his mouth as she sighed regretfully.

Again the hand was extended and this time Mina held out a sorisell, a type of spoon, into which a good amount of the infusion had been poured. Apologising for the awkward procedure, Ikella carefully dribbled the Merishwhen wash into one exposed eye feeling the tension in him release as the liquid flooded the socket. He trembled violently, but kept his head in her lap, until, with uncommon gentleness she dried his face, whispering into his ear, "Well done my boy.", as she tended to the other eye.

He lay still, savouring the freedom from pain as Ikella quietly explained the known properties of Merishwhen in a subtly rhythmic voice, while Mina, who was keeping one finger on the pulse of the Source, felt her bring a calming influence to bear on him, gentling his mood, testing the strength of his awareness of her skill, through their mutual connection to the Source.

Finally, he relaxed and his mouth quirked in amusement as his mother remarked,

"You need a shave young man.", as cupping his face in her hands, the Sorceress ran her thumbs along his jaw line, feeling the stubble of at least a ninenight spring back along her fingers. Ikella gently turned his face, this way and that, observing the clear, pink imprint of a small hand on one cheek, which she touched lightly, commenting,

"No damage to anything but your dignity here. You are a man full grown and I suppose that a beard will hide this sort of thing the next time.".

The Sorceress grinned maliciously as she spoke, but Mina nodding silent agreement observed Daro's embarrassed flush.

"Young Jalni won't take any nonsense from you and no more will I.", his mother warned him, hands gentle on his hair as she told him.

"We found a Scroll of Prophecy, which indicates that an infusion of Merishwhen will help this problem with your eyes…" and was given no chance to finish her sentence, as Daro sat up, hope blazing from a chalk white face. His lips moved, he gasped and neither Healer needed magic to detect the flare in his aura. Tenderly, the Sorceress took his hand in hers and said slowly, patiently, as if to a child.

"No my dear. I haven't the power to change this for you. We can stop the physical pain, but you will have to adapt to life without sight. You just have to give it some time.",

He sighed deeply and Ikella had to bite her lower lip to stop it trembling. Tears welled in her eyes and even Mina had to swallow hard as he lifted his head resignedly, saying simply,

"Well, there it is. I knew what I was doing, just didn't consider the consequences of doing it.".

He lay back down, allowing Ikella to bathe his eyes with a stronger solution, before she put a pad over each eye, binding them in place loosely. Finishing the bandage with a neat bow at the back of his head Ikella turned him on the edge of his bed, saying softly.

"Lie still and rest now my boy. Sleep will do more good than I can. If you need help, I will arrange your personal care while you rest. Hanna will make sure you are attended until then.".

He swung his feet up obediently and snuggled down as she gently covered him with a blanket.

"Sleep, regain your strength. Selesh will still be here tomorrow, then you can tell us how we can help you.".

She gazed down at him, but he had withdrawn, so they left him and went about their duties.

"I think that was a start.", Mina confided in Satra as they returned to the treatment room. Ikella looked considerably more relaxed and Satra beamed as Mina continued, clearing the treatment tray as they talked. "He let her bathe his eyes and listened to her, without any protest.", Mina confided, placing the tray in a rack to be steamed that evening. "He seemed rather resigned to the fact that Ikella intended to get her own way.",

Mina described Daro's apparent capitulation saying, "He has likely stressed himself to a standstill. He needs rest now, but I should try him with a little food later.", and Satra grinned, adding slyly, "Soup? I could send Jalni to help him!", at which Mina rolled her eyes wickedly.

"Yes.", The Sorceress interrupted, continuing thoughtfully, "He needs a carer who can help him establish his independence. There's a certain justice in my solution to that problem.".

Confused, Mina followed the Sorceress back to her own quarters, but as they descended the ramp to the next level, along the corridor from Daro's room, a door closed softly.

Chapter 13 - A Diversion of Magic

Closing the door as the Sorceress departed, Jalni decided to visit Duvell, on her way to Ikella's study. A small diversion brought her to his workroom, where the blind shoemaker sat in the doorway, gently tapping a gilt pin into a tiny slipper. The work apparently finished, he hung his hammer on his workbench and replaced the pin vice in a meticulously tidy toolbox, before dusting and handing the slipper to Beneva. Jalni's curiosity drew her forward, the unusual quality of the slippers revealed as she edged closer and the Guardian of Knowledge smiled at her whisper of admiration.

"Oh… Those are exquisite.", she breathed, as Duvell's deft fingers checked its partner. Beneva agreed wistfully.

"Ah yes. They were never made for feet like mine.".

She held out the slippers in gloved hands, remarking, "Go on then, look, but don't touch. They are very old and incredibly fragile.", smiling, as Jalni promptly put her own hands behind her back.

The delicate slippers under Jalni's envious gaze, were made in gilded leather, set with stones to represent flowers. They must have fitted the tiniest of feet and wondering, Jalni noted the laces, finished with tiny silver bells. Then Beneva confessed.

"These belonged to Feydora, the last Sandsinger, who once lived here in Selesh. However, because we can't read the records yet, the last Age of Mystery remains just that: mysterious! We don't even know her Sand of origin, but I have high hopes of getting Lord Daro's help eventually.".

She withdrew the slippers and prepared to leave, then added in a thoughtful tone.

"I'm working on a new haul of Scrolls right now. They appeared just before Spring Rites and I have had no time to look at them, because Ikella guards then so jealously, you'd think they'd materialised in that old worktable she's restoring!".

The hair on Jalni's neck literally rose as Beneva continued softly,

"They're clearing levels last used in Adaria's time now. The One only knows what will come to light as they go deeper! Still with a live Sandsinger in our midst, things may get even stranger.", a bell on the slippers tinkled as she turned away.

Jalni thought sourly, "Yes…and we won't necessarily hear that one approaching.".

The Guardian smiled almost as though she heard the thought, then with a swish of her robes, swept away towards the end of the corridor, where a woman waited. As Beneva passed (with no hint of acknowledgement), to disappear round a corner, the stranger raised a hand to Jalni, with a slow sweet smile, before following the Guardian and vanishing from view.

Jalni turned back to the shoemaker who tipped his head up at her.

"Mistress Jalni.", he unerringly identified her. Don't tell me you need another repair already?", he enquired and Jalni winced, remembering how he had scolded her over the rough treatment she gave her work boots. Mildly distracted, she glanced back up the corridor but Beneva and her companion were no longer in sight.

She asked curiously, "Duvell, do you know the name of Beneva's friend ?", for to her knowledge, she had never seen the woman before. The blind shoemaker looked bewildered, saying slowly, "There was Guardian Beneva. I know her by the scent of wax and parchment.", he smiled as he said gravely, "She studies too much, she'll turn into a scroll one day, or so she says!", He raised his head enquiringly, as Jalni said, "No Duvell, I meant that other woman with her.".

A guarded expression crossed his face and Jalni would have bitten her tongue out, rather than humiliate this kind and friendly man. She reached out and touched his hand lightly, "No matter. I'll find out later.", she said, despite a sudden conviction that she would never identify the mystery woman. The shoemaker relaxed as she turned to her reason for calling on him.

"Duvell, I need your help. My current patient is a man, twenty Rotations old, who has lost his sight. He's angry, withdrawn, yet resentful of any help. He has stopped eating, barely drinks and won't talk about his experience, which doesn't help me work out how to approach him. Will you help me? Tell me what it was like to lose your sight? How you felt. or how you behaved?".

She saw the pain and reluctance in his face, but waited patiently. At long last, he sighed and nodded agreement and Jalni relaxed as he moistened his lips, preparing to speak.

His hands found a piece of leather, which he turned over and over, until he was sure of the shape. Wordlessly placing it on the last and taking a scriber from his pouch, he concentrated on his straight-edge, incising a sure line down the material. His head lowered, brows drawn together, he spoke gruffly.

"I had thirty-five summers when the great Storm came, blinded me and turned me into an old man before my time. We lived in Maraken, the trail stop on the western Fringe.", he raised unseeing eyes and paused, looking back over the Rotations to another time, another life. She crouched, kneeling in front of his stool, listening attentively as he picked up the thread of his story again.

"I had a good tavern, brewed my own gris and I loved the life. Then came that accursed Storm.", he cleared his throat and Jalni instantly regretted her intrusion, but Duvell continued with a wry expression on his face.

"In those days I was married to Asnith, my boys were small and this story doesn't put me in a good light Mistress, so forgive me if I tell it quickly. The Storm had blown itself out and we were all exhausted. None of us knew which way was up and to my shame, I left my wife and went to bed, leaving her with the children and a tavern full of stranded travellers.".

His hands busily stationed the scriber in his pouch and deftly retrieved a punch as he told the tale of his own private tragedy.

"I woke, sick and headsore, to her pulling me from my bed, demanding that I uncap more barrels, but my eyes were afire and my throat burned. It was pitch dark and I didn't understand her anger until I asked her to pull the drapes and open the shutters. Only then did she tell me that although it was dark and hazy outside, the new glowstone light was full on my face!".

Jalni saw through this matter of fact description to the scream of terror as the appalling realisation dawned. She felt her blood run cold, as he forced himself to continue.

"In that moment, I lost my mind.", he swallowed painfully, continuing in a low voice.

"I blamed poor Asnith for not waking me earlier. For not being able to fetch a Healer. I blamed myself, my own brew, anyone and anything. The children's noise, the Storm, the Sands, for I, like you, am of the Azure.".

He chewed on his lower lip and tipped his head upward towards Jalni, as if he looked into her face.

"Mistress, they say that blindness is a curse on all men, but then, we didn't know that we weren't the only ones. Terror overwhelmed many, who fought each other. I know of others who killed themselves and their families. More, who just lost hope, turned their faces to the wall and died of despair.".

The pain of that time etched his face briefly, as he gathered his thoughts again, lifting down his hammer and positioning the punch, he continued to mark out the shoe upper that he was creating as he talked.

"Eventually plague came. It took my wife before I understood that I couldn't manage alone. My youngest was dying when Patris and the traders brought us here. The Sorceress saved my Chrism and gave us a home. Later, I fell in love with a novice who'd studied here. Shanna learned to train the newly blind to earn a living. We married and I began to live again.", he paused, brightening as he suggested slyly, "Perhaps if you want to save this man, you must make him love you?".

Jalni, covered in confusion, thanked him and retreated towards the main halls and Ikella's study.

When she entered the ante-room, a poker faced Jashell admitted her, telling the bemused novice,

"Good day Healer Jalni. Seris Ikella was hopeful that you would share her Sunfall meal. Will you join her in her robing room?".

At her discreet tap, Mina opened the door and Jalni was confronted with piles of ceremonial Opalwear, laid out along a couch. She hadn't thought of the Sorceress as a follower of fashion, but hanging from doors were cloaks, Opal encrusted robes and tunics. Pants and shirts lay neatly folded, piled according to style. As Ikella's eyes fastened on hers, Jalni recovered some poise, saying hastily, "Forgive me Deshun, but I forgot the ceremonies that accompany a full Council. Are these yours?".

She fingered the fine cloth, marvelling at the change of colour under her hand, until Ikella snorted.

"Child, I may have a reputation for eccentricity, but I do not intend traipsing the Halls decked in male attire! These, have been held by the Guardians since time began apparently. Guardian Beneva retrieved them from one of her repositories recently.",

She pointed out a plainly cut set. Pants and tunic glimmering, the severe lines ornamented only at wrists and shoulders.

"What is your opinion of these? You would know what young Clansmen are wearing these days.".

Jalni flushed. It was really none of her business, but she asked guardedly,

"Are they for Daro?", and Ikella to her astonishment blushed.

"The Opal Sandsinger should wear the Colour of our Kind.", she said defensively, and Jalni nodded agreement. saying,

"However…". She hesitated, then threw caution to the Winds. "I don't think he's ready to think of such things for himself.", she stated firmly.

"Men generally don't think about clothes, leaving the decisions to their women. Although I believe that his "ceremonials" will need to be as dramatic as his arrival, if you want to please him. Daro would like the flowing robes of the past. They would certainly accentuate his look.".

Mina covered her mouth with a hand and even a muscle at the corner of Ikella's lips twitched as Jalni mused.

"I think he will wear some of these for ordinary activities, caught at the waist with a really ornate belt, but he will want extra drama for Council meetings and any ceremonial functions.", she warmed to her theme, thinking of Daro's uncomplicated masculinity.

"I think anything that allowed him to walk amongst Healers unnoticed will eventually be his choice, but for now, robes should suit him well.".

Ikella nodded her approval and then to the students amazement, she found herself being ushered into another room and offered a chair to sit in. Ikella herself sat facing her, as Mina made tassin, a hot sweet drink with an odd roasted flavour. Jalni sipped at it cautiously (for it was rare) and said to be a stimulant of some kind.

"How is my son?".

The Sorceress's question caught her by surprise and she glanced at her foster-mother out of the corner of her eye and saw Mina, smiling and nodding encouragement. Jalni took a sip of her drink, cleared her throat and placed the cup on a small table nearby.

"Impossible, is the only word to describe him Deshun. ", Jalni began. "If I'm not sorry for him, he sulks like a child who needs a spanking. He has obviously suffered a terrible shock, he grieves for his friends genuinely, but he is recovering.".

She paused, almost thinking aloud.

"Those minor injuries are already healed, but his mental health may be another subject. Hanna says he arrived in "a state of fugue, which I wouldn't know how to treat, but it seems that he is running away from something he just can't face.".

Mina's eyes narrowed and the Sorceress looked up as her novice suggested, "If he is more emotionally distressed, than physically disabled, we could promote recovery by distracting him in some way. I wondered if getting him away to convalesce in anonymity isn't perhaps the answer?", she blushed, for she was on very uncertain ground, however Ikella nodded.

"He always took things to heart and as a small boy, was nearly killed as a result of trying to ransom his pet Dolcan! At one point I thought he would never make adulthood. Of course he is grieving, as he always did and not just for Ahnell, who was the only brother he knew, but for his own loss, but he must get over that! One has to.", she seemed to look inward for a long moment and then said briskly, "and how are you child?"

Jalni stared blankly, "Deshun?", she questioned, to which Ikella said with a smile, "I hear from Hanna, Satra and Dorra that you have made a remarkable recovery. Hanna says that you have acquitted yourself well as a supportive Sister and a talented Healer. Is that still what you want?".

Jalni hated being the subject of other people's conversation, even if they meant well. Ikella noted her scowl, but went on calmly.

"I think there is a way that you can fulfil your training, provide a service to the Guild and help rehabilitate Daro.", she announced and Jalni waited, her nails dug into the palms of her hands, the death knell of all her hopes ringing in her ears, as the Sorceress continued more thoughtfully, "Are you ready to return to the Azure?".

Jalni leapt to her feet, face chalk white and blazing, but the Sorceress regarded her with equanimity.

"Yes.", she said pensively, "still a bundle of unresolved anger. which may affect your ability to treat patients impartially. However infuriating Daro is, he needs your help and so do the children of Scartel. Are you woman enough to try and solve two problems with one cast of the dice?".

Jalni scowled balefully, silently snarling to herself, "So that's the way Mirayen blows is it?", all the time staring stony-faced at Ikella, as the Sorceress continued.

"Complete the task and I will see you advanced in status to Healer, or maybe more. I wondered if you should have been tested for Sorcery when you arrived and I still wonder if a more independent role is what you need.".

Ikella's next words confirmed Jalni's worst fears.

"In this next Rotation of your continued studies, you have to be detached from your Hall, independently living with and serving the needs of a permanently disabled patient. Your responsibilities extend to daily medications and practical assistance. You must be aware of emotional distress, working out strategies that will permit them to live independently, while building their confidence towards integrating with the able bodied world. This is according to the plan that Dorra sets all our fourth Rotation students. There is no bias for, or against you. Your only problem is that the patient concerned is probably the most powerful mage since Cataclysm!".

Silently hating her, Jalni dipped her head, but the icy blue stare did not disengage and Ikella stood to pace her floor as she elaborated.

"We must send help to Scartel. The One only knows that there are too few of us to spare, so we must send our most powerful, to bring the children back to safety. Solana, (your own Senior Healer) has managed to send a runner to Tirjella, but in so doing, deprived herself of her only assistant. From Scartel to Darnesh, the Azure is quarantined, this is your opportunity to show us your true worth.".

Dourly, Jalni watched the elaborately tattooed hands telling off the positive effects to her reasoned argument.

"The borders are closed, the trails though usable won't support a large party. We need a Healer to estimate what trail stops need restocking, so the journey itself has purpose. You are almost fully qualified and can assist Solana in ways that only the release of a fully trained Healer could improve on, further to that, you are going to your own Sands, where you would have advantages that others might not be able to employ.".

Mina nodded enthusiastically, while Jalni seethed. It was all signed, sealed and settled, yet only now was she being consulted. Was she living a life designed by others for their benefit, or hers?

Ikella noted the passive resistance as Jalni stretched an overly tense neck, but continued, seemingly impervious to the barely suppressed fury, etched on every muscle of her novices body.

"Despite his depression, we believe that Daro is capable of supporting a weave for a number of children.", her voice changed.

"However much you want to deny this, you are part of some scheme. You were the one who could read the Scroll of Prophecy. You are certainly able to link to a patient psychically. We are convinced that had you not been there to call him back, Daro would have died on that first night. You are the first person that he connected to and hard though this is, I mean you to take him to Scartel, so that you can both complete your destiny. You may kill or cure each other, but you are going to take our Sandsinger from the Opal into the Azure and safely back again.".

Jalni stared at her dumbfounded and as she did so Ikella moved and the desk where the scrolls were kept came into Jalni's view. She gazed blindly at it for some minutes before she found her focus and as she did so, she became aware that she had seen that desk before, in the labyrinth of old Selesh, where she had secreted the scrolls from which her downfall had sprung.

Catching the direction of her gaze, Ikella opened the drawer and took out the Scroll of Prophecy. As she did so, another, caught on the tie of the first and it slipped from Ikella's grasp. Jalni felt a deep sense of resignation flood through her, as Ikella reached for it and it opened, displaying for any and all to see a depiction of the crater of Scartel. Immediately, it became obvious that the

Sorceress had made enormous strides in her ability to read the ancient scripts, for she said, "In late Spring we find Merishwen at Scartel.", and then abruptly continued saying thoughtfully:

"Well, that's a bonus, for you can pick it at the right time. Fresh it is stronger and a little Merishwen goes a long way.". She laid both scrolls on the table inviting Mina and Jalni to join her.

Immediately, Jalni asked,

"What is that?", Pointing to the second scroll, she barely breathed as the Sorceress peered at the faded drawing.

"It looks like another Sandsinger, with a Sorceress.", Ikella grunted, peering short-sightedly and Jalni scowled.

"Well, I'm not going then.", she said decisively. The two older women glanced at each other, " I've already had enough trouble with one of them, without looking for another.", Jalni declared, glancing at the large sand glass on Ikella's desk.

"Can you send up some of Daro's ceremonials so that he can be presentable in Council?", she asked, and without waiting for an answer, she headed for the door.

Afterward, when Jalni recalled how rude she had been to Ikella she squirmed with embarrassment, but she was not going to apologise! Defiantly she thought, "It must have been the tassin!". Then remembered to ask Dorra for Daro's clean bedding.

The bundle lifted into her arms left her over-laden, but Jalni stoically headed towards the Infirmary, her mind fully engaged in plotting her escape. Possibly, the height of the additional burden caused her to miss a turning, or possibly the rebellious mood that took her mind far from Selesh was to blame, but she suddenly realised she was lost. Anxiously retracing her steps, she became more confused with every turn.. Having walked these halls for four Rotations without missing her way once, the cold fingers of fear touched the nape of her neck. Bewildered and angry with herself, she paused at an insistent tinkle, but before she could find out what made it, she was heading up the ramp that led to Daro's rooms.

Hastily, she knocked at his door, but he didn't answer, so thinking him asleep, she went in quietly, to a room devoid of Sandsingers. Anxious enquiries with the first Healer she saw, solved the riddle as the girl explained.

"Lord Daro? One of the Elders came for him ages ago. It won't be long until they're ready for you to bring him back. I'll take that bedding and make his bed by the time you return if you like.", she lifted the bundle from Jalni's unresisting hands and made off with them, just another Healer in a Hall full of faceless women.

Jalni, already on her way to the level below, caught sight of the great sand glass in the hallway and gaped in disbelief. According to that, she'd been wandering. lost in the labyrinth for three complete turns of the glass. She consulted the infallible sense of time that came with the practice of Healing and found it was true, but Jalni being Jalni, refused to believe.

"That's impossible.! As impossible as Sandsingers!", she grumbled to herself, quickening her pace, to come out, opposite the Sorceress's privy stair to the Inner Sanctum, just in time to see Daro, resplendent in flowing robes, being led towards her by Ikella herself.

He seemed quiet, but as she joined them, Ikella said in mild rebuke:.

"Jalni, you shouldn't let visiting Healers lead Daro.". The novice stared mutely as the Sorceress continued purposefully.

"You must prepare yourself to go to Scartel with Lord Daro. You will act as guide and Healer as required, until your arrival. After which, he will make the necessary decisions. You are to help Solana.".

She regarded Jalni seriously, noting the mutinous scowl. "I know this turns your expectations upside down, but lives depend on you for the first time. Parentless children and your own Senior Healer will starve if not relieved. I dare say you don't want to go, but with this one task, you could complete your training and take full Healer status, until then you are bound to Selesh and I say you will go.".

It was a command and Ikella's Staff blazed, but Jalni didn't feel any compulsion to obey. She glanced at Daro and there was a brief flicker of amusement on his face, then she realised that the power, streaming from Ikella's Staff, was being diverted to Daro's hand. Half hidden by the cuff of his flowing sleeve, Daro was casually rolling up a ball of light, as a weaver balls yarn. His face was averted from Jalni, who seethed silently.

"Does he think I need his help?", scowling savagely as Ikella said (not unkindly).

"I know it galls you to be bound Jalni, but this is for Daro's protection, as well as yours!".

Jalni forced herself to bob in deference to Ikella, then stepped in to take Daro's arm. For a moment he resisted her then Ikella said warningly:

"You have talked yourself to a standstill my son. I will come and see you later, but for now, we both need to rest. Go with your guide as I advise and don't be difficult.", at which Daro muttered reluctant acquiescence and Jalni led him away.

At the first turn in the corridor, Daro pulled his hand from the crook of her arm, opening his palm to display the glowing ball. Tilting his head (as if listening), he waited until, far in the distance, a door closed. Nodding to himself, he released the ephemeral orb from his hand and it hovered briefly, before Jalni's eyes. Then it disappeared, leaving a small but visible trail of smoke in the air. She giggled, as a smile touched the corner of Daro's mouth, then he held out his hand.

Without thinking, Jalni took it and instantly knew her mistake. As they touched her eyes flashed to his face and were caught in a hypnotic gleam. She remembered trembling, then she woke, staring at the absorbed look on his face, then stubborn fury flooded her

"Deo me!", she sputtered enraged. she was being used as some sort of experiment in magic! She didn't Follow these strange Opal beliefs, she wasn't sure of the Way anymore, but she was not going to be the subject of a battle of wills between the Sorceress and her son either!

Before she knew it, she was walking away from a newly blind man, when a voice… "His voice?", sounded in her inner mind.

"Jalni?", he pleaded. "Don't leave me. I won't intrude, but I must make you hear me!". Her feet stumbled to a stop as he begged, "Don't fight me. If you hear me, come back.".

She was astonished, but returned protesting through clenched teeth, "Go away! Get out of my mind right now and leave me alone!".

As suddenly as he had established the link, Jalni felt it close (like the door they had heard earlier), then he was in front of her, saying quietly.

"There! I have gone now, but in emergency I can return.", his voice and smile was gentle, but Jalni thought angrily.

"You'd better not try.", and missed seeing the quiver at the corner of his mouth.

She mused inwardly, as she guided him back to his room.

"I hope he doesn't think he can get into my head whenever he likes.", she thought, guiding Daro to a handrail, at the foot of the ramp to the next level, telling her silent companion.

"Just put your hand there my lord.", she suggested, deliberately being as formal as she knew how.

"Your lady mother had these installed to help blind patients or blind visitors. They extend right down to the undercroft where the villagers are living temporarily.".

She guided his hand to the rail and he complied without protest. A glanced showed him leaning on the rail, those brilliant mysterious eyes closed, and in simple compassion, she slowed their progress. She thought he looked rather forlorn and quite vulnerable, but couldn't resist asking herself silently.

"So how in Sundreth's Hall did he stop her?", half wondering what Ikella would do to him, if she found out, realising rather ridiculously that she would champion Daro any day, as they neared Daro's room. Stopping to allow him to re-orientate himself, she studied him closely, a thought flickering through her mind.

"At least he looks the part! Robes suit him, although it'll take more than a pretty face and party tricks to convince me he's a Sandsinger!", wondering silently at his nerve, her thoughts flew on.

"Which ever way I reasoned it, Ikella is still Guardian of the Way, Keeper of the Nine Sands, Warden of the Winds, yet he treats her as someone he can run rings round. ".

Sobered at the thought of the risks he was taking, she conducted Daro to his room, and helped him to lie on his bed, without a word. Her brain went on with the silent argument.

"He defied his mother in front of me.", an awed refrain repeated. "Ikella, Mistress of all Magic, Guardian of the Ways, Sorceress of the Opal Sands, and lately Tiraj di Schpeller (whatever that means)?".

Daro turned a beatific grin on her. His voice chimed in her inner mind again, silencing her private thoughts effortlessly.

"Tiraj di Schpeller?", his smile broadened at her gasp of horror. "In this case I'd try Spanker of small boys!".

This suggestion tailed off with a sly chuckle, as taking her disbelief in Sandsingers with her, Jalni fled to prepare for the most amazing journey of her life.

From the following day, Jalni established a new routine. Mornings were spent on domestic duties, preparing both herself and Daro for the journey ahead of them, afternoons she spent plotting. During this period, deliberately devoting long hours erecting mental barriers against that Voice. Succeeding only in exhausting all but her irritation with life, she taught Daro to negotiate the Infirmary floor safely, forcing herself to endure as his moods swung between high elation and black despair.

She had no doubts about her own abilities, but if getting to Scartel was relatively easy, she personally questioned what one novice Healer and a blind man could achieve. She badly wanted to understand the purpose of this mission, but as the coils of another's machinations entangled her again, Jalni's resentment grew, until she had all but decided to leave the Healer Hall, if any more demands were made of her.

On the third day following Daro's induction, she spent the morning, gathering herbs and other plants from the plateau above Selesh, returning to Ikella's private workroom, where the Sorceress taught advanced classes. The novice watched Ikella strip fire bush leaves, after boiling them to destroy their poison loaded hairs. Under instruction, Jalni split the stems, extracting the resulting fibres, from which they produced a strong (if sticky) twine. Ikella, said brusquely.

"You will need your wits about you. With Scartel out of food in days, you must live off the land. Camping, foraging, even trapping your food. Fire bush leaves make good soup, fire bush twine makes snares or nets. Trust the Sands they will provide.".

She opened a draw as they spoke, producing a couple of greased paper packets, folded tightly into squares. She spoke thoughtfully.

"You should learn this one.".

She held out the apothecary's slip, instructing, "Smell it dry, taste it wet, but be careful, it is highly active.".

She nodded encouragement to Jalni, who, noted a drawing on the outside of the packet. A tall grass like plant, with a plume where she expected a flower. She looked up at Ikella curiously.

"What is it called? What are its properties?". Ikella answered her briskly.

"It is Ritash and no sensible traveller goes without it.".

She paused to let Jalni sniff at the substance cautiously. The grey granules still had a pungent smell and the novice suggested. "Poisonwood?", to which Ikella nodded.

"A less dangerous relative, with many more uses. With the smoke from poisonwood, you can fumigate sickrooms. With an extract of Ritash you can wash dirty wounds, rid a patient of head crawlers, neutralise scab and alleviate the itch of rash, but…" her voice dropped dramatically. "It is not for internal consumption. It has been used as a weapon before now, thankfully, it has the most distinctive flavour.".

The Sorceress took a tiny spoon and carefully selected five small grains from the rest. She scooped them together and placed them into a grinding dish then (using a tamp), ground them to a fine yellowy powder. Folding away the remains of the Ritash while a kettle boiled, she added a drop of hot water to the contents of the dish. Stirring the minuscule compound together. To Jalni's surprise the colour disappeared, although the result was not absolutely clear, she could see that it might disappear in a glass of water, or wine. Ikella scooped a droplet into a clean spoon and indicated that Jalni should taste it.

The novice hesitated, but a raised eyebrow from the Sorceress prompted Jalni's memory. The silent accusation in Ikella's eyes, recalled her voice to Jalni's mind.

"You administered a substance, untried and untested, to your sister Healer!", and she knew that she deserved this lesson (which would be remembered long after this day).

She dipped the end of her tongue into the mixture, with all her senses alert. There couldn't have been more than two drops in the spoon, but immediately, a distinct, sharp, yet acrid taste flooded her mouth . She pulled a face in disgust, but rolled the Ritash round her mouth, comparing it with other substances she knew.

"Woundwort?", she suggested and Ikella, pleased that she had made the connection, nodded, before making Jalni wash out her mouth with a distillation of honeyberry. They worked on. Jalni learned about Daro's diet, collecting several useful additions to her pack. She watched attentively as Ikella sketched edible fungi, unfamiliar berries and Yanni, a huge spineless cacti, which was not only a source of water, but could also be eaten. It had a fresh but slightly sour taste, comparable to the citrines of her childhood.

Several other substances were produced. One, (a fruit seed from the Malachite Sands), could be ground to produce an oil with remarkable curative properties for burns. Another (resembling dried breadcrumbs) affected the throat, and Jalni was persuaded to smell and taste each one in turn, working her way through every variation present. She examined ointments, sweet, sour and bitter, smelling and tasting each one as Ikella advised. She peered at powders, ground fine and coarse, and several like baked crumbs which tasted of nothing in particular. Names and treatments filled her head and note tablet until she yawned, at which point, Ikella raised an eyebrow and said considerately,

"Well child, you are tired. That's enough for now. No doubt I shall think of something we missed later, but you have done well today. You are looking a bit pale, why don't you go and take a breath of fresh air, eat your noonday meal and rest? We can catch up later.", and so saying the Sorceress brought the training session to an end.

Jalni had the beginnings of a headache by this time and having missed breakfast, felt slightly sick. Ikella, on the other hand seemed quite pleased with her efforts, so Jalni took the opportunity to escape.

Unaccustomed to the fiercer heat at Height of Sun, the novice went to the room allocated to her, next to Daro's. Cool and dark, it welcomed her aching head. Cold linen kissed her feverish face as she collapsed on to the bed. Too late she realised that she was ill, as her head swam and darkness descended. Rousing from a feverish dream, she found herself struggling against a strangely tilting world.

Stomach lurching, she was only dimly aware of calling for help, before the cramps left her writhing, groaning, overwhelmed by nausea. She was aware of a cool hand pressed to her head and a voice saying,

"Don't fight it, relax, hang on to the bowl.", then with one inelegant retch, she vomited.

A horridly long time later, as the pain faded, she realised that her vision was clearing, the world had steadied and a drudge was mopping her floor. A sharp clean smell permeated the room and as she jerked into full awareness, she exclaimed angrily, "Ritash!", and the man sitting on her bed chuckled.

Jalni was furious.

"O, that's the bitter end!", she cried in distress, "I can't even be ill without you being involved!", and as the weakness of the moment overcame her she sobbed helplessly.

"I'm always in trouble and I've tried so hard to put it right. I can't do anything to please Ikella and now I have to take you to Scartel. Well, be aware that if I'm involved, you are doomed. Does your mother really hate you so much?".

She rolled over, face down, snuffling into her pillow, barely conscious of the delicate unlocking of old grievances in her mind as she wailed.

"Why me? Its not fair! She could have given me a Healer post at Darnesh. She could have stilled me! Anything would be better than this continual torture!".

If she had not been so self absorbed, she would have seen her pain reflected on his face, but she missed it, as she wept.

"I didn't mean to hurt anyone. I just need peace, to be left alone! I thought that was all over, why is she punishing me now? I've worked hard, she said so herself. Just because I don't want to go to Scartel, or because I don't conform to her idea of a Healer. Well, I don't believe in Sandsingers anyway, I won't be a Healer if I don't want to, and as for Sorcery...", she sounded regretful for a moment, before collapsing to sob , "Why me? Why me...".

Covering her face she huddled on the bed as Daro cautiously stood. With one hand tracing the wall he left her weeping, a bitter twist to his mouth.

"So much for establishing a better relationship.", he thought gloomily. His was going to be a long, lonely road and unless Jalni adapted, he could imagine that applying in both directions.

Returning to the meditation from which Jalni's cry for help had roused him, he tucked his legs underneath him, cleared his mind, slipping into a reflective trance, quietly re-visiting the day of his induction. While his mother had been exerting her authority over Jalni, he had Surprised himself with his own reluctance to permit a stranger to guide or robe him. When Jalni failed to collect him, another Healer, (who seemed peculiarly perceptive) had appeared. She spoke quietly, calming him as he robed.

"True power can't fail you. You will know what to do, what to say or sing at the right time. Don't struggle with it, relax and the One will guide you. It is the same for all of us.".

He understood that her awareness of his need for reassurance came from the physical connection as she led him, and resolved to ask his guide, a few more questions the next time he met her. However, as the thought promoted the bitter realisation that he couldn't tell one Healer from another, he also knew that the one Healer he would always be able to find, was the one, who wanted none of him.

He set himself to working out his gains and losses over the last few days. Surprisingly, he had found it easy to dress himself, if someone laid his clothes out ready. He smiled, remembering the robes he had worn to his induction, letting his mind drift.

His guide had apologised for a missing belt, but the garment that he shrugged on moulded itself to his body settling on his shoulders as if tailored for him. As the loose sleeves slid down his arms like familiar friends , he suddenly felt alive, confident, ready to face the world. His hands had strayed to a faint pattern in the weave as his guide made him tilt his head up, while she fastened the ties at the neck. She folded ornate cuffs on his sleeves, helped him put on a hooded cloak, then stepped back as he adjusted the cowl.

"Looking me over.", he had thought wryly, but there had been no patronising intonation in the voice that said apologetically,

"There was no time to arrange the boots that go with these robes, but they will come later.".

Then it was done and he was ready. She placed his hand on her arm and said, as if reading his mind,

"Every time you walk with a guide, you will adjust, until you hardly remember a time when you didn't need one. If you have a good guide, you will quickly regain your confidence.".

He remembered replying, (as though he hadn't intended anyone to hear him), "But I will never run again.".

As they reached the doors of the Great Hall, she whispered words that left him astounded.

"You ran, all the running that you needed to do in a lifetime, in returning here, you ran for yourself, you ran for Sararrh and you ran for Ahnell. All the running for three lives in one moment. It is not surprising, that you set up such a vortex, that you broke the Gate in the Rock, unhinged the doors to the Healer

Hall and swept the skies clear of the debris left by the Storm on the night of your birth.".

As Daro considered this statement in awe, she said, "Don't forget the book, fetch the book.".

She left as the Inesh guards opened the newly rehung doors of the Healer Hall and he heard the measured steps as the Elders processed to greet him.

He turned his head, seeking his companion, but she had slipped away and in that moment Ikella joined him and taking his arm, led him up the Way of Challenge to the Sacred Circle.

The tiled hotfloor, Mina's late husband's legacy, made deeper, echoing sounds as the Elders proceeded to their allotted places along the Way of Challenge. Daro listened intently, as he waited at the door, trying to hear when they crossed the hammered brass rail that surrounded the Sacred Circle and then Ikella, sensitive to his hesitancy whispered, "Now us.", and stepped forward.

He had forgotten the way silence sang to him, but as he entered the Hall, he could feel the song of long ages waiting to greet him. He almost heard the moment the Hall recognised his presence with a soft flush of colour, evoking a note in his head, like the sigh of a weary child being welcomed home.

Ikella spoke softly. "The Hall seems alive, or is that you?".

She paused before the Sacred Circle, turning towards the Book of Rule, as the memory of that strange night when she found him there, threatened to destroy his calm. Remembering how it had been, standing here with every fibre of his body intent on bringing forth the melody that the Book had sung to him, he had trembled. Not yet sixteen Rotations old, awed and desperate to see if he had imagined that summons, as Ahnell (confused and terrified), hid in the shadows. He recalled Ikella choking back tears as she challenged him and beside him, felt her falter as she remembered it too.

His head had turned, as though he would gaze precisely at the place where Ahnell had knelt, then he gracefully inclined his head, his lips silently invoking his friends name as Ikella followed his lead, for the spot was indeed blessed. Then Daro moved forward a pace, and Ikella took him into the Sacred Circle, up to the Book of Rule, which no man in living memory had ever touched. In profound silence he ascended the steps unaided, and braced himself on the lectern in front of him, hood shadowing his face. His voice whispered in his mother's inner mind.

"Go mother. Sit with the Session of Elders for a while. Just let me be here and gather my thoughts.".

High above the Hall in the depths of his Infirmary room, the memories streamed as if imprinted indelibly on his mind, then he was in the moment that the Book stirred under his hand.

Ikella had left him, occupying her usual seat, placing her Staff into its holder, signalling Sorrill to close the newly rehung doors .

He knew nothing of the faint glow that had flooded the walls of the immense cavern, lighting up the place where he stood shimmering in his cloak of Colour.

Absorbed in the thrall of the Book, he had raised his hand above the cover, feeling it open under his hand. Once more, its power streamed upward, lighting the vaulted roof, touching his face, illuminating him so that his Opal infused eyes were visible to the awe-struck Elders.

Then the melody began to filter to the watching Council, as once more in the Hall of Selesh, a Sandsinger sang. He remembered the joy as his voice (a melodically lyrical tenor) built in power. He remembered, that as it lifted into that special augmented arena they knew as *"othervoice"*, he had used language unknown to this time, yet they understood that he was dedicating himself to their service.

Gradually, the inflections in that othervoice had changed, he remembered the moment when instead of the Book controlling what he sang, he had followed a suggestion, and sent his voice searching. Locked in his memories, Daro recalled the feeling of satisfaction as something materialised in his hand, and he turned to the Council with a small golden key in his palm.

The pure mischief of that moment tugged a small smile to his lips as he recalled the sound of every woman rising to watch, (not that any of them moved closer). Even his mother had preferred to peer from a safe distance, rather than get in the way of High Magic. Daro thought bitterly that even with eyes permanently closed, he could see more clearly than they.

"How frightened they are.", he extrapolated thoughtfully, "Not of higher power, but of power in the hands of a man, yet are we not half of humanity?", forcing himself back to the events in Hall rapidly, lest his treacherous mind question whether he was still human. He felt his fingers exploring the sides of the lectern. He recalled the watchers holding their breath, as a low tone caught his attention. He felt warmth as a glow came from the lectern, which seemed to be shivering under his hands. His eyes flared into life like the aura which had revealed him outlined in opalescence. The memory of every inch of his body suffused with power, caused him to tremble as he dreamed and remembered filling the Sacred Circle with a growing chorus of sound, which swelled seemingly from the stand itself. Then, the silence, followed by an audible "click!"

He had pocketed the key, after inserting it into one of the carvings in the stand. Casually lifting the immense Book from the reading slope, (still chained to the stand where Feydora had left it) he had let it fall. To him, what symbolised the end of an Age , filled those assembled with terror. Even Ikella shuddered, for every day those who entered this Hall passed beneath an inscription, which ran close to the hearts of the faithful.

It read, "Let not the Book of Rule fall.". He knew now that she could hardly believe that it was her son who had defied that instruction, and had feared to see what he would do next.

He had pressed another carving causing the stand to slide apart, revealing a small, dark aperture, no more than four fingers square. His hands performed a complex gesture, as he revealed the hiding place of the true book of Rule, then, the sound of a bell echoed, pealing down the centuries, as a small book leapt from the cavity into his hand, and the Second Age of Mystery began.

The small, board bound book, held together with simple leather ties felt strangely familiar, as though he had been bound to it. He had run a thumb over the front cover finding an inscription, which he knew from his mentor at Tirjhinar must read, "For the Singer of the Song.". It seemed at that moment, as though a burden had been surrendered, for he felt as though warm lips had touched his brow, then a gentle sigh filled the air.

Apparently Ikella also heard that sigh of relinquishment, her head came up and he felt her gaze on him as the stand slid back together and closed. Hearing the gasps as the book from which he had sung raised itself to the reading slope, He'd remembered struggling to stand as the power ebbed away, leaving him clinging weakly to the lectern. Head bowed over his hidden treasure, as though he hardly dared to touch the sacred relic, he'd eventually suggested plaintively,

"If someone will come and get me?", and Ikella moved swiftly to his side. The meditating man smiled gently thinking that every movement of her body proclaimed, "This is my place. He is my son, my Sandsinger!", as she took his arm, guiding him from the Hall, onto the stairs that climbed to the Djellim, to join the High Council.

As the sand-glass turned, Daro's meditation grew more profound. He found himself reviewing the most important part of his induction as Sandsinger, as though he stood outside his own experience looking on, as an impartial observer might have done. It was really odd, he decided, knowing how he had felt, yet aware of how his friends and family felt too. Then he realised that understanding had produced images that he could follow and sunk in trance, he studied them closely.

At the doors to the Djellim, they had been greeted by the full Chapter of his own Honour Guard, headed by Diras, resplendent in the finery of full Guard Commander. Her eyes had blazed triumphantly as she ordered the salute. He recalled Ikella's reaction as she heard for the first time, the familiar name by which he would henceforth be known.

"Ichspeller Selunsanni.", they chorused. presenting spears in an elaborate display. He felt the tremor of Ikella's secret amusement, his Guard turned slightly bewildered eyes on her, before repeating the salute. However, she noted their reduced enthusiasm, accepting albeit reluctantly, that an Opal Sorceress was of small account alongside a living Sandsinger.

The Elders, who had preceded them, stood around the Council Table, waiting for him, but now he understood the secret of this room. The images that Ikella had broadcast to him at the time, began to make sense to his dreaming mind as he realised the Chamber could grow to accommodate many more than it presently contained. The Council table (also possessed of this unusual property) gleamed. The chairs stood ready and the ceremonial chair, (in which another Sandsinger had appeared to Ikella) now occupied the place in which her state chair usually stood. He could feel its familiar glow, and needed no fingertip inspection to see that his own name appeared below the Opal panel on its back. He remembered wondering how it could be here, knowing he had last seen it in the High Hall in Tirjhinar, then his mother asked formally.

"Ichspeller, may I have your permission to convene this meeting?",

Daro remembered how surprised into silence, he had simply inclined his head, then (improvising wildly) murmured.

"If that be the will of you all.".

Slightly dazed he had allowed Ikella to seat him, then he had struggled to gather his wits as she sank into her chair and the assembled Healers and Council joined them.

"Will you speak to us Ichspeller and tell us how you came to this?".

Ikella threw down her opening gambit. He knew she was dying to know what had happened to him, so determined not to flinch, he gave them a partial explanation. He had pushed back the hood of his cloak in reply, so that the enormity of his sacrifice became evident to his Clan Elders and the only family he had ever known. He had revealed his strange opal eyes, showing them his badge of identity, his brand and his disability, in one blaze of fire, praying that he could withstand their pity.

Shocked by the uncompromising nature of his revelation, an awkward silence had fallen, into which Hanna

rose to the occasion. She had spoken factually and as interest replaced the tangible wave of sympathy, he was grateful he belonged to a community where practical solutions outweighed pity.

"Daro is totally blind. However, his rehabilitation is coming along well. He has magic on his side of course, but, in order to allow him to adapt, it is (in my considered opinion), essential that no information should escape.".

As Hanna sat, Ikella spoke quietly.

"My enquiries showed an unusual lack of othersand's visitors to Spring Rites. We therefore sealed all knowledge of our Sandsinger within Clan and Sand. This ensures respect for his privacy, allowing him to develop an understanding of his power and purpose.".

Daro's trance was lightening and only the discomfiture of his autocratic parent kept him riveted on the moment that Dorra said idly,

"You two make him sound like a novice, not a Sandsinger.".

At which a hush of consternation fell, and he recalled chuckling.

"Listen to all of you!", he had exclaimed.

"I'm only Daro you know. Not some visionary in holy orders, anxious to go around flinging bolts of lightening, terrifying old women and Zeglurs!",

That was the point he remembered asking Mina where his Songfather was, but Mina didn't know. However Ikella had seized the moment, telling him brusquely.

"Your Songfather went to Malos to evade your return, leaving a dearth of old men and Zeglurs to practice on. However, all those here saw your entrance!", she said tartly. Even the memory of that acid tome caused Daro to feel ill at ease as he remembered apologising like the scapegrace boy he had once been.

He had spread his hands with a self-mocking gesture.

"Unfortunately, my anger at the waste, the injustice of it all, engaged before intelligence, so you will have to mark up the damages to my account and protect me, until I have paid in full!".

His mother quietly responded.

"I think I speak for us all when I say that your debts account to little other than a few broken doors. No person or animal suffered anything other than inconvenience, we are used to rebuilding and we now bathe in the light of Seleus again. It is our debt not yours and we are but your children in power.".

She spoke softly, but there was a concerted wave of agreement around the Council Chamber. Daro held her hand in his and drew her to her feet, saying lightly.

"I will try not to let you down again, but Dorra was right. I am only a novice and novices often get things wrong.".

It was as if he had flicked a switch in Ikella's brain, she turned and exclaimed,

"Jalni, where is she? Why didn't she bring you to Hall? She should be here to collect you!".

However, she had not been present, nor did she arrive and eventually he found himself being drawn back down the stairs, on Ikella's arm. He remembered touching the small board bound book that he had slipped into his pocket and that very action tore his dreaming mind back to the present.

He was sitting in his room, in the growing dusk of late afternoon. On the other side of the wall, Jalni was recovering, though he doubted the wisdom of telling her that she had called him in her distress, he was pleased that he had been able to help her. He wondered idly, who was going to help him make sense of it all and took the book out of his pocket and it called to him.

Chapter 15 - Blind Man's Bluff

Daro moved to his table, holding the Book that would dominate his life, and resisting its allure, sat deep in thought. At first, the light tap at his door didn't register, then, when it did, he called "Enter", before realising that the sacred relic lay where anyone could see it. He moved to shield it, as quick, light steps sounded, and the fragrance of old wild rajas surrounded him. He recognised his unknown Healer almost before she bent over him, exclaiming in delight.

"Daro, did you find my book, you didn't forget it did you?".

There was a thrumming note and Daro felt the book move. Quick as a flash, his hand shot out grasping her arm roughly. He kept his voice low, yet it dominated, pulsing with restrained power.

"Madam, explain yourself!", he commanded, feeling the tingle of power rush through his hands as his visitor giggled deliciously, wriggling out of his grasp. He heard, no… felt, no… heard, a strange shivering note in the air, then she was on the other side of him. He didn't attempt to conceal his annoyance at such capricious behaviour, frowning reprovingly, as he spoke.

"If you want to play Blind Man's Bluff, it would at least be polite to ask! Besides, I think you're cheating.".

The gentle thrum of power in his blood sang, then died away, as she said lightly, "Of course I'm cheating, I always cheat.".

He sensed her merriment and tightened his grip on the book, but her mood had changed again.

"Now I suppose you want to know everything! You're no fun at all!".

She sat abruptly. Her hand brushed his, then he became aware, that he could feel a soft vibration in the air and that somehow, she was fading away, dissipating like a dream vision, seen in smoke. It was most extraordinary and yet he was not surprised. Her voice sounded in his ear.

"I have been called, I have to go.".

Her voice came from a distance, "Keep the Faith Daro.", but the laughter died as she said, more faintly still, "Keep the book safe, keep it with you always!".

 Then her voice dropped to a barely audible whisper.

"Goodbye Daro, Ichspeller Selunsanni. May the Light of the World truly return.".

The Source within him shivered and she was gone.

He strained to hear her again, to feel her hand, as empowered as his own, but there was nothing, she had gone. His voice hardly wanted to obey him, replying softly

"Goodbye.", then less hesitantly, "Goodbye Feydora.", as the door opened and his mother entered, followed by a wan, but recovered Jalni.

If Ikella heard, she showed no sign of it in her manner and voice. She simply pounced on the first thing that she could criticise and started tidying up, instructing Jalni as she did so.

"If you are to make a good carer, you must keep everything and I mean everything in the same place. Remember, you have eyes to find things, Daro must use his memory, and it isn't easy.".

She picked up the clothes Daro had discarded that morning, handing them to Jalni to hang, then sitting, she arranged items on the table in front of him.

"Platter, cutter, wedge and spoon always in the same position. Food always arranged the same way, grains to the top, vegetables to the right and bread to the left. In that way, Daro won't be unpleasantly surprised when eating.", she paused, then said briskly.

"On to other things my girl. Your packs contain dried rations, spare clothes and medications for Solana's use. I prepared your scrips with my own hands, but they need checking. Plain lightweight desert wear will suffice as you will discover, neither of you is accustomed to the heat that Seleus generates, having been born during our time of twilight. You must shelter during Height of Sun and at night, your first overnight will be at Fronish.".

The Sorceress referred to a deserted Healer training post, but she wasn't finished with them yet.

"Jalni.", she warned, "Do not stop to light fires until you get there. I had a disturbing report this evening, it seems that Wanderers hunt along the Dreken Pass and since they now have light days and travellers to prey on…".

As her voice trailed off meaningfully, Jalni reacted as Daro might have predicted, (had he been given the opportunity). Lips curled scornfully she demanded,

"You would send me, with your blind son out there, while madmen and worse hunt that area?". The young Healers voice was shrill with contempt. "Have you nought but sand in your heart?". The tone was glacial and Daro's head lifted, scenting battle lines being drawn up. He said as lightly as he knew how:

"Don't worry about me Jalni, I can pull my own weight!", His attempt to soothe her was rejected like a slap in the face as that tangible glare hardened and turned on him.

"Yes.", she agreed flatly. " So can those Wanderers and more than likely they will pull yours dead on a rope behind some trek beast. I hate to think what they would make of your pretty robes! Have you any idea how to fight when you won't see the first spear? You couldn't run, or even hide and yet you expect me to take responsibility for your safety?".

She was wild and white with anger, blue eyes blazing in a stubborn face. Ikella, astounded by Jalni's behaviour, summoned power without so much as taking a breath, but before she could bring her wayward novice to heel, the urge to do so left her. She stared as Jalni, completely unmoved, continued to pressurise Daro.

"You have to stop this. We can help the children another way, they are putting too much faith in magic. Do they think that if I get you there, we can transport those children without a hundred times the risk. There must be another way!".

Daro stood, calmly picked up the Book of Rule and said quietly, "You only know half of the story Jalni. It is not your place to know the other half yet. We are going to Scartel, at the behest of the Council, in answer to a call from one of my dearest friends.".

He calmly ignored his mother, saying encouragingly,

"Of course, if you want to stay here and be a drudge until you mature that is your choice, but if you want to show everyone how wrong they were about you, come with me. We both have a lot to prove. Let us do it together.".

Jalni didn't see Daro make any gesture, but she felt something "shift", as Ikella calmed. Taking this opportunity to make a swift departure, she couldn't resist remarking (over her shoulder) as she left,

"I will guide Daro under protest, but if we are strung up by Wanderers, be aware I fully intend to come back and haunt you!".

Ikella faced her son,

"You snared my bond on her!", the Sorceress accused, as Daro nodded.

"She has to do this for herself. Having learned to distrust and hate, given the slavery and abuse of her youth, I can understand her reasons, but she must learn to let that go and find a new path herself.". His vehemence surprised Ikella, who studied him curiously as she asked:

"She confided in you then??".

Daro, recalling the afternoon's distress and the horrors that his casual probing had uncovered, said tersely, "Not exactly. She was more than a little worse for wear due to your meddling with Ritash!", and for a moment his mother looked thoroughly disconcerted. Recovering swiftly, she continued.

"I have my reasons for distracting Jalni from recognizing her part in an experiment. I will tell you more later.", she closed her lips firmly and could not be persuaded to enlarge on this topic. She was thoughtful, wondering whether this new maturity came with his experiences, or his power, but she was cautious as she warned him.

"She is a wild thing, with a strange lonely soul. Take care not to anger her, for I fear for your safety while she is free.". She sounded so worried that Daro relented, confiding softly.

"Mother, though she doesn't know it, she is bonded to me!", he took the Book of Rule from his pocket and repelling all further questioning, said firmly:

"Now I must study, before I sleep. Tomorrow we leave.".

He quite deliberately turned his back and sat at his table, the book still closed. It lay in front of him and completely ignoring his mother, he held a hand over the cover and it opened. Once more, he was cloaked in the opal glow streaming from the pages and Ikella, excluded from the realms of this higher magic, quietly departed.

A turn of the sand-glass later, when Daro lay quietly in his darkened room, waiting for sleep to still his restless mind, there came a quiet tap at the door. He sat carefully and called softly "Enter", hoping that Feydora had returned to him, but no, it was a quiet, slow moving, man.

"Who is it?". Daro was startled to here the quaver in his voice, but this was the most unnerving part of being blind. A mature, masculine voice answered him.

"Master Daro, we apologise for disturbing you. We are looking for Mistress Jalni, we have a gift for the Sandsinger, but I must have miscounted and we have the wrong room.". Daro sat up, intrigued.

"Wait.", he commanded and the men, for there were at least three of them stopped by the door, shuffling uneasily.

"Close the door and come in all of you.", he ordered and as soon as they obeyed, he asked curiously, "What is this gift?".

A younger voice, said hesitantly,

"Master Daro, it is not important. We are not Clansmen, being born of mixed Sands. We weren't in Hall during Spring Rites, and have never seen the Sandsinger, but we heard that Mistress Jalni travels with him soon and we thought that by pleasing the mage, it might help the girl who got us housed safely before the storm struck Selesh.".

Daro stood slowly, as a flood of thoughts came into his head.

"How is it possible that our own villagers don't know the identity of their Sandsinger?", he questioned wildly, followed by the thought that somehow, in her urge to protect him, Ikella had used magic, but he knew he was wrong. Nothing would conceal the presence of a Sandsinger for long, it was just coincidence that left Clansmen in the possession of the facts and the very people that he wanted to help, in ignorance.

He covered his disconcertion by asking lightly:

"Who is this paragon of virtue? The one that brought you all into safety?", but in his heart, he already knew the answer, for she had not been in Hall herself, an inexcusable lapse in a fourth Rotation student.

"Mistress Jalni!", they chorused and Daro feeling for the chair beside his bed, lowered himself awkwardly into it.

"What help does Jalni need?", he asked them curiously and the elder amongst them spoke again.

"Master Daro, I do not want to cause more trouble for her! She is a good girl, though I think she is troubled. We only wanted to speak with her, not to disturb your rest.".

Daro maintained an imperious silence and the younger man said hurriedly, in a stage whisper.

"Father, just tell Master Daro. He might help us.", and Daro, feeling the stubborn integrity of the elder, felt for the edges of his certainty and trickling just a minuscule amount of power, "pushed", at the man's conviction. There was a clearing of throats, a hesitant rustle and Daro said graciously:

"I am afraid that I only have one chair, but you may sit if you like. I don't know your names, perhaps you'll introduce yourself.".

There was a momentary silence and then the elder spoke softly from the floor area.

"Mistress Jalni came to me, to ask my help for one of her patients.",

There was a solemn dignity in the man as he confided, "She thought that my experience might help her nurse a young man, who has also lost his sight. You probably don't remember me Master, but I am Duvell, the shoemaker. This is my son Lown and this great lump is my youngest, Chrysim.".

Daro sensed movement amongst them and then, the younger man, Lown, spoke urgently.

"Father, this cannot help us.", and sensing that they were moving towards the door, Daro said quickly,

"Don't go, tell me what you were trying to do?".

Footsteps approached him and Lown spoke again.

"My father found out that the Sorceress and the Sandsinger are making Mistress Jalni go back to the Azure Sands. She is frightened, for her family are all dead and she has no-one there she knows. We thought that if she gave the Sandsinger something of value to him, he might take another Healer and let her stay here with us.", he paused, then Duvell interjected.

"With you Master?", and Daro heard the implicit question, but chose to ignore it, saying abruptly:

"What is this thing that you think a Sandsinger may place value on?", and Lown continued the explanation.

"Rotations ago, my father had a tavern in Maraken. One night he took in a man who was clearly dying. Even with no money for a bed, he would never turn anyone away, even calling a Healer. However, it was too late and he died.", Lown's voice lowered. "Before he died, he gave my father the only thing of value that he owned. He told us that he found it out near the Silent Sands.

Daro felt the wings of destiny fan his cheek and thought he heard just the faintest trace of a mocking chuckle as Lown continued gruffly.

"My father loved it the minute he saw it and later when his life changed, he learned to work a craft, that allowed him to repair it.".

Duvell stepped closer, his hands outstretched, his fingers clicking gently and Daro reached forward and found him easily. The shoemaker placed something light, something redolent with the scent of worked leather, across Daro's right arm and wordlessly guided his left hand to touch an ornately tooled belt.

Daro laid it gently on his lap, letting his fingers track the symbols of his own high rank, reverently, picking out the pattern that matched the design woven into the robe of colour hanging only two paces from him, hidden in the shadows of his darkened room,

"This is quite extraordinarily beautiful. Such an elaborate repair does you honour Duvell."

He sensed the pleasure in the voice of the shoemaker.

"Thank you Master. We hoped that the Sandsinger would like it, enough to release Mistress Jalni. If he really liked it, we thought he might be able to heal the young man that Mistress Jalni has taken to. She says nothing, but I think she fair broke her heart over how unhappy he is.".

Duvell's voice tailed off uncertainly as Daro, quite overcome by the irony of the situation choked back mixed laughter and tears.

"O, Duvell, Duvell!", he eventually exclaimed, then he said quickly, before he could change his mind, before the courage deserted him,

"Lown, turn up the light will you?", and as Lown removed the shield from the glowstone and the light fell on his unshaded face, he heard Duvell ask quietly,

"Is it as I fear? I only realised when I showed Master Daro the belt, that he couldn't see it. He had to use his hands to feel the tooling!".

The steady voice held nothing more than practicality when Duvell addressed Daro directly.

"That is very hard fortune Master, but you have the support of all of us. If there is anything that the Healers can't tell you, let me, or any one of us know and we will find the answer for you.".

Lown reached out quite naturally and lifted the beautifully tooled belt from Daro's lap and as he did so, just as naturally, Daro opened his eyes, fixing the little group with his eyes glowing Opal. There was a deep silence and then one by one they knelt on the floor before him, heads bowed to the ground.

Lown cried out, "Master forgive us, we meant no harm. Only to please Mistress Jalni.", and his face was one of anguish as he turned, embracing his father and his slow, silent brother, placing his arms protectively about them as the full enormity of realisation hit them. Daro was the Sandsinger and their Sandsinger was blind!

The mage waited for the rage to engulf him, the power to take him beyond the pain that he had inflicted on himself and now, on these kind good men, but nothing happened. He sighed gently and as he did so, he felt his powers flush through him in a calm, healing torrent, killing the anger and the hurt before it was born. Astonished, he finally understood. The anger and despair that had fed his power wasn't the source or even the key to that power. His disability didn't matter to his new friends, he was not being measured by the value of his sight. What really mattered was that the quiet one, Chrysim, was crying, huge tearful sobs, such as a frightened child might make and Daro, at one with his power at last, carefully stood and took a pace towards him.

Gently placing his hands on the huge man's head, he "listened" intently. As Duvell and Lown raised their heads, Daro radiated reassurance, until they disengaged their arms, releasing Chrysim into the hands of the Sandsinger.

Daro touched the Source delicately, looking for a note, a gentle lullaby rhythm, a pain relieving melody and wielding all three, carefully integrated them into one healing surge of song. He looked beyond the empty space behind Chrysim's eyes and found the spirit, the intellect and the voice that had never developed, opening the compartment and filling it with light, with love and healing melody.

Afterward, when he had sunk exhausted on to his bed and Duvell had been persuaded that Chrysim needed him more than Daro, Lown returned, looking down anxiously at the Sandsinger. He placed the ancient belt awkwardly into Daro's hand, whispering into the dark.

" If we offended you Lord, we apologise.", he said humbly. "My family can't thank you enough. My stepmother is beside herself with joy and my brother…", he smiled a trace self-consciously, "My brother, has a life now thanks to you.".

Deft hands found a blanket, covered Daro's shivering body tenderly. "We owe our lives to your mother who took us in and fed us. Now Chrysim has a future too, so I will pledge my life, all our lives to your service.".

Daro held out his hand to Lown, who took it without hesitation. The Sandsinger allowed a little trickle of power to touch the man, he was honest, brave, loyal and at last Daro understood the ancient term "Sandsworn".

Lown stood to leave, whispering:

"I forgot, Mistress Jalni isn't pleased with any of us.",

Backing towards the door, as Daro drifted off to sleep, he said,

"She says that you have an early start in the morning. She doesn't mind all male

parties, but do you have to sing so loudly?".

Chapter 16 - Darius Reborn?

As Seleus rose, Daro woke, feeling (perhaps for the first time since his return) refreshed and ready to face life again. He lay idly wondering about his late visitors, then resolved to find out how much help he had been to Chrysim before he left Selesh. It was early. Only a few drudges about and taking that into consideration, he slipped out of bed and turned to face the wall that accommodated the linen press, where his robes were hung. Devoutly hoping not to knock his recently healed legs, he made the short journey across the room, surprising himself with his own temerity. He was amazed at how slow he had become and, how much the loss of certainty was affecting him. Silently resolving never to be so impatient again, he measured the area by counting paces. However, gauging the size and relative positions of the furniture was tortuous, knowledge reinforced by painful reminders inflicted on exploring hands and unwary feet. Long before he felt equal to opening the press and finding suitable garments, he was thoroughly frustrated with himself.

Dismissing the idea of involving Jalni, he sighed, wondering how exactly he would choose clothes without vision, and remembered the strange runic patterning worked into the garments the Guardians had provided.

"There's nothing else for it.", he mentally grumbled, "I shall just have to work my way through all of it, one set at a time.", and he began, removing the first robes he came upon from the hanging bar, trying by feel to work it out for himself. He grinned ironically, imagining the shock on Nadra's, or Ahnell's face if they were to discover him, sorting out his own clothes, without their help and the usual raucous comments on his appearance. The pain of recollection brought him back to sand. Ahnell was dead and Nadra was far away, being nursed back from the brink of grief induced insanity, over the death of her adopted son. He grew still, his face clouded and then, more slowly he began the task he had set himself.

He found his ceremonial robes from the feel. A fine silky fabric, with a subtle pattern worked in a manner which imparted a shivering movement under his hand, as though the robe was in some mysterious way, "aware" of him, his proximity, his power. He "felt" it quiver and sigh under his exploring fingers and smiled. Imagining himself descending to the undercroft decked out like the puzzle tree the Inesh erected to amuse the children at Jentaroth, he abandoned that idea immediately, sliding that hanging bar to the left in pursuit of more suitable garments.

He sensed a flurry of movement to his right and found a set of garments that seemed better suited to his purpose, swinging towards his searching fingers, and lifted it down. He had considered using magic to help with this task, , but unable to summon power, he'd Supposed that this meant the task was not important enough to warrant it and paused considering that problem. From the moment he'd become Sandsinger, he'd been struggling with it. His hands mechanically lifted down the next hanging bar as he contemplated the nature of the beast he must master. Casually hooking the chair that silently glided to his side as his palms passed over the knap of the released garments, he found that he was holding on to a serviceable pair of desert pants. Investigating the waistband and fastenings, he was relieved to discover these unfamiliar garments were definitely male attire, blushing as he considered the total humiliation of inadvertently cross-dressing!. Ruefully reminding himself that they could be any colour, he was forced to suppress spluttering laughter at the thought of roaming abroad, dressed in the hideous pink shade adopted by his mother for nightwear.

Sobering, he folded the pants and laid them on the seat of the chair, while he examined the long tunic and thought deeply about the nature of magic. It seemed ephemeral, like mist on a mountain, there within reach,, but gone in the instant he sought it. Still, it could flood through him when he least expected it, so wondering if he would be able to invoke it when necessary, he thought carefully about the previous night, as his night robe unbuttoned itself and slid to his feet.

Deep in thought he stepped out of the tumbled material and stretched, unashamedly naked. Completely unnoticed, His robe gathered itself up, tidily removing to his pillow, as realisation dawned. Up until now, power had invoked itself, (usually when his emotions overrode his ability to analyse how he accessed it). As this revelation occurred to him, he frowned, then his new tunic lowered itself over his head. Emerging from the discreetly self-adjusting fabric, he muttered to himself.

"Yes! I'm nearly always as mad as a Myst-cat when it happens!", and vaguely wondering if he was missing something that would allow him to focus his powers, as Ikella did through the powerstone on her Staff, he stood, oblivious of his clothing as it settled about his person.

Recalling the night of his return in horror, he realised he'd been so angry it still frightened him, determined though he had been (at the time)to pick a fight with his mother. That time, he'd scaled the pinnacle of power, propelled by his emotions (and Ikella's provocation) and he stared bleakly into the abyss of his own ignorance, knowing that episode could never be repeated if he wanted to survive. There simply had to be something missing that he needed to find. His jaw set while his tunic buttoned itself, paused, then undid the top buttons to reveal just a hint of his masculinity. He tried to remember how he'd invoked the power to help Chrysim, absently pulling the wrist ties on his tunic together, as he concentrated on the dilemma. They fastened themselves unaided, as he sat on a chair (miraculously devoid of clothing) and as unsuitable garments discarded earlier, rehung themselves neatly, the Sandsinger tried to analyse the path to the place from where he could summon his power. Despairingly, he ran his hands through his hair, in a combing gesture and the required implement slapped into his palm, so he combed his hair and mused inwardly.

"When I couldn't reach the Source, whatever did I do?".

He slid his bare feet into the well-worn sandals that had nudged him, standing preoccupied as the straps adjusted themselves to his feet, sitting again to search a bedside table for the things he needed, totally unaware of the silent accommodations that his furniture had made for him.

Pocketing the Book of Rule, he slid it out of yesterday's robe and into the tunic of today's, never questioning the subtle adjustments he felt the pocket make to accept the precious relic, so totally absorbed was he, by concern over his ability to safely channel power.

"Just what did I do?".

Almost as though she had whispered in his ear, he remembered Feydora's words.

"Relax, if you don't struggle with it, you'll find the power easily.".

He snorted derisively, thinking that it was all very well for her. She had lived in a time where Sandsingers were trained in the use of magic, and a touch of self pity invaded his mind. Smoothing his hands over loose pants, he discovered that even these had been made as signature pieces, for as he caressed the weave, it sang to him. Feeling the shimmer as the wakening sun touched the rocks surrounding him, he touched the wall with relief, drinking in the power of the Source. Thus absorbed, he suddenly felt the magic flow, like the blood in his veins, singing a melodic accompaniment to his life. There was a sunny cinnamon scent in his room and he smiled, thinking with absolute certainty, that if he knew the perfume that Feydora used, now he knew his own. In that moment, he heard the glacial chime of crystals and a sense of approval enfolded him, like a physical embrace.

A soft clatter outside his door broke this spell, as a passing drudge took her mop and pail into the corridors and with a growing sense of urgency, Daro adjusted his new belt round his waist. The smithworked clasp came easily to his hand, the tongue "snicking" into the oval locking plate as if they had never been parted. He felt it close about him, as under his hand, there was a sudden warmth, in wonder, he traced the outline of what had been a comparatively unadorned anchorage.

No more was it the central tongue of a simple clasp. Now, sited over his navel it blazed in imperial Opal and he settled the belt into place with a deeply satisfied smile. Neither of them would ever see this, but he knew that Duvell would understand the true value of his gift when Daro showed it to him.

Using one hand to guide himself and the other for balance, he made his way to the door, then before he lost his confidence, out into the corridor beyond. He knew this part of the journey. Now all he had to do was to find the ramp that would take him down to the lower levels. Here, a main corridor led into the undercroft and with a renewed sense of confidence, he walked quite briskly to the top of the sloping ramp. He could hear the sound of voices and he moved steadily towards them, but they stopped abruptly and then suddenly his newfound confidence evaporated. He paused, taking deep breaths as he tried to fight down the panic and disorientation, but he caught himself thinking morosely,

"How could I be so stupid? What use is magic without sight? How will I get to Scartel and back when I can't find a friend in my own home?".

Perhaps it was only his own fear pursuing him, but he was suddenly filled with the idea that he was surrounded by hostile whispering. He seemed to be heading down, down into the dark and his thoughts went with him. He heard Ikella snort in disgust, saw Beneva's lips compress and felt Shiarjha's eyes on him as he descended ever deeper, uncertainty, misery and panic hanging over him, invading his thoughts.

"That boy will be the death of me! How could he think he can just roam around unaided!". Ikella's voice echoed in his mind, overlaid with comments from old adversaries.

"Pride is the harbinger of the greatest fall Daro!", he imagined Indeera saying, followed by the self-satisfied tones of the only girl he had been hurt by.

"How sad. You will be nothing, long before I can show you my magic!", Suraya, Sorceress in training taunted him and at last he understood. He was blind and that was that! He might have found the magic, but without sight, he would never be able to wander at will. Without sight he would never be able to use the Talent and that thought brought him to a shuddering halt.

Footsteps approaching his position unnerved him further. He felt the power in him diminish and by the time the other was close enough to touch, Daro was almost quivering in apprehension. He tried to get a hold on himself, for in less than two turns of the sand glass, he would be walking towards the Dreken Pass, in the open, with no protection but a novice Healer. Managing to force a response, when a man greeted him.

"Fair day to you Master.".

He stood shaking, until the man paused to ask, "Are you well? Shall I fetch a Healer?".

Daro pulled himself together briefly answering the question.

"I'm well enough friend, just a little tired, thank you.".

Every muscle in his body was taut and he could hear himself screaming silently, "No Healers! No fuss! Don't even look at me! Go away, please go away.", but he managed to hold himself together, until the man said soothingly:

"If you are sure Master, but I can send someone for you when I reach the kitchens if you like.". Daro ached with terror at the thought of his weakness being exposed to all and sundry and barely in control of his nerves croaked hoarsely:

"No, no my friend, thank you, but having escaped the Infirmary, I don't want to go back straight away.". The other man chuckled confidentially.

"I bet you don't.", he added, "When I lost my sight, I fought nail and claw to get out of the place, I wouldn't go back either.".

Up until then, Daro had been hanging on to his composure, but that was the last straw. He fled, driven by those demons who thrive on demonstrating how anyone other than yourself, can manage a little grace and more acceptance.

He found himself in a narrow corridor, but something in the echoes around him brought him to a sweating, chest heaving halt. A junction turned steeply downwards, where it was cool and quiet. His feet seemed to stumble out of his erratic pace and he tripped, coming to an inelegant stop against the wall, his breath sobbing in his throat. Beyond caring who saw his distress, he slumped onto his knees, in a shallow alcove and exhausted beyond thinking, slipped into a kind of reverie, in which he was running, endlessly running, pursued by the demons of the outer reaches and only a dark void in front of him. He threw an arm across his eyes, wondering where could he run, where could he hide… and slept.

Far above, in the comforting antiseptic corridors of the Infirmary, a bewildered novice

was doing her best to explain the Sandsingers absence to an outraged Sorceress.

"Jalni," she said severely, " I am used to my son being difficult, wilful, scheming and totally disobedient, what I am also used to however, is my son being visible.".

Her comment carried clearly to the Healers and novices who had been unsuccessfully searching the settlement for the Sandsinger. Satra winced as she exchanged silent glances with Hanna. Dorra, aware that a full half of her class was missing, slowed to a walk as she joined the group, hearing the mornings news second-hand.

"Daro's missing, no-one has seen him anywhere since last night.".

The bubbly Novice Mistress looked at them in round-eyed amazement and whispered.

"Has our Deshun thought to search Diras's barrack room yet?", and escaped with her charges as stifled giggles were hastily converted to coughs, but the Healer Hall in general understood that sometimes, lightening the load with humour often renewed those whose appetites for trouble were growing a little jaded.

Jalni answered, spitting fury in the face of the Sorceress.

"Oh no my Deshun. Daro is not my responsibility until we leave Selesh. In Hall he is all yours!".

Hanna's mouth twitched, Amah whispered:

"I can see that one being melted into a puddle if she doesn't back down.".

Dorra, anxious not to infect her flock with Jalni's rebellious attitude, had already ushered the novices away and now, only a dwindling group of Healers remained curious to see what would happen to Jalni, who holding the door open for Ikella, rolled her eyes at them and followed the Sorceress into Daro's empty room.

There was a sound of furniture being moved, doors opened and closed and in the corridor, an audience dispersed.

Ikella reported, "His journey wear has gone, so he is fully clothed. His sandals have gone, could he have been getting ready by himself?".

Jalni said quietly, "That's unlikely. So far, he has done little other than sleep. He's barely willing to feed himself or explore what he can do. What if he thinks this task too much? Would he have run away?"

Ikella said scathingly:

"He is a Sandsinger, sworn to the Opal Sands and its peoples. Whatever his personal difficulties, he would never run away. That would go against his nature.".

Jalni said blankly, "His nature?".

Ikella replied sourly. "Male! Natures exhibitionist. Spends three days talking up his abilities, two days swearing undying devotion and four days beating his chest, before attempting a job that a girl of ten Rotations could do in two sectors of the sand-glass. All that before claiming the bragging rights on the completed task until next Jentaroth!".

The Sorceress sat on the corner of her son's bed, holding her Staff loosely on her lap. She appeared to be fiddling with the great Opal mounted on an elaborate curving finial below the wings at the head of the Staff. To Jalni's immense surprise the stone came away in Ikella's hand and the Sorceress glanced up at her.

"Pull the table over girl.".

She stood as Jalni moved the table to the centre of the room, untying the cord that served her as a belt, connecting it to the clasp of the Opal. Placing the stone on the table, she folded back the wide sleeves of her robe and Jalni saw the silver wristlets of Guardianship, fully displayed for the first time.

"This is serious.", the novice decided, as Ikella sat close to the table, clasping her hands together, leaning on her elbows, staring with unblinking green eyes into the heart of the glowing powerstone.

"Open the door Jalni.", Ikella commanded and Jalni lifted the latch. As the Sorceress focussed on the stone, a low hum filled the room, then the stone elevated, hovering just a finger span above the table. It pulsed and a steady stream of light started to flow from it, lighting Ikella's wristlets until they glowed and pulsed as one.

As though following a draft the great powerstone drifted towards the open door and rising silently in its wake, the Sorceress and the novice followed it. Ikella, connected to it only by the cord of her belt, walked steadily behind the Opal, clasping the naked staff in her left hand. Jalni leapt to open doors wide and the stone lifted a little higher, hovering in the hallway, then moving faster, drifting to the left and down the ramp towards the undercroft. Ikella followed, walking swiftly, an expression of the utmost concentration on her face. Jalni ran alongside her, removing obstacles from the path of the entranced Sorceress, putting out a guiding hand here and there, all the time thinking grimly:

"Where-ever Daro went, if he got this far on his own, then he either did it with magic, or he is better than I thought he was. Wait until we find him. If he hasn't broken his neck, I might volunteer to do the job for him!.".

They continued their progress downward, ever downward and then the glowing stone stopped, hesitated and slipped into a side passage, one that Jalni remembered with a rush of sweating terror. Praying silently to herself, she followed Ikella, heart pounding with apprehension.

"May the One preserve him. He can't see marks on doors…", ran the litany in her mind, in remembrance of a floorless room. She noticed several marked doors, most of them barred, to prevent accidents. However, she need not have worried, for as the powerstone started to turn into the passageway, it hesitated, the Sorceress gave a sort of gasping sigh and the stone dropped to the floor, hovering for just a second and then the flaming light in it died away, leaving the two women in the dark.

"Light", snapped the Sorceress and a flame flared into life as if a torch had been lit. To Jalni's surprise Ikella had extended her hand (palm up), from which the flame leapt (apparently painlessly). It cast enough light for the women to see their way and their Sandsinger, huddled on the floor, curled in quivering misery.

"Daro, stand up.", Ikella commanded impatiently. Jalni, acutely embarrassed by the tears streaking the face of her patient, bent to his assistance and gasped as their hands touched in the dark. Ikella continued to scold him.

"Whatever were you thinking of?", Ikella dusted him down one handed, "You should know better than to go wandering off in such a dangerous place. If you behave like that in the desert, it could get you killed!".

"Yes.", agreed the novice fiercely, her words echoing in the Sandsingers dazed mind. "By me if no-one else volunteers!", but unable to respond, Daro hung his head, acknowledging their right to be angry with him.

Ikella shone the handfire round the corridor, prodding Jalni with her stoneless Staff and the novice jumped as Ikella said, "Hold out your hand girl.", as she poured handfire into Jalni's palm, chuckling at Jalni's disconcertion.

"Strange isn't it?", she commented and Jalni had to admit that it was very strange.

"A bit like having a very cold liquid melting swiftly into your hand.", she remarked and the Sorceress smiled, before turning her attention on her son.

"Are you hurt?", she demanded and Daro shook his head mutely.

"Then pull yourself together.", Ikella barked unsympathetically. "I can relieve physical pain here, but I am not dealing with nervous breakdowns in the dark!",

The Sandsinger was struggling to balance, so Jalni supported him, ignoring the defiant voice that rang out in her mind.

"Then its just as well I've no intention of indulging in nervous, or any other kind of breakdown! Everything I do will always be in the dark from now and if I have to manage that, by the will of the One invested in me, I will,!".

The great Opal, reuniting with the Staff, blazed into life as Ikella said sombrely:

"You don't have to shout! I may admit to one hundred and more Rotations, but there is nothing wrong with my hearing. Now, for the sake of the One, let us return to the Infirmary, Jalni, care for your patient!".

Every inch of her back radiating outraged dignity, Ikella stalked away from her astonished son and didn't speak again until they reached a gallery near the turning to the undercroft. Here the corridors were lit and Jalni feeling Daro falter, released her hold on the handfire, to clasp his waist more firmly, drawing him to one side, where he could prop a hip on a shelf and catch his breath.

Ikella raised her voice,

"Beneva and I have been reading the records, such as they are. It is clear that something comes, something foretold in the First Age of Mystery is upon us, which requires a Sandsinger to prevent.".

Her voice carried like a prophecy.

"We believe that you must go forth, away from this place to find your true destiny. This foolishness must end, your wild and wilful ways must cease.".

She faced them, eyes blazing like great Opals and unsure of which of them she addressed, the novice and the Sandsinger bowed their heads and listened.

"You are drawn into the circle of the Spell, charged with a task, return to Scartel. Seek the Heart of Selesh and bring it safely home, for the love of those who have cared for you.".

In the main pathway to the under caverns, a man paused listening, in his head the words, "You must leave this place", burned like fire as he hurried away muttering, "She sent him away, she sent my Sandsinger away!".

On their return to his room, a relieved Hanna supplied them all with breakfast and Daro

explained his adventure to his mother,

"Duvell, the shoemaker was looking for Jalni late last night and brought his boys with him as guides. They wanted to ask her to pass on a belt that fell into Duvell's hands Rotations ago and instead, they fell in through my door. We had a bit of a chat and I think I might have helped Duvell's youngest. His mind and tongue are still locked in infancy you know. I was on my way to say my goodbyes and see how he fared when I lost my Way.".

His illusion to the compulsion of the Way, was not lost on Ikella, who murmured reassurance.

"The Way is changing Daro, too fast for some of us, but your youth and stamina will carry you through!", and apparently reassured Daro relaxed.

Ikella admired his belt, exclaiming over the workmanship and on being told how it had reached Daro, pressed her hand to the silver wristlet, summoning Beneva, to see it, although neither of them could have predicted the reaction they got. Jalni left to collect her freshly packed medicine scrips from Hanna, passing the Guardian on her way out. Daro had risen to his feet and was facing the door as Beneva arrived. She was obviously distracted, her hair fell down from her more than usually severe bun, giving her abstracted air real strength. She bustled in, wax tablet and enscrasure at the ready and turned from closing the door to face Daro across the room. Catching sight of Daro in his journey wear, belt buckle blazing Opal, she raised a trembling hand to her mouth and sat abruptly, staring as if she had never seen him before. Her fascinated eyes wandered over him, from his clothes, to his lengthening hair, his brilliant unveiled eyes and smiling mouth, then she whispered.

"O my! Darius Selunsa reborn! Seen like that, you're his double Daro!", she announced, not making much sense to either of them..

Chapter 17 - Of Small Books and Sandsingers.

Ikella raised her eyebrows and Beneva hastened to explain.

"In the repository, there is a life-size portrait of another Sandsinger. It is he only known likeness of an empowered mage as far as I know.".

However, Ikella knew of another! Magically concealed for the twenty Rotations since she had discovered it, carved into the roof of the caverns below Caranchar. She felt her son's amused gaze on her, as she dragged herself back to the present and found herself wondering just how much he knew of that episode.

Beneva was saying thoughtfully, "I have known that portrait all of my Guardianship. In it, the mage is wearing that weave, dear me, yes, I could swear they are the same garments, though that would be impossible!".

Her voice dropped into a disjointed mutter, as though she was making mental notes (to Daro's amusement).

"That's my Beneva. Ever the scholar, fitted absolutely to her role as Guardian of Knowledge.", he thought, as rousing from these private contemplations, she announced.

"The impression is all the more marked because Daro bears an uncanny resemblance to the most fascinating man ever to walk the Opal Sands.".

Daro's lips twitched as Beneva' grew pink, confiding crossly, "The portrait is enchanted, though how I do not know. Its impossible for one who went to the Sands a thousand Rotations ago to exert such an influence, but I know what I am saying. The eyes follow you, wherever you stand, I feel as if I could walk through the frame and into personal contact with the mage himself.".

She sounded defensive, saying softly, "It isn't fair! He has no right...", her voice and eyes dropped.

Schooling her features as though she addressed some novice with a crush on a village boy, the Sorceress spoke severely, "Has this fascination got a name?", and Beneva said in a low voice.

"Yes indeed he is called Darius. with the familiar names, Selunsa which I, (albeit imperfectly), translate as ...", here Daro smoothly interrupted softly:

"The Light of the Sun!", as Beneva looked up quizzically..

"The Inesh called you "Ichta Selunsanni", after you left. I heard it many times and your Songfather was incredibly moved and comforted by that accolade, though how they came by that title, I will never know. Their legends are still a closed book to us and until they choose to reveal the knowledge, I cannot claim it.".

Daro's eyes rested on the Guardian as she offered her translation tentatively.

"The language is undeniably from the same source and with the evidence staring me in the face, I think it translates (however loosely) to "The Light of the Sun Returned.".

At this, Daro bowed his head in tacit agreement, then lifted it, magical eyes glowing and smiled. Beneva gasped, flushing with exasperation at the wild surge of long controlled emotions, as his gaze found hers.

"Will you please stop doing that?". She demanded crossly and Daro nodded, as if he had tested a theory and found it valid. He patted Beneva's hands in apology, his voice murmuring softly:

"I'm sorry Aunt Beneva, I don't mean to tease you. That was unfair of me, but no object can exert such an influence without the active engagement of the mage concerned. Perhaps, Darius created a weave to which you were particularly vulnerable, but such enchantments die with the enchanter and no….". He raised a hand to quell the barrage of questions that Beneva plainly wanted to ask, "I have no idea how you could connect with energies a thousand Rotations old, but they must have been intensely powerful and I think augmented by some artefact that magnified their focus. We can investigate this later.".

He saw Beneva's resigned shrug, as she settled to take notes, humour touching his eyes as she said impulsively, "Kella, you will see what I mean. The impact is phenomenal.", she gazed at Daro absorbed in recording every detail to compare with the portrait of his mysterious predecessor.

Ikella snorted derisively. "Yes Beneva, Daro is very pretty for a man, but before you turn me into a moon maiden with your own private mage, tell me why Jocasta was so interested?".

Daro chuckled at Beneva's discomfiture.

"Dear Beneva, you are still being teased.", He said it lightly, but Beneva's reply sobered him.

"Lord, the resemblance is frightening. I wonder that I didn't see it before, but with the Opal upon you, the effect is very potent.".

She shrugged admitting, "Seris Jocasta of beloved memory, felt that we were being influenced towards another Way and sought to ensure that it was a fit and proper direction for our world. She had become aware that particularly strong personalities were capable of deviating from their adherence to the Way. When that ability was detected amongst the Sisters of Sorcery, she decided to seek enlightenment in the records of the past. Change however, was upon us too soon for us to prepare the people.".

She turned to Daro and said softly, "but she saw you before she died and I believe she knew your destiny even then.".

There was a brief tense silence, then Ikella said shortly, "The revelation amongst the Sisterhood? Did she suspect Adruna even then?". Incredibly, Beneva raised her eyes to Ikella and without a blush said comfortably:

"Oh no my dear Sister. The changed one in the Sisterhood was you!".

Hardly had Ikella taken in what her fellow Guardian was saying, when Beneva concluded her minute inspection of Daro and remarked.

"I am glad that only we Guardians have access to the images of the past. If everyone could see the relics as we can, there would be many who would start believing in phantoms. Speaking of which, has anyone seen Feydora since Daro came to power?".

Daro murmured quietly, "She brought me to Council four nights back and visited me again later, but she took her leave very abruptly when Mother and Jalni arrived.". He paused and then said quietly, "I don't think we'll see her again, although I could be wrong.".

They stared at him in astonishment, then Ikella demanded, "How long have you known Feydora?", and Daro grinned.

"All my life, in one guise or another. She was the nursery drudge who sang me and Ahnell to sleep, the guard who shadowed my every move. We have all met her, in many forms since my birth.".

He sobered, remembering his nursery-mate. "Ahnell never realised who or what she was, I didn't know myself, until I discovered the Assendarium.", as he mentioned the great elevated platform from which he had sung, Beneva pounced on the new word with alacrity.

"Assendarium? The rock above the Sacred Circle?".

He nodded saying briefly:

"I will show you one day, but only an empowered Sandsinger can open or use it. I still don't know how Diras and her crew got me down.".

Beneva interrupted. "May I make a suggestion?", and in her voice even the Sandsinger heard the authority of the Guardians.

"Seris Beneva.", he acknowledged, "Speak freely, always.".

He smiled at her and Beneva said sternly:

"If you leave mysteries open, others may explore at their peril. No-one is in Hall at present, could you close it?", she added hopefully. "That would announce your absence from Selesh to the greater population also?".

"Is that wise?", Ikella demanded. "We'll be inundated with questions. Where's the Sandsinger? Why has he left us?".

Daro frowned, then smiled ironically and into Ikella's mind came his mocking voice. In the intimacy of this communication, she heard a rueful chuckle.

"I seem to have gone from having the eyes and ears of Selesh track me, to encouraging the entire Opal to join in! Of course, it will get worse as word goes off-Sands, but you don't have to worry about that for a while!".

She suddenly understood that he must have prevented that himself, but nodded silent agreement as he commented, "We can't avoid that.".

He drew a long breath and Ikella felt the Way shift under her feet as he spoke.

"I have other concerns, which you will have to address in my absence.", he took Ikella's hand and said quietly. "The worship of the One is universal. All our people should be welcomed and in Selesh, there will be no divisions. All are welcome, be they Clansmen, Felmin, Greeyeyn, or Wanderer.".

Ikella said faintly, "That is too much change Daro, the people themselves wouldn't accept it and the Hall would never accommodate the numbers.".

He said serenely, "The people will accept the will of the One and the Hall will accommodate all who ask admittance. Everyone must learn the truth together, in that lies our strength. Even here in Selesh there is division and unfair advantage, it must end if any of us is to survive.".

The Sorceress and her sister Guardian, looked bewildered as Daro elaborated.

"Think Mother. The identity of the Sandsinger has become the great Clan secret and that won't do. Confusion reigns. Everyone knows that I'm back but ill. Everyone knows that we have a mysterious Sandsinger, but only Clansmen know who the Sandsinger is. I have been split in two by all of this secrecy! To further complicate matters, my loss of sight seems to be a secret too, which is hardly practical management of a serious complication. All I want is to get on with my life and be treated as always. There will have to be announcements before I return from Scartel. I suggest the Zenitheon Gather as an appropriate venue, but you can choose what you say.".

He turned away from them briefly and they saw his body stilled in momentary concentration. The silver wrist bands of Guardianship were tingling, the air was electrified with some sort of static build up and then Daro said softly, "Surisha!", and a light shudder went through the walls, a soft groan was followed by a distinct "thud" and the Sandsinger, turned back, eyes dimming from the blaze of exertion. He smiled calmly at the thud of pounding feet headed in their direction and his eyes glowed brilliantly again. To Ikella's amazement, Diras's voice rang out, the feet slowed to a steady tramp and the Guard Commander spoke abruptly.

"Stop. Lord Daro commands that we place a guard on his Eyrie. He knows that the Assendarium closed. it was as he commanded and shortly he will leave us. Before then he is in conference with the Guardians and must not be disturbed.".

The marching feet retreated and the Guardians glanced at each other, but said nothing and Daro said:

"Before Jalni arrives, there is much to discuss. I will take up residence in the Eyrie upon my return. I know it intimately and, it is large enough to suit my purpose. To divert Diras, I have declared this journey as a pilgrimage. She is not happy, but I am directing my Chapter of Guard to pass the word to every community within the Sand to gather. We need a Master Builder to prepare for that, so the Chapter are also to act as escort for applicants.".

Ikella nodded, but he saw her mouth thin, her forehead pucker and said swiftly,

"I am only freeing you to work with Beneva, researching this Darius. Perhaps we can identify the task I must complete that way.".

Beneva, lifted a hand to free the door once more and Daro said urgently:

"Wait Beneva. Tell me what you want, I will fetch it faster.".

Beneva said faintly:

"A scroll. It is in the Council Chamber, on the first shelf to the left of the dais. It has a silver scroll rod with a blue hide cover.", Daro nodded, holding out a hand and suddenly, there was a shivering peal of chimes and the scroll materialised.

Ikella greeted this, with a helpless shrug. His command of power was so easy, so awesome, her mouth thinned and turned down at the corners. "If he is so easy with the use of small magic,", she reasoned, "No wonder he seems intent on taking over!".

He laid the scroll on the table and taking her hands in his, kissed them, whispering softly, (privately, his *othervoice* just brushing her conscious mind):

"Not at all. You will always be at the heart of the Opal. You just need my help. What comes is outside all current knowledge and power, but together we can overcome anything our world faces. Without the shift in power that Jocasta recognised in you, I would never have survived to take my place. I owe you so much, please don't fight me Mother.".

She gazed at him silently, this stranger son, so immensely changed, so immensely powerful, as his voice echoed round the room.

"I believe that my power will grow daily.", he said, then hesitated over his next statement. "I don't need sight to study my role, it will be revealed to me, as the knowledge is needed, but there are things that I have to ensure that the Guardians hear. Jalni will come for me soon and I have much to show you.".

He delved in a pocket and placed on the table the true Book of Rule, Ikella stared at it, her thoughts reaching Daro in a soft wistful murmur.

"Such a tiny thing, is that why Adaria never found it? How can it hold so much information?".

Daro spoke softly. "You know that the Sanctuary Chest is really a repository?", and Ikella's swift grasp of all things magical revealed the truth before he spoke again.

"Yes, in this book lies the wisdom of the Sandsingers. It cannot be read by anyone other than the Sandsinger to which it belongs, unless of course, that someone is me! That provision incidentally was intended only as an emergency measure, but now, so many Rotations later, it may well result in some re-scribing if any of the books are missing.". His hands lovingly wandered over the little book as he said softly. "This is mine now, can you read what it says on the cover?".

Ikella looked at the ancient script doubtfully, but managed an attempt. "For the Singer of the Song.", she read gruffly, her voice shook as she added the words, "My son.".

Daro responded in high good humour. "Yes. You are my mother Ikella. You may be Guardian of the Way, Sorceress Keeper of the Opal Staff. and Mother of all Sands, but most of all, you are my mother and don't you ever forget it.".

Ikella blushed as his *othervoice* added for her ears only, "Tiraj di Schpeller, Scourge of Sandsingers, or Spanker of small boys to one who loves her dearly.".

The warmth of his smile suddenly enfolded her, as if his arms were about her, supporting her as tears stung her eyes, then his beloved *othervoice* was tenderly murmuring little endearments.

"Sssh, little mother, it can be our secret!".

Long seconds passed as she realised how life would change. He would go about the business of a Sandsinger, whatever that was, wherever that took him, in this inhospitable world. She was old, getting tired and suddenly she saw down the long Rotations of her life, wistful for the things she would never do now. A warm breeze tickled her nose suddenly and she felt her hair being stroked gently. She pulled herself out of her reverie and looked at the small book in her sons hand.

"What does it say Daro?", Does it tell you anything that we can hear?". Beneva was staring at the Book of Rule enviously. He held it out to her, gently and reverently Beneva put down the scroll she had just picked up, taking the Book of Rule in shaking hands. She turned it over and marvelling at the fine leather ties that held the simple binding together. She spoke regretfully.

"I am afraid that too many records are missing from the repository for me to advise you further. There are only two of us empowered to act, though Shiarjha is confirmed as Guardian - Elect, which places the power of the Guardians firmly in the Opal, a situation I believe to be indicative of the level of threat we face. However, Shiarjha is not presently in Selesh, any threat is not overt and I think we have time to confer before that happens.".

Daro looked perplexed and then he said softly:

"I will reinforce the warding with one of my own and then we will consult the Book.".

There was a soft hiss, the walls flushed Opal and the door flickered out of sight, leaving only a bare rock Opal wall in its place. Ikella centred her thoughts and the table slid to centre of the room, allowing the two Guardian's to sit, using the edge of Daro's bed as a bench, leaving the only chair in the room available for the Sandsinger.

He sat, opposite them, his shimmering garb now assuming the look of simple desert wear. As they watched a light dusting of sand sprinkled his hair, producing an aura of shabbiness. It was the look of a commonplace man going about an ordinary life, but there was nothing ordinary about his eyes. Like fine fire opals they blazed green and blue as he opened his eyelids. Both women trembled before this magical othergaze. When he accessed his power, it was hard not to feel a shiver of apprehension and Ikella wondered soberly, how much harder it would be for ordinary people to withstand.

His voice, when it came was remote, entranced, as if another spoke through him. The Guardians listened in awed silence.

"This is the Way of the Opal Singer, as decreed by the Council of Guardians. The Opal Singer shall respect all Women of Voice and hold them equal in their endeavours, to the end that women may also come to our Hall in Tirjhinar, or Sanctuary and aspire to their own Sands. Each Sand has its Singer who is overlord in his own Sand. They shall appoint their own people from the Sands of their Rule. These shall be known as the Sandsworn, who will be the Singers followers. The status of Sandsworn is open to all men and women, be they Clansmen or not.".

Beneva was thinking wildly, "Oh for a set of tablets and enscrasures, I will never remember this word perfect.", then out of her reach, a tablet lifted itself and without any enscrasure script appeared on it, beneath her widening eyes.

The remote voice chimed into the fiercely concentrated silence. "The Opal Singer's duty is to seek out and empower all Singers of Colour, to bring them into the fold at Tirjhinar and there to train them. Their duty is to serve the Sands, to repel evil and to protect the lives of all our peoples, even unto the loss of their own.

The Opal Singer is of them all the most powerful and combines within his one power, the powers singular wielded by all colours. In his submission to the Higher Source, the Opal candidate must be of so pure a purpose that all iniquity will be burned from him, though he suffer the fires of torment, will he remain true to his purpose to the brink of death itself. His powers shall be like no other known to man and for that power he will pay dearly, yet in attaining it let no other being, magical or mysterious though they be, doubt his truth, his honesty and his very oneness with the Source. The Opal Singer will serve all the Peoples of this world, until the true purpose of his empowerment is revealed.".

The voice was strengthening, there was a strangely crystalline note in it, like the chimes of sand-paste ornaments, tinkling in the wind and Beneva glancing up from her absorption with the remote note-taking, drew a ragged breath and rose respectfully to her feet, dragging Ikella with her.

There was a shimmering aura about Daro, he seemed to be taller, the same but different and Ikella glancing at her Sister in Guardianship knew that she saw another in his stead. Every nuance of his voice chimed as he said fervently:

"Live not in terror that a Singer is amongst you, but in joyous anticipation of a long life spent in harmony, safety and love and when the time comes for him to know his

purpose, be sure that in everything he does, his life will be sacrificed to the protection

of Pelshar before a single human life is lost.".

The fire in Daro's eyes died away and his eyelids lowered again, the Book of Rule lay in his grasp. The ties were undone and his finger was inserted in between the covers, as if he had read the proclamation directly from the page. Ikella was gazing at her son in awe and wonder and as

Beneva moved the blind Sandsinger gasped and sank back in his chair.

Beneva unrolled the scroll that he had brought from the Council Chamber and wordlessly laid it in front of the Sorceress. She pointed to a lifelike drawing, boldly coloured with some

extraordinary tints, of a man stood high on the Assendarium. He wore robes of the kind that Ikella had hung on the back of Daro's chair. This mage had his arms outstretched and from his fingers there seemed to be an indication of colour flowing. Beneva pointed to a single line of script, which read clearly "Darius".

Ikella gazed at the picture soberly.

"Is this the one you mentioned?", She spoke softly, so as not to disturb Daro, who was plainly gathering his thoughts and strength as he slumped in his chair.

Beneva seemed surprised.

"No, no, this is only a sketch. The one I spoke about is life sized, almost three dimensional. It is painted so realistically that I once thought I saw him breathe! I dare not remove that from the repository, it bears a very solemn warning not to do so on its frame, but I sometimes go and look at it and wonder if the mage could speak, what he would say?"

Ikella grunted, not greatly surprised, for she had always known that Beneva saw more romance in the past than in the present. Despite the sketchiness of the scroll, if she had not known better, she would have thought she was looking at Daro, she followed the historians finger and saw the belt that encircled her sons trim waist. She bent over the picture, there was a fob, a silver orb which hung from the belt of the Sandsinger in the drawing. Ikella could see a loop which now held a cleverly knotted piece of leather, so intricately worked that it could easily pass as the original and instantly understood it had been repaired. Beneva looked at Ikella.

"I would give anything to be able to hang that fob back in its place.", she remarked, as Daro sat forward seemingly refreshed.

Ikella blinked. With such an eventful dawn, she had expected him to be exhausted, considering privately that the planned journey should be postponed, but that hardly seemed the case. She said in a cautious aside to Beneva:

"Did you learn anything from the scroll?", and Beneva replied quietly.

Not really. The writing on this one is so faint that little other than the drawing is of use to us.". Daro seems to have identical robes to Darius, the belt may even be the same one and, I don't have the faintest idea what or where that fob is.".

Daro cleared his throat and then said gently: "Find the fob Beneva. The one that belongs to my belt. You might have seen it when the chest was packed, but not known what it was. When you can, look for any representation amongst the papers. It is important, without it I cannot complete my task.".

There was a soft sigh as the doorway re-appeared and unsealed itself and Daro rose to his feet, this interview over. If Beneva had heard command in his voice, she gave no hint of it. Picking up sand tablet records and the scroll, already rerolled and covered reverently, she briskly prepared to return to the Djellim, but not before Daro's *othervoice* reached the Guardians ear, as she strode between the Infirmary and her precious repository.

"Beneva, if you know where my Songfather is, get Driss to fetch him home. I have need of his wisdom.".

As Beneva left, Daro stood, languidly picking up small items and stowing them about his person. He spoke absently to Ikella, as she sorted clothing on to his bed.

"I have to keep the Book with me, I cannot allow it out of my sight, for I must study it carefully. It tells me so much that I need to know and I am sworn to keep it with me…", (His voice lowered), "till the end"

Ikella nodded simply.

"You must do what is demanded of you," she concurred and then, "But the Council will be afraid if they knew the Book of Rule is no longer in Selesh. I should have asked Beneva if she has anything that we can keep in its place?", She grew thoughtful, "I mean no disrespect, it may well be that nothing other than the True Book can be kept in the Great Hall?".

As Daro paused considering this, Ikella said briskly, "We must not keep falling behind in getting you and Jalni on your way. Are you able to journey today?.

Daro looked at her seriously, "Mother, I gave myself a fright, nothing more and Jalni is coming with me, so I will be safe. I am still not strong, but I have time and youth, on my side. The sooner I am on my way the better.".

He raised his voice in the plaintive wail that Ikella had never thought to hear again, "I'm bored! I've got to get out of here.", he grinned impishly and Beneva reappeared, holding a small blue board bound book, tied together with leathern thongs.

"Will this do 'Kella?", she asked, innocent of the consternation in her sister Guardians eyes.

It was altogether very similar to the True Book of Rule and Beneva placed it directly into Daro's hand. The dusty little book fitted his palm neatly and almost as soon as he touched it, his head lifted, utmost surprise on his face. He rubbed the cover gently and beneath his fingers a line of script appeared.

"It is not written in any language I know" Beneva commented and the line of faint script seemed to fade as she spoke. Daro loosened the ties that kept the cover closed and inside the covers, a fine spidery writing filled the pages. He held the book open on the palm of his hand and with the other hand held just a finger from the page, he hummed a long silvery note, almost at the top of his range and the pages started to turn. Faster and faster they flickered, a faint blue glow lit his face as absorbed in his spell casting, he bent towards the pages. Towards the end of the book, a small fragment of parchment fell out and Beneva retrieved it, placing it on the table, ready to

be examined and Ikella stared at it, something tickling her memory. The last page turned and Daro chuckled as he exclaimed a single word.

"Schontish!".

The use of the word that had all but stilled Mina, galvanised Ikella into action. She grasped her son's hand in spite of the power running through him and said clearly:

"No Daro, don't say it again.", and as the light died away and silence fell, the Sandsinger and the Sorceress looked at the little book, as she hurriedly explained.

"I believe that word, to be part of a medicantric.", At his enquiring look she said sternly. "That is a use of magic to which neither the Sisterhood of Sorcery, nor the house of Guardians would subscribe. It is woven by combining elements in a way that we don't wholly understand. That one, applied to Mina, very nearly silenced her *othervoice* for good.".

She paused, looking at Beneva bleakly, until her fellow Guardian nodded.

"Jalni found the recipe on a piece of parchment, I thought that I had burned it, but it seems that it is protected, otherwise, how could it have re-appeared like that? She understood some of it, made sense of the rest and used the recipe against Mina!".

She met Daro's eyes levelly, no expression in her voice she stated:

"She has trained here, long enough to know that to administer to anyone, a substance without full understanding of the consequences is to court death.". She drew breath, focussing sharply on Daro, who was frowning.

"In mitigation she immediately confessed and showed true contrition for her actions. She has been on probation ever since and has not only performed every version of drudgery designed to humiliate her cheerfully, but was instrumental in recovering you, from whatever place you took yourself into, after First Rites. She has been punished, is very contrite and Mina has forgiven her. We thought that this journey with you would rehabilitate her thoroughly, as well as give her a chance to return to the Sand she fled and find them free of threats, whether she returns as a Healer, or as something else.".

Daro raised the book in his hand and in front of them, the ties refastened themselves into an elaborate knot.

"It would be safer if this is hidden away, until it is needed then.", he said and with a complicated gesture of his free hand, he unleashed a stream of bluish light, which filled the air and dissipated through the floor. Daro's eyes showed opal fire before his eyelids closed masking his power and involuntarily, Ikella and Beneva glanced at his hands, knowing that they would be empty of small books and they were equally certain, that no one but Daro could recover it from where he had concealed it.

At that moment Jalni arrived. She was ready to go, with one travel pack on her back and the other ready for Daro to carry. She took note of the scene in front of her, but remained unmoved, though she did cast a hard glance at Daro's eyes. She noted the robes immediately, taking note of his fine new belt and snorted in disgust.

"You won't get further than the outskirts of Selesh Minoria wearing those, before the Wanderers grab you!", and Beneva turned, startled eyes on her.

"Daro will protect both of you.", the librarian said staunchly, at which Jalni rolled her eyes, taking the robes and carefully placing them in the second travel pack. Unavoidably they touched and as they did so, Daro was uncomfortably aware of Jalni grumbling, deep in the recesses of her rebellious mind.

"Who is protecting whom? What from I wonder? Oh dear, here's a wall, a floor, a tunnel! No better not go near any of those, they scare him too much!".

He drew a steadying breath as a rage he thought he had forgotten flushed his veins again. It was no time to create a scene, to delay still further. Already the sun would be high and they would be hard pressed to make Fronish by nightfall and he was beginning to understand that the journey would test his abilities to the full. He bit his lip, but from the moment that they left Selesh, Daro was aware that the situation between them had to be resolved. He felt waves of fury and resentment emanating from her, permitting him to sense, almost to a finger-width, the distance between them.

She shouldered the small travel pack on to her back and Ikella who had ascended to the gates of Selesh with them, touched Daro's arm gently, lifting his own back pack on to his shoulders as she did so. Reaching up, he adjusted the straps until the pack settled on to his shoulders in the old familiar way. Ikella, came round in front of him, and tucked straps into place and made sure that his cloak was fastened securely, lifting the hood of his travel cloak into place to shade his face.

Abruptly, he clasped her hand in both of his and to the great astonishment of his foster mother, lifted it gently to his mouth, burying a kiss into the palm of the hand that fearlessly wielded power over the Opal Desert and its thousands of inhabitants. Her other hand came up and briefly cupped the face, that shadowed in the cowl of his cloak was all but hidden from view, tears shone in her eyes as her glance fell on his closed eyelids, beyond which lay only pain and darkness.

Inarticulate suddenly, the Sorceress of the Shalhanhi bade her fosterling goodbye and turned back into the cavern system of Selesh. Daro stood for a moment following her footsteps on the rocky path and then resolutely turned towards Jalni and said gruffly, "Let's go.", but Jalni was already ten paces away, head down, marching defiantly down the track that led to the Azure Sands and whatever fate awaited them.

PART 2 - DESERT OF DOUBTS

Jalni's voice echoed him maliciously, "Let's go? Yes, let's go!".

She stalked away, her pent up fury communicating itself in an unrelenting mental assault, until he hissed. Desert boots scrunched on the path, then, she grasped his arm roughly. As he jumped, she taunted him.

"Come on then, don't just stand there .", and pulled him forward, giving him no chance to gain his balance or bearings.

At first he resisted, pulling against her, but she was angrily determined. Slowly, realising that his life lay in her hands, he began to work with her, as they trudged through the deserted centre of Selesh Minoria. At last, her pace began to moderate, as her mood shifted from fury to sullen resentment. He struggled on silently, a pace behind her, wrist avoiding the bump and sway of her pack, arm aching from the unnatural posture, but she gave no quarter, stalking past Emblem Rock (in a manner that broadcast her distain for all things Opal),as Daro became painfully aware of the proximity of thornbush. The track roughened beneath his aching feet, but still she maintained her relentless progress, as Daro wondered whether he could trust her with the equanimity that his mother had displayed.

As they passed from comparative safety into the wilderness, they were skirting the Great Divide, on a rising track to the Drekken Pass, beyond which lay the Azure Sands. Here, the path levelled out briefly and Daro detached himself, doubling over to catch his breath. He stretched his thighs, easing leg muscles that still felt as though they didn't belong to him and Jalni came to a halt. As the brisk creak of her boots ceased, he was suddenly aware that when she swung round a chain chinked on her bag and grinned. He adjusted his sandals, shaking the last Opal Sand from them into the palm of a hand, as she began jogging impatiently on the spot. He pocketed the sand, straightened and in his hand he held a stout unornamented staff.

Jalni blinked, not having seen the brief flicker of Opal as he conjured it and scowled ferociously, calling out, "We can't stop here you know. Come on!".

Hearing the impatience in her voice, he dug the staff into the rising ground ahead of him and walked slowly forward, leaning into it, hoping to ease his legs. He smiled wryly to himself, doubting the wisdom of breaking this wild, angry, mood of hers. He consulted the inner clock that accompanied his power, amazed to discover that they were approaching Height of Sun already, but they were still so close to Selesh! Appalled by the enormity of this task he wavered in his stride, steadying himself with difficulty. Crossly muttering, "What now?", she came back, grasping his hand, as fatigue threatened to topple him. Daro was immediately engulfed in a scathing tirade.

"Oh for the sake of the One.", she hissed. "Sandsinger? He can't even walk alone! How is he going to help these children? He's a superb magician, but he's no more a Sandsinger than I am a blind man!". Abruptly her rage spiked, her voice strident as she demanded of anyone who could hear her, "All I ask is to be left alone! Now I'm lumbered with this so-called Sandsinger. Huh! Anything less magical would be hard to imagine.".

He froze in outrage and in the ensuing silence, she gave him one brief burning glance and scrambled up the rise, sinking to her knees, in a patch of scrub. Her inner voice ranted on and on and Daro, irritated beyond control, thought viciously, "Hadda take this stupid, ignorant child! How is her life ruined by three ninenights of frustration? I must always walk alone and blind. Everyone I knew and loved dead, my greatest triumph denied me, for I shall never see the Sands I love again!".

In horror he heard his own voice, loud, roughened with emotion, shouting his own grief, anger and frustration at her, then in shock he sat on the track overlooking the Great Divide, knees to his chest, arms encircling them, head buried. He heard her foot on the path behind him, but didn't move as she spoke, her voice low, as she murmured:

"You know nothing of me Sandsinger. I only know that you are supposed to be a great mage and in that I must place my faith. Well, if you have command of magic use it, for we have company!". Her voice shook as she tapped his hand in the Inesh manner, demanding that he listen to her.

He nodded, hearing the hoarse whisper. "Get out of my head, you are driving me insane. I can hear everything you think. Now, use your cloak to merge with this rock and for the One's sake stand still. Whoever follows, is not far behind!".

She clasped his wrist loosely, lifting his hand to one side and he felt the rough surface, which thankfully loomed above him. Almost holding his breath, he stood slowly, allowing his hand to travel up the rock, until he was sure that it overtopped him. He huddled, face turned in, touching the Opal through the sand in his pocket, until the unusual properties of Opalwear mirrored his surroundings. In the cover of this perfect camouflage, he slid into a gap, placing the rock between himself and whoever followed them.

Using only unenhanced senses to track Jalni, he was hampered by a gentle breeze so, thus reduced to examining his immediate surroundings, he cautiously slid a foot to one side, finding himself in an area about three paces square. He slid down, back to the rock and sat cross legged, waiting. Time passed and Daro knew that his rock shaded him, for one side of his face was hotter than the other. Height of Sun was upon them and wondering if those following were also resting, he quietly shuffled further into the shade, before letting his mind drift, remembering the times that he had walked alone. Great canyons opened up before him, massive stone pillars towered above him, loose brush blew and the cry of a bird on an evening wind filled him with a deep melancholy, then he woke to Jalni's voice, which whispered hoarsely in his mind as her hand clapped over his mouth.

"Sssh. Company coming.", and he relaxed against her legs, trying hard not to let her feel his consternation as he realised that she was perched on the rock above him. Her voice sounded very calm.

"Quiet! They could walk right past without seeing us here. I think there's only one.". He nodded agreement and remained still, although his legs were burning where he had brushed up against fire bush earlier. The enforced rest was welcome, he was so tired and thirsty. He could feel Jalni slipping into meditation, her mood changing again, as the sand drizzled through the sand - glass of his mind. There was a rustle, a "chink" of passing feet, but Daro knew better than to break the silence and Jalni,(observing him from above) nodded her own approval.

He had placed a small, clean pebble in his mouth, (encouraging natural salivation to relieve his thirst). Now, he leant back against the rock, and his breath soft and regular, told her that he slept, a good strategy, so long as he didn't wake suddenly or move while their stalker was in the vicinity. She drifted herself and was roused by Daro gripping her foot, as he rose to warn her. He was standing stock still below her, when the grating sound of boots on rock came to her ears. One walker, followed immediately by a slow stumbling stride, muffled by desert boots.

Silently, she slipped off the rock and slid the length of a hard, masculine body and his arms closed around her, clasping her firmly, merging their outlines in the dappled light of Sunfall. His hand cupped her head, pressing her betraying blush against his chest. His throat quivered as she clung closely, trembling as the others passed them oblivious to their presence.

Jalni, aware only of an intoxicating scent and the warm pressure of his hard body, felt him shiver as her eyelashes brushed the base of his throat. She studied the bronzed vee revealed by his tunic and held still, trying to ignore the rising heat. She was afraid to think of this man, so dependent on her, yet so masterful. She tried to hold herself away from him, but his voice said mildly, "Jalni, hold still. They are quite close. Any noise, any movement will alert them.".

He rested his chin on her head, his beard tickling her forehead. Strangely breathless, she curved her body against his and after a lifetime of tingling awareness, Daro raised his head, nodded, then gently lifted her back to her vantage point. Only then, did she realise that he had held her in mid-air the whole time.

She waited, cautiously listening for sounds off the trail, thinking wildly, "How can someone so helpless, be so powerful?".

There was no-one in sight, but painfully aware that she could be under scrutiny herself, she decided! "There was nothing else for it, they would have to make the dash to Fronish and hope that the others on the trail were only innocent travellers.".

"Daro?", he was still stood below her. "If you wriggle round the rock to your right, you could lift me down to join you.", she suggested, but he raised his face, asking quietly, "Can you get down by yourself? I have needs that must be attended to.". He didn't sound embarrassed, but Jalni was. Her face flamed as he continued meaningfully, "I only need a moment.", but Jalni was already muttering furiously to herself.

"Deo. I'm a fool!". She hadn't considered this problem! It had never been discussed! but recovering her equilibrium, she said lightly, "Oh, I can manage, if you can.", and as he turned away seeking privacy, she struggled down the smooth rock face, that in terror she had climbed in a single bound.

By the time she had lowered herself backpack and all, Daro was waiting on the path and she ran a quick glance over him. He simply stood to one side to allow her to pass him but she surprised him by reaching up and straightening his travel cloak. She explained:

"One of the seams would have cut into your neck and given you a painful sore. We can't afford that out here. Tell me if you need to stop for anything. If you need help you can hold on to the fact that I am a Healer.".

His face was completely serene as he countered with, "My thanks Healer Jalni. If you can't manage something alone, please don't hesitate to summon me, remembering that I am a Sandsinger!", and turned the most beatific grin on her. Thoroughly flustered, Jalni took his hand and placed it in the crook of her elbow, guiding him as she had been taught and without further incident, they regained the path and set off towards Fronish, the last outpost of the Opal Sands.

It was close to dark when they came to the start of the Drekken Pass. The high track began below Dorenard Plateau, at the base of a soaring cliff where the small cave system of Fronish had developed. A Healer post and overnight stop, deliberately positioned to support large trek trains ascending the well made Dorenard Trail between Selesh and Scartel. It had, like the trail, suffered irreparable damage in the great Storm preceding Daro's birth. Now maintained for emergencies only, it lay warded, but deserted. They mounted the last fifty paces of the track fronting the entrance. Jalni walking on her toes, lightly slipping between deepening patches of shadow, Daro sliding naturally behind her, soft footed, only too aware that at least three were on the trail ahead of them. She paused, heard nothing and slipped into the short dark tunnel that should have caverns to the right and the warded Healer post straight ahead.

Daro drew back, into the concealing rocks beside the entrance, letting her sidle into investigate unhampered by his clumsiness.

He crouched, aware that he had some sense of what Jalni was observing, as she quietly padded into the small complex. His hand tingled curiously and he realised that she must be tracing the wall in the dark, fingertips barely brushing the surface, as she explored towards the communal caves. He sensed rather than felt her knock a foot on a protrusion, grinned at the silent invective as hissing with suppressed pain she nursed the injured limb, them his own breath caught in his throat as a distinct "chink", sounded ahead of her.

Jalni froze against the wall, where a buttress of some kind afforded concealment. She dared not cry out as a large ungainly shape shambled towards her and then, to her horror, two men, fast and determined leapt out of the communal caverns and pinned the large one to the wall. there was a breathless heaving of strong masculine bodies, a soft curse and a yelp as the attackers pinned their victims arms to his sides and then the walls exploded into view as a cold voiced and exceedingly angry Sandsinger demanded:

"Back off. Stand clear whoever you are!", and he was there, a torch held aloft, his garments rippling and sparkling in the light and nothing very magical other than his stout Staff swinging in his other hand, with which he plainly intended to defend her. She managed to take a breath as he passed her, then fell in behind him, reciting the fragment of an old skipping rhyme to remind herself, of the warding key, so that she could open the Healer hold, if they needed an escape route. It was totally incongruous, that part of her mind chanted,

"Nine times one for the Opal,

Nine times two for the blue", as she followed Daro down the tunnel towards the Wanderers, who were plainly vicious characters, who had lain in wait for and who were clearly intent on attacking and robbing another innocent traveller. She was still struggling to assert a sense of reality, when the light fell on a familiar figure in front of her and as she cried out.

"Duvell!", Daro said, "Lown! First of my Sandsworn, what are you doing here?".

As the answer to that question lumbered to his feet, advancing on Daro with incoherent cries of joy. Then, their relief turned to horror as the faint glimmer of the warding was eclipsed by a huge shadow.

An immense, snarling feline form , leaping from the shadows had borne Chrysim, (Duvell's youngest) to the ground. However, its brilliant eyes seemingly dominated by the gleaming othergaze of the mage, it simply lashed its tail and made strangely enquiring sounds as Daro held it immobile.

Jalni was the first to react. Catching the torch from Daro's hand, she held it up to illuminate the unusual sight of a mystcat crouching on the back of its "victim". Duvell's head swung in her direction as she murmured calmingly:

"Don't be afraid Duvell, Daro will protect us.", and winced at the dry laugh she heard from Daro, as following the feline snarl, he sat, slowly lowering himself until he could bring his remarkable eyes to bear on the animal. He placed a hand on Chrysim's outflung wrist, and the shoemaker's son's struggles subsided. Jalni began running scales in her mind, seeking Chrysim's energies and found them surprisingly intact. He was frightened, but unhurt, now he had his breath back. She felt something touch her and opened her eyes with a start to see that the Mystcat was staring at her, an expression of confusion on its face. Suddenly realising that it was not much more than a kitten, with hugely immature paws, softly tufted ears and milky blue eyes, she began to relax inwardly.

She "reached" for Daro and found him communing with the cat.

"Yes.", The mage was soothing, "You are big and brave, but you won't get any supper if you pounce on my friends like that!".

With a sense of wonder Jalni saw the animals teeth lift from Chrysim's neck, heard the note of enquiry in the soft rumble and saw the lashing tail, quiver and drop. It slunk forward on its belly, burying its head in Daro's hands and Daro gentled it, setting up brilliant opalescent lights in its fur as it sank its head into his lap. In the flickering light, Jalni saw him smile tenderly as he fondled the enormous creature, then Daro said quietly,

"Jalni, open the warding and find Echo some food. He has come a long way to find me!".

With those words ringing in her ears, Jalni found herself shut out of the continuing conversation with the cat.

Shaking from a mixture of cold, frustrated fury, and fright, she rose to her feet. Reduced from companion to menial drudge, she stalked in dignified silence to a rough bracket where she lodged the torch before summoning handfire to light her way to the warded cavern ahead. Mentally snarling, "I wonder who died and pronounced you God!", as she reached her objective. Daro was too absorbed with the Mystcat to notice, as she moodily raised a hand, striking a metal plate, silently reciting the keywords.

"Nine, One, Nine, Two.", followed by the required note to lower the warding. Escaping with her misery intact, she set about acting as drudge, cook and servant to the very mixed company she had lowered the warding for. A mage, his blind shoemaker, a herder, his disabled brother and a Mystcat! Her cup of misery was full to overflowing!

They ate their fill from the rather generous ration packs she uncovered, then long before she'd finished cleaning the neat kitchen in the Healers quarters, the men drew aside, talking amongst themselves. Duvell sat smiling indulgently at Chrysim who sat on the floor of the storeroom, with the cat draped across his legs, while Lown and Daro, sat on a pile of sacks and talked, hands waving expansively. Jalni sat in the kitchen area and brooded on her woes. She couldn't hear what they were talking about and studiously refused to "tune in" to Daro, preferring to stoke her temper, fuelling it with their random requests for lights, sweetdrinks and water for the cat. She stoically endured their apparent disregard for her own weariness, but her responses grew sharper and less friendly with every task, until Daro said something to Lown and they all looked in her direction, as Daro stood, producing his Staff from nowhere. Donning cloaks, they walked towards the entrance to the Healer hold, once more warded to keep their party safe.

Jalni stared impassively at their backs thinking morosely in a parody of Daro's voice, "Jalni, come and release the warding. Jalni watch the cat while we relieve ourselves outside.", but the request didn't come. Puzzled, she rose to her feet, picked up the bedding roll intended for the Sandsinger and went where she could see the gently glowing barrier to the hold. When she realised that they were nowhere in sight, she thought that they might just have gone to the small chamber designed as a Healers sleeping space, but it was empty. Only the pallet lay mutely begging to be dressed with the blankets she carried. Now cross and alarmed, she went through the chambers of the Healer hold, finding as she did so, a treatment area with a bench bed and a four bedded ward, but of blind shoe-makers and Sandsingers, their companions or the wretched Mystcat there was no sign.

She took herself back to the small dormitory, where thankfully there was a small cramped necessary, for the use of the patients. There was running water too, so she spent a short time making herself clean and comfortable and then, somewhat doubtfully she unwarded the entrance and went in search of the men. She approached the communal caverns cautiously, but they were still vacant, so stepping briskly past that entrance, she walked lightly down the tunnel and stood in the opening. They were all there. Not twenty paces away, backs turned towards her, facing Jenta. The light from their brilliant moon streamed down, bathing Daro's head and uplifted hands in its silvery glow as he knelt in prayer. Behind him the shoe-maker and his sons raised fervent faces and behind them crouched the Mystcat, its fur rippling, shot through with opal flecks.

In silent misery, she tried to access the Source, hoping to lift her spirits, but the connection remained obstinately closed. A long sigh shook the mage and Jalni watching breathlessly , saw him rise to his feet, finding his balance more easily as he turned towards Lown. His hand hovered above the man's head and Jalni was surprised at the flash of a silver medallion set on his obesh, which he had bound to his brow. Mystified, the novice saw Daro stoop, placing the kiss familiar on Lown's cheek and saw the glitter of proud tears streak the man's face. Daro stood again, took two careful paces to his left, raising Duvell gently until the shoemaker knelt erect, his head held high. This time Jalni saw the mage slide a new obesh over Duvell's head, allowing it to rest on his chest, a bright flare of Opal, marking yet another medallion. His voice carried to the bemused novice.

"Faithful friend of the Shalhanhi, brother to my Sand, I grant your adoption into our Clan and render you Sandsworn.".

The mages hands streamed light over Duvell, but Jalni didn't wait to see the rest. She fled back to the sanctuary of a small Healer hold and sought the solitude of the kitchen. This at least had a folding screen door, which she pulled shut as she entered. Here it was quiet, clean and ordered and she sank into the deep soft chair, wrapped herself round in the quilted blanket that covered it and closed her eyes against a world which she felt had rejected her.

"I'm beyond redemption I suppose.", she thought drearily.

"Wasn't I the one that revived him? Didn't I connect him with his Sands, protect him from these others?".

These incoherent thoughts, (punctuated by sobs) asked only one thing.

"Why have they become Sandsworn? What have they done to help him? Why doesn't he want me?", then, snuffling miserably, she slept.

Chapter 19 - Mina Avenged

Jalni woke, sweat scalded by dream sensations she refused to acknowledge. Rising, she washed swiftly, then ventured into the hallway where Chrysim and the mystcat curled about each other, across the threshold of the Sandsinger's retreat.

Wondering briefly how to get to her patient, she peered into the dormitory, where a glimpse of discarded clothes and recumbent figures persuaded her to go about her own duties, escaping to the treatment room, scrubbing her hands before turning to the medicine cupboard.

She grimaced, detesting this part of Healer routine. However, the Way dictated that visiting Healers check the stores, note deficiencies and pass on the information, so with weary resignation, she licked the end of an enscrasure, lifted down the tablet provided and began the thankless task.

One part of her mind occupied itself with counting fever drenches and another argued that despite being the mage's Healer, she would soon be the sole member of this company, with no experience of his power. Dismissing his ability to communicate directly, (along with the peculiar effect of his touch as "parlour tricks,"), she sullenly noted the number of stomach powders, before counting the pile of medicated bandages, continually tallying her grievances as she worked.

"He obviously prefers the company of men, (including the benighted Mystcat).", she gave a savage twist to a pot lid, thinking, "He hadn't asked her to attend him once, not even for prayer.", and glared at a tub of innocent tarifin wraps so aggressively, she half expected them to burst into flames as she counted. "He favours Chrysim over me!", her resentment almost burned her mark and the sigil of Selesh on the sand tablet, as she absently recorded her findings for Solana's use. Then, aware of a break in the rhythmic rumble from Chrysim and his feline friend, she went to find them stretching out the creases of the night. Chrysim smiled sunnily and to Jalni's surprise said clearly, "I'll fetch this mornings sweet drink.", wandering off as he spoke. The mystcat remained, staring at Jalni, tail lashing, huge immature paws flexing as it kneaded a nest in their cushions. She stared back resolutely, tuning the voice of her inner mind, as it lay down, pinning her with a baleful glare. An opal mounted on an obesh "collar", gleamed against its throat and she thought severely, "Has it come to this, you, creature of the Ashgenar? Did you come slinking on your great belly, just to get an Opal collar? You should be ashamed of yourself!".

The great head lowered submissively, as though the kitten heard her and he let out a "Prrrow?", of enquiry before rolling to display its soft under fur, begging her indulgence. She couldn't help smiling, for these shy animals were seldom seen. The incongruity of kneeling on the bare floor of a little used Healer hold to tickle a kitten, who measured in length the height of a grown man, caused her to forget her sour introspection, but not for long.

By the time she had swung herself upright, folding away Chrysim's blankets from habit, the fragrance of hot stemmis permeated the air, so abandoning the cat to its solitary guard duties, she went in search of Chrysim, who beamed at her as he closed the cover on the firestone.

His whole body language had changed. His hands were steady on the tray of drinks. His face bright, the eyes below the obesh of his allegiance were alert, the Opal gleaming softly. She sipped her drink, thoughtfully taking fresh bread from the oven, as he went to wake his father and brother. She thought crossly,

"So, I drudge while Daro collects his ill assorted army. Well, that's no business of mine! In fact, once I'm in the Azure, Hadda can take him and all his minions!". Her mood swung blackly. as Lown looked in through the door and she saw the Opal blaze on his forehead.

"It is nearly dawn Mistress. We can eat breakday on the way home, where I must deliver Lord Daro's messages but...", he paused, looking around before continuing,

"He hasn't risen then?".

Jalni hardened her heart against the inferred request.

"No, not yet. He is very tired. Must you disturb him?", and thought defiantly, "If you think I am going to wake him, think again.".

She made no move to detain them and if they were disappointed by Daro's continuing absence, they made little of it. Gratefully accepting the bread she had made for their breakday meals, they left quietly, the brothers flanking their father, followed by the mystcat.

"I am to care for Echo until Lord Daro comes home.", Chrysim confided. "He will live with me in the old herders hut on Mount Torrenesh. He will keep pests from eating all my brother's crops, but he mustn't eat the coatan herd. He will be good company and the other boys won't tease me anymore now I am Sandsworn.".

Jalni wondered for a fleeting moment, if she had underestimated Daro's perceptiveness, appreciating the unusual kindness shown to this simple soul. However, considering the devious nature of men and suspecting an ulterior motive, she took her companions through the warding, out to the cave mouth, before quietly returning to the real source of her irritation.

He sat in the chair where she had dreamed of him and she paused, noting his guarded, secretive face. His hair was unkempt, fastenings tied awry and one sandal strap was twisted, but he had risen and dressed himself, which was good. However, his head lifted imperiously, his face stern as he said reprovingly, "That was unkind Jalni. They only wanted to say goodbye to me.".

The rebuke sparked her temper, which she turned on the kitchen. Washing utensils in water that mysteriously heated as she poured it into the wash-buck. She slammed his cooling drink in front of him, hard enough to make him jump, unrepentantly snarling, "If that is the only unkindness they receive after giving me such a fright, then they are lucky.".

161

Scrubbing furiously at the working surfaces, she ignored Daro's attempts to engage in conversation and was relieved when he stood and found his way to the screen door. Her fury escalated, heartbeat by heartbeat, until she was gritting her teeth on every breath, but eventually she threw the skirler into the wash-buck and demanded angrily.

"How come you only do things when I am not there to see them? How can you possibly expect me to believe what I have only heard from others?", the hurt in her voice clashed in his ears like metal striking anvil, as she angrily demanded, "Am I not good enough to be Sandsworn?", and he appeared to consider this seriously, responding with a question, the meaning of which eluded her angry mind.

"Didn't you see me walk the warding?", he asked and Jalni, who had not, felt utterly deflated, but refused to acknowledge it, spitting savagely, "Small magic!", leaving him to shoulder his own pack.

As she brushed by him, she was uncomfortably aware that she was being entirely unreasonable, but she couldn't stop to save her life. She collected her own pack, feeling far too contrary to help Daro, who was half a step ahead of her as she entered the hallway. Instead of waiting for her to lead him, he obstinately ignored her and kept going, setting in motion that day's nerve jangling contest of wills. As she bit back the impulse to warn him of his danger, Daro walked straight through the shimmering curtain of power, careless of anyone seeing him.

Persuaded that the warding wasn't working, she followed his example until there came a sudden rushing in her ears. Her breath caught in her throat as a dreadful blow struck her to the ground.

It was her painful exhalation that alerted Daro, who, having let his temper provoke him into showing off, turned abruptly, almost as she fell. Dousing for her with his bare hands, using the bond that he had imposed on her, he returned through the sizzling barrier and knelt, to find her dazed, but determined to rise unaided.

She protested the hands that lifted her, set her back on wavering feet and began to check her over. He held her head, rotating her neck gently, then ran his hands over her chest ignoring her furious protests at this indignity. She pushed his hands from her breast crying, "No, no! Leave me alone, I'm alright.", realising as she did so, that her nose was bleeding profusely and that he had only been making sure she was not badly hurt.

She stumbled, then sat on the floor, trying to make sense of what had happened as he withdrew, leaning against the wall, the cowl of his cloak hiding his face.

"Are you truly alright?", he asked and feeling stupid and angry both with him and herself she muttered obstinately: "Yes, I said I was. Don't you ever listen? I just got the warding wrong. It is no more than I deserve and no more than a child of ten Rotations can stand.".

She got up, ignoring the contrition in his voice and staggered to her feet, a mutinous expression on her face. She was feeling queasy as she approached the barrier, but this time dispelled it with ease, remembering to reset it as Daro walked through unaided, his Staff in his hand. He placed himself two paces behind her, copying her mood of wilful self-reliance, spurning her hand coolly, using his bond on her to sense his way.

Heading into the dawn light outside Fronish, Jalni adjusted their packs roughly. Her neck and shoulder ached, she still felt nauseous as she handed Daro his breakday bread and led the way eastward, eating as they travelled.

It was not long before his slow progress irritated her into broadcasting her dissatisfaction on an empathic wave that he couldn't avoid overhearing.

"This journey is torture.", she declared, listing her grievances. "Treated like a skivvy and supplanted by a mystcat.", and as they climbed higher into the Pass proper, she continuously lamented her plight. Fragments of dream sensations, coupled with a burning sense of injustice washed over him, in a soul destroying litany of despair, until he could hardly think of anything else. However, he followed this doggedly, feeling his own spirits sinking even lower as he struggled with the world he could no longer see.

He caught the moment that her mood worsened, as they entered the Fall Field. It was the most treacherous part of their journey, where rocks changed to the basalt blue of the Azure Sands. Here the trail had collapsed, leaving a single footpath ascending the towering spoil, where soft shale had split away from under an ancient tamped and pinned track. By this time, Daro was tiring, though he sensed improvement in their progress.

Jalni however, plainly thought otherwise. She had completely ignored him for the last two sectors of the sand-glass. Yet, somehow he had followed her, keeping a rein on the bond, despite the loose scree that slipped beneath his feet. One of his sandals felt loose, but as Seleus rose towards its zenith, Jalni had refused to let him rest, or strip off a layer of clothing. They were climbing ever higher, nearly at the top of the Pass, when Daro stopped, too exhausted to maintain his balance as he stumbled and fell on the treacherous surface.

He resolutely picked himself up from a series of such falls, ignoring the scrazes that covered his knees and found that she was standing within arms length of him. The Sandsinger sighed as she launched an irritated tirade at him.

"Can't you do better than that?", she demanded scornfully, " We have only two days water left and if you can't walk faster, we may die before we get there! Why can't you use some of that

magic to keep you upright?".

He stifled angry words, shielding his inner voice from his perceptive Healer as he thought, "I could definitely use power to block my ears!", and snapped back incautiously,

"Perhaps you should close your eyes while walking up this!".

The precipitous incline loomed threateningly as he added, "I remember how dangerous this track is for the sighted. Now I need a guide, mine doesn't want to play!", and slid as he attempted the next step and Jalni retorted,

"May the One protect us!", she said scathingly, "Ikella's precious little brat needs a guide! So I get volunteered! No-one asked me what I need! I needed my mother and she died. I needed a home, I was hunted out of mine, right to the doors of Selesh by Grandparents determined to steal my legacy. Tjerri would have been my friend, then she died, so I wouldn't get too close my lord Sandsinger!".

The storm broke over the astounded Sandsinger, as tears broke through the surface of her control.

"I needed peace and quiet to think, to mourn and I got Mina!".

Her voice climbed towards hysteria, two octaves higher and she stalked away from him crying bitterly.

"I wanted to be a good Healer, but my *othervoice* frightens me. It is too unpredictable, I think they will still me. I can't go forward and I can't go back.", Her inner voice chimed in, confusing him for a moment, then he heard the whisper, "and I can't go on with you!", This is your journey, I want no part of it, no part of you. I can't do this, I can't look after anyone.".

Her voice was in his head as well as his ears and he followed the sound cautiously, still stumbling from time to time, until he found himself off the scree and on a rocky trail, where she stood.

"If I am to be any use at all, I need to use my *othervoice* but I can't control it and I might hurt someone. It seems so big, it wants to burst out of my chest and drown me, but I don't want to be a Wanderer, I have had enough of being the odd one out!".

Abruptly she clenched her fists screaming her frustration to the Nine Winds and the Azure echoed her bewilderment and fear.

"Grrrrh.", She snarled a parody of a mystcat's roar.

"I am wasting everyone's time! What good can I do? Who will help me? Certainly not you!".

She had all but talked herself out now and he could take no more. He felt the simmering mood she had engendered come to boiling point and somehow failed to control it. He was shaking with his recent exertions and the cruel strain of concentration. and suddenly convinced that he would never descend from Drekken Pass unless he imposed some peace and quiet for himself, he drew on his last reserve of strength and raised his *othervoice* until it carried just a sliver of power in honeyed persuasion. He staggered to stand before her and unerringly reached out one Opal cloaked hand, placing his fingers gently to her lips and said sweetly,

"Hush. Jalni, you talk too much. Rest now. Leave it alone, let go of your bitterness and just be here, with me and see what happens.".

He was looking forward to some peaceful co-operation until he could get her to think straight, but he should have known better, for strangely immune to his power, Jalni took a deep breath and bit the hand that silenced her.

His outraged roar rang out over the blue horizon, as clutching his hand in disbelief, he felt a flush of triumph flood through her. He nursed his injured fingers deciding on an altogether different approach.

"Jalni bin Selesh" his eyes flew open, pinning her like a moth against a glowstone. This voice left her reeling in shock as he reached out and seized her face, bringing it close to his, battering down every defence she had erected, with casual ease.

"I won't be tormented like this any more.", he announced, "You will remain silent
until you can speak sense, show common courtesy and perform your duty as guide.".

She glared at him, furious and frightened, hanging on his power, but rebellious just the
same. He felt her grit her teeth, drag breath enough to enunciate with painful effort, "I... will... NOT!".

Daro fought his own temper back, knowing that he could break her so easily. While she faced his othergaze with fearful defiance, he searched his memory for the word that would bring her to heel, finding it with a smile of unholy joy. He said in an ominously gentle voice,

"O Jalni,", pausing until he had her undivided attention. Then lifting
his *othervoice* he sang that word, "Schontish!", and the Drekken Pass echoed it.

He wanted to laugh at the wave of terror that radiated from her, as he used her own medicantric against her, but then she relaxed and he felt her chest heave as she pushed herself away from him. Through their psychic link her voice sounded triumphantly.

"Huh! Fat lot he knows, I don't eat cake!".

Silence fell on the frozen tableau, followed by a wail of terror as into her mind flashed an image. A few brown crumb like grains, a sample urged on her in the safety of Selesh. She made the connections one by one. The watchful eyes of the Sorceress, her instinctive knowledge that she would remember this lesson, then the novice shrieked in the moment that her inner voice faded.

"Ikella!", she wailed disbelievingly, " I trusted you..." and Daro chuckled grimly.

"I gather that you're not talking to me?", he said with deep satisfaction. "So Jalni. Let's go.".

Chapter 20 - Second Prophecy

Jalni turned stiff-legged, too terrified to react as Daro caught her arm. Half helped, half dragged to the crest of the path, he doubled over catching his breath as she silently lifted his backpack to the ground. He heard the shuffle as she crouched, then the taut "whirr" of straps being undone, before her hand guided him (none too gently), to a flattened rock. He sat, conscious of a breeze wafting strange scents along the scrub, then she opened his flask and poured a drink. He was trying to identify a sharp, spiky scent, when she tapped his arm, silently warning him to "Prepare", as she placed his cup in one hand, simultaneously pressing the flask into the other.

In the moment that he realised his own vulnerability, she was up and running like the wind. With the voice of her mind rendered inaudible, he hadn't suspected a thing, but now he sat, energies too depleted to prevent her slipping past him. The air moved as his backpack bounced down the lower trail, then there was silence, broken only by his self-mocking laughter.

Raising his cup in a wry salute, Daro murmured, "Well little one, if you must leave to seek your destiny, so must I.". and drank. Both flask and cup were secured to his belt when he stood, "calling" his staff to his hand. He leant on it, considering the dividing trail ahead, remembering the precarious path to the north with a shudder.

Wondering if the slope to the Sands joined a Fringe track, he ruefully decided that as his pack had taken the downward plunge, so would he, (but hopefully not so fast). A few hesitant steps using his staff to locate the cut into the basalt cliff, brought him sweating to the top of the downward trail. Cursing himself for a timorous fool, he found the worn rock face with one hand and slowly descended, pace by painful pace on to the northern edge of the Azure Desert.

He baulked for a moment fighting indecision. He had no native "feel" for these Sands in the way that he felt the Opal, but sensing a compacted flatland track beneath his aching feet, he turned until the wind touched the back of his neck as before. Keeping the open desert to his right and the basalt ridge to his left, he trudged forward swinging his staff ahead of him. Tortuously slow by sighted standards, he stumbled along, maintaining a light rein on Jalni, who unaware that he held her in his power, negotiated the upper path.

She had whooped with malicious glee as Daro's pack tumbled down, but her joy was curtailed by the sound of silence. With no way to tell if her condition was permanent, her freedom meant nothing and she slowed her pace with a growing sense of unease. She wondered if she was being watched, but unable to pinpoint the cause of that sensation, she climbed onward and upward, taking the crumbling Dorenard trail, but growing more concerned with every step.

"He'll be fine if he stays where I left him.", her rebellious half thought, while the Healer argued quietly, "What about Height of Sun? He has no shade!".

Slowing to a stop, she stared bleakly at the derelict track, seeing his danger, acknowledging her guilt. She had planned to press on to Scartel, help Solana rehome the children in their own Sands, before disappearing into anonymity. However, this imposed silence thwarted all such plans and she hunched in misery, all her triumph spent as she thought, "If silencing me is Ikella's revenge for what I did to Mina, how will she avenge her son!".

Daro, far below and out of her sight, had stopped to wipe the sweat from his brow, when he heard a fluting whistle from high overhead. The sound "rolled" oddly, dying echoes "pinged" off rocks, swirled down gulleys, then muffled themselves against the Sands. Curious, he opened his inner mind allowing the Source to flood in, hearing heights and depths as the response from craggy contours sang in his blood. Realising that information was almost as good as a guide, he pursed his lips and mimicked the cry of the snow raven, enhancing his whistle with power. A shadowy terrain appeared, not sight exactly, just a fleeting impression of the land formed in his mind. A barrier to his left, open desert to his right and ahead of him, a track. All too soon it faded, but encouraged he whistled again and his shadow-land reappeared. With his attention diverted from Jalni and his thoughts focussed on his surroundings, Daro sought the cause of this revelation flying high above him. Gravely wishing the Cuirax a safe migration, he emitted another piercing call.

This time he knew what he needed to find and having turned back a pace or two, soon located a rounded shape, unlike any boulder, only a few paces away and thankfully retrieved his backpack. The relief left Daro physically drained, so finding a niche at the base of the rocky hillside, with shade in which to shelter, he set up camp. In the shadow of a rocky overhang he spread a blanket, cautious of scorpions or sandrigals and sat to drink (straight from his flask) before rolling himself over to sleep.

The sound of voices woke him and hoping these travellers would pass by, he lay still, but before he could "shift" the colour of his cover to match his surroundings, he found himself in the midst of a family group. A young father, mother with a baby who patted him, investigating until he sat up.

"May the One bless your day.", he greeted them courteously, inviting them to join him, grinning cynically at the traditional response.

"Yea and the light of Seleus always brighten your path!".

While the young man stamped to disencourage insects or more deadly visitors, Daro felt the air move as someone spread blankets. His new friends introduced themselves as Trellin, who sat nursing her baby and Bernot. Daro offered his flask, thankful for the power that allowed him to replenish the water it contained magically, but when he held it out, the young man commented in a voice unaffected by pity, "Man, you're blind! We have our own flask, you need yours more than we do. How come you're here alone?", and before Daro could answer, a low

sweet voice said, "Husband" and to Daro's amazement, a great slice of Tarin bread coated with berry-paste was placed in his hands. He hadn't realised how hungry he was and thanking them, he ate the offering with relish.

Trellin said quietly, "We couldn't walk through Height of Sun with a baby and it is good to share food with a new friend. I thank you for the shelter, but you shouldn't be here alone.".

Her husband said firmly, "No indeed! Have your guides deserted you?", and Daro, reluctantly "embroidered" his explanation, for the death penalty would be exacted from Jalni, if the truth was ever known.

"No.", he said (crossing his fingers like a child with a secret), I've twisted my ankle, so she has gone ahead to look for shelter so I can rest overnight.", he added innocently, "I hope she isn't lost!". Sensing their puzzlement he added, ""This is my fault. I was neither fit to travel, nor adjusted to my situation.". He impatiently indicated his eyes and hearing understanding in the man's soft "Aah", continued gruffly.

"She is not a trained guide. Only a novice Healer from Selesh, where I am a patient. I wanted to test my recovery and she is trying to get to Scartel.". His grim chuckle startled them all as he admitted, "You see what a fine mess I've made of everything, I over-reached myself and she needs help managing me, which is not what we came to prove.".

Bernot said softly, "O man, you have no idea of the risks you take. The Drekken is no place for the blind and unwary. You both walk into peril for there's plague in Scartel. There's no-one left to heal, they've all gone to the Sand!".

Despite his confidential murmur, his voice reached Trellin, who said wearily,

"Bernot! You can't protect me from everything, I knew about Scartel before you. What do you think the women chatter about all day?". Her voice was muffled and Daro knew she had buried her mouth in her child's hair as mothers do. Bernot went to comfort her and in his minds eye Daro pictured the young parents gazing sorrowfully at their own child and giving thanks for his safety. Wondering how he knew that, he decided to tell them more and thought, "Perhaps I can do as much good by spreading the story. Jalni wanted the orphans to stay in the Azure. Better to get the matter dealt with on their own Sands than pile more responsibility on Mother.", he surprised himself with the fierce pride he felt in that association and smiled as he said softly, "The children survived.", and Bernot came back, resuming his seat by Daro, questioning him by his very presence.

"My companion was to help Solana heal any that are ill and prepare them for fostering, away from Scartel. The town must be cleansed by fire which can hardly be done in front of impressionable eyes. The Guardian of the Way will make decisions about the distribution of the children when the time comes.".

The young mother said doubtfully, "How can the Opal-born understand our culture? Those children will know nothing of our Clan, they'll return as strangers.", she was very direct and Daro valued this insight into the way the Zurias thought, but her husband was horrified and protested saying, "Trellin, Sssh!", Daro, sensing his embarrassment grinned and Trellin ignored both of them.

"I'm right Bernot.", she insisted immediately and Daro felt her burning gaze fall on him, examining him closely.

"You're a Clansman.", she accused. "I didn't notice your braid under that hukvah.", and Daro hastily concealed his rank more effectively. Her tone grew bewildered as she demanded,

"How come a high-born Shalhanhi male busies himself with Zurias orphans? Just who are you?", and Bernot chuckled suddenly.

"You'd better come clean man!", he suggested and Daro hearing the smile in his voice knew that Bernot at least understood that this was some sort of adventure.

He sighed, holding out a hand, allowing his status ring to slide round his index finger to show his seal. The device, designed by Shiarjha and blessed by his mother blazed against a field of blue and Bernot became very still as he realised who his companion must be.

"O man! You're Deshun Ikella's son? Truly?", he sighed with deep satisfaction, but no hint of apology as he explained who Daro was to his astonished wife, before asking anxiously, "The children? Will you take them to Selesh, or can they remain with our own kind?".

They were standing now, gathering their things together, ready to leave. Daro's heart sank, he didn't want to be alone again. He hid his dismay, saying easily,

"They only go to Selesh, so we have room to sort them out. Relatives will have first claim, but Ikella won't give a child to anyone who asks. They must prove their ability to love them, teach them the Way and raise them, as she did me. It is a huge undertaking.".

As Daro folded his blanket Trellin spoke, her voice puzzled, "Room enough? However many are there then?". Her voice died away as Daro replied, "More than a hundred Trellin. Brothers, sisters, cousins, the entire progeny of a small town.", and the stunned silence emphasised his own astonishment at the monumental task before him.

Bernot, surfacing from that mutual well of contemplation said decisively, "Then we must help you. The old pack route to Cathlea is easy walking. The trails cross close to Shoranal, you'll be safe and your guide can't miss you. We may meet her coming back with help if we hurry.".

Daro didn't hesitate, accepting Bernot's arm and found himself walking more confidently. They talked, took turns carrying the sleeping child and gradually Daro "tuned in" to these Sands, discovering he could sometimes "hear" Bernot's thoughts. They ran a bakery in Dovodan, a farm community not far from Shoranal, where the fact that they had married "across the Clans" was ignored. The Azure was sparsely populated, most of the inhabitants living on the Fringe since the ravages of the Great Storm and ensuing plague. The few major settlements, like Scartel, Darnesh and Anempor lay days apart, with many of the population too afraid to leave ancient villages ruled by warlords. Many feared the fostering of children would lead to the death of the Clan, especially where it took the children off-sands.

Daro concentrated, listening to vital information for Ikella, as he strode out, making intuitive connections in his own mind, only realising that he was walking at nearly his normal pace, as they entered the stop at Cathlea. He heard the echoes of his feet, as he walked on to the paved forecourt of the gathering yard and paused listening for other voices, but there were none, Cathlea was empty and he would be alone once Bernot and Trellin turned homeward.

He quite expected them to leave him immediately, but they had other ideas, saying that there was time in plenty for the short distance that they had to travel and with immense pleasure, he found himself being guided to a seat. Trellin left the baby with Bernot and went on a tour of inspection, returning cheerfully to say that she would cook for them. Into Daro's mind flashed the ominously long list of things he couldn't eat as he accepted hesitantly, "That would be wonderful, but…" and the wistful tone in his voice was not lost on Bernot, who laughing demanded, "Come on man, out with it, she won't bite!", as Trellin returned asking swiftly,

"Is there anything that you can't eat?", and gratefully Daro explained.

"I don't eat animal products.", he said apologetically and there was a perceptible pause in the conversation, as Bernot and Trellin chorused eagerly, "Are you a revivalist then?", and Daro could feel their eyes burning with interest as Trellin sat on the bench beside her husband. They leaned forward eagerly, while Daro felt his way through the maze of this strange conversation. He decided that he would have to speak truthfully, but was half holding his breath as he did so.

"I'm not sure what you mean by that.", he said quietly, "but you can tell me and I will answer as well as I can.". There was a shifting of bodies on the bench opposite and Daro was intrigued to discover that he could quite clearly follow their movements. They were looking at each other, unsure of what to say, but Bernot spoke carefully into the lengthening pause.

"There is a movement among those of us born after the Storm. We are not organised yet, but we believe that the Storm was a warning, a way of making us look at what we are doing to Pelshar. Some of us even believe that we are about to enter another Age of Mystery. Even now in the Amber Sands, a precognitive predicts the return of the…", he coughed as Trellin nudged him in the ribs. He continued, in a more subdued voice, "but I talk too much friend.". He watched Trellin go to start the cooking.

Daro sat contemplating the radical beliefs of othersands. He was not prepared to find a world waiting for the return of the Sandsingers and not sure that he was the one they would want. Bernot hesitated, then said softly, "If we have offended you friend I apologise, it is just that with the baby we want to look forward and it is hard to see what future there is for him in particular.".

There was a peculiar inflection in Bernot's voice, at which Daro raised an eyebrow and Bernot whispered hurriedly, aware of his wife approaching.

"Our baby is blind.".

His words stabbed like a knife in Daro's soul, but Bernot continued before he could speak.

"My wife won't admit it, but he can't follow the light. I checked it myself and a Healer confirmed it. There is no disease, he was born too soon. Just born too soon. We will be lucky if he survives long enough to be named, for the dangers he faces are too vast to number.".

Since the Storm, a series of plagues had been responsible for an increasing number of blind men. It was strange, didn't seem to affect women or children. Daro thinking of the young couple's generosity to a blind stranger was humbled as Trellin served their food and sat to nurse her child.

She laughed without embarrassment as her son smacked his lips at her breast.

"Ah, I have one appreciative customer at least.", she teased and Daro hearing the love in her voice marvelled at their strength. They had none of his advantages and yet they were taking their babies burden in their stride. Quietly resolving never to feel sorry for himself again, he ate with relish.

Trellin added, "There is nothing in this that you can't eat. I use plant oils in my pastry and the filling is made with grains, dried vegetable and fungi. As we met you today, I made a greenfruit cake.".

Later, with Bernot guiding him, Daro explored the facilities. Basic beds, a washdown, the necessary, learning how to lock the door and get a drink. Cathlea was all he had hoped for, he could safely wait for Jalni and suddenly realised that he hadn't thought of her once since he first met Bernot and Trellin. Reflecting on his mother's maxim, "that you only measured the severity of pain, by the pleasure of its absence", he suddenly saw that there was a difference between solitude and loneliness.

The men returned to the table where Trellin dozed beside her baby, under the shade of an extended roof. Bernot went to inspect them, re-joining Daro with the comment, "That is what makes me a revivalist! The hope that one day, we will be able to get help for our baby. We need to stop what is happening to our world. Friend, I truly pray that this is indeed the dawn of another Age of Mystery and that men of science, women of Sorcery and all practical craftsmen, can reach agreement that we all inhabit Pelshar and that we should be building a future for our children together, not just sitting around waiting for that someday, that somewhere a Sandsinger will return.".

His voice was low, emphatic, as he declared his beliefs, then he laughed saying lightly, "Man, if my mother had ever heard me, she would have shaved off my ears and used me as a pot stand.". Daro grinned, understanding those sentiments exactly.

Trellin rejoined them sitting sideways on the bench, as she lifted her son into his travelling pouch. She spoke severely, "Bernot! You will make a preacher one day.", but Daro heard the smile in her voice. "Don't get him started friend, I warn you. He will recite the prophecy next and you'll die of boredom or become a convert.".

Daro smiled in the direction of her voice and she sat, suddenly placing her hands on his. He "shielded" instinctively, but there was no power in her to detect his. She only asked him quietly, "Tell me friend, what is it like to be blind?", and Daro fought down his instinctive reaction and tried to tell her.

"For me, it is like being in a darkened room. Only hearing to tell who is nearby, smell, taste and touch to reinforce immediate impressions. All of those senses have to be used to replace the sight you lost. Some days are hard, some days are easy. That is what it is like for me, but it is different for everyone.", he felt as if he had let her down, but he had told her what he could. Still, she turned her head into her husbands shoulder weeping. Daro knew the scent of sorrow and he patted the hand he still held as she spoke defiantly.

"Our baby isn't blind. I don't believe it, I can't believe it!".

Daro rose quietly and walked away from them, as Bernot murmuring comfort into his wife's hair said softly, "Help will come. If the One wills it, help will come!".

It was cooling when they gathered their things to leave, Bernot lifted the baby's sling and hearing these preparations, Daro who had settled on his blanket, stood and came to thank them. Trellin told him where to find her shop and Bernot clapped him on the shoulder, shocking Daro by hugging him in a way quite unlike the manner in which the Opal-born conducted themselves. The baby, sandwiched between the two men cooed happily, as Daro said, "You still haven't told me this prophecy.", and Trellin groaned.

Bernot pleaded with her, "Just a few words from the Second Prophecy?", he begged and she relented. They stood, heads bowed for a moment, then chorused,

"Honour to the One, keeping only to his path.", asTrellin sat and Bernot lifted his speaking voice.

"From the Second Prophecy of Man, the true word of Revival.", he paused, assured himself of their undivided attention, then proclaimed, "He walks in the night, the one who comes. Sired by no mortal, birthed in the Storm. Touched by infinity, loved beyond life, gifted in power, the Voice, the Light of the World returns.".

There was deep silence. If Daro's hair could have stood on end, it would have done. He thought bitterly, "I measure up so badly by those standards! If that is what they are waiting for, they are about to be so disappointed!", but he couldn't leave them to their sorrow. He couldn't.

He held out his arms for the baby and Bernot shook himself out of his trancelike state and smiling placed the boy securely in Daro's arms.

"Hold his head up friend.", he said, putting his arm round his surprisingly silent wife and Daro obliged. Tilting the child into a more secure position, he drew breath, filling his lungs with enough for one impassioned plea, seeking beyond magic, to the feet of the One. As if forewarned, Trellin raised a shaking hand to her mouth in wonder, as Daro summoning power was encircled by a glowing opalescent aura. Bernot stood transfixed as Daro lifted his *othervoice* into a torrent of sweet melody and the magic began its work.

He could never remember the words afterwards and sometimes not even a snatch of the music he sang. It was as if he had become an instrument of power, channelling it to his will, sculpting the object of his hearts desire. Weaving a spell of such deep enchantment, that mortal flesh had to give way and reshaped itself to his bidding.

He was certain, that he heard Trellin cry.

"My baby, my baby.", as the Opal glow died away. He found himself on his knees, holding the baby aloft in absolute supplication.

As the power of the Opal left him, Trellin took the baby reverently and Bernot lifted him to his blanket, as he let his power depart in trickles that left him shuddering.

"What have you done to yourself man?", Bernot's normally steady voice shook and then Trellin was there, holding their child, holding him on the other side and covering his hands with kisses of gratitude.

"I don't have the words.". she faltered, "but my baby sees, he reached for me, he pulls my hair, my baby sees!", Tears were falling and Daro wept too, with exhaustion and joy. Bernot spoke solemnly, his deep voice filling the whole of Daro's horizon.

"Now I understand.", he said, returning to the prophecy. "He walks in the night!", It is you man, You are the one who comes. A Sandsinger?", and Daro nodded, simply too tired to prevaricate.

"Yes. I am Daro. Opal Sandsinger, born in the Storm at the gates of Tirjhinar.", He felt his own voice change subtly.

"Not quite power.", he thought critically, "More as though another speaks through me.", and powerless to alter the words, he went on:

"I am the Voice, who men call Ichta Selunsanni and yet I am but a man who must walk in the night and alone.".

Bernot stood still and Daro had an impression that he was simply staring at him and then he turned to his wife and catching her hand, he said:

"We must make haste and tell the others.", and then they were gone, running down the narrow pathway to Shoranal and their celebrations. Daro sank on to the blanket and slept the sleep of the dead, from sheer exhaustion.

He slept so soundly, that he missed the keening of the Cuirax warning him he had company and never heard the grating of desert boots on stone.

Jalni stood, hands on hips, staring down at him in bewilderment trying to work out how he had got here. He had eaten well she noted and even prepared a bed, so this was plainly more evidence that this "Sandsinger" had hidden from her.

"Well, it seemed that I'll be in your company a while longer my friend.", she gritted through her teeth, "but if you think I am waiting on you, you can forget it.".

She covered him, leaving him to sleep where he lay, in the open, going in to the Traveller stop and happily used the prepared bed herself.

Chapter 21 - Solana's Last Journey

With less than a day's journey before him, Daro painstakingly ran his fingers over firebush blistered legs, hissing as he prodded them gingerly. He had stripped to wash and now sat naked on his blanket, dabbing on barrisweed balm, too engrossed to bother when Jalni approached from the direction of the sleeping hall. Her inner voice sounded weak but familiar as she exclaimed sympathetically.

"Oh my!", she observed, "What a mess you are my Sandsinger". He detected a queer note of victory in those words as she added, "Now you'll have to let me take charge.". Completely irrationally, he decided that was the last thing she would ever do!

Scowling, he swung his legs away from her, turning until she backed off, squatting half a span away as he finished treating himself. He stood, careless of modesty and heard her wince, then dressed, thinking with perverse satisfaction, "That bad!", and completely ignoring her packed methodically. Wash cloth, towel, food, medications, rolled blanket, then he slung his backpack over his shoulder took up his staff and went to fill his flask.

Jalni stared after him then ran to her bedspace, gathered her belongings, filled her flask and rushed back to the courtyard, just in time to see him disappearing into the distance.

An angry torrent formed in her mind, but unable to deliver it, she shut the door and ran down the track, as a party of travellers approached from Shoranal. She ran lightly, overtaking Daro at the end of a rocky path, joining him as he stepped out on to the Sands. He missed a stride as she passed him, but stoically plodded onward into the grey blue dawn.

So the last of the journey went. Jalni danced ahead, not able to talk but rejoicing in her connection with the sands of home. Daro trudged his own path, pausing every few steps to whistle, seemingly able to gauge his direction as a result. Gradually drawing away south east of the border now, all visible landmarks faded from view, no directions to Scartel, except the cloud gathering in front of them and the track beneath their feet.

Jalni's pace slowed. Daro had stopped whistling, his attention on something else and she took the opportunity to get him to acknowledge her presence, by standing in his path. However, just when she thought he might speak, he whistled again, nodded to himself and walked round her before she could react. So it was Daro in the lead as they came to the strange break in the crater of Scartel, known as Gateway.

In full view, Daro (ignoring her warning hiss) removed his cloak, letting his Colours blaze against the rich blue Sands, as they were surrounded by laughing children, many of whom already knew Daro, greeting him rapturously by name.

Largely ignored, the novice waited until leaning on a stick, walking with perilous care, Solana came to greet them. Remembering her manners, Jalni dipped in formal greeting to the Senior Healer, who kissed her cheek, quavering in obvious relief, "Young sister, it is good to see someone other than these rogues.".

She poked her stick at one of the children, smiling as he pretended to run away, then slowly led them past the pallid huddle that was Scartel village.

Following Jalni's questioning glance, Solana murmured briefly, "All gone. Not one survived.", then on a gasp, "Warded to keep innocents safe.". Seeing that even speech exhausted her, Jalni took Solana's arm, supporting her Sister Healer with genuine concern.

They slowly ascended the long curving ramp to the caverns above the town and Jalni looked around curiously. These were rumoured to be the oldest habitations in these Sands and Jalni was unusually "aware", as they entered the great Home Cave. Then Solana caught hold of Daro's sleeve, peering up into his unguarded face.

"So what became of your dreams boy?", she demanded and Daro answered softly.

"My dreams Mother Solana?", he paused and Jalni not knowing the full story was struck by the tragedy in his face as he muttered, "O, they became nightmares for those who dared to dream. Too high a price was exacted from all of us.", and into the old Healers mind came a picture of three adventurers, heads together, eyes sparkling with laughter. She said softly, "Look with the eyes of your heart boy and your friends will always be with you.".

A single tear tracked Daro's face and as Solana's withered hand reached up to brush it away, Jalni, uncomfortable in the presence of so many shared memories and such affection wandered off with the girls. So they entered Scartel, unaware of the mysteries that lay within.

They spent the next two days resting. Jalni (still silent) gravely learning the old Healer's routine and hearing (in mild disbelief), about Daro's birth. Solana, noticing Jalni's preoccupation with the sleeping man, made her jump by cackling mirthlessly, "Some lover's tiff is it? You don't need that one girl. Let him find another fool!".

However, she had broken off in mid sentence, shuffling away muttering to herself and Jalni saw that the old Healer had all but reached the end of her days.

Soon putting names to faces, Jalni made note of Lallee, Solana's favourite, Marran, the eldest boy, Terris who loved to cook and Brus, who, fascinated by Daro, hovered solicitously at his elbow, making sure that he didn't fall. Watching the routine tasks of each day, even Jalni began to feel at home, at peace once more.

On the fourth day, the wind crept round until it rattled small pebbles along the frontage of Home Cave. Restless under that influence, Daro asked Brus where Orto had gone and was dismayed by the answer. It seemed that the deaf mute had never returned from Darnesh. They had gone outside to talk privately and the boy said sombrely,

"We try not to talk about Orto in front of Mother Solana, she misses him terribly. A runner came from Darnesh with medication and told us he was quarantined. He would have returned by now, if he'd survived.".

Brus was quiet for a moment and then greatly daring, slipped his hand into Daro's and asked conversationally,

"You've been ill too. Was it plague that took your sight?", and Daro, recognising in this gawky man-child, the adoration of a younger brother, said gently,

"Not plague Brus, just the result of disobeying my mother!", and he felt the solemn dark eyes scan his face anxiously, then an awed voice remarked, "Cor! I bet you caught it!", and an image of Ikella, scornfully facing him in all her power flashed into Daro's mind.

He choked back hysterical laughter long enough to agree that his mother had been very angry, before Brus scampered away to tell his friends. Then he leant against the hitching rail and wept, a lifetime of sorrow dissolving as he whispered into the rising wind:

"Tiraj di Schpeller, Spanker of small boys, I love you mother!", and returned to his blanket, knowing his words would reach the Warden of the Winds and tell her that he was safe in Scartel. He had taken Solana's advice seriously, when the Healer had forbidden him to talk further on the evening they arrived. She had grumbled,

"Now young man, if you think I can heal you of your own carelessness, think again. I am too old, too tired to mend your legs, they will do by themselves.". She glanced at Jalni and said provocatively, "I suppose that one will get her tongue back? Cheeked your mother did she?", and Daro decided not to rise to the bait, but permitted Jalni to salve his legs with Solana's own remedy and slept like one dead, recovering with indecent haste, to Solana's indignant comments and Jalni's silent amusement.

"Men!", Solana's eyes tracked Daro round Home Cave. "They die of a chill, just to annoy, but given a nap and a pot of salve, they'd recover from a severed leg and go hunting the same day if you let them!. Why can't they be born with the sense to stay in bed when they need sleep?", but her eyes had rested fondly on Daro as Brus led him to eat.

She handed Jalni a twist of paper, decorated with a leaf, drawn in a familiar hand. Jalni stared at it and then with care unfolded the Apothecary's slip.

There was a fine grey powder in the folds and Jalni remembering exhortations to, "Smell it dry, taste it dry. ", raised questioning eyes to Solana's face and the Healer cackled.

"I told Carolus you wouldn't recognise it and I was right!", She triumphed, then said soberly.

"You're holding the treasure of the Azure Sands girl. This is vetali, dried, ground, boiled, dried and ground again. Nowadays we use it steeped in alcohol as a tonic for minor illness, but once it was part of our ritual life, for the plant is dedicated to Jenta.".

At Jalni's blank stare of incomprehension the old woman explained.

"Pick mature leaves on the Eve of Jentaroth. Fast dry them with fire. Pass them through the purest water vapour as it boils in a sand-paste chamber, then dry the residue in the Height of Sun, on a basalt slab. Store until Zenitheon, then grind it once at dead of night. Store until Jentaroth again, grind once more at Height of Sun and serve it to any passing Sandsinger you encounter.".

Solana smiled grimly at Jalni's astonishment, saying tartly, "Some of us know the old ways. Others know how to work. None of your "shoddy soak it in wine and let the spirit do the work" remedies here. Besides, in this form it can be compressed with oil to make tablets. This tonic was once known as Sandsinger's friend!", she announced and Jalni blinked, thinking with some alarm, that the Healer (in her vague way) might accidentally betray Daro, but just then Solana chuckled at Jalni's bemused expression saying,

"Some believe the old prophecies and yon mad Apothecary has been refining the cures and travelling amongst trusted friends "preparing the Way.". She broke off, shuffling away, lost in her own private thoughts again and Jalni folded the slip around the contents and took it to Solana's workroom.

On the table stood an intriguing box, labelled in the upright script that she associated with the Apothecary's scribe. Deducing that this was where it belonged, she opened the lid. Inside, neatly arranged, were other slips, a few packets and an intriguing envelope inscribed "For the Singer of the Song". She stared at it, but having replaced the Sandsinger's Remedy, she closed the box, thinking, "Perhaps not now.", and went serenely to her bed, without disturbing Daro.

She lay contemplating the Apothecary's secret belief in Sandsingers and smiled without a trace of malice, on the hope that she would be present when the old man learned the truth. As she slipped into the naturally light sleep of a Healer on duty, she wished she had seen Daro sing in power and her previous resentment was replaced by a wistful longing to believe in the impossible.

In that night, Solana passed from their reach into a wandering reverie, responding to no-one. Frail hands clutched a shawl around her shoulders, as she stood gazing out over the warded village muttering. During the morning, she called piteously for Orto, wandering the Home Cave crying because she couldn't find him. Terris told Jalni in a frightened voice, that she had sent a runner to fetch Marran, (out foraging with the teens(and Jalni nodded as the girl persuaded Solana to sit by the fire. The ancient Healer restlessly plucked at things, examining them mindlessly, before she abruptly rose to her feet, saying urgently, "Where is he? They promised me help!", before her strength suddenly deserted her. Face sagging oddly, eyes rolling, she collapsed into Jalni's arms with the faintest of sighs.

Unable to call for help, Jalni was suddenly aware of a flare in the Source, as Daro reacted to the crisis. Her eyes welled in gratitude as his voice said simply, "I'm here.", and she transferred Solana's limp body into his strong arms. Brus, shocked and silent held Daro's sleeve, guiding him to the Healers alcove and so, on the fifth day, carrying his old friend as he might have lifted a weary child, the Sandsinger set Solana on the first leg of her last journey.

Marran arrived at a run, swiftly disposing his group to heat bricks, draw water and find more pillows, effortlessly translating Jalni's flickering fingers, as the shadows lengthened across the crater floor.

Terris kept the daily routine. Bed rolls were aired, meals were provided, water was drawn and washing was dried, but there was an anxiety in the air, an emptiness in their eyes, as they contemplated their lives without Solana.

Quietly gathering his strength against the coming task, Daro deliberately "withdrew", into the small, quiet space of meditation. Cloaked and cowled, he sat cross-legged in the corner of Solana's alcove, trying to ignore the pulsing ache behind his eyes, regretting the Merishwhen treatment left in Selesh, in the knowledge that tonight he couldn't afford distractions.

At Sunfall, Jalni drew back the privacy curtain, with Terris in tow. She bent over Solana, sighing as she recognised the approach of death. Quietly conducting a gentle examination, she reported, "Pulse slow and thready", then he heard the scrape of enscrasure on tablet as Terris made notes. Someone approached him warily, then her voice touched his mind, saying apologetically,

"Daro, if you can hear me, Terris and I need to change Solana's bedding and you need to eat. She can bathe your eyes with the Merishwhen Carolus left here, while I relieve you and care for Solana.".

He appreciated this delicacy in her approach, but shrank inwardly at the thought of anyone unknown touching his eyes, he caught Jalni's hand, placing it on his closed eyelids. Shaken by his mute appeal, she lifted the curtain and he sensed her hands flickering. After a moment he heard Marran say, "Brus, bring Daro to get some food. Jalni needs boiled water to bathe his eyes, so sit him on a stool near a table, while I help Terris.", and Daro relaxed as that operation took effect.

He couldn't face food, but took a hot drink, sitting isolated in the midst of a cacophony of questions, until Marran returning, apologetically shooed the little ones to bed. Daro drifted as the teens gathered on the apron fronting Home Cave, where Marran put the boys through an exercise routine, accompanied by a slow hand-clapped rhythm provided by the girls. The song of the rising wind, the rhythmic beating of hands, the slither of posturing bodies, occasionally punctuated by the staccato tattoo of feet stamping, gradually sent Daro into a deep meditation, from which he hardly roused, as Jalni bathed his eyes.

He woke to the cool relief from pain, to find Jalni, holding an apothecary's slip in her hand. It rustled, as she unfolded it and he reached out a restraining hand, only for her to tip, a single freshly pressed tablet into it. He tilted his head inquisitively and a picture of his Songfather appeared in such detail that he paused, but Jalni was struggling to convey what she wanted to tell him. He deduced that the medication was for him and shook his head violently. He felt her rueful shrug, then, a mental image of an Azurian warlord surrendering and he laughed softly, as he interpreted her usual snarl of "I give up!". He was still amused by this change in her approach when abruptly, she picked up the tablet, snapping it in half, replacing one half on his hand, the other went to her own mouth and he realised suddenly that she suspected him of refusing the medication from fear. She carried his free hand to her throat as she swallowed and he sensed her daring him, prodding him urgently, until he said quickly,

"I do trust you Jalni, but I dare not take anything to help me sleep tonight.", and she tapped his hand, signalling an emphatic "Wrong.".

At his demanded "Tell me!", she first shrugged, then tried making the universal signal for "friends" and "one more word". She prodded him pointedly, repeating the silent code against his hand. He touched himself and said cautiously "Me? Daro? or..." and the suggestion of his rank was reinforced by the disclosure of an Opal ring, as his other hand curled to form a mouth. She touched the back of his hand, indicating "Nearly". to which Daro deliberately raised an enquiring eyebrow. She rapidly signalled "Right!", then she put his hands together and held them tightly. He sounded totally bewildered, whispering, "Sandsinger's Friends?", to her evident delight. She traced and tapped, "sick", followed by, "Well", followed by, "Tired", then pantomimed taking the tablet, placing it in his hand, with a drink. She was thinking of Carolus again and he hazarded the term "Tonic?", to a round of applause. He took the half tablet, wondering why it tasted vaguely familiar and allowed Jalni to lead him back to Solana's alcove, where in the rustling of drying herbs and the scents of summer gatherings, the old Healer dozed fitfully.

She would return to consciousness, but her mind wandered and she lay muttering, doubts and fears, confusion and sorrow as the sands of her life trickled slowly away. Around the middle watch, she became restless and Jalni, who had hovered nearby for some time, surprised Daro by sliding round the curtain and gently bathing the sick woman's face. She sighed as she dried the withered cheeks tenderly, then came to stand by Daro and impulsively touched his hand. He "saw" an image of her walking the Home Cave, checking the children and was grateful to know where she would be. He smiled as she pictured him running round the Cave at top speed, realising that the tonic had taken effect and that physically at least he was ready to perform his last sad duty.

Solana woke suddenly and Daro knew that this was his one chance to tell her that the one she waited for was here. Focussing the eye of his mind on the well remembered image of an enormous Opal, he sought the Source, commanding Jalni's attention urgently.

"The Spellbinding begins!", he spoke solemnly, "Sleep now, don't disturb the others. I will call you if I need you.", and again Jalni was excluded, but this time, she understood why.

He leant towards the bed, opening his eyes and allowing his magically empowered othergaze to penetrate the bewildered maze, through which Solana tottered. She sought that power eagerly, her lined face flushing with joy as she saw the aura surrounding him. Then bewilderment filled her eyes again and he withdrew a little, allowing comprehension of what she "dreamed", to remain in her waking mind, until he could sit on the edge of her bed and take her hand in his, confirming in his mastery of this magical element, that her Sandsinger had come to the rescue.

Reluctantly Daro put back the hood of his cloak, exposing his face fully to her searching gaze. She gently traced his eyelids, the Healer still responding instinctively.

"Is it You?", she asked and Daro nodded as Solana's wits wandered again.

"They told me they'd found a Sandsinger.", she muttered to herself, "but they sent me a blind man and a girl child.". Daro "reached", pulling her blanket aside with the power of his mind. Eyes snapping open abruptly, Solana saw his clasped hands in clear view and the blankets once again tucking themselves around her and made the connection.

"You are the Sandsinger? You, my Daro?", and her voice cracked, as she searched his face, understanding at last, the terrible price he had paid for his power. The wind moaned, anchoring him in the moment and he raised his left hand, kissing the Opal of his ring, murmuring the traditional summons to this most solemn ritual.

"Solana, preserve the knowledge with me.", he commanded and she sighed, then began to share a lifetime of knowledge, passing all she had learned to the one she had waited, begged and prayed for. Smiling up into fire opal eyes that couldn't see her, Solana was at last content.

As the children slept, the sound of the wind moaned softly through the caverns and Solana shivered, for soon she would surrender her powers, into the hands that Opal cloaked clasped her own so tenderly. She knew that she was dying, she had known for some time, but now, for the last time she would sing in power, creating a library of warded chants that would drain the dregs of life from her. For so it was with all Healers. She would weave an incantation, that would prevent loss by the messenger and she would lock forever her magically empowered *othervoice* in her last spell as she died. She felt the power throb in the hands that held hers and comforted she raised her voice in a prayer she had once heard on the night of his birth.

"'Gurayen sek moyen, Gurayen noi shominen' (Gurayen shelter us, Gurayen defend us). The first line of the prayer for the dead would once have filled her with dread, but now, hands held in the clasp of a Sandsinger, she shared her life in joy.

Towards dawn, Jalni brought a drink for both of them, but Solana was beyond drinking. The novice patiently moistened her lips, sitting quietly beside Daro, listening intently as they perfected the work. Daro was singing back to Solana, who lay gathering her strength in the glow of his aura. For some reason, Jalni was drawn to place a hand firmly against his back and only became aware of exhaustion as she did so immediately wishing that she could give him her power, or just lend him some of her strength. In that moment, she felt a connection form, enveloping them both. Fighting back her instinctive desire to shut down, run away or hide, she forced herself to lower the barriers that resisted this strange intimacy and sat entranced, power flowing freely from her hand to Daro.

Sleepy, warm and comforted, she heard someone murmur her name. "O, yes.", her mind agreed, her name was Jalni, but she was too tired to talk. Someone lifted her, floating her effortlessly as a cloud to her bed. Someone tucked blankets round her, someone brushed the hair from her face, dropped a kiss on her forehead and left. She roused a little, looking across the cavern to the Healers alcove, registering that Daro still sat with Solana, on the other side of the fire. Smiling sleepily, she snuggled down, thinking, "Help a Sandsinger Jalni? That's a good dream!". In sleep saturated bewilderment, she "saw" Daro's face smiling down at her, there was a soundless click in her mind and she felt the speech-binding dissolve. Recognising that she had dreamt Daro "floating" her to bed, right over the fire, she decided to tell him as soon as she woke and slept.

Around dawn, the children woke very subdued. Slipping from their blankets they dressed rapidly and came as if summoned to surround Solana's bed. She rested quietly, face serene, her hair combed out, spread across her pillow. Lallee whispered to Jalni,

"She looks beautiful.", and Jalni had to agree. The worry, the fear had left Solana's face,

and she was calm, waiting for her children to hear her. Marran, lifted her up and placed more pillows behind her and she smiled up at him patting his hand gently. Daro, moved to sit at the head of the bed, holding her right hand in his, Lallee on the other side, held her left, then they were all gathered.

Solana spoke gently, but clearly,

"Children, you knew that this day would come.", The children groaned softly and Solana's voice took on a deeper, sterner tone.

"Don't let me down now!", she instructed, "This is, as it should be. Now, I will tell you myself, what is going to happen.".

Her voice quavered and she closed her eyes, fighting back tears. Daro squeezed her hand gently, strengthening her resolve and she tried to sit up. At that, Daro slipped into the space behind her, raising Solana so that she lay back against his body. His hands were on her shoulders and she turned her face up toward him, seeking reassurance. He let a little trickle of power flow between them, as she gathered her defences, then her eyes opened and she spoke again, her voice empowered as she bound them to her will.

"You will wait here.", she instructed firmly, then devastatingly, she revealed.

"Till the Sandsinger comes for you."

Jalni heard the children wail in protest. Solana waited for the furore to die away before continuing firmly.

"I have been promised a Sandsinger.", she paused, fighting for breath, "and it pains me to say, that it would probably take the strength and wisdom of two, to get you ruffians safely to Selesh where the Guardians can look after you until you are claimed.".

The children murmured amongst themselves, siblings drew close to each other, the younger ones crept into the arms of their elders until Daro interrupted the buzz, for Solana was breathing oddly now, her presence in the Source was very tenuous and she still had much to say. Rousing from the torpor she was slipping into, Solana's last spell was on her breath and in her heart, but she and she alone must say it. She tried to attract their attention,

"Children, Obey me, Attend me!", The familiar Voice of Command rang out once more, . but she broke off coughing and Jalni alarmed that the old Healer would die before she could finish, moistened her lips. Solana leant back against Daro and asking with a trace of her old humour. "Am I dying well Ichspeller?", and his shock at her use of the ancient title seemed to give her great amusement, for she chuckled suddenly, eyes lighting up with laughter.

She eased herself back into Daro's encircling arms and spoke again. The cavern grew still as Solana commanded.

"You must remain here , until the Sandsinger claims you!". It was her last weave and with it the tiny presence in the Source of all Souls flickered and faded. Her *othervoice* stilled forever. She smiled hazily at her charges, knowing that there was only one task left and her heart was full as her gaze wandered over the solemn eyes and quivering lips. She had done well by them, she thought, she had always shared her home, her wisdom and love, deep within her she knew this was right and gathered her strength as the dawn light poured through the Home Cave entrance. As the song of warming crystals chimed in her blood, Solana turned her face towards the light and started her long journey home.

Chapter 22 - The Children of Scartel

At the moment of Solana's death, Daro felt a flood of warmth wash through his frozen bones. He had been so engrossed in supporting the dying Healer, that he had somehow lost touch with reality, no longer knowing if the bitter chill of death was in his blood or hers. He was calm, yet joyful, all his pain had melted away. He, (or was it she?), hovered at the edge of existence, no longer troubled by sorrow, time or the constraints of life. Wanting to sing he went to draw breath, but could no longer breathe and knew (instinctively) that he too, was dying.

Too late to withdraw, too late to call for help, he felt himself floating free of his body. Too weak, too entranced by the sensations he was experiencing , he tried to say goodbye to Jalni, who kept the vigil across the room and she roused. Staring into his sightless eyes perplexed, Jalni wondered if Daro had called her, then, as she watched, a bead of cold sweat dropped from his brow, as she finally understood what was happening.

"Deo!". She grabbed Marran's arm. "Help me quickly.", she commanded. He jumped at the sound of her voice but fully engaged in Healer mode, it came to her aid, crisp and decisive once more.

The boy needed no prompting, lifting Solana's body, so that Jalni could pull Daro aside. As she gave new orders, they were obeyed, thankfully, without anyone seeing the panic in her eyes.

Picking the four strongest boys unhesitatingly, she commanded briskly, "Simbel, Lladro, Torvin, Rann. Lift Daro out by the fire. I need to treat him urgently.", and as they swung into instant action, she turned to Terris. "Nimah can look after the children, I need you to go to the workroom. Bring me the blue box from the second shelf on the back wall. Now run!".

She ran herself, after the boys who lifted Daro to the warmth and space that she needed and joined Marran, who grim faced, turned the Sandsinger's head to the side and checked his mouth.

"He didn't choke, but he isn't breathing right.", he reported and Jalni felt at the base of Daro's throat for a pulse, before starting resuscitation.

The spark that was Daro gradually came back to a world of pain and panic. His throat burned, his chest was bruised and some young ruffian was still pounding on it. He groaned, then realising that his assailant was Jalni, relaxed into her hands. He could feel a "presence", so he sought the Healer who hunched over him and was confused by the faint musky scent of wild raja's surrounding him. He whispered,

"Feydora?", and heard the chuckle... "Whose cheating now Sandsinger?", she taunted and was gone, though there was reminiscence in Jalni's aura, which thought abruptly focussed his mind as he tried to orientate himself.

He lay by the fire, his sweat soaked clothes had been stripped, as she roughly towelled him dry. He could hear Marran's voice organising, he thought hazily and pictured Jalni, as he remembered her, lower lip caught between even, white, teeth, worry lines creasing her brow.

Marran stepped in closer, his boots scuffing the ground beside Daro's blanket, as he crouched, asking curiously,

"What happened ?", Daro felt Jalni's gentling hands pause in their ministrations.

"Exhaustion.", Jalni answered shortly, tracing an energy line on Daro's naked chest, her fingers constantly checking his pulses. "Sorrow, plus the fact that he came here, fresh from his own sickbed.".

She glanced up at Marran, seeing the shocked look on his face and reassured him. "He's fine and will recover with sleep and a tonic I will mix for him.". Daro caught the grim determination in her voice and thought, "The bloody Healers win again.", and winced as she pinched him discreetly.

Completely unable to help himself, Daro suffered the indignity of being lifted in Marran's strong arms and taken to a raised pallet. Cocooned in soft warm blankets, he could only smile weakly, when the boy said gruffly, "Glad you're back with us again. You gave your Healer a dreadful fright, enough to bring her voice back anyway.", he paused uncomfortably, then said, "Ah, you'd better call me if you want to get up. Nimah, Asher and Rianna are fighting over who washes your clothes and you're mother naked under those wraps. We don't want to frighten the children do we?".

Chuckling, he sketched a salute and left Daro, who, too weary to speak, simply went to sleep, oblivious of the activities around him.

Jalni began instructing Terris in the use of simple medications. She lifted the lid on what she had decided was the Sandsinger's box and retrieved another slip filled with the vetali powder, explaining sternly:

"Daro has to observe strict dietary rules. Absolutely no animal products, such as milk, meat, butter, cheese, nothing cooked in or containing fat.". She checked, looking at Terris's wide-eyed look of disbelief, sternly.

"This is serious Terris, he cannot tolerate these things. He might die from the reaction and I wouldn't want to be the one that killed Deshun Ikella's son!".

She smiled grimly at the girl's horrified response, saying lightly,

"Yes, well, now you know who he is, keep it to yourself. He likes to be free and doesn't want special treatment. Mother Solana knew him from birth. She was a good friend to him and took care of him for a while, not long ago. She wouldn't have stood for any fuss either.".

Terris said cautiously,

"I saw him before, but never spoke to him then. He seems quite easy round us.", and Jalni continued on the theme of food.

"Yes, he is easy with people and he is used to his diet. If you are unsure, he will know what he can eat. It is the same for medication, which is why Master Carolus left it here with Mother Solana, "just in case".

She saw the girl relax and the crease on her forehead smooth out, as Terris said quietly:

"I thought that these had been left for the Sandsinger!", she blushed and looked away, saying gruffly,

"I didn't think it through properly I suppose. A Sandsinger wouldn't really need medication would he?", and Jalni sighed, thinking that she had just walked into another morass of her own making, but she could deal with that later.

She smiled at Terris.

"Oh, I see.", she said easily, then, "We need to make up a tonic for Daro. It has vetali powder in it and I have to release the power of the plant by making an infusion. Do you know what that means?", and Terris smiling said quickly,

"Like stemmis? With boiling water poured over the powder?", and Jalni nodded agreement,

"That's a good start, but you need to know how much water to add, or the infusion won't be the right strength. I usually measure by the gouche. I expect Solana have one somewhere.", and so they worked together, boiling water, measuring ingredients, steeping, then straining the resultant liquid into a cooling jug, until, in the Height of Sun, the smallest children drowsed and the Home Cave quietened.

Jalni and Terris stood, nodded to Marran and slipped discreetly into Solana's workroom. They worked swiftly, lifting the small delicately flowering plants that Nimah and the other girls had picked whilst foraging that morning. They pulled up stools and plaited several garlands together, adding the sweetest smelling herbs from the drying bunches over their heads to the growing pile. There was a discreet tap on the door and Lladro stood there. He kept his voice low, plainly not wanting to rouse the little ones.

"Healer Jalni, Marran says that hot water, the oils you need, clean linen and helping hands are ready.". He paused awkwardly and said,

"We lit the beacon at Height of Sun. Just as Mother Solana wished. It burned clear and bright for one sector of the sand-glass, then Rann put peloance to the flame until it burned blue. We saw the station flame so the message will be passed to Lady Tirjella.".

Jalni was amazed by Solana's strength of will. Not only had she planned the way for the children to leave, but recognizing the approach of her own death, had calmly prepared her children, these children of Scartel, for the task of letting her Sorceress know that the Senior Healer of the Azure Sands, was no more. In wonderment at the old woman's fortitude, she found herself wishing she had known Solana better. She looked around and said as calmly as she could,

"Thank you Lladro. Now, do any of you know where Mother Solana's robes are? She was of the Council of Nine and should be dressed according to her rank.".

Terris said gently, "There is a chest. It is very old and smells funny, but Mother Solana kept her best blue there. Shall I fetch it?", and Jalni much relieved nodded. Terris rose and placed her finished garlands in Jalni's arms and turning, took Lladro away with her.

Jalni lifted the garlands in a sheet to stop them shedding florets and went to the workbench where Daro's tonic was cooling. She studied it anxiously, but although it seemed a horrid muddy colour, it actually smelt quite pleasant so she strained a cupful and lifting the garlands in the sheet, went back to Home Cave. As she approached Solana's alcove, Daro woke. He didn't move, but she felt him wake, just like a torch lighting the dark and went to his side. She bent over the pallet bed and whispered.

"Hello. Do you feel better?", and he snuggled deeper into the blankets for a moment, before he roused, painfully aware of his naked body. His colour rose, as Jalni said comfortably, "Don't worry. I have stripped you, bathed you and done many intimate Healer services for you before now. There is no need to be embarrassed.", and to her astonishment he froze.

"What? What did you say?", he demanded furiously, rigid with indignation.

Jalni's voice was very patient as she explained, "Who do you think took care of your every need when you collapsed at Selesh? Didn't you realise that it would be a junior Healer who acted as your body servant when you were unconscious, rather than a Sorceress? Neither Ikella nor Mina could risk using power on you, nor could they sit with you, all day and every night and there were times in your delirium when two senior Healers were not enough.", she paused recalling the intimacy of those moments, then said awkwardly, "I was on probation, they were desperate and you responded to me, so I nursed you, under strict supervision. They would hardly have let me accompany you if I knew nothing about your well-being, or hadn't proved myself capable over a period at least equal to this journey, now would they?".

She saw the stain of acute discomfort flood his cheeks and continued softly, "I know that's difficult for most men to hear, but I am bound by oath to Healer service until I have leave to depart and you seemed to respond to my *othervoice*.". He blinked and said slowly, "I don't remember that, I don't think I ever heard you healing. How strange.".

She placed the beaker she bore on a ledge and he grinned saying,

"You'd better get Marran to attend me before I drink that.", and with great dignity she sent Rann to fetch his captain, while she and Terris went to prepare Solana's body for her funeral rites.

All too soon the pitiful task was done. Fresh sheets covered the fragile bones. Her pale face and body was cleansed according to the Rites of Zurian and Terris and Jalni combed out Solana's hair, spreading it out on her pillow like a young woman's and threading tiny blossom's into it. Jalni carefully worked the Healers braid into one long lock, threading the Azure ribbon into it, denoting the Seniority of this Healer, before raising Solana's slight form, to enable Terris to robe her. The faintest aroma rose from the chest as they removed the light blue under robe and Jalni bent her head and breathed the scent in.

"The perfume reminds me of the way Ikella's robes smelt when Beneva produced them from storage.", she remarked and Terris stared at her, wide-eyed.

"Jalni!", she exclaimed, in a shocked voice.

"You can't speak about the Guardians so casually. They exist to protect our whole world and they should only be named by their familiar names, by those who are privileged to serve them.".

Jalni glanced at her solemn face with amusement,

"Goodness me!", , she remarked as one impressed. "You have been listening to Solana closely. Do you want to enter training as a Healer yourself?".

The girl blushed. "Not exactly. I want to be an Apothecary.", and Jalni stared at her, for of all the healing arts, this was the longest training and not half as exciting as Healing. She finished the elaborate braid and began making another finer braid, working into it Solana's clan beads and then as a finishing touch, put the Healers Source Beads on one thin wrist and her Song Beads on the other. Both girls rose, took the deep blue cloak and laid it gently over Solana, then they bowed silently to the still form and took themselves back into the Home Cave and made themselves rest in the stillness of mid afternoon.

Before Sunfall, Home Cave filled with waking children and Jalni was amused to see Marran draw his particular group aside in low voiced conversation. He was obviously giving instructions and still feeling an "outsider", Jalni sat on her bedroll and observed. Torvin seemed to act as Marran's second, she saw with interest and watched as the taller boy gathered a group of younglings together. All boys, they diligently packed away bedrolls, tidying them into one remote corner of the cavern and lined up holding small bundles under their arms. She watched in mild amusement as one older boy stepped forward, ran his eyes over his cave mates and stood in the position that Jalni knew as "at the ready", from the Inesh guards at Selesh. She had to hide a grin as Torvin came to inspect them and when he gravely insisted on looking at their hands and behind their ears, she engaged her magically augmented hearing to catch what was going on.

"Sandrigal patrol, stand easy.", Torvin said and the boys, standing so stiffly to attention as their elder approached, relaxed, adopting a much easier posture, as Torvin said gravely:

"Today, our Mother Solana goes to the Sands. She must not be shamed by grubby hands or faces, clothes or bodies. This day, we will bathe as she taught us, together and in the special pools beyond.".

He turned solemnly to the leader of the group and said gruffly. "Lead off Sandrigal's" and Jalni abruptly sobered as she saw the military precision with which the boys gathered themselves to bathe, touched by the determination of the children to honour the Healer who had loved them. She realised with approval that the entire complement of the cavern was being marshalled in the same way. Simbel, Lladro and the taciturn Rann, gathering the remainder of the boys and taking them through a narrow gap at the back of Home cave, Nimah, Asher and Rianna similarly gathering the girls, followed their counterparts example and Jalni suddenly realised that she was alone, apart from Terris and Marran, who stood in the cavern entrance, scanning the horizon protectively.

Daro's voice suddenly interrupted her thoughts.

"Jalni?", he sounded a little anxious, so she rose quietly and went to his side. He was sitting, swathed in a blanket which preserved his modesty, if not his dignity and she saw that he was more comfortable and had taken his tonic.

She spoke gently. "I am here.", and waited, at which his eyebrow twitched in an unconscious mimicry of his mothers facial habit. Jalni grinned, pleased to see that he was getting back to health again. He interrupted her thoughts, his voice saying quietly,

"Jalni, they need time to grieve before we take them back to Selesh.", His voice murmured in her ear and she flashed him a glance, saying reprovingly,

"Don't just talk "in silent mode" Daro. At the moment they are afraid of anything different and they are very aware. Terris incidentally knows that you are Ikella's son. She is very impressed!".

He considered this grimly, then said soft - voiced,

"They have been trained by some-one to be ultra- observant and obedient to orders.", He remarked, "Solana was a remarkable woman, that training will be the difference between life and death when they travel back to Selesh!".

He raised his head listening and Jalni heard his voice in her head saying swiftly:

"Marran comes, he has no feel for magic, but Terris may be a problem. Just follow my lead, we have to keep them together, not allow them to panic or run and I need to think about how I handle things so that none of them suspect the identity of the Sandsinger, before I can work a weave.".

Jalni nodded and said brightly,

"Oh, here is Marran and Terris, I hope we can bathe too?", and heard Marran say in an easy tone of voice.

"Terris, I didn't know who he is. Stop worrying, if he wanted us to know, he could have told us himself but he didn't, so I just treated him as one of us! So he's a Clansman? Stop fussing .".

"Quite right Marran.", The mage agreed and Terris laughed, "Men! They'll gang up together whatever the outcome. I'd leave them strictly alone if I were you.".

Marran said invitingly, "The ancient bathing pools are the reason for Solana deciding to move in here in the first place. Some have restorative properties and I think that Daro and I could do with a dip before sundown, so if you ladies will excuse us?".

He sketched a bow, then picking up a bundle that Jalni hadn't noticed he said curiously:

"Do you have any other clothes?", and Daro said smoothly, "Yes, I have my Clan colours with me. Tonight, I represent the Guardians for Solana's Rites, so these are entirely appropriate.".

Jalni suddenly thought,

"He makes it sound so likely, so probable and tonight these children will see the Sandsinger and not know who they see!", and Into her mind came the soft *othervoice.*

"If that is the will of the One.", he said and blithely allowed Marran to lead him to bathe and Jalni found that she was in no way jealous and went with Terris to prepare herself, glad that she had spare robes and a blue sash to identify with her Sand of origin.

Chapter 23 - On the Wings of the Wind

Jalni slid into Healer robes and brushed her damp hair. Taking a section at her left temple to create the elaborate braid of her calling, she rapidly plaited several fine sections together, feeling for the first time, a sense of identity and pride in her vocation. She stared into the ancient mirror plate, periodically estimating the lengthening braid, until she had two-thirds completed. At this point, she began adding embellishments, working a strip of blue tape (salvaged from an old tunic) into her hair, thus honouring her Sand of origin. Arranging the intricacies of the braid to show she had entered the final Rotation of training, she glanced at her reflection, wishing she had a pretty ribbon that would sufficiently honour Solana's memory and froze, staring in disbelief at the filmy star spangled strip that materialised.

"Impossible!", said her eyes. "Unbelievable!", said her heart and her mouth muttered crossly,

"Stop it Daro, you'll give yourself away!", before she smiled hugely, appreciating the Sandsinger's gesture, without resenting the fact that he still read her private thoughts.

The ribbon returned to tape as she touched it regretfully, but she was still smiling to herself as she stood in the entrance, letting the air dry her hair. A cinnamon scented breeze kissed her cheek and the ribbon re-appeared stealthily. Catching sight of it, she startled a passing child by exclaiming, "Defiance will get you nowhere young man!", in a parody of Ikella's manner, but answer came there none, so she returned to Home Cave, intent on recapturing some sense of normality.

Terris knelt with a gaggle of children, amassing a collection of their childhood treasures into a scarf. This outpouring of love contained brightly coloured pebbles, feathers and beads and impetuously Jalni added a bracelet of threads from her father's loom on to the pile, as Terris gathered the scarf and the children slipped away. As Jalni joined her, Terris beamed at the novice saying, "I told you the water would revive your skin. You look wonderful Jalni! Your robes, that ribbon, you honour Solana and our Sands. I wish I had the gift of it.", and hung her head tongue-tied. Jalni, belatedly realising she was the subject of hero worship, smiled as her stomach growled.

"What smells so wonderful?", she asked, remarking honestly, "Anyone who cooks is truly gifted.", and lifted a bowl suggestively. Terris, flushed with pride said dismissively, "Cooking's easy! That's only a blend of vegetable, grains, fungi and herbs. The children are fed, washed and resting, we can eat now or wait for those men.", and plunged a ladle into the fragrant stew.

Still mopping her bowl when Marran brought Daro back limping, Jalni saw that his sandal strap had finally parted. They sat at a table opposite Jalni's, while Marran made running repairs with a leather thong, muttering disparagingly, "Sandals aren't much use on rocky terrain anyway. You need a pair of boots.", and he grinned at Terris, who picked up bowls to serve them both. Daro stopped her gently saying,

"Not for me Terris. I can't eat now. I must prepare for Solana's Rites. Sunfall is upon us and there is no time, but I'll look forward to it later.". He stood, letting Marran refasten his sandal and was guided to his blanket and sat, hugging his knees as Marran draped a cloak around his shoulders. He retreated into the privacy afforded by the cowl and Jalni was sobered by the bleak expression on his face, as the shadows shut her out once more. However, as Marran cane towards her, the Sandsinger's voice murmured quite privately, "Oh Jalni, I always found that defiance could get me anything I wanted!".

Choking on her drink, she refused the invitation to reply, glaring at Daro's back instead.

Daro turned towards the lowering sun as he sank into trance. Marran studied him surreptitiously for a moment, then tiptoeing past the rapt mage, came to eat at the table. Jalni waited until the boy had cleared his bowl, then hissed at him.

"I am Daro's guide.", in a challenging voice. She stood, hands on hips, at which Marran cleared his throat cautiously: "I told him you'd object, but Daro wanted to give you some time on your own.". He gestured at the remote figure. "He doesn't want to be in the way of preparations either. Has anyone any idea where we should bury Solana?", he asked in a fairly obvious attempt to change the subject.

Jalni scowled, "You don't know the first thing about Healers do you?", she said scornfully, "Well! Understand this. I am Daro's Healer, guide and body servant. This is my duty, to which I am honour bound.". Her teeth were clenched with the effort to remain polite as she explained.

"You don't know his needs and I am trained to look after him. Unless I am indisposed then his care begins and ends with me.", she declared and Marran had the grace to blush as she said firmly, "He was entrusted to me at Selesh. I brought him to Solana and I will take him back home soon. You are Cavern Captain, I am Daro's Healer, don't try to do my job as well. Now let's have an end of it.", then, over her shoulder she remarked enigmatically, "We don't bury Healers, Marran. We send them forth on the Winds!", and his bewildered face was all the reward she needed, as she went to lay garlands around the bier.

As she neared the bed, Solana's cloak shimmered through every shade of blue, from sky to deep midnight, catching the last rays of light, as Seleus sank westward towards Sunfall. Her white hair threaded with tiny blossoms seemed to stir in a faint breeze. Jalni laid the blue and gold sash of the Senior Healer across the body for the last time, threading one end into Solana's right hand. As Guild witness, she passed to the end of the bed, standing head bowed, her own right hand caressing her Azure sash, subconsciously aware that she too, would one day go to the Winds like this and beside her, Terris wept.

The children watched solemnly until then, tiptoeing closer, to lay their treasures down, each determined to say goodbye in their own way. Jalni's eyes welled, tears spilling down her cheeks, so engrossed with the heart-rending farewells, that she was totally unaware that Marran had brought Daro to her, until with infinite tenderness he laid an elaborately plaited and embellished braid of dark hair on the bier and startled, she saw that he had cut his Clan braid, signifying his own grief and loss. His hand gripped her shoulder in mute sympathy and his voice was in her mind, saying simply, "To grieve for any mother is to grieve for your own.", and she leant against him for a moment thinking,

"How strange you are! I only just told myself that I shouldn't weep for a stranger, when I never wept for my own mother. How did you know?", but he was on Marran's arm and Solana's Rites had begun.

A hush fell over the cave as six older boys lifted the Healers bed, carrying it towards the cave mouth. Daro took Marran's arm, collecting Jalni with his free hand as they passed and together, they walked the Home Cave with Solana for the last time. The cavern swept and strewn with herbs seemed to sigh in Solana's wake. The empty fire pit hidden beneath a garlanded cover, the lights dimming along the path of the bier as it was processed. Muted sobs and little murmurs of farewell rustled in the dark as she passed, then the bearers went through the arch and out on to the front entrance and turned resolutely towards the Beacon Point.

Jalni felt a small hand clasp hers and looked down to see Lallee, head turned hopefully. She was perhaps only ten Summers old, plainly of Greshe extraction and Jalni smiled into her tear-stained face and remembered her own mother's death. She tucked the child's hand firmly under her arm and said gently.

"You should stay by me Lallee. Mother Solana would want you near while we send her home on the Winds.", and swinging her own cloak over Lallee's shaking shoulders, she found herself whispering to the devastated child:

"She feels no more pain. Her legs and back don't hurt her anymore. She was so tired Lallee, so very tired and now she sleeps in the arms of the One. She will never be cold, tired, or hungry again and she was loved to the very end. Death is not our enemy my dear. sometimes, death is a kind friend and Solana knew him well and was never afraid.".

The child clung to her mutely for a long moment, but left her in company with Solana's favourites and Jalni watched her go, absently picking up a cloak as she passed the bench on which it lay, before following the cortege up to the Beacon point overlooking Solana's home.

Marran led Daro to the very edge of the Upper Watch level, where the Beacon stood at the head of a stone plinth, they paused, conversing quietly as the bearers gentled Solana's bier on to the slab. Jalni looked at the fire basket towering over Daro. It stood ready, laid with kindling and her eyes swept the well maintained observation point with interest, noticing that glowstone containers were filled and three stone jars stood nearby, tanbark stoppers covered in metal paste, painted the colour appropriate to the warning. The substances they held changed the colour of the flame, red for attack, green for disease and blue to mark the passing of a Healer. In her minds eye, she saw the beacon burn blue, sending its sad message across vast tracts too inhospitable to travel at speed, then, a pale glow rose around the bier and her senses tingled as Daro turned from contemplation and raised a silencing hand.

The Sandsinger stood alone, his cloak fluttering palely against the blue desert floor and the deepening hues of the evening sky. As if on cue, a steady breeze keened across the Sands, wuthering along the Heights of Scartel and Jalni moved closer to Daro, but he seemed totally absorbed, as if he listened to some internal clock.

One hand raised slightly and the solemn faced bearers withdrew to join the throng and utter silence fell. Daro traced Solana's body, following the line of her shoulder to the hand that held her sash, before gently lifting the free end in his own right hand. Facing them, he asked in a voice rough with emotion, "Who will follow her? Who will learn her spells, who will be the Healer of Scartel when man lives here once more?", and there was a muted shuffling as bemused children looked at each other.

"What does he mean?", Jalni heard Terris whisper, "what should I say?", and the novice moved until she could touch Terris, but the girl was staring wide eyed at Daro, her attention riveted, as he repeated the call from beyond the grave.

"Who will follow, who will become the next Healer of Scartel?", then Terris seemed to come to a decision and stepped forward, head held high.

"I will follow Solana.", she said softly, "She always wanted me to, but I thought it too hard. I will try my best for Scartel and in the memory of her love.".

Jalni felt a lump in her throat as the girl's clear voice carried to the others.

"What must I do?", she asked and Daro reached out, fumbling as he clasped both her hands around the free end of the Healers sash. Jalni felt a tingling awareness and saw them silhouetted against the most brilliant Sunfall sky she could remember. Midnight blue graduating through smoke grey to surround the ball of Seleus with streamers of amber, gold, flame and sepia, the last lights glinting off the Healer's sash, then Terris bowed her head humbly.

as Daro placed one hand on her golden hair and the other on the Healers body. Turning his face to the setting sun, he raised his voice in prayer.

"Divine One, grant that as Seleus sets on the life of your servant Solana te Nazurian it will dawn over the path of a new Healer. Let the wings of the wind carry the mortal remains of Solana to the Source of all Souls in peace and tranquillity, for her path has been long in your service.".

Jalni was aware of the children bowing their heads solemnly all around her, as Daro said gently,

"Look up Children of Scartel, look up and lock this memory in your hearts forever!".

He paused, as if remembering another happier time himself and then said softly, "Welcome Gurayen.", as his cloak billowed and Solana's bier began to glow.

There was a low hum, a hint of gathering energy and the children looked up and gasped with amazement, for Solana's sash was glowing, in Terris's hands. Blue, gold, turquoise shot with sapphire stroked the girl's rapt face as Daro turned towards the dying sun. As the children stared in wonder, Solana's cloak lifted, the scent of cinnamon perfumed the air and the rocks hummed a chorus of deep tones. Jalni gazed at the young woman's face as the Healers sash flared into a band of incandescence. From the bier came a coruscation of colours, flowing towards the children, who lifted their hands into the sparkling stream of light. Gently borne to them on the departing breeze was a whispering sigh "Farewell.", and Solana was gone, her body dispersed to the nine Winds.

As Seleus sank below the horizon and the colours faded into the night-time sky, Jalni came to herself, just in time to catch Terris who simply collapsed weeping into her arms. She stood holding the sobbing girl, as Marran guided Daro towards them. The Cavern Captain handed Daro's arm onto Jalni's shoulder, then placed his own, (somewhat possessively) Jalni thought, around Terris, persuading her gently to join the children below. Carrying Solana's cloak, Terris leant against Marran asking tearfully, "Why me? Am I right? She picked me?", and unused to such a display of emotion, Jalni was relieved when Daro suggested Marran take her quietly to his blanket, where he would come and talk to her.

Marran was subdued but watchful, ready to leap to his feet the minute Daro moved a muscle and for once Jalni was grateful for that attention. She felt awed and humbled by the simple ceremony, but throughout had not been able to see what if anything, Daro had done to create the illusion. She had attended these solemn Rites during the last plague and in the hands of the Sorceress, knew magic when she saw it. She was deeply troubled at the thought that she had seen no difference in the ceremony tonight, except that she had not recognised power when she should have felt it. Could Daro be wielding a force far greater than any ever imagined, one that she couldn't discern? Sighing and retreating into her hide bound belief that no man could use magic, more in defiance than anything else, she suddenly recalled (with deep confusion), earlier conversations regarding defiance. Without thinking, she summoned hand-fire (to check her own abilities were not astray) and kindling a table mounted travelling trivet, made hot drinks for the company.

She was still sunk in such thoughts and didn't see precisely how it started, but suddenly a fight broke out and mayhem was spreading as she leapt to her feet and made for the source of the disturbance, followed by Marran, Daro and Terris. The boys facing up to each other, already bore injuries. One had a nasty gash over an eye and the other sported a bruise on the left cheek, but knuckles clenched and bloody, they were oblivious of the gathering audience.

The boy with the gash was shouting, "I won't stay. I won't stay for some old wizard to get me. My mother said only bad children got sent to the Sandsingers!".

The other child was panting, holding his side and saying very little. Panic was showing on several faces and it was obvious someone had to intervene. Marran and Quaryn came swiftly into the circle that had formed around the sparring partners, grabbing one boy apiece and forcing them to their knees with a move reminiscent of Jalni's humiliation at the hands of Jashell and Indeera. Swiftly grabbing her scrip, she saw Terris grab a washcloth, both girls bearing down grimly on the struggling combatants.

Terris got there first, picking the boy Quaryn held and demanding crossly, "What have you done to Brus Calar? We know you two can fight over anything, but what started this, tonight of all nights! We should be in harmony, remembering that none of us would be here but for Solana! She would be ashamed of you both.", as she spoke however, she was deftly applying pressure to the bleeding eyebrow and Calar subsided moodily into her hands.

Jalni, pulling up the jerkin on Brus, looked at a swelling on his ribs, she could feel the angry anxiety pouring from both boys and concentrated on generating a dampening field, humming softly to herself as she ran skilful diagnostic fingers over his chest.

"Never a good combination of moods, even in adults.", she thought, tracing an energy line to its source-point and stimulating it. Only then did she realise that Daro was squatting carefully nearby, determined to talk at the child's level.

"What was that all about Brus?", he asked mildly, "You shouldn't be fighting tonight. We should be together, talking and remembering Solana and preparing for tomorrow.". The boy shrugged and Jalni felt the sickening pain as he blenched, trembling as Daro took his hands, but before the mage could speak, Calar interrupted.

"That's exactly what's wrong.", he shouted furiously ready to fight, ducking away from Terris and advancing on Daro, hands clenched.

"You can't help us, you're blind! How are you going to fight a Sandsinger and why did Solana send for him anyway? I hate her!", and shocked silence filled the cave with apprehension, as Daro began to see that somehow he had to hold them together until he could break the news, that the Sandsinger they all feared was already in their midst.

Chapter 24 - Laced with Magic

The night crept in slowly. Lamps were lit and soon the handful of babies lay drowsing under watchful eyes. Daro absently fielded one small crawler, playing with her till, draped across his lap, she slept as he held court. The older boys surrounded him, listening to his adventures in other Sands, while Terris visited each small "patrol" of weary children and Marran went about some duty out of the cave. Jalni however, was quivering with apprehension, some indefinable sense "prickling" at the nape of her neck.

She drew apart, curious about the small trickle of children gathering in one corner and decided to investigate. Following them, ostensibly to fetch water from the spring, she quickly recognised the air of suppressed excitement amongst the youngsters. Patrol captains and their seconds were filling water flasks, while several backpacks lay suspiciously close to a curtained wall. Keeping her face expressionless, she queued for water, noting the swift concealment of a bed-roll amongst the shuffling crowd, thinking to herself that it was becoming obvious that they planned to hide in the caves that riddled the Heights of Scartel. Filling their own flask to the brim, she made an unhurried exit, but sent an anxious thought winging to Daro immediately.

"Something's in the air!", she "thought" at him and leaving their flask by her own backpack she crossed the cave, heading directly for the Sandsinger's blanket. Marran's group, with Brus and Calar hovering, had left Daro, and noting Marran vigorously shaking his head (a look of near adult disapproval on his face), she knelt by Daro, catching his hands in hers. Directing his attention as Marran's group grew vociferous in disagreement with their young leader, Jalni spoke swiftly, as the Sandsinger raised his head in enquiry.

"Daro, we have to do something.", she announced quietly. "We're going to lose half of them in the caverns above and beyond here. They are dangerous, according to Solana. Surely her weaves will dissipate now? They are so vulnerable."

She was so intent on engaging Daro's interest, that she didn't hear the quick light step behind her, but Daro did, silencing her with a flicker of his hands, as she released them.

"Solana's weave will hold until the Sandsinger comes. She promised us that.", said Marran firmly and with Calar and Brus bringing up the rear sulkily, he came to a halt with a stamp of his foot, standing braced at the "alert" as he faced Daro. Jalni was amused to see Daro's sketchy salute to the young man, but turned her head to hide her smile as Marran greeted him.

"Lord Daro.", Marran requested formally. "May I ask your Healer to look at these two again?", Daro, accepting that the children now saw him as their leader, sighed, then nodded, saying swiftly:

"Call me Daro, Marran. At the moment I am lord of the broken sandal, or lord of the worn old blanket. I am out of my Sands and my mother would box my ears if I was to "Lord" it over anyone. We are all in the same basket here, just young people trying to get back home safely.".

"I might be able to replace that sandal later then Daro.", Marran offered as he squatted near Jalni, holding his hand out to her, where she saw that he had a bruise forming on his knuckles.

Out of the scrip slung round her waist, the Healer took a small salve pot and rubbed staunch root cream onto the affected area, intending to draw the bruise out. She was humming a low note under her breath as she "worked the Source", feeling for the edges of the contusion, softening the surrounding tissues as her thumbs rolled over the injury.

Daro tipped his head quizzically,

"What happened?", he asked and Calar shuffled forward a little, looking embarrassed, nevertheless he faced Daro truthfully.

"It was probably my fault.", he admitted. "I went up to the next level, to see if I could find a way round the binding.",

His voice was exceedingly small and Jalni noticing that he held himself very stiffly, simply altered the pitch of her voice and fixed Calar with a diagnostic stare.

"He guards his right side and that shoulder is very painful.", she thought to herself and Daro nodded, as Calar looked at the adults, shamefaced. The boy went on.

"I was running because I thought that I had passed through the barrier.", he paused awkwardly,

"Go on.", Daro instructed, reaching for the child's arm, running his hands over Calar's shoulder, feeling him flinch.

"You've taken quite a knock.", he said conversationally and Jalni grinned as Calar squirmed under Daro's probing fingers, but her smile faded as she sensed Calar's arm being warmed, soothed. She grimly followed the Healing flow, swelling reduced, tissues reforming, ligaments eased as she felt the Source flush the child's arm and realised what was happening.

"Deo! The man's entirely unaware that he's healing him!", the thought nearly sprang into speech she was so dumbfounded.

"No effort, no loss of concentration, no herbs, no preparation, no Voice.".

She stared at Calar and Daro smiled, relaxing his hands and saying gently:

"Is that better Calar? You must have run into that warding full tilt!".

"It was nothing, honestly" the boy demurred, stretching his hand and circulating his arm at Daro's instigation. He winced at one point and Daro passed his hands down the boys injured side. Jalni saw that the Sandsinger was not even touching the child, but was obviously effecting relief all the same. Calar leant trustingly against Daro, smiling.

"Is that better?". The blind man lifted his head towards the child, not bothering to obscure his face for a change, easier in his manner with children, Jalni thought, happier in their uncomplicated company, than with the schemes and plans of the adult world. The boy replied slowly,

"Yes, thank you.", the child was instinctively polite, but his next question was devastatingly insightful.

"How did you do that? Are you a Healer?".

Jalni held her breath.

"What was Daro going to say?", she thought frantically, but he just smiled mysteriously,

and said,

"Not exactly, but I am good at massage and fixing tangled ribs. I always used to have them and it's a handy trick to know.".

"Did I have tangled ribs?", Calar was round eyed, but keen to impress the company, with his fortitude.

"It didn't hurt much.", he announced and Jalni, who had seen the white line of pain touch his mouth and the shadows grow under his eyes, sang a thread of pain relief into the boys arm and gently touched his shoulder to make sure of the Healing.

Brus joining them said cheerfully, "So why did you pass out then?", and Marran cuffed him lightly on the ear and said,

"If he hit the barrier half as hard as I did, he can't call it nothing.".

Marran showed his other hand to Jalni, who noted the scuffs and grazes which she dabbed with salve, telling him briskly to rub it in, before Daro asked curiously:

"What is on the next level Marran?",

The young man screwed up his face, answering slowly:

"Well,", he said thoughtfully. "There are quite a lot of small rooms with doors. Some are open, others are locked and there are signs that roof falls and some floor collapse has taken place. The rooms are carved out of the soft rock, along a tunnel. My father said that in the Dark Days, this was a fire mountain. Fire, stones and melted rock flowed through here like an underground river. Some say, that is what made most of the caves, but others say that the Sandsingers lived here and they made the caves. It is too long ago to know which story is true.", he shrugged and grinned.

Daro nodded, "I've heard of Fire Mountains.", he paused thoughtfully asking:

"Are there any rooms we could use Marran?".

The boy creased his brow and said doubtfully:

"I don't think so. Solana told us that although many people lived here before us, they mainly lived in a city, built in the crater. My Grandfather was a Ranger on the northern border and he said that Scartel was old before his time and had many secrets to show those who had the eyes to see!". He coughed apologetically, but Daro ignored the awkward pause and said mildly:

"Rangers? Aren't they the walkers of the Sands? Those who know the trails, the animals, the natural foods and all the habitats of man?".

He spoke respectfully and Marran responded with pride. "Yes Lord Daro, we are one of the few Sands that still have Rangers and I was to train with my

Grandfathers company and join them after my seventeenth Rotation.", sudden grief flooded his face and choking back the tears that threatened to unman him, he said hoarsely, squaring his shoulders as if facing a fact for the first time.

"All that future has gone now. I cannot enter the service without a sponsor. My place was secured by my Grandfather's name, but all Rangers have to secure sponsorship from settlement, Clan or Guild and I lost that with my father's death.".

There was a taut silence, as Daro and Jalni began to realise that most of these children had not only lost their parents but futures settled on, apprenticeships agreed and the bright promise of the continuance of Scartel itself, for once razed to the ground as it must be, only the caverns would remain to tell that anyone had ever lived here.

Daro considered the options carefully.

"Marran is well versed in the past of these caverns.", He thought, "Perhaps the compulsion to come here is for a reason beyond my understanding.", and was rewarded by a faint perfume, which left him thinking grimly.

"Feydora!", but could make no sense of his belief in that lingering presence. Marran was telling Jalni something interesting and with difficulty Daro brought himself back out of his reverie and heard him saying cheerfully:

"Oh, yes, people used these caves once and there are still useful things to find here, but it is very dangerous now and I ask you not to wander without guides.",

He sounded embarrassed, but Daro said swiftly:

"It is the same at Selesh, which is much bigger and harder to control. Do you run the cave as the Rangers run their companies?", and Marran nodded agreement.

"Just after my parents died, we came here, but Solana was already very frail. When she sent Orto for help, she couldn't manage alone, so I told her that I knew a game that all the children would play. I made up my own patrol and they all wanted to join in. When she saw how it worked, Solana made me Cavern Captain and I selected the most responsible ones as patrol leaders.".

Daro dipped his head in what Jalni perceived as a nod of respect and murmured,

"With both you and Terris as her elected seniors? Am I not right?", and Marran relaxed. They talked a little about the ancient rooms, Marran declaring,

"It is strange, but nothing seems to decay here. Perhaps the caves are so dry that things last. Solana's chair came from the third level. We might even find you some sandals or a set of desert boots if we search!",

He grinned wryly at Jalni, who looked at Daro's bare feet, then at his damaged sandals hopefully, for they certainly wouldn't be leaving here anytime soon unless they replaced the originals. Marran hurried on.

"Anyway, here is my idea. I think I know where the barrier runs now. All the children want to go up to Lookout Cave.", he blushed and looked at his hands, not meeting the eyes of the others as he explained.

"When we lost our parents, many of us just wanted to be alone and cry. We found a cave high up on the inside of the Heights, overlooking the crater.", Catching the look of puzzlement on Daro's face he continued, "Half of it is open to the sky and from there, you can see Gateway, the village below and all the stars at night. Solana used to come and sit with us. She told us that the stars were our parents eyes, watching over us.".

The tall boy, in his homespun Ranger garb, ducked his head, looking ashamed of this fancy, but Daro nodded, comfortable with this concept, so Marran continued, gruffly.

"When we got tired, she warded the lookout wall and we just took our blankets and slept there. Orto made sleeping benches, another fire pit and a room for Solana. I took extra blankets up there. We have food, fuel and supplies also, so that if marauders came, we would be able to defend ourselves, or hide. It would take someone who knew the Heights to find the way in.",

He paused.

"The children want to go up there tonight. They want to see if Solana's eyes are watching over us too and we would all feel safer if we didn't have to meet this Sandsinger on his terms. After all, we don't know why he is coming, or what he is going to do with us. We may not wish to be split up, or sent to Selesh anyway!",

This last comment was spoken in half defensive, half defiant voice and Jalni looked at Daro, but his head was lowered and she couldn't help wondering what he was planning.

Daro was occupied in quietly probing the thoughts of the nearest children. Feeling quite drained by recent experiences, he reached for those in the immediate vicinity, surprised as he discovered that all seemed to be of one mind. Struck by the solidarity of their conviction he lost track of the conversation raging around him and was only brought back to reality by the baby, stirring restlessly in his lap.

Marran looked at Jalni, as though searching for the right words.

"What about you two?", he asked, while closely examining his boots, (clearly not wishing to meet her eyes). He continued rather uncertainly.

"You are very welcome to join us, but I think you might want to remain here. The climb up to the Lookout isn't for the faint-hearted and you two are still tired, not yet recovered from your journey. I don't want to leave you here, but it isn't going to be easy or safe for Daro.",

Daro, who was shifting the sleeping baby, bridled immediately and Jalni found the breath stilled in her throat, at the momentary spark of irritation that lit Daro's eyes, but thankfully the mage controlled his temper.

"I can assure you that the only part of me that doesn't work is my sight.", He said mildly enough, but Jalni caught the edginess behind the words and so did Marran, who grinned as he said gently,

"I meant no unkindness Daro, but you can't judge heights anymore and some of the path takes us in places where you might hit your head on the roof.

There are parts where we need to wriggle through narrow gaps as well. I told you that it would take someone who knew the Heights to find the Lookout !".

Daro received this information in silence, but Jalni groaned internally. At the first pitfall, it looked to her as if their enterprise would be going nowhere. She had underestimated Daro's difficulties and only now realised why she had been sent to assist him. She quietly reached out and took the blind man's hand, sending through a physically re-enforced link.

"Where you go, so go I. It is for you to decide, I will help you all the way."

She felt the Sandsinger quiver with suppressed laughter and closed her eyes as he reminded her of her "devotion to duty", with an image, half hazarded, of a backpack tumbling down a precipitous track. She scowled and he let her see his frustration tinged with sadness.

She got to her feet, towering over Marran.

"Where I go, Daro goes with me, I have taken an oath to protect him and he is your guest also, so if you go up to the Heights, we both go with you."

Marran stood abruptly.

"Then, lets be practical.", he frowned. "I just remembered Solana saying something about boots. Daro can't go anywhere until we settle that problem, so while Terris sorts the children, packs the bread and you get your own kit packed, I'll go looking.".

Jalni, gathered their meagre packs together, returning to Daro's side as Terris and Lallee approached him to take the sleeping baby up in a travelling pouch. He was apparently thinking, his head drooping over the Jhirelle child, as if listening intently to something. His closed eyelids revealed a sweep of thick eyelashes that most women would kill for. She watched Terris bend over him, saw his smile as he lifted the baby up to Terris. The other girl straightened rocking the baby over one shoulder. Then she said something to Lallee, who skipped away towards the storeroom. Jalni hefted their packs and returning to reclaim Daro's blanket, raised an eyebrow in mute enquiry and Terris laughed explaining:

"I just sent Lallee to remind Marran about a pair of boots that Solana hid in the spice store.", She grinned at Jalni's sceptical expression, saying cheerfully,

"No silly, they didn't smell that bad, its just that Solana raided rooms for special items and she found some containers that she said had preservative qualities. Orto brought loads of them down and Solana packed them with food and her medications. One of these had a pair of boots in, so she kept them in the barrel, saying that she didn't need them yet.".

She slipped the baby into a carrying pouch and handed her to a passing girl as she spoke and stood with Jalni, shaking out the last blanket and rolling it, as Marran and Lallee returned, rolling a medium sized barrel between them. Jalni smiled as they turned the barrel over at Daro's feet.

"Is that what you remembered?", Marran asked Terris. "I can't get the lid off the snarrelled thing.", he complained. "I think that it is cross screwed, or I could have just brought the boots out.", and the two girls pounced on the challenge, with cries of "Let us try.", at which Marran retreated, seating himself on the floor beside Daro, grinning at Terris, who poked her tongue out at him.

Jalni touched the stout wooden barrel. Despite its ordinary appearance, she could feel a tingling under her hand, as if the barrel were ensorcelled. She grasped the black iron band running round the rim with one hand and the clasp on the lid with the other and twisted, but if anything, the tingle became a positive vibration. With a gasp of frustration, she was forced to give up the attempt.

Terris tried next. Her eyes widened as she too, felt the strange tingle, but she said nothing, other than to complain that she had hurt her wrist.

Jalni was examining her, when Daro reached out his hands to Marran, who guided them on to the barrels lid, with the cheerful comment, "We'll need to smash that, it won't come off in a million Rotations! Its that properly wedged!", as Daro applied his hands to either side of the barrels lid. They didn't see precisely what he did, but suddenly it made a sharp "clicking" sound and like a cork, the lid popped open.

"You must have loosened it Terris.", he murmured and the two girls leaned forward to see what lay inside.

Neatly wrapped in a piece of linen, was a pair of desert boots. Made in soft leather. Tooled patterns worked around the tops, attracted Daro's sensitive fingers and he smiled, hearing in memory a soft voice saying,

"I couldn't find the boots, but no matter, they will come later.", and he sighed with pleasure.

"They are a fine pair of boots.", Marran was eager to look at them and Daro smiling handed them over to the boy, who said to Jalni in a slightly puzzled voice,

"Look at all the patterns Jalni.", He lifted them for the Healer to see and she thought with a shiver,

"They remind me of Daro's belt.", which she had no doubt that the enigmatic Sandsinger heard. Declining to react, he ran his sensitive fingertips along the tooling and declared:

"This is Opal work. I recognise the design and they seem to be in fine condition, I hope they fit!".

The two girls leapt to Daro's rescue and amid many giggles and much tugging and pulling the boots were eventually in place on Daro's feet.

Jalni sighed internally, as the Sandsinger paraded before the admiring group of boys. She didn't really understand anything anymore she decided, resigned to her fate. There was definitely "something in the air", something which she was only just awakening to and wondered if she had imagined the size of Daro's new boots altering to fit his feet, recalling the subtle shift as she finally slid them home. She watched his confident laughing face turn to the boys and felt a touch of the familiar old resentment return.

"There he is, suited, booted and ready to enslave another group to his will!", she thought grumpily and his Colours shimmered and flared in silent acknowledgement of her accusation, a muted aura forming around him , fading even as she caught it out of the corner of her eye.

There he stood between Jalni and Marran, a group of children before and after him, excited voices raised as they headed to the rear of Home Cave and the secret passage to the Lookout Cavern and only Jalni knew that they were taking with them the person they feared most.

PART 3 - SCHOOL FOR SANDSINGERS

Chapter 25 - Sandsinger Revealed

Jalni, while not underestimating the difficulties of the transfer to the Lookout Cave, found that even her vivid imagination had not prepared her for the actuality. She watched jealously as Marran, overriding all protestations, undertook to help the blind man negotiate the twists, turns and variable roof height of the ancient passageway, which, as she had suspected, started behind the curtained wall near the spring. Walking in patrol groups, the exodus was orderly, mid-teens placing themselves at intervals between the "smalls", led by Lladro and Torvin, carrying torches. Every child carried their own backpacks and hand lights. Terris, carried a pitcher filled with glowstone embers to start a fire and looking down the line, Jalni could see the evidence of careful preparation. She was to walk just ahead of Lallee, who acting as a runner, would constantly change position in the queue, which, far from reassuring Jalni, left her nerves quivering as they entered the narrow passageway. The small lights bounced and flickered, casting long dancing shadows ahead and behind them, then, Home Cave stood abandoned to the winds once more.

In the depths of the passage, the blue -black basalt was flecked with colour, revealing rare and precious mineral deposits, but with night falling fast, there was no time to pause and study them. Almost as that thought crossed her mind, the upward gradient of the passage increased and the roof descended. Behind her she could hear Marran's voice, a constant rumble of encouragement, interspersed with Daro's curses as he stumbled. She frowned, the claustrophobia she had felt in the depths of Selesh, seeped into her bones and she paused, sensing danger. Lallee touched her shoulder and whispered quietly.

"I don't like this bit Jalni. It is very dark and my light doesn't seem to work properly here. Can I hold your hand?".

Jalni held the child's hand firmly, as they entered this dark field. There was a faint musty odour, against which she took a deep breath. Battling the inexplicable feeling of oppression, she emerged abruptly where the passage ended at another curtain, beyond which the others gathered as the passage levelled out into a richly decorated chamber.

Jalni stared around her, realising that there were openings to her left and right. Intrigued, she raised the glowstone lamp she carried and peered into the shadows beyond. She stood in what seemed to be an ante-chamber, furnished with one or two chairs, a wall hanging, over properly cut flagstone flooring. There were bare patches, revealing where other hangings had been and dimly visible, through the gap in the wall to her left, were other entrances, old and tantalising places to explore. The party behind her came through the curtain, Marran half supporting Daro, who slumped on to a seat, ruefully rubbing his back. Jalni moved towards him, one hand on her scrip, but he was surrounded by young men keen to tell him about previous explorations of this level, so she went to look at the most inviting view, through an open entrance to her left.

Across a dark gap, a richly embellished door stood ajar, beckoning her and the temptation was too much.

"While that lot chatter, I could get there and back.", she thought and turning her back on Daro's small "court", she stepped forward, through the entrance and the ground under her feet lurched.

Marran exploded into action behind her. Only just in time to catch her as she stumbled, he flung her back with an exasperated shout, from where she had been teetering on the brink of a yawning chasm. She gulped, clinging on to his strong, brotherly arm gratefully as he drew her back from the shadowy entranceway, then, she turned abruptly, staring down into the depths below.

"What in the Nine Sands is that place?", she peered over the edge of the fall. Below her was a fathomless void into which small trickles of rubble continued to slide and Marran explained.

"We don't know exactly, we think it lies beyond the Bathing pools and probably on a lower level. Solana thought that it could be an underground river. You can hear water running, but because the passage has fallen through in places, we've never been able to get into those rooms.".

Marran's grip tightened, as he propelled her away from the chasm and she followed him, reluctance in every pace she took, her attention riveted on the mysteries beyond.

"We don't have time for that Jalni.", Daro said mildly as they returned to where he was sitting and Jalni blushed as she resumed her place in the orderly queue that wound up through the Heights of Scartel. Somehow, she found herself just behind Marran and Daro and had to bear the attentions of Brus and Calar as they jogged backwards and forwards encouraging and exhorting their visitors.

She heard Daro curse fluently as his head hit an overhang and she was alarmed in the next heart-beat, when the cursing stopped and he cried out involuntarily.

"What's happened Brus?", she demanded anxiously and Calar called back.

"Daro just banged his shin on a rock.", came the airy reply, which was spoilt by Brus adding, sotto voce, "The pain of which was not improved by him deciding to kick the rock with his other foot!".

The child's merry eyes met Jalni's and they stood together, struggling not to giggle as the party ahead moved on.

"Advance!", the stentorian bellow from Marran eventually galvanised the Healer and her escort into action and again the corridor climbed. with relief Jalni saw a glimmering of light ahead, climbed three stone steps and found herself in a grand ante-chamber thronged with children. Here a wall sconce held a flaming torch aloft and she looked around her at numerous passageways off this hall and listened to Marran, who, with deliberation, drew the company assembled to order, by sticking his fingers into his mouth and whistling shrilly.

"Cavern Heights to order.", he commanded and Jalni was touched as all the children glanced around and then fell into their patrol groups. Marran began a simple roll-call.

"Nestlings?", he asked and Marl, a pretty pre-teen looked along the line of elders carrying sleep-slings. She counted swiftly and replied, "All present.", followed by groups named as "Stars", (all girls of about eight Rotations), "Chaffrills", (their maile counterparts), right up to the half - dozen young men named as "Nightlingbys", by their suddenly self-conscious Captain. However, Daro who had stood quietly while this check took place, said seriously.

"Marran, I can only find one fault with that process and that is very simply addressed. Healer Jalni will show Terris how to make a note of all your patrols. You should call them to order before a journey and check them regularly. You didn't include yourself or Terris, or your visitors, which you could do easily, by associating them with one of the existing groups. I could be a Nightlingby, what would the girls like to be?", and almost simultaneously Jalni and Terris, thinking of the tiny trefoil leaved vetali plant, symbol of the Azure Sands said, "Vetali?", and so they were, attracting jealous glances from Nimah, Marl and Motri, girls of the same age, who were heard to mutter, "Why didn't we think of that?", as they turned and ducked through an oddly shaped doorway and disappeared into the Lookout Cave.

Jalni hung back for some reason that she couldn't immediately fathom, but once Marran had instructed Daro to "Step down carefully.", she accepted the friendly hand held out to her and turned to face the most amazing sight of her life. The drop into the Lookout was fairly deep, almost twice the depth of a normal step-down, but as she discovered this formed a natural barrier, beyond which the smallest children couldn't explore, she understood the wisdom of that provision. Beyond the step, the cavern floor sloped naturally to a level area, where the basalt blossomed into paler shades of blue and then she realised that incredibly, she was looking at the night sky, where stars were just beginning to appear.

"Oh my!", she exclaimed to the obvious delight of Marran, who took her hand and led her forward, right to the edge of the rift that gave them a bird's eye view of the great crater of Scartel. She drew back nervously, but Marran laughed and said comfortably.

"This whole side of the cavern is warded. Some of them think that Solana placed that warding here, but she told me, that it was ever the same. Even in her childhood this has been a place of retreat and my Grandfather certainly knew of it also. If you look out across the crater, you can see Gateway. That is where the rim of the crater is all that is left and from here, it forms a natural entrance which we can watch, so that we will be safe from slavers, marauders and Sandsingers alike.".

Jalni's heart lurched as he spoke in simple sincerity and she felt shame flood through her.

"He trusted me and I have brought their enemy into their midst.", she thought painfully and stricken, she stared across the cavern, to where Daro, laughing, lifted children onto cunning sleeping shelves, cut into the walls and lined with wooden retainers for their bedding. He patted a passing head here and there, happily chatting as the little ones snuggled down to sleep and reassured she turned back to see Marran spreading her own blanket out, next to his.

She sat, keeping an eye on Daro and the other teens, who happily assisted Terris in transferring the glowstone embers into a ready laid fire-pit. Children neatly arranged themselves into patrols and Marran wandered checking on all of them. She felt, for the first time in her life, that she had found a place in which she belonged and stared around her, marvelling at the immense proportions of the cavern. There was no hint of cold, she decided that possibly the ancient warding kept the weather and the chill of night at bay. The walls here were faintly luminescent, permitting natural night vision some kind of extension and she thought sleepily, it was as if the cavern welcomed them and wonderingly saw the wall nearest her flush, (As if with pleasure). her half dreaming mind mumbled, as outside, the wind sighed, "Sssh," and Jalni felt a gentle touch on her arm.

She turned her head slowly, to find Daro sitting at her side. His voice effortlessly penetrated her mind, his words shattering her mood of peaceful introspection.

"It is time!", said the Opal Sandsinger, "Time for the Sandsinger to stand revealed.", and half fascinated, half terrified, Jalni nodded her agreement, for the children were all relaxed, happy in their surroundings and if ever there was a moment, in which none of them could take fright and run, it was now. She stared at him mesmerised and from the shadows, he continued,

"You know that I must tell them who I am.", he murmured, lower still, his voice redolent with pain, "What I am.", He paused, "Even you, Jalni, even you, know but are as yet unaware of my real power. When you see the Opal on me, you may be afraid of me, but you should know that the man I am, is also the Sandsinger I must become. What I care about, who I care about doesn't change with the power.".

His voice usually so melodic, roughened with emotion.

"You came back to me of your own free will, but before I take the next step on this journey, I need to know that you won't leave me again. From now on, all these innocents will depend on that.".

Jalni was shaken to the core.

"He's afraid.", she thought, aware that part of her glowed with the knowledge that at long last she had become indispensable to someone, that she, Jalni was wanted.

He was waiting for her reply, his anxiety sharply defined by the very stillness of his posture. She took both his hands in hers, "Daro, I won't leave you.", she said simply and with no magic involved felt the weight of his relief. It flooded through him, transforming him utterly. His head lifted as if to some summons, she caught the gleam of teeth as he smiled at her and her senses swam as she became aware of his masculinity. Her hand was still caught in his, as the electricity between them flowed, tingling from fingertips, to quivering breasts. Her face flooded hotly with a sweet pulsation and she felt her breathing change, from restive to rapid, following the odd syncopation of her heart. She had no idea of time passing. Was it ten seconds or ten hours later that Marran coughed discreetly and she came to herself again, realising that a fire was lit, children were chattering quietly, pointing out their family stars to each other and Terris had made sweet drinks for all.

The tall would be Ranger smiled at their confusion and somehow she stopped her face crumpling into her usual scowl and greeted him with composure as he teased.

"Sorry to interrupt you two.", Marran remarked innocently, a wicked grin on his face. "But, you

mentioned a bedtime story and some of the young ones will be asleep before you get a chance to tell it.".

He addressed himself to Daro, "Are you still up to it?".

"Oh yes.". Daro smiled at him and pressing Jalni's hands gently, he let go of her and rose to face the waiting children.

Marran sat down beside Jalni, who watched Daro make his way to the centre of the cavern, guided only by the encouraging comments of his audience, to a position where, framed against the night sky, he could be clearly seen and heard by all.

Marran huddled back to the wall, his knees pressed against his chest, blanket draped round his shoulders. Jalni pulled her own blanket round her firmly and while the last child was chased into bed and everyone settled to hear the storyteller, she thought about her strange conversation with Daro.

"What had he meant by her knowing, but not understanding his power?",

She considered his comment and for one brief moment she was reminded of the sensations she had felt when he first touched her, on his return to Selesh. She remembered the assertion that the Sandsinger had been responsible for the return of the sun and instantly dismissed the idea, as being too fanciful for words, but part of her wondered and another trembled. Whether that was fear, or something else she couldn't tell, nor did she intend to find out at that time. She therefore ignored Marran's bright knowing stare and watched as the Sandsinger stood for a moment tall, still and remote, until the little noises associated with the settling of tired limbs and fretful minds ceased and an expectant silence filled the Lookout.

All eyes were on the palely glowing figure, clad in the Colours of the Opal Desert, he stood, ready to begin , Jalni listened intently, aware that something was about to happen, she could feel Power building, building. The fire glowed warmly and lit the whole of the arena in which Daro stood, in that moment he moved and suddenly she understood, as if seeing him properly for the first time.

He had thrown off his cloak and stood clad in his simple desert garb, which changed under her gaze into the brilliant cloth of Colour. At his waist the ornate Opal wear belt blazed, where an immense Opal clasp held it in place. On his feet the boots shone and now she could see how they matched the weave of his garments and then the magic took him. A brilliant aura shot with flecks of turquoise and gold fire danced around him and into an awed silence, Daro threw back his head and Sang.

The children were enthralled, the teens transfixed, as was Marran beside her. She stole a glance around the company and saw that they were watching colours flickering from the rock walls and Daro himself, entranced, as a gentle melody was coaxed from the basalt rocks of Scartel. She saw a child relax back into her seat and wondering vaguely what Daro had done to them, she felt a pair of loving arms slide around her. Tears sprang to her eyes, as she recognised the feel of her fathers arms and the gossamer touch of her mothers hand on hers. Awash with emotion, she relaxed back, safe, protected and listened to her Sandsinger's story.

It began, as though she dreamt, of a world, filled with the sounds of life. Images filled her mind and like the children she gazed enraptured by the sight of green fields, abundant crops and so many people that her brain rebelled. Great areas of silvery sparkling water washed up against familiar coloured Sand and as these images dwindled and the night sky filtered into her consciousness, she saw recognisable star formations, felt the thrum of a world's energies and realised that she was looking not at a strange new world, but at the past of her own beloved planet. She gazed in awed silence as the visions changed to familiar places, to this very cavern and she watched incuriously as a man appeared, pottering about, peering at plans, then approaching a centrally positioned fire-pit and bending to operate the bellows attached to some forge. She watched the tale unfold as long-dead children tiptoed into the room, climbed onto sleeping shelves and snuggled down to listen as the other, also robed in Opal wear let the magic take him, lifting his head to Sing. Jalni felt the gaze of that other sweep across her, tracking away and then returning, lingering on her face until she lifted fearful eyes to meet the opalescent fire and in that moment felt herself transfixed, held motionless, drowning in the magically enhanced othergaze of a sighted Sandsinger and mercifully fainted clean away.

When she roused herself however, Daro was still in Song and she allowed the images of strange animals, singing flyby's and great sailed objects floating on water to flow through her mind. She watched another story unfolding now, of a girl with a powerful Healing voice, a girl who matured to womanhood in front of them. She felt the power in the hands of the Healer and the love of many children, including a tiny baby rescued from the most terrible of storms, it was then that she saw Solana's face and there was a collective sigh from the grieving children, as Daro held out a hand to catch two bright teardrops as the woman aged and faded.

The Sandsinger held Solana's tears reverently, showing the tiny reflective points of light in his hands, until they grew, filling the cavern with an unearthly light. He gently raised them, blew a visibly opalescent breath across them, sending them spinning and pulsing up into the night sky, to hang above the crater. Twin stars to represent Solana's eyes watching over her children. As one, they sent a collective sigh of satisfaction after them and Daro still sang, now of the world he wanted Solana's Children to live in and they dreamed and drifted with the magical cadences, until Jalni became aware that Daro was gently withdrawing the power, backing it down from a roaring torrent to a trickle, allowing the children to slip from their thrall into natural sleep and those who could, waken to the knowledge that their Sandsinger was amongst them and would protect them against any harm, even at the cost of his own life. In the great cavern, an awed silence fell.

Eventually, Marran took a long shuddering breath and turned a tear stained face to Jalni, smiling ruefully, but he spoke without rancour.

"Jalni?", He said tentatively, "Jalni..." His voice shook as he finally found the words to frame a question. "Daro. He's not a priest, or some new fangled Healer either! He's a Sandsinger, isn't he?", and rendered speechless with emotion, the Healer bowed her head in silent assent.

Chapter 26 - The Sentinel Appears

Jalni responded with infinite care, anxious not to alienate her new friends..

"Yes.", she confirmed, "Daro, (Ichspeller Selunsanni), is the Opal Sandsinger and the most powerful mage in all Pelshar.", and thought wildly, "A ninenight ago, I'd have laughed myself sick. Whatever's happening to me?", and found herself apologising.

"I'm sorry Marran. I couldn't tell you. Daro had to tell you himself.", but incredibly Marran was smiling, though the tears were still wet on his face as he confided shyly:

"It was wonderful! I felt my Grandfather hug me, heard his voice again and that was a gift beyond price. How did Daro know I never got the chance to say goodbye?".

She didn't know, but found herself saying softly,

"The same way he knew that we all needed to feel a loved ones arms around us again. I hope he enjoyed the same experience!".

The boy's gaze tracked to the Sandsinger, who stood wavering, under the anxious scrutiny of Terris. At his cautionary "Uh-oh", Jalni, rose abruptly, grabbed her scrip and reached his side in a few strides and Terris, relieved by her appearance, relinquished him to more knowledgeable hands. Jalni knelt at Daro's feet and found him shaking. Focussing sharply on his face, she saw the sheen of sweat on his brow and instinctively raised a hand to his throat, checking his energies, sensible of the fact that she dare not engage the Source this close to an empowered mage.

She frowned, concentrating on bringing erratically racing wrist pulses into balance, reviewing his symptoms automatically and thought, "With the Opal upon him, I doubt there is any power to equal his. Why does he collapse when it fades?", but before this inner consultation could continue, his voice whispered urgently, "Jalni, I'm going to be sick!".

He could hardly stand when Marran slid an arm under his and half carried, half led the faltering Sandsinger through a doorway at the rear of the cavern. Surprised, Jalni followed, into a room which she had passed, oblivious of its existence.

The door overlaid with basalt-blue stained leather, opened silently, the atmosphere (redolent of age) welcomed them, as the tall Ranger swung Daro onto a high bed and grabbed a bowl from a stand.

Jalni needed all her Healing skills to combat the racking nausea that pinned Daro to the bed. At first she wasn't concerned, hearing the self - mocking laughter in his voice as he recovered from the second bout of vomiting, "Magic?", he groaned involuntarily, settling back on roughly heaped pillows, "I'd call it Ritash for Sandsingers!", and grinned in rueful recognition of their role reversal, but the nausea continued and despite her best efforts, he seemed like a shadow of his former self in the pale light of early dawn when at last it eased.

Marran, shocked by Daro's shivering exhaustion, went into the main cavern to tell his night watch to heat a brick for the Sandsinger's bed. Then, briskly gathering Daro, he guided him, firmly wrapped in a blanket, towards a far door, saying out of the corner of his retreating mouth,

"I'll help Daro take a bath. That's something I can do for you. You're dead on your feet Jalni, go sit by the fire and take a break.".

Jalni bristled from habit, but too tired to argue, slid the warmed brick into the bed and obeyed. She smiled grimly, imagining Ikella's outrage had she known one of her Healers was preparing to share her son's bed if his body warmth remained so low, but as it happened when she tucked him into bed, he was recovering. Marran went to inspect his Dawn Patrol and the cavern slept, with the exception of Jalni. Perhaps it was the aftermath of too much magic, but she lay wakeful as the deep night departed and Seleus returned to make the rocks sing. She grew stiff, cold and miserably resentful of all those who shared "her" space and abruptly fell asleep as the others woke.

She was roused cross-tempered, by Nimah bending over her. Jalni's sleep-sodden brain refused to work, the girl was demanding answers to questions as she blinked in confusion. Staring blankly at the dumpy teenager, she sat up, to the repeated motif.

"Sorry to wake you.", exclaimed Nimah (exhibiting no sorrow at all), "but Terris sent these for...", (she broke off, struggling to remember Daro's title), finally thrusting a pile of clothes into Jalni's unprepared arms, saying, "We found spare clothing, plain and Opalwear, will they fit?", and faltered to a stop at Jalni's expression.

Head spinning with unresolved fatigue, Jalni snapped, "I don't know do I? Do you see him here? Perhaps when he wakes, I'll find out. However young lady, I an Healer Jalni, you will address me as such. Ichspeller Selunsanni, Sandsinger of the Opal Sands, you won't address at all, unless it is through me. Further to that, I am not his robing drudge, but his Healer, you could pay both of us a little respect!".

She irritably threw the neatly folded clothes on to her blanket as Nimah burst into tears and fled.

"Oh, Deo give me strength!", she thought irritably. "Teens should be known as Sundreth's kind! Moody, defiant, angry, irritable and I can't abide snivelling!",

From the exalted heights of eighteen Rotations, she dashed away angry tears, braved the glances of the Cavern Captain and his crew, before stalking off to bathe.

Even in this contrary mood she could see that the children were happier here and thought about the situation as she bathed alone in the deserted pool. Acceptance of Daro as a Sandsinger seemed total and she had noticed as she passed amongst them, children clustered in small groups, a constant stream of chatter filling the air.

It was Daro this and Daro that, spoken in awed tones of wonderment at the sights they had seen the night before. Not one derogatory reference to the

"Sandsinger" was heard, yet when Jalni sat, freshly bathed, on a discreet terrace, overlooking the desert floor below, she was still stiff with resentment. Where she had been admired by Terris and enjoyed the brotherly companionship of Marran, now they all seemed to be ignoring her and the talk was only of magic users. She sat brooding, while she mentally consigned each Sorceress, every Guardian and all Sandsingers beside, into Sundreth's deepest mine, while she munched on dried citrines that she had found in her travel bag. She wondered vaguely whether Daro responded this badly to using his powers all the time and a frisson of alarm stirred the air as she considered his puzzle.

"I don't know what I could do with such knowledge, were I able to find someone to ask about Sandsingers.", She decided, "I don't suppose that even Ikella knows the answers to those sort of questions. I can't form a valid theory, but his use of power is totally different to anything I've experienced before.".

Her mind briefly recognised that candidates for Sorcery had always been selected from the Guild of Healers and wondered why, before a delicate chiming sound distracted her. Wearily, she reverted to thinking about Daro.

"His power seems greatest when Voiced.", she thought, "but he seems unable to control the volume of power he uses.".

A chill settled over her as she contemplated the enormity of a Sandsinger unable to control power, wondering how an aberrant Sandsinger could be stilled. As though another had spoken, a dreadful picture formed in her mind. A great cavern, so lavishly decorated that it could only exist somewhere that she had never visited and many bodies, lying where they had failed to prove themselves equal to the task. Her reaction was almost a physical recoil, then a soft voice intruded.

"Don't be silly!", it whispered. "Cathedral Cave is littered with the bones of those who tried and failed. The Opal is the most powerful and whoever inherits that mantle is tried beyond mortal endurance before his training begins. He is everything that he promised to be, but he is in danger until his Seguidor is found!".

She went completely still, looking around her wildly, for something out of the norm to register, but apart from a faint perfume where she sat, there was nothing, so she rose and went back to the Lookout and began to sort out the pile of clothes for Daro. She was still musing on her strange thoughts, working out how to tell Daro he was in danger, when Marran led Daro to the table and instantly aroused such a sharp flare of jealousy, that it was a physical pain. She ground her teeth as her words came back to haunt her, then as she set her jaw against them all, a cheerful voice announced proudly,

"Thank you Healer Jalni. I was just coming back for those. Daro...", the gawky teen grinned self - consciously, "I mean, Ichspeller Selunsanni, has made Brus his guide and I am his robing drudge. Marran is his body servant. Isn't it wonderful?", and Jalni, jolted out of her comfortable niche, was further unsettled by the sight of Daro surrounded by petitioners of all ages. She felt the dark rage descend and obstinately refused Daro's discreet summons.

"Let him see how dependent he is on me.", she thought resentfully, "Perhaps he'll stay out of my head and bother them instead.!".

As soon as the thought left her, Daro adjusted his position, turning his back to her. She watched in mounting fury as Terris and Marran served a sweet drink and kept the children at bay so that he could eat in peace. She knew she was being unreasonable, but somehow she didn't care. She didn't want to help him, didn't want others to either. She laid her muddled head down thinking she didn't want to be near him, but longed for him to touch her and confused by these feelings, she pulled her blanket over her head, drifting and despite the bustle of the day, fell heavily asleep.

Daro "reached" for her, but she slept soundly. He tried a little persuasion, concentrating on "summoning" someone to talk to, until he felt a light touch on his hand. One of the children, he thought and in amazement heard a clear voice, sounding in his mind as though she spoke in reality.

"I'm Lallee.", she said and waited for him to respond. He followed her voice, tracking until she appeared in his thoughts, as she must be in life. She was a slender child, inclined to melt into the crowd. He reached out and Lallee, stood quite still as he touched her hair, thinking ruefully,

"I still can't interpret what my hands tell me. I am so attuned to colour.".

Then suddenly he felt a soft rushing sensation and his whole body cried out the joyous recognition of green. "Malachite green.", he thought numbly and heard the child's respectful voice say softly:

"Ichspeller Selunsanni, you are reminded that you are not alone.".

His thought processes turned cartwheels, as he fought for control by resolutely refusing to contemplate what he suspected was happening, choosing instead to indulge in a picture of auburn hair, a tightly woven Healer braid and an Azure ribbon dotted with stars.

The child's inner voice said patiently, "You're thinking of Jalni. My hair is the colour of hakesh flowers in winter. Not white and not yellow, but somewhere in between.", and he sighed with pleasure at the memory of the creamy blossoms as she continued carefully, "Marran is nut brown. Skin and hair like coppa nuts, Terris has gold hair, like sunlight, Calar has black hair, Brus is a fire head and you got it right about Jalni.".

Daro hoped that no one else saw his jaw drop, but Lallee caught his astonished thoughts and giggled.

"How long have you been able to do that?", he asked sternly and Lallee grew quiet, biting her lip as she confessed. "My tutor taught me, though Solana said that there wasn't anyone else here.", her head lifted, voice defiance insistent, "but he sings me stories at bedtime and teaches me tricks in our school..." and her voice dropped to a whisper. "Shall I bring him to see you?", and Daro, feeling his sense of reality slipping away, nodded mutely. Allowing Lallee to exact a promise of another bedtime story, Daro asked Brus to take him back to his room, where he intended to catch up on sleep and knowing that he wouldn't be missed during Height of Sun, he gratefully retreated.

Pacing the simple room to get his bearings told him little, he was too tense to explore, so he lay down and must have drifted off and woke to utter silence. No sound from the outer cavern penetrated and he sat with his head in his hands as he shrugged off the reluctant tendrils of sleep, astonished at his own lethargy. He wasn't quite sure when he became aware of Lallee's inner voice chattering telepathically.

"Look Grandfather, I told you he was here.", the child's hands patted his shoulder and he felt the bed shift as she climbed on to it. There was a small grating sound, as someone sat in the rickety chair by the bed and then another voice entered his bewildered mind.

"Well my boy.", it said, in the richest velvety baritone, "You've come a long way to find a school for Sandsingers, but you are right. You need a mentor and so I came to help you.".

Someone patted his knee gently and a hand took his in an oddly familiar way and every sane thought departed.

"It's like touching the Source itself.", he thought numbly. A gentle warming, a scent like sun ripened berries flooded through him, then his perception of reality dimmed away and all he could feel was the sensation of being connected to who knew what, His mind reeled in disbelief,

"Another Sandsinger? Was he dreaming and where had Lallee come from?", he "reached" out into the outer cavern, wondering how Lallee and this man had passed the Watch. He prepared to ask, when the other placed a cautionary finger against his lips and the voice sounded again.

"Daro, where is your Seguidor? Without it, you must control your power by sheer force of will. It is dangerous to call the Sands without a means of focussing the power!", the deep voice demanded. Lallee shifted awkwardly and then the child said reluctantly,

"He can borrow mine, but I want it back! I won't be able to talk to you without it. Promise?", and then a small hand slipped a metal object into Daro's palm. His hesitant fingers traced it awkwardly, until she closed his hand around it, locating his thumb and forefinger within a central whorl and touched the Sand. Gasping, "Malachite.", he allowed the cool green wash to flood through him and felt himself "centre" and relax.

He was near Malos, walking the ancient woods again, hearing the sigh of the wind across the Sands and as Lallee leant against him, he caught the sharp clean scent of the Eldowan trees and knew that his earlier presentiment had been correct.

He found his inner voice and said quietly, "Lallee is the Malachite then?", and the child giggled, throwing her arms around his neck, whispering in his ear.

"Not yet silly. I must be called in order and at the age of responsibility. Don't you have a mentor? How came you Opal to the Sands knowing nothing?", and Daro said quietly,

"I was called to Tirjhinar, but had less than six ninenights to learn it all. I am sorry to disappoint you, but I am only a novice myself.", and the old man chuckled.

"Well young lady,", he said drily, "You had the advantage of being fostered by a convert. Solana's power, though poor by our standards, nevertheless served to guide you. Now I must mentor both of you until we must settle the matter of Daro's Seguidor. Only then can you leave the School for Sandsingers " and Daro turned the small metal ring in his hands, feeling its shape carefully.

"Is mine different?", he asked, "Does it have sections inside and a loop to hang it on my belt?", and the old man chuckled grimly, "Oh yes, Ichspeller Selunsanni. Now where did you last have it?", and Daro was forced to explain that he had never had it in his possession, but, that his mentor had told him that he had to find it. His companion tutted under his breath, sounding dismayed as Daro explained the current social structure.

"Dear me!", he murmured as Daro enlarged on a world without Sandsingers and, "The One protect us!", in comical horror, as Daro told of the matriarchal society of Sorcery.

"Harrumph! Yes, well, lets get on with it then my boy. You can't force Power, you can only channel it and for that we Sandsingers developed the idea of carrying the source of our powers with us, but we found a pocketful of Sand inconvenient and difficult to focus through. Darius Selunsa, of blessed memory, took counsel of a very wise scientist and together they forged the Seguidor. Each Sand is attuned to its own and the Opal is attuned to all. It has another function as well, but it is imperative that you are reunited with yours before you kill yourself.".

Daro listened, trying to picture his visitor. He thought he must be about hands span shorter than himself and not young, idly wondering how old he was, hazarding a guess.

"Seventy Rotations, eighty?", and the other chuckled.

"Not even close Selunsanni, not even close.", and unaccountably Daro was reminded of his mentor and shivered, thinking of immortality.

The old man interrupted his musings with an abrupt, "By your leave?", and took Daro's face in Healer trained hands. He tilted Daro's head, pressing gently on his cheekbones, just under his eyes and despite his delicacy of touch, Daro hissed in pain. His eyes felt scalded dry most of the time and as if he had spoken aloud, his visitor responded.

"Mmmm, we must do something about that.", and to his astonishment the old man started to hum. It was a quiet melody and Daro mentally filed it for further research. There was a feather touch along his eyelids and then cool, cool liquid seemed to well in his eyes and the pain eased. Daro felt his heart rate return to normal and his earlier alarm diminishing. Lallee leant against his arm and he could hear her talking to the other, who still cradled Daro's head in his hands.

"Grandfather, why are his eyes like that?", Lallee was asking her companion,

"Sightless, do you mean child?", the old man kept up the flow of mental conversation with the girl as he gave Daro's eyes a complete examination. Lallee considered this and then her voice said softly,

"No Grandfather, he has special eyes, you must look at them, they are Opal. Show him Daro.", she commanded and her companion tutted deprecatingly.

"Child! You cannot command the Opal like that. Sha'el Marosjh, you must show more respect for your elders and superiors.", he said reprovingly. "Where are your manners? you should use his title calling him, "Ichspeller Selunsanni, as I taught you.".

Daro caught the sudden image of a severe, yet fatherly face, as the voice continued gravely:

"Furthermore, you shouldn't hang round his neck like that. It is unbecoming in a young woman.".

Lallee shifted her position, swinging against Daro so that he was forced to support her with one arm as she faced the old man.

"He's not Sandsinging now is he?", she demanded, not at all abashed by her mentor's attitude, "He's my Daro when he is not in magic.".

Daro suppressed his amusement as a picture of a tall handsome man flashed across his mind, ruthlessly refusing to look at the heroic image the child had conjured of him. Putting her gently to one side, he spoke solemnly, but firmly.

"Lallee, while we are together like this, you will defer, as I do, to our mentor. You will do as requested at all times, for your own safety!".

He hoped that he hadn't been too severe, but acutely aware of the perceptiveness of this girl, he shielded the thought and felt the approving pressure of his visitor's hand. Lallee abruptly settled herself, adjusting clothes and behaviour without comment. Daro cleared his throat.

"I am sorry if you think me rude, but I don't know who you are, your titles or what I should call you? Won't you tell me?", and paused, aware of fatigue washing over him. The old man replied quietly, "Find the Sand, use the child's Seguidor.", and Daro did as he was told, centring himself and letting the refreshing rush of the Malachite Sand renew energies sapped by concentrating on this telepathic conversation.

The old man sighed, saying, "Eyes first.", and tilted Daro's head up,

"Open your eyes boy.", he commanded softly and Daro lifted unwilling lids to the gaze of the other. There was a profound silence and then the visitor said quietly, "I have never seen anything like this, I'll try and find out more, while I coach you further.", he touched the centre of Daro's forehead as if in blessing and then released him and returned to his chair and began to question Daro closely.

"At your induction, what rite did you choose to perform?", He asked gravely and Daro respectful of the ancient rites of accession said hopelessly.

"Oh, I didn't know what to do. We have no experience of Sandsingers, so I threw a tantrum, broke the Gate in the Rock, trashed the doors to the Healer

Hall, challenged my mother who rules the Sand and then used the Assendarium to relieve our skies of the clouds that have hidden Seleus since my birth!".

There was an awed silence and then the old man said mildly,

"Ah, a demonstration of command of weather, supplemented by imposing a touch of natural terror?", and Daro hung his head, as the other continued.

"To resort to anger, is to taint the purity of the power, but I read beyond your words Ichspeller and I see your pain. What other High Magic have you sung?", and while Daro shifted uncomfortably, Lallee answered for him.

"I told you Grandfather.", she trilled, "Men don't Heal, men don't magic, men don't do anything much. Only my Daro is different, he can Sing, I heard him, he Sang Solana's tears into stars. He even sang me rivers and seas, like you do. He magic's too. He fixed Calar and Brus after they bashed each other, he mended Calar when he ran Solana's warding.", She frowned searching her memory before saying triumphantly, "and he put Jalni back to bed when Solana was dying! I saw that too. He stayed with Solana and Jalni went up in the air and back to bed, right over the fire, I saw her floating. She was hopping mad, but too tired to hit him, though she thought about it.". Her friend grunted in answer, he was examining Daro's eyes closely as Daro clung to the hand of the other and was dimly aware that he was drawing strength from the contact itself.

"When did you lose your sight?", he asked softly and Daro felt the memory of Cathedral Cavern burst from him, in a torrent of pain, reliving the whole experience. He felt the death of Sararrh, heard Ahnell's last words, then the terror, the darkness enfolding him. Of his anguished race across the desert he remembered nothing, only the confrontation with Ikella, feeling the whole experience played out in front of him, as though he was seeing again, through another's eyes.

When his companion released him, he realised that he had Sung the entire experience empowered and etched in his mind was a picture of someone that he had never seen before.

He was old, hair as white as the snow on Dreken Pass, with a long flowing beard to match. He wore colours, Opal colours and an amazing surcoat of some sparkling weave, at his belt hung a glowing crystal, as though this Seguidor was formed from star dust. The man seemed shadowy, insubstantial, yet strangely compelling and suddenly Daro felt quite awed, humbled, he bowed his head in gratitude for the relief from pain.

"Ichspeller", he murmured and the old man dropped his hands on to Daro's head for a moment and confided,

"As you asked, you may call me Sentinel, or Grandfather if it makes you feel more comfortable. In your case it is almost accurate, but for the passage of time. You may not know more than is necessary for each stage of your journey, but that is the Way of Magic and no-one I care to know has ever succeeded in going against the Way. I must go and put this one to bed, or she will miss her midday nap and I have interrupted the flow of time for long enough today!".

He lifted Lallee, who had been drooping on Daro's knee, before the startled boy could react to the comment about time.

"Don't worry, I will return and we'll talk. Rest while you can. You have to raise the Azure to power before you need worry about young Lallee!".

His voice dropped to a hypnotic murmur as he glided effortlessly away.

"You're feeling sleepy, your eyes are closing.", He passed through the door, but Daro never heard it creak, as he stretched out on his bed.

"You must sleep, close your eyes and sleep.", the disembodied voice drifted away, as Daro yawned wearily and slept.

Chapter 27 - Plain of Shadows

Daro woke refreshed and sat up, deciding to become more independent and dressed. Standing, he felt for the wall, wishing he had a Staff. Simultaneously, he "felt" an ephemeral shaft take shape in his hand and the Sentinel's warning came back to him.

"Have a care Selunsanni.", the velvet voice echoed, "High Magic must be avoided until we find your Seguidor.". Unsure what constituted "High Magic", he paused to consider before plunging a hand into the small leather pouch he wore under his clothes, touching the Opal Sand he had secreted within, as he channelled power to form a slender Staff.

Plain yet elegant, lightweight and flexible, it thrummed sympathetically as changes flowed through him into the shifting shaft. As it lengthened to a hands breadth above shoulder height, he ran inquisitive fingers over a metalwork mount at the head, picturing something like his mother's Opal, then sighing he grasped the bare shaft, steeling himself to explore.

He walked forward, swinging it ahead, but only took two paces before he stopped, intolerably conscious of his own vulnerability. On the point of giving up, he remembered Solana's children, abandoned, often disabled, sharing their frugal existence with the orphans from the village. Less than a Rotation ago, Solana had welcomed his band of outcasts, given them shelter, food, advice, despite her own poverty. As he thought of those he had compromised in his obsessive search for power, he gritted his teeth, vowing to repay their courage with some of his own.

"I can neither hide my disability, nor hide from it any longer.", he finally acknowledged, "Anyone can see I'm blind, that in itself provides perfect camouflage for the short time that such a thing is useful.", and absurdly cheered by this thought, he spent the next turn of a sand-glass mapping the room where Solana had worked and slept, while she comforted those she had entrusted to his care.

Eventually, the plain rectangular room revealed itself. The door was almost at the junction of a short side. The Healer must have had a workbench and he delighted himself by finding out where it had once stood, following the rub line engraved into the rocky surface of the long back wall. He was sufficiently aware of herbs to know that the collective scents of common plants hung in the corner, just above the missing workbench and he confirmed his suspicions, smiling as his probing staff caused a light rustling above his head. He imagined a drying rack, grinning when his hand encountered a cleat which secured a strong oiled rope. Deeply satisfied with his mornings work, he decided not to be the one on whom a sturdy drying rack descended and turned along the back wall, towards his bed.

He counted fifteen paces then when the Staff struck the bed-frame, turned again until he found the end of his bed, where a thin pallet leant against the wall.

He stopped , imagining Solana extracting each child in order to give private counselling and in that moment, became aware of a distinct lack of normal activities in the main cavern. He stood for a moment listening to silence and then, removing the chair from his path, he made his way to the door, opening it on what could have been the night aspect of the Lookout Cave.

He listened intently, but there was no greeting from a willing helper, no welcome from Marran and yet, the cavern wasn't empty. He could detect the faint glow that revealed Jalni and feel a tentative flicker of a Source empowered gleam near the fire and thought, "Terris". He sought Lallee, until a prickle of panic gripped him.

"Just where is everyone?", he puzzled, "Why isn't anyone awake?", the only answer was the swift rustle of movement, then blurrily, a pallid ghostly figure appeared.

Daro dropped his Staff, clapped both hands over his eyes, exclaiming wildly, "O Deo! I'm dead and walking. I've killed myself. It's too late, I've already failed!", and Sentinel chuckled. He felt the old man pass, catching his unique scent as his Staff was returned to him and then the low voice said kindly, "Shut the door boy, we don't want to rouse the Sands while we talk!". He complied in a daze, numbly returning to hitch himself up onto the high bed. He shuffled backwards, intending to lean against the wall, but found himself pressing into a recumbent body and froze in horror, somehow knowing that "the body" was his own.

He fought the instinct that crawled through his mind babbling: "Wake up, let me in, O Deo, let me not be dead!", as he sat taking deep breaths, until his heart steadied and the rushing noise went from his ears. The Sentinel said very gently, "Well done my boy. A trifle disconcerting isn't it, but I have no doubt that you will adjust quickly to the Plain of Shadows.", and the pale glimmer that Daro had shied away from, shimmered and consolidated into the figure of an old man. Daro's mind reeled as his visitor muttered, "However, True-vision is another matter. Because you have lost the knack of seeing, you may find this training difficult, you must remain aware at all times that this is a function of High Magic. It is not intended to replace that which you have lost, but it may help you more than a sighted Singer.", and he smiled directly at the bemused man.

"Plain of Shadows?", Daro demanded and Sentinel leant forward, absently summoning a table on which he rested his elbows. He smoothed his beard thoughtfully and Daro whispered shakily, "I can see you Grandfather!".

The words came in a breathless rush and Sentinel raised his head smiling into Daro's face.

"I hoped for as much my boy.", he said, "This is the tool we call True-Sight. You can use this to identify good from bad, the honest from liars, strength from weakness, or ensorcelled. What you see in True - Sight can be trusted and will show as you might see it in real vision. What appears shadowed is to be avoided. It will reveal secrets also!", he said enigmatically, chuckling at Daro's confusion.

"Look.", he commanded and where Daro had found bare walls, suddenly he saw compartments filled with paraphernalia the purpose for which eluded him utterly.

"Just some odds and ends.", Sentinel muttered, "Your Seguidor would blaze like Seleus if it was there. I would have detected it long ago.".

"The best we can hope for is to trigger some event that will reveal its location. I am bound to Scharatel, to those I mentor and although it may be possible for me to search Selesh once you have returned, I can't leave unless summoned by Seguidor!", adding ruefully, "If I only knew where to start looking!", and sighed heavily.

Daro said gently, "Well then, let's do something else. I know nothing remember, not even how to find other Sandsingers, or will they find me?". The old man was shocked. "Opal calls the other Shades.", he said bluntly. "That's why Opal doesn't use power in another Sand unless absolutely essential. Empowered as we are, we might rouse another Sand before they are ready."

Each Singer comes to maturity at a different rate. None can take power until they are matured by the Source. They may be young, old, or in the mid Rotations of their lives. Only the One knows who they are and when they will come to Sing, but they will come again, have no doubt and I can tell you that I have already identified a few. I know the Azure, the Malachite and the Amber, as well as you who will know them in time, but don't ask me!"

He held up a hand and a deep ripple passed through the crystalline surcoat and a shimmering chime underlined his command. Daro acquiesced with a sigh and then said plaintively,

"Do I take it that this Plain of Shadows is an altered state of being? I seem to be asleep in my bed and yet I am talking to you. Will I remember all this when I wake?", and the wise old face smiled, as the Sentinel began to explain.

"We, who have command of the Higher Powers, believe that power is derived from Seleus and the Source, focussed on or through our home Sands. One amongst us realised that though we can't always see the sun, yet it is still there, even under the shadow of night. He too came Opal to our world and learned how to pass beyond the confines of his mortal frame, into that shadowed place between life and death, between sleep and dreaming, where you accidentally strayed today.".

"Do you know how I got here then?", Daro asked and the Sentinel looked a trifle flustered as he admitted, "Ah, well, that was possibly my fault. Young Lallee was determined to show me "her" Opal! Otherwise, I might have visited you at a less vulnerable time. However, we came because this room being warded in a number of ways, protected everyone.".

He indicated the hidden cupboards and their precious contents, his eyes twinkling as he remarked, "Well, I was astonished when it became obvious that you could see us. I must research some of your rather unusual qualities. In some instances practitioners have been known to enter "The Plain of Shadows", without preparation...", he broke off abruptly and stood, pacing about muttering. "You could have been teetering or leaving some state of profound exhaustion…", he swung about exclaiming, "Dangerous my boy, deeply dangerous. I will show you how to protect your sleeping body before you indulge in the practice again."

Daro feeling like a schoolboy, said cautiously, "What dangers Grandfather?", as his companion said mildly, "Let's start at the beginning, shall we?", and Daro settled back, more comfortable about leaning against his sleeping body, as the Sentinel placed Daro's hand around his own shimmering Seguidor, saying quietly,

"Focus on the Opal to fully recharge your strength.", and Daro obeyed, floating on an endless tide of power as the Sentinel directed his thoughts.

"Imagine that you are walking a long corridor.", Sentinel's words hypnotically spaced and Daro yawned, as his companion continued. "There are doors behind you and doors to each side of you, but the light in the corridor is getting brighter as you walk.".

Daro nodded, the picture was firm in his mind's eye. Wall hangings glowed, door handles gleamed and there was light around the architrave ahead. The voice came softly to his ears and he followed the instruction unerringly.

"When you get to the door at the end of the corridor, the light around you will be as bright as day. When you walk through that door you will wake and be yourself once more.", Daro mumbled sleepily, yawned and woke in the dark, confused and trembling, thankful that the room was warded, for he was sure that he had heard a fretful cry, "Don't leave me Grandfather.".

"Gently my boy.", the Sentinel was bending over him. "Be still a moment and drink this.".

He held a gouche filled with Jalni's remedy to Daro's lips and said, "Drink as much as you can. It is weak stuff, but well made. You could also do with a few square meals on that scrawny frame of yours.".

Daro took the gouche and drank directly from it, feeling the tonic reviving him and said reprovingly.

"I think our world is very different now. Food is scarce, for twenty Rotations we have been rationed, it is only since I came to power that Seleus has shone on our world. The children here will be starving soon, I must get them back to Selesh, or somewhere that has food, rooms to house them and parents willing to foster them. That is why I came here.",

There was a long considering silence and then Sentinel said softly.

"You came because I summoned you. You came to gather your Singers and until you do, you will walk the Sands forever searching!". Daro shivered, feeling as though one long dead had cast a long shadow over his life.

They worked on, Sentinel showing Daro how to ward his sleeping body, triple ward his room and keep vetali tablets to hand. Miraculously he proved adept at leaving his sleeping form, slipping onto the Plain of Shadows with an alacrity that had the old man worried.

He grumbled,

"You must take care Selunsanni. Dark forces are at work and should they detect your presence before we find your Seguidor, I doubt you could escape their attentions.", He refused to say more on the subject, but intrigued with his ability, put Daro through his paces time and time again, until the Sandsinger was white and trembling, uncertain on his feet and falling asleep as the Sentinel brought their lesson to a close. He patted Daro's arm kindly, as Daro, once again in his own body, sprawled inelegantly, limbs too tired to move.

The old man murmured confidentially, "I will find your Healer some extra strong vetali to mix with that other. You must concentrate on controlling her temper though. She behaves like a spirited woman, but she is not yet mature in body or mind. Why does she fight you so much? Tell me.", and Daro leant on his elbows, puzzling .

"I think it has something to do with the way she was compelled to nurse me. I overreached myself thoroughly when I returned to Selesh.", and he dredged through his memories of Jalni saying thoughtfully, "I remember someone holding me.".

Then in a wondering voice, "She wouldn't let me go. I couldn't hold on alone, so she held me until the sun rose. She put my hand to the wall, I remember nearly drowning in the rush of power, but I don't know what happened next.", and the Sentinel paused in the doorway, his head lifted, his voice questioning curiously.

"Have you impose a bond on that girl?", he demanded, "Surely she didn't fight you so much?", and he grimaced as Daro yawned

"Yes and yes.", he mumbled and the old man snorted derisively.

"Tried to subdue a lightening rod didn't you?", he jeered, "Well my boy, if you want to ride a wild Zephryn, you'd best put sweet oil on its horn before you slip a bridle on it. Make her want you in her head before you issue orders!".

He looked back at the recumbent Sandsinger, but Daro was asleep and dreaming.

.

Daro lay considering Jalni's "touchiness". Having come to no firm opinion on the subject, he rolled out of bed, dressed and was pulling on boots, when she tried the door. There was a hum, then her bewildered voice said, "Oh!", as he dispelled the warding and the door opened. Marran, Terris and Jalni trooped in, facing him through a veritable cloud of disapproval, as Jalni spoke.

"I apologise for my absence Ichspeller.", sounding anything but contrite. The tight little voice continued, "I understand that you have found alternative help during my indisposition. However, now I am recovered, I will be ready if you call.".

The stilted little speech emphasised her sense of estrangement, startling Daro into wondering why he hadn't told her she deserved a rest and that others must learn to shoulder his care soon, so that she could help lead them back to Selesh. Jalni took a breath and continued into the silence in which he had received her complaint.

"Furthermore, Marran and Terris were worried about you and couldn't open the door to see if you were alright. After last night's episode, that was both dangerous and inconsiderate. You could have been taken ill again and the children think they have done something wrong!", she stared at him challengingly and Daro, recalling Sentinel's description of his Healer, stood and attempted to make peace.

Voice grave and formal he said slowly, "Jalni, I apologise for not having communicated my intentions clearly. I further apologise for the misunderstanding which has obviously caused deep offense, where none was intended.". The tension in the room dropped considerably as he felt for the pale glimmer of Terris, who stood beside Marran and addressed them formally.

"Marran, Terris I am sorry to have brought disharmony to your house.", he said feeling Terris exhale with relief. Marran surprised Daro, by clasping his arm silently, then they left to continue their chores, leaving Jalni with him.

"Thank you.", she murmured, "They couldn't bring you a breakday meal, Marran thought you had fallen victim to sickness. Terris thought you were sulking and Lallee said you were fine, snoring like a verneg in the sun. I couldn't get to you either and...", the tentative smile in her voice was replaced by consternation

"Deo me!", she exclaimed, "I forgot, I went back to sleep and didn't warn you.".

She sounded so outraged, he found himself sitting on his bed, saying mildly, "Sit and tell me now then.", and she told him of her lonely, miserable morning bath. Of how she had used her ration pack rather than share a breakday with those whom she had seen as supplanting her in his affections and how this had led to the peculiar "warning" that she had received. She explained in an oddly convincing way, the sequence of events, answering his questions simply, until she reached the perfume that she had smelt.

"I caught it very clearly. It is one of my favourites and comes from a flower called a raja. It is very rich and heady, sweet and long lasting, but for an older woman. I will wear it when I find a rich lover, or when I finally work out what I am to be!".

She glanced up and saw without surprise that his eyes were glowing, "Feydora!", he exclaimed in tones of deep disgust, then wearily, "Well, tell me the worst!".

She blinked, "Who's Feydora?", she demanded blankly, but Daro, scowling, shook his head and waited for her to tell him what she had heard, so marshalling her thoughts she spoke hesitantly.

"I don't know whether I heard a voice, or caught a thought, but I was left thinking that you were in danger and should refrain from using High Magic until something with a funny name turns up.", she sounded doubtful, but he was smiling as he said,

"Aah. Would that have been a Seguidor?", he asked.

Despite not knowing what a Seguidor was, Jalni appeared relieved and nodded furiously suggesting, "If it can't hurt them, the foraging parties are going out to look for useful things, like blankets, carry bags and spare shoes, so couldn't they look for this Seguidor too? If you could describe it to me, I'll tell them. They won't know its properties any more than I do, they're so unaware of magic here.".

Daro nearly choked suppressing laughter.

"Scartel,", he thought, "has more exposure to magic than she thinks!".

He had heard Sentinel use the ancient name, "Scharatel", understanding that as, "School for Sandsingers!", where apparently the Opal, Azure, Malachite and Amber were currently resident, with a tutor, not to dismiss that ghostly presence that haunted him.", he chuckled to himself, "They appeared to be sprouting Sandsingers and Jalni thinks this place unaffected by magic!", he smiled, hands flickering until he had conjured an image of the missing belt fob.

"Oh.", she said blankly. "I saw something like that back at Selesh. It was plainer.", she sounded doubtful, "Perhaps it wasn't the same thing at all and I can't remember where I saw it, I'll have to search for it when we get back.".

Daro reached out and she instinctively moved towards his seeking hands. He took her left hand in his right and with the other he gently cupped her cheek, tilting her head towards his. She stared into his face anxiously and he said softly:

"Don't be afraid little one, lend me your thoughts.", and his eyes opened.

Pinioned by his othergaze, she swam in Opal. Alternately bathed in turquoise, flamed in rose and seared to the soul in a wild rush of communication so deeply invasive that she felt that he knew her, as no other could. His hands tenderly cradled the back of her head, holding her imprisoned, his othergaze brushed her quivering eyelids, stroked her tears away and then he withdrew, leaving her kneeling, heart-pounding and uncertain of what had just occurred.

He smiled gently and changed the subject abruptly as she stood, struggling to remember what they had been talking about. He said conversationally, "I feel a lot better. For the first time since I returned to Selesh, my eyes don't hurt.", and sensed her professional interest engaging

"Let me see.", she ordered, standing so that she could tip his head against her body with a cool hand. He liked the feel of that and submitted meekly when she said, "Open your eyes.".

The lids lifted reluctantly, until Jalni found herself gazing into his eyes. and Daro steeled himself not to recoil from the intrusion. Jalni, kept her inspection cool and professional, observing the healthy sheen and failed to notice the opalescence forming until it obscured the natural colour of his pupils. Swirling through all the jewel tones of opal his eyes changed slowly until she was looking deep into the eyes of an empowered mage. Fascinated she stared at him, then Daro, very tentatively opened himself to the Source and felt a strange compulsion seize him. He was teetering on the brink of a high place, surrounded in Azure, a soft shiver ran through his body and the hands that cradled his face seemed to tremble. He hastily withdrew from magic and let her complete her inspection, shielding his thoughts fiercely as he numbly accepted that either he was falling in love with this awkward unawakened girl, or she had answered his gentle call.

"In which case", he thought mournfully, "Pelshar is in grave trouble, for the fire in the Source was Azure blue.".

She was saying gently, "Thank you Daro, that was most instructive. I am very pleased with your eyes. Provided I can replenish the salves I brought with me, they will remain well. I am off to look at Solana's medical store with Terris. If I find soapwort and peliswrack I can provide the other ingredients for an eyewash, but I will be busy with Healer duties in the Lookout as well. Will you be all right for a while?".

Daro, shielding his concerns, nodded, as she said quietly, "I am sorry we were cross with each other. I will try harder if you will.", and left.

She slipped past Marran, joining Terris at the fire-pit and watched Marran collect two packs and the Sandsinger. They were chatting as they left the Lookout Cave and Terris seeing them go, said sweetly, "Good. Now they've gone adventuring, we can have our breakday, even if its half way to Height of Sun.", and completely in harmony, the two girls sipped their drinks and ate a rough porridge.

The older children, marshalled into foraging parties by Torvin, came and went. Terris organised babies and toddlers and Jalni received the finds, sorting and storing in between corralling those too tiny to help. Bumps and bruises, knocks and scrapes abounded and by Sunfall they were tired and Jalni was on the edge of black depression. Daro and Marran had been exploring the open areas, bringing back small books, blankets and some brush torches that they had literally stumbled over. Marran chuckled as Jalni tutted over a badly skinned knee.

"That's nothing Jalni. Do you want to see my other scars?". Daro, laughing, suggested she didn't, much to her indignation. Discovering that Marran had slid nearly ten spans on a scree covered slope, lacerating his nether regions, she shook her head over their puerile humour and watched them gloomily as they trudged off on yet another foray. Daro confidently swinging his Staff, Marran carrying supper in a backpack. She was blisteringly jealous of their freedom as Terris, remarked indulgently, "Aah, just like men, leave us with the children, while they go off and have all the fun.", and Jalni's mood plunged down from dismal to depressed.

Was this all she could expect? Drudgery, children, mending cuts and bruises, strains and sprains? Which way should she turn? That question unresolved, she moodily helped put the young ones to bed, then headed through the entrance, passing beyond the hallway and into the secluded rooms beyond, determined that she would be the one that found Daro's Seguidor.

She went through an open doorway, into a small room, comfortably set with a table, chairs and interestingly a sort of window, set in a deep embrasure angled so that she could see Gateway in the distance.

She sat in solitary state, feeling perfectly miserable and not having to hide that fact from all and sundry, began to list her woes, reliving the most hurtful. One by one she mulled them over, until she wept quietly, tears flowing unchecked, until she found herself reaching out for something to wipe her face on.

As she reached blindly towards the curtain beside her, she touched something that clinked, discovering a niche behind the fabric which held a bottle. She reached in, withdrawing a slender blue shape, stoppered with a carved stone and filled with liquid. She had left the Lookout with nothing to eat or drink, intending to return shortly, but here she was and here she was going to stay in peace and comfort. She had torches, with spares in the hearth, so she lit the one already ensconced and using her teeth to withdraw the stopper set about investigating its contents.

At some point Marran wandered in and found her holding up the bottle, to see how much of this wonderful stuff was left, having catalogued her miserable existence to date under its influence. She was gloomily imagining a fatal fall followed by solemn mourning and her subsequent obsequies, when Marran ambled in saying, "Oh, there you are. Don't you want to eat and hear the bed-time story Daro is going to tell?".

She looked up, bedraggled, tear stained and hiccuping inelegantly said, "No, I shall shtay here. I'm planning my funeral rites, an I don't want to be dishturbed.".

Marran looked at her critically, "You're drunk.", he said enviously. and returning the look through narrowed eyes, she said accusingly, "An' you're a man, not a Shandlshinger.", and burst into tears exclaiming, I don't want to go to bed. I want a drink.".

Leaning forward to waggle the bottle under his nose, she said provocatively, "Thish'ld even knock the pants off Jashell! Think you're man enough?", and giggled as he took the bottle from her. It was nearly full, so he took a swig, hoping to placate her long enough to get her back to safety, for plainly she would never make it on her own feet. However, the moment he swallowed, he knew he had made a dreadful mistake.

"This isn't just potent.", he thought muzzily. "Its lethal!".

He felt as if the top of his head was open to the sky. His eyes were on fire and his throat boiled, before the flavour sweetened the pain. Then the intoxication hit him, flowing like lightening through every vein in his body. He took another swallow, the flavour was so intense this time that he hardly noticed that his legs no longer worked. He felt his belly clench on liquid fire, but by then, he no longer cared. Dimly, he heard her say.

"S'not fair, I'm too young to die, but leasht my Shandshinger will mourn me too.", and vaguely picturing Daro and Terris weeping over their biers, Marran blacked out.

After Daro had sung the story of the night, the children had settled down to sleep. Terris thanked him prettily, but he could tell she was anxious. When his enquiry elicited the fact that Marran had gone in search of Jalni and that they were still missing, he disguised his concern as Terris chattered.

"Marran knows the Heights better than any of us. He won't attempt anything silly without lights and more help.", she acknowledged bravely and then it dawned on him that in his world of twilight shadows, he hadn't noticed the Fall of Sun, now it was dark, Jalni and Marran were in real danger.

He discreetly touched his pouch of Sand, turning from the task of conjuring up fanciful visions of herds of Zephryn, riding the storm clouds, to conducting a discreet search and found them almost immediately. Calming the anxious girl by saying lightly, "Jalni knows the rules. Selesh is very much larger than this settlement and she leads exploration teams regularly. They are close by and may have found something interesting. Why don't you get Nimah and Motri to help make a sweetdrink, Quaryn and I can go and call them back.".

He called Quaryn over, saying quietly, "I need your help Quaryn. Brus will mark where we go and run errands if necessary.", he smiled sunnily spreading reassurance as he said, " We won't be long.", and left the Cavern on Quaryn's arm. Concentrating on remembering their path, Daro was conscious that in the dark, he was the guide, the boys only needed to stop him banging his head on low thresholds. A short corridor and two rooms away they located the missing couple and an embarrassed Quaryn found himself peeping into the room where Jalni lay quietly sobbing and Marran sprawled unconscious on the floor.

He backed out of the doorway, into Daro, who aware of Jalni's muddled emotions, was standing quietly in the passageway outside the large ante-room off which the Lookout lay.

"Daro.", Quaryn spoke urgently. "Don't think we should go in there.", and to Daro's amusement, he felt the boy's colour rise, without any use of power at all.

"I'll go and tell Terris that we found them and that they're fine shall I?", and without stopping to think about the needs of a blind man in a rabbit warren of caves, the awkward adolescent fled.

Mildly disconcerted by Quaryn's perception of the situation, Daro stopped, probing to see if he was intruding on an intimate moment, before entering the room. Despite the sense of warmth and comfort, his underlying concern for Jalni made him less aware of Marran stretched out on the floor, until he tripped over him and fell almost on top of Jalni. Enthroned in sorrow, she lay on a pile of luxurious cushions, so absorbed in misery, that Daro landed almost in her lap before she knew he was there. He immediately realised why Quaryn had reacted so badly. He was lying less than a span from Marran, who snored in drunken stupor, completely devoid of all interest in the proceedings.

Daro regained his breath, rolling on to his elbows, to investigate the cause of Jalni's misery. He heard something clink and reached out to see what he had knocked against, finding the warm body of his guide. She was too absorbed to care when he ran inquisitive fingers up her body and found the source of her sorrow, allowing him to remove it from her grasp and breathe in what seemed to him to be the nectar of life itself. The honeyed call of the liquid was beyond him to deny and he carefully took a sip from the bottle, gasping as the fire pervaded his senses. The wonderful flavour hit the back of his throat and he drew breath, considering Marran in a different light, hoping that his new friend would survive this experience, then, hiccupping like a weary child, Jalni nestled against him, relaxed and pliant melting into his arms as he secured the stopper on the bottle once more.

"Hello.", she said happily, "Are you my friend?", and patted his face softly, giggling as she found stubble.

"No.", she said dreamily, "My friendsh over there. He hasn't got a beard like yoursh. Do you want to be my friend?", she breathed invitingly, burying her face against his throat, nuzzling into him. The strength of instant arousal quite took Daro's breath away. He had been drunk before and was no stranger to women, but this was a completely new sensation. His body ruling his head, he too was caught in some thrall in which he simply didn't know what to do, then Jalni solved the problem for him by bursting into tears.

Half drowned in her sorrow, he found himself comforting her, uncomfortably aware of her body pressing against his. She raised herself up on her elbows, half lying against his chest and forced back into the cushions, Daro knew her face hovered only a finger span from his. Her breath was sweet, sharp and spiky, reminiscent of the great trees above Darnesh. Her tears trickled down her face, soaking his chest, her gaze almost as distinct as any touch as she sobbed.

"S'all his fault. I shouldn't be here, s'all his fault!".

Daro asked curiously, "Whose fault, dearling? Who has made you so unhappy?". Internally vowing to drag Marran to the Dreken Pass and personally stake him out to die, if he was the culprit, Daro was suddenly aware that he could do no such thing and that tearstained eyes and quivering lips hung within a breath's touch of his own.

As the tumult in his blood refused to subside, she laid the blame at his own door.

"That Shandshinger, that's who.", her voice was scratchy, her words slurred, but she could still list her grievances comprehensively and Daro almost offered to tame the Sandsinger before catching himself in mid sentence, forced to consider the potency of the drink very soberly, as Jalni turned on him herself.

"No, no you mustn't, he can't fight you, he can't see.", and then, "You mushn't hurt my Shpeller.", she twisted her hands in his hair, pinning him back against the pillows, until confused and just a little intoxicated, he felt the slow heavy warmth of true arousal sweep through him and slid his hands behind her head drawing her to him. Just before his lips touched hers, Daro felt apprehensive, then swept away on a surge of desire so strong he almost forgot to breathe, he was kissing her, holding her, murmuring little endearments as she responded eagerly.

As his hands caressed the nape of her neck, her own fluttered against him and he groaned softly, caught in a dizzying rush of desire, as he rolled her over into the pillows and resumed his exploration of her mouth. Her hands entwined in his hair, as he caught the tears that trickled beneath her eyelids with his lips until they stopped. She clung to him as he ran his lips down her throat, feeling the pulse beating frantically until she was shivering against him, peaked breasts all too willing to be explored. Then in mid kiss, sobriety returned with the warning, "Have a care Selunsanni!", and he hurled himself from her, shaking.

"What am I doing?", he questioned himself silently, "I read her signature in the Source this morning and seduce her tonight? I think not Ichspeller Selunsanni. I think not!", and turned to face his tormentor, still fighting for self-control and finding it, caught the bright thread of an idea. "If I was bonded against my will, I would fight with teeth, claws and nails to secure my independence. Perhaps, one day she will submit, but never unwillingly.".

All this time he had kept the throb of the Source gently pulsing in his mind and almost instinctively he felt the flush of the blue spectrum and made the decision it demanded. Careful not to fall over Marran again, he towered over her, his face illuminated by the magic glowing in his eyes and held out his hand.

She had sobered the instant his lips left hers. Though she was still shaking with the fever he had aroused in her. Now, she was aware of him, she realised that what she had considered "an awareness of men in general", compared very dimly to the sensations Daro had awoken in her.

Breathless and confused, she stared up at him, seeing his frown and wondered what she had done to displease him. As he bent over her, hand held out, exhausted by the wash of conflicting emotions, she finally accepted that Daro knew best and slipped her hand into his. He pulled her to her feet, feeling his bond on her tighten as they touched skin to skin. She turned to face him as he asked softly,

"Am I really to blame for all your sorrows little one?".

His voice sounded less certain, the hands that stroked her hair were shaking. Wordless she clung to him, unwilling or unable to stand unaided and in mute reply she shook her head, as he spoke careful that she should understand clearly.

"Jalni, I will release you from your bond, because this.", his voice shook a little, "This cannot go on, at least," he amended, " Not now. If we are to have a future to offer these children, we must have clear minds, uncomplicated hearts and no misunderstandings. It will be a hard journey and I cannot.", he spoke almost to himself. "Will not be, distracted from my purpose.".

She was cold, trembling, as she said slowly. "What bond?", and a picture of the day that he diverted Ikella from enforcing her will on Jalni crossed her mind, along with the moment that they had touched. He watched her carefully as he said, "As Opal Sandsinger, I run the risk of accidentally imposing my will on others. It is rare, but not inconceivable that I could "persuade", another's actions to mirror my own desires, which in the last Age of Mystery resulted in the election of the Sandsworn. All devoted by bond to their Sandsinger, they formed a hedge against ordinary society. Unable to risk touching another, the Sandsingers lived in seclusion, surrounded only by their Sandsworn or their bond mates. I thought I could be different and I fell at the first obstacle.".

She looked at him oddly and whispered, "If only you knew how much I wanted to be Sandsworn and you chose anyone but me, even a snarrelled Mystcat.", and impetuously he touched just the tip of her nose and said very gently, "Being Sandsworn is not for you dearling, you mean far too much to me for that!", he stroked her hair and then the strangest memory came to his mind, as she caught his hand, sending him an agonised glance.

A picture of a bed, then a young girl bending over his own unconscious form. In this silent vision, his eyes flew open, strange shimmering Opal eyes. His hand clung to the girls bare arm and Daro wished desperately for Sentinel to interpret the vision as it faded. His *othervoice* speaking within her mind, was rough with emotion, but the words came clearly as she steadfastly stared up into his face.

"Oh Jalni, I didn't know. How you must have suffered, but why didn't anyone tell me? The bond I set deliberately is what kept me safe in the desert. That allowed me to follow you. It is what allows us to do this, "speech without speech" we call it. It is the practice of Sandsingers to bond their trusted companions so that they cannot be parted in life or death. However, I had no knowledge of the natural bond, formed when you treated me and so I must free you and then you can make your own decision. Become my willing bondmate, or stay with the children. You will find your true path soon and I will exert no compulsion.".

She spoke softly enough, but there was steel in the voice that responded.

"I won't be bonded against my knowledge or will.", she said and Daro believed her, knowing it would have taken an empowered mage to detect the tiny quaver in her voice, or the quivering sigh as she lifted her chin defiantly.

Her voice in his mind whispered wistfully, "I am used to you in my mind and I will miss you, but I have to be free!".

She knelt at his feet, submission in every line of her body and held her hands up in appeal.

"When I know my vocation, I will tell you. I cannot remain here in the Azure, for something draws me back to the Opal. All I know is that I will be stilled before I fail you again!".

Daro felt such a rush of tenderness for her that he knelt himself, facing her and gently brushed his mouth against hers in the traditional kiss of peace. He settled himself and reached for her saying softly, "Open your eyes Jalni, look at me, look me in the face and see the man, see only the man.".

She moved and Daro felt her burning gaze on him, abruptly an image of her swept into his mind's eye. Huge lilac tear stained eyes, quivering lips, but full of courage, hope and determination. With relief he gathered his power around him and took her hands in his, feeling a rush of something so powerful through their doubly linked hands that his head swam, then he murmured:

"Let all compulsion be removed, let all links be severed, take from this one the shackle of bondage,".

She cried out, swaying dangerously, seeking him blindly, struggling to free her hands. He supported her as she muttered, "Daro? I can't "feel" you any more.", then she said desperately, "Oh no! What have I done? I can't be so alone again. Oh, why did I fight it?".

He steadied her, holding her hands firmly in his own, aware suddenly that his own head and heart were hurting, that she had left him, that he couldn't "see" her in his mind any more. She leant against him weakly, until he gently coaxed her.

"Jalni, open your eyes. I am still here and you can hear my voice properly. This is what you wanted. To be like everyone else. Living only with your own thoughts and under no compulsion of mine. Now, if that is still what you want, look up and tell me so!"

He could no longer feel that burning gaze on his, but with his hands on her shoulders, he felt the lift of her head and braced his heart for the ultimate rejection. It didn't come. Instead he heard a very subdued voice say, "Will it hurt if you put it back?", and he felt every muscle in her body tense as if she too expected rejection.

Incredibly she was clinging to him, attempting to place her arms into the double link again and he bent his head, brushed her cheek with his lips, saying thankfully, "Are you sure?", and felt the relief flood through her.

He cleared his mind, solemnly vowing to remember this moment and folded her willing hands into the ritual double link. He filled his mind with the gentle rhythm of the Source and bent a smiling mouth to hers in a tender kiss familiar, murmuring, "Jalni, look at me.", and as she timidly obeyed him, he opened himself fully to the power that surged and soared between them like lightening flickering in his veins. Jalni looked up into the fire opal of his magical othergaze and found herself hanging from his supporting arms, flooded with sweet joy and hearing him again.

This time his voice was clear, his presence certain and there was none of the tenuous hold that she had sensed and fought. She listened to him saying with tender solemnity, "Jalni bin Selesh, will you be my bondswoman, give me your fidelity, your life and limb until we are parted by the Divine. Will you share in my tasks, keeping me only to the Way of the One? Will you hear my sorrows and share my joys and give yours in return that our bond be mutual in value, desired by both, to the end of our mortal existence.".

Jalni suddenly knew that her life was about to change beyond anything that she could ever have imagined, but uncharacteristically she didn't flinch, run, panic or hide. She quietly and without a backward glance committed her life to him in one simple acceptance, that at last she had found her place. Almost too low to hear, she whispered, "Yes, O yes.". At his touch, she opened her heart and mind fully and was bonded to his will. Her eyes filled with tears of relief, the floodgates opened and she was held in his strong arms knowing that she was safe at last.

Chapter 29 - Second Sight

Jalni never found out how she got back to bed that night. She woke with a feeling of purpose and finding the bathing room deserted, stripped and sat in the bubbling pool. She had no memory of getting drunk, she only knew that Daro had found her, that he had seen her pain and freed her from it. Terris wandered in still half asleep and grinned at her, as Jalni rose from the water and dried herself, thinking how nice it was to have a friend almost the same age. She had wrapped herself modestly when Marran and Daro arrived chatting comfortably and to Jalni's surprise, Terris quite unselfconsciously, stripped to her nether-wear and entered the large pool.

Marran left Daro with Jalni at a stone basin and taking the mage's clean linen and wash things Jalni turned to assist him and was bathed in the warmth of his smile. His inner voice enquired calmly, "Are you well today?", and Jalni realising she was and oddly happy too, heard him chuckle. He could manage quite well by himself, but she leaned close by, handing him items as he needed them and was so absorbed with Daro that she didn't see Marran strip and join Terris in the pool.

Daro turned an ear in their direction, then wickedly, pressed his mouth against her ear and barely breathed, , "Do we all join in or what?", and she couldn't resist teasing him.

"Of course. Its an old Azurian custom.", and grinned at his delicate shudder, totally unprepared for the mental image that flickered through her mind. Two bodies entwined on a pile of cushions, followed by the impression of a sensual mouth commanding hers. Her face flamed as he commented dryly, "Speaking as an experienced woman of the world?".

His inner voice sounded amused, but he was sufficiently aware enough to duck as she swatted him lightly with a towel.

Terris noted Jalni's face as Daro touched her shoulder and nudged Marran, who stopped soaping his hair to watch. The tender amusement in the Sandsingers mouth, Jalni's blush and their body language told its own story and Marran watching her lead Daro out of the room, a new confidence in every line of her body said, quietly, "I was going to ask him if he was married. I never thought about Jalni! ".

His voice died away and Terris giggled, "Jealous?", she asked and Marran splashed her.

"Not me!", and pulled a face confessing, "My woman needs a sense of humour. She's far too moody and I'd prefer a good cook!".

Giggling Terris ran back to her sleeping space and hummed happily as she dressed, noticing the sweet curve of Jalni's lips as she folded blankets, which told the astute teenager that her mind was far from her task.

That morning Marran formally lined up the patrols and Daro fell into place with the Nightlingbys as the Cavern Captain called them to order.

"From now on, you will work, sleep and eat in patrols.", he announced gruffly, "Soon we will journey from our own Sands to Selesh, from where we will receive help to find living relatives and counselling. Daro has promised that families will stay together, so lets get used to travel rations, stowing bags properly and helping each other.".

He put his fingers in his mouth and whistled shrilly. "That signal's "Stand Still". It is the most important whistle to listen for and obey immediately.". The children shuffled as he whistled again, this time twice, the last note dying away on a falling tone.

"that means "Shut up and listen!", Marran said shortly and Jalni was impressed by the alacrity of obedience. "Right.", said the Cavern Captain, "Let's get to it. "Fly-bys, Sandrigals, Vetali" pack. Nightlingbys and Skimmers draw and distribute ration packs. Nestlings and carers check your supplies and carry on as normal!".

It was a valuable lesson, Daro was stationed at a table with Torvin. As each child collected their rations, Torvin marked a long list on one of Solana's wax tablets, tongue-tied with concentration. Rann controlled the traffic, marshalling the children and Daro solemnly stamped each hand with a bright blue dye, using this chance to elicit information about each child, mournfully accepting that they would all have to go back to Selesh, few knowing of living relatives and none of anyone who would foster them in their native Sands. The children were solemn and silent, the Sandsinger delicate and reassuring and the Opal Sand in his pouch dwindled with each subtle probe.

Height of Sun came and went, the children eating cold rations, drank from flasks, before unrolling blankets to sleep on the floor, as the adults withdrew, leaving Marran's crew in charge. As they sat listing the most frugal requirements to make their journey safe Terris asked Jalni directly, if she and Daro were bonded. For a second the Sandsinger froze, startling Jalni with his vehement demand for "Privacy!". His inner voice reminded her starkly of the barriers she had erected around her own feelings, but she knew only one way to stop speculation. Calmly, she looked Terris in the eye and said, "How clever of you. We thought we had hidden it so well.". She deliberately leant forward and took Daro's hand in hers, hoping that "speech without speech," would convey her meaning clearly.

"This is to keep private those things they don't need to know, so help me.", she pleaded, weighting the thought with an image of a burning village, diminished food stocks and dangerous trails. His head lifted and a smile curved his mouth, softening his expression gently as he answered, "Yes, we are bonded" and that was the end of that conversation.

They returned to essential planning, Jalni and Terris worked back the days, to be sure when Solana's quarantine would expire, as Marran's crew tallied rations and Daro meditated.

That Sundown, as the children packed meagre belongings back into carry bags, Daro returned (for the first time that day), to his sleeping quarters. He had

239

hardly gone, when he shocked Jalni by shouting for her. She was used to a discreet summons, had even expected one, so when his voice cut through the chatter in the Lookout, she nearly dropped the scrip she was checking.

"Attend me woman.", he bellowed and colouring, she leapt to her feet, to meet Marran's laughing gaze. She headed to the Sandsinger's sanctum, shutting the door on speculative eyes with relief, turning to find Daro resplendent in his ceremonials. There was no magic present yet he still radiated power as his inner voice said firmly, "Jalni, get your bedding, for you must sleep with me from now on.", and she flushed as she took in what he had said.

"I mean you no dishonour my Healer, but we must maintain the illusion you created, particularly if we need privacy to deal with emergencies.", and she knew that he was right, as she scolded herself for not having thought of that before, but as she left, she noticed his hands cradling a rapidly dwindling amount of Opal Sand and wondered why he seemed to cling to such a strange souvenir. Feeling at last, she belonged with the Sandsinger, she collected her belongings and returned, slipping silently in, to kneel behind him as he prayed, wondering what he was planning to do this Sunfall and added her own prayers for his safety, sharply reminded of a handful of Opal Sand, although she didn't understand the connection until later.

She was rested quietly back on her heels, studying the way his hair curled, when he took a deep breath and rose to his feet, holding out his hand. She took it naturally and felt her connection to the Source form through him, as she opened the door leading him out to the waiting audience.

A low two toned whistle hushed the buzz of anticipation as the children stood facing the Sandsinger. Jalni swept a glance around and saw the cave glowing warmly, the basalt blue of the walls reflecting the flame of the torches on the faces of her friends. In the deep shadows where they had their beds, the tinies woke and crawled forward into the light. The deep blue of the night sky framed Daro to perfection, as clad in the aura of the Opal, he lifted a hand and summoned them to listen.

They came to the edge of the huge fissure, where they could see across the mighty crater, the shadow in the centre that had been their home. From there, in the light of their twin moons a pathway gleamed softly to Gateway and beyond into an uncertain future.

Jalni shivered, whether from excitement or fear she didn't know and it was the same for the children, many of which still hadn't taken in the fact that there would be no return to their little village, no parents smiling at the door of their own house and that the darkness that they knew to be Scartel only housed the shadow of Death itself.

Daro paused for a second, allowing the children time to let their eyes adjust to the star strewn night sky and then he signalled with a hand that they should all sit and as they did so, Jalni felt the rush of a mighty wind, heard the peal of long silent bells and Daro took breath and lifted his *othervoice* and sang of the first Age of Mystery.

It started with a vivid image of Sanctuary, gleaming in all the colours of the Sands as it slowly materialised like a painting on the back wall of the Lookout Cave. She felt as if they were all soaring with the Bridge of the True Believer as it spanned the great chasm that had swallowed the Sanctuary of their time. Then as if they had crossed that ephemeral bridge, the view seemed to rotate and there were men and women, clad in the Colours of the Clans, ranging from Opal to Onyx and Jalni gasped, craning forward trying to catch a glimpse of the Sandsingers as the image faded. Then tumbling one by one the images flickered and flowed, on every wall, surrounding them with immense trees, fabulous plains, great expanses of water and unbelievably fertile fields. Daro seemed to be conducting the events that unfolded and Marran watched with bated breath as crops failed, heat shimmered off the Sands and there were no more scenes of open water.

Dried riverbeds snaked across the Sands they viewed. He saw a huge rift appear in the land and lightening flickered a constant reminder of the power of natural forces and still Daro sang. He sang the Winds of each desert, incorporating a muttering tempo as the Winds rose. Jalni looked around swiftly to make sure the children weren't afraid, but she saw that the teens had gathered their travelling groups together and in each group, one girl, one boy, acted as surrogate parents. Awed gasps and whispers were definitely heard, but no terror, the youngest nestled with the oldest and felt safe, even laughing as the restless winds gathered in the visions of the Voice that Daro created.

Then he showed them the Storm, a tiny baby being rescued by the Sorceress Ikella and she suddenly saw, in the gentle loving picture of his own nursery and the soft liquid croon of his voice how he perceived the need to reassure the children that they would be loved, for even the greatest Sorceress of their time was waiting to welcome them.

Jalni, every bit as entranced as the others, leant against the perimeter wall that protected them from accidental falls and watched as the images began to show Selesh.

As images of the Opal Desert flickered brilliantly, the Healer was overwhelmed by the feeling that they were not alone, that "another" watched with them and cautiously turned her head to see the ancient Sandsinger Daro had shown them the night he revealed his own power. This time however, the old man was no illusion and as she turned to welcome him, he stared at her quizzically, glanced at his bare feet and vanished into thin air. Inevitably, her eyes found Daro again and enthralled, she forgot time, place, visions of old men, until it was over and sleepy children snuggled together in patrol groups.

Marran helped the flagging Sandsinger towards his bed, Terris brought a sweet drink, onto which she had sprinkled a dose of the "Sandsingers Friend" remedy, stirring it swiftly as she handed it to Jalni. Seeing the emerging Healer in the girl, Jalni smiled, as she saw the colour come back to Daro's face with no evidence of the racking nausea he had previously suffered, although he shivered from a combination of cold and fatigue.

She heaped the pillows on his bed smoothing blankets and thought about the illusions Daro had conjured. A snatch of melody ran through her mind, bringing with it, the memory of their ghostly visitor as she sat at the feet of the Sandsinger, removing his boots.

"Should I pay you for your thoughts?", Daro's inner voice roused her from reverie blushing, but unable to dismiss the vision, she remained pre- occupied, hardly noticing when Daro removed his robes.

He was shivering when she finally responded to his appeal for help, her manner oddly subdued as she guided him to a deserted bathing room and carefully pitching her voice told him,

"You will have to tell me when you need help but you should understand, that until I qualify, energies are dedicated to Healing. I can't enter a relationship with a patient because I have taken the oath of respect. Our Deshun insisted on that before we left. So, you are quite safe in my hands, as I hope I am in yours.".

She plaited her fingers and her meaning was plain.

His face smiled down into hers and Jalni quite irrationally wished he could see her, but she maintained her cool professional exterior, while her heart pounded in an altogether disconcerting way. His lips were tantalisingly close as he whispered, "Jalni, we are bonded, hip to hip and heart to heart. I can hear your thoughts and you need not fear me as a man. It is not the time or place, besides I respect your rights.".

She stared up at him, one hand resting on his upper arm, as he lowered his face, brushing her cheek against his. She heard him then, very softly, "If you listen you will always be able to hear me, I can hear you in my head and my heart. The time for us will come, but we are here for these children, our time is later.", and silenced, she led him steadily back to their room.

Much later, lying on the pallet beside his bed, Jalni's mind turned back to the old man that she had seen and suddenly it came to her. The older man could be Daro himself. The shape of the head, hands and body all fitted but what did it mean? Had she seen an vision of the future? If indeed this was Daro, where were his boots? Why was he so distressed by the images of the city past? She struggled with her thoughts, but they kept slipping from her, replaced by an image of firm strong limbs, smooth golden skin, a well-muscled chest, a ruefully smiling mouth and a voice saying softly, privately,

"Jalni, this I simply cannot manage, can you come and wash my back?", yawning and sighing wistfully over this stupid yearning for him, she rolled over and fell deeply asleep.

Above her, Daro waited quietly in the dark, monitoring his breathing pattern so that she was unaware that he was still awake, listening for her to relax into full sleep. She was restless, shifting on her pillow and sighing to herself deeply. He probed her thoughts gently and was shocked by the images that filled her dreaming mind and withdrew. At last she fell into a dreamless sleep, so setting a light hold on her and curled into a natural sleeping position, Tuning into his inner voice, he began the soft chant Sentinel. had taught him and gradually his awareness faded. He drifted, seamlessly sliding into trance as if he had been doing it all his life and woke, calm but tired and the old man was there, striding about in an agony of impatience.

Daro sat up, feeling his limbs strangely leaden and performed the ritual "warding", of his own sleeping body, aware that his mysterious companion was not in a happy frame of mind. Still unused to "true sight", he gazed around for a minute, before he caught the Sentinel muttering to himself.

"Too soon, too soon.", he mumbled, as Daro entered the Plain of Shadows and he turned a truculent expression towards Daro as he stood to join him.

"You don't listen to anyone do you!", he admonished and Daro stopped still, aware that Sentinel was really alarmed.

"I told you very clearly, not to use High Magic until we locate your Seguidor and here you are, luring the Azure, bonding the woman, driving yourselves insane on that dratted Feydora's Cloudberry Wine and then, you dredge up the past for the entertainment of children? Are you quite sure that you don't really want to kill yourself? I can think of more painless ways to go!".

Daro said placatingly,

"I am sorry Grandfather, I didn't lure the Azure! I'm not even sure that Jalni is the right person, but she is very powerful and she was the one who found the drink. She was drunk and I only decided to try it to find out why. I intended no disobedience. I deliberately grounded myself in the Sand before I sang and it was important that the children know that they will be safe and loved in Selesh, now, was that wrong?".

For answer, Sentinel drew Daro forward and despite his chronic fatigue, they walked to the door, out into the Lookout and over to the great fissure that revealed the crater below.

Daro was flagging by the time they leant on the barrier wall and Sentinel smiled sardonically, as Daro collapsed against it, panting.

"Weak as a Myst-kitten.", he crowed, "No wonder your love-life depends on Feydora's muck. Never used an intoxicant like that before, I'll warrant!",

Daro stared at him,

"Are you telling me that cloud berries are aphrodisiac in nature?", he demanded and the old man chortled.

"Combined with various herbs, distilled and bottled with a moonstone stopper, you'd better believe it. Sandsinger's can't reproduce without it, but they can only reproduce with a mortal, boy. You'll never get a child by that one, for she is rising Azure, if not Azure ascendant. Too late my boy, too damn late!".

"So why were you saying "Too soon," as I arrived?", Daro said nastily and Sentinel groaned. "Aah. You will be leaving far too soon for me to teach you all the tricks of the Seguidor, but I have an idea, where to find yours now, I am just waiting for the weather to change and we shall see!".

Daro felt too exhausted to respond to this. His brain was numb with all the things he had been forced to learn in a hurry. He hadn't had the time to explore Selesh properly before he was being hurried out through the door, expected to absolve himself of what Ikella had perceived as sacrilege, by getting all-Sands treatment for his obsession. This had seen him travel Sand to Sand in search, not for the artefact his mother sought so diligently, but of the past, of the secretive Sandsingers of the past and now he had encountered another of the ephemeral mentors, he was on his way again.

"Its enough to make a man giddy.", he thought resentfully and then realised that he was indeed giddy and dreadfully nauseated once more. He said nothing though, preferring to cling to the wall of the cave, using this weird "true-sight", to stare at the crater below. He couldn't trust what he perceived now, he decided. The night seemed filled with deep shadows, a strange green flicker marked the warding that still held good at the village, protecting the dead that lay within and the living that slept without. He observed with interest in the odd perspective that true sight gave, the great entranceway and the desert beyond, straining to see more. The effort caught the notice of the Sentinel.

"You seek the path that you must tread,", he stated gravely, "but it is not a path that any vision can follow. It is not a thing of highways and hills and perils are just as likely to accost you where you feel safest and amongst those you trust!".

He turned and looked over the desolate landscape below, brooding darkly. Daro looked at him steadily. The cold, old planes of his face gleaming silvered by moonlight and the Sentinel raised his eyes and for a second Daro saw himself mirrored, then his visitor moved and the strange moment and the strong feeling of connection was gone.

The Sentinel spoke, his *othervoice* peaceful.

"She can see me you know.", Daro immediately thought of Lallee, but before he could voice his thoughts, Sentinel interrupted him. "No, no, not the child. Jalni can see me. This makes life very difficult."

Daro choked back a laugh.

"That's nothing new for Jalni!", he observed, "How do you know she can see you. When did that happen?", he asked curiously and the Sentinel let out a short bark of laughter that made Daro flinch. He somehow couldn't get used to the fact that no-one in the cave would have been able to see them asleep or awake and yet he could stand amongst them, see them, touch them. it was most confusing. He persisted,

"What is so funny, I mean, how do you know that Jalni can see you? When did she see you? She never told me.".

His voice faded in the face of Sentinel's hilarity and he paused, if only to give the man a chance to recover his breath. He eventually sobered, saying with some asperity, "By the powers boy, don't you think when someone looks straight at you and takes a step in your direction with welcome on their faces and wonder in their hearts that you don't know it?", He hitched a hip on to the wall and disposed himself comfortably, turning towards Daro as he spoke,

"By the stirring of the Sands boy! Don't you know your own powers? When a Singer summons all to hear they come, whatever they are doing. I came, standing just against that wall and the Azure in her saw me.", He continued,

"I was just standing, at one with the spell,", his voice dropped a little, remembering, "Seeing Selesh again, I thought had made me careless, but I looked and I was still on the Plain of Shadows, yet she saw me, for like others of her Clan, she has Second Sight.", He wrinkled a brow, brushed his face wearily and said softly, "A thousand Rotations since I was called to mentor and then I am woken as you rose Opal, then along comes the little Malachite, with no guide of her own, so I mentored her until you came. Then the place is positively overrun with Singers. Lallee, that Amber child, an Azure rising and now I find an Opal, with no formal training. Whatever is Sanctuary thinking of and how came those at Tirjhinar to let out a whole herd of untrained Singers at once? Tell me that young man.", He turned a burning gaze on Daro, who struggled to escape in vain.

Daro shivered violently, not just with cold, but with some internal shock. How could he explain that the world that Sentinel knew had gone? That there had been no Sandsinger for a thousand Rotations. How could he tell this lonely ancient that whatever his time had dreaded, had occurred and that none of his line had survived the resulting Cataclysm. He might not understand that not only were there no records, but that Pelshar had deliberately forgotten and knew, from Sentinels ashen face that he already had.

There was a strange disturbance in the Source, Sentinel sagged back, , his eyes blazing crystal bright, Daro quailed before him feeling the power surging through his companions othergaze and tried to respond to the command, "Tell me Selunsanni, bow before the power, but tell me all" and Daro told him what he knew of Pelshar's past. It was ripped out of him, torn from every corner of memory. From scrolls he had never unrolled, to sand tablets he had merely glanced at. It poured from every twist and turn he had explored in the depths of Selesh. He remembered even things he didn't know he knew and when the Sentinel released him, he suddenly saw what he hadn't seen before and that was the faint aura of purest crystal, sparkling on the skin of the ancient mage and then his true-sight left him and he was alone, in the dark, without the strength to return to his sleeping body.

"What's happening?", he begged in a whisper, as he collapsed and knew that he was dying. Beyond speech, the voice of his mind whispered, "Jalni…Lallee" and the air around him blazed as they ran to him.

There was a bell tolling somewhere, a Voice chanting softly and lifted on the Source he listened attentively. "There is one who walking in the night comes amongst us, bearing power absolute, yet unknown. His gift is the greatest, sprung from his sire borne on the arms of the wind, seeded in the storm and raised with the sun. He shall bear pain, summon joy and taste infinity. His love shall be beyond love, his voice shall be the honour and the saving of Pelshar.".

The voice disconcertingly faded as Daro realised that the prophecy would never be carried out if he died. He fought the spinning blackness grimly, floating free of the pain in his chest to see Jalni sat by his bed, holding the hand of his otherself, weeping bitterly, murmuring little fragments,

"I should have known. He was so tired. Please don't leave me Daro. Oh, Ichspeller come back. We need you, I need you.". She wearily rested her head against his chest, kissing the bare skin beneath her trembling lips. A shudder of grief tore through her and she raised her head in such a convulsive move that Daro felt the howl of anguish before she launched it, as whatever power suspended him, stilled the cry before it began.

It was painfully slow, but as he was lifted to lie alongside his sleeping body, his last thought was, "Jalni, Jalni I am here, I am not dead. Be still little one, be still.", and summoned all his remaining energy to close his eyes and slide back into that space in time that was the door from the Plain of Shadows to normal existence.

When he awoke, her mouth was clamped to his, breathing sharp citrine scented breath into his body. Daro took in the fact that her scent had changed from the fresh pine fragrance that he associated with her and wondered vaguely whether this was the scent of anxiety. Then, he thought that this was very pleasant, to wake in the arms of a woman, even if she was pounding on his chest as if his life depended on it. He moved to reach out to her but the only trouble was, that he couldn't summon the energy. His head was swimming, his heart hurt and the effort of breathing was just too much. He was choking, his limbs were leaden and his body was fading away. He had only the time to thank the One that he had unwarded his body, as Jalni shrieked for Terris and he felt himself fading, floating, spinning in a sea of lilac blue.

When he awoke, she was there and with her another. He felt the glow in the Source, as Terris, Jalni and Lallee, bathed his face. Someone strong was holding him, much as he had held Solana and the sensation of being surrounded by loving hands, overcame him again and instinctively he knew that this must be the last time that he over reached himself. He relaxed into Jalni's hands and was immediately aware of a voice, an *othervoice*, as she lifted her head and Sang for her love.

When he felt her tremble and take a breath, he was quite unprepared for the reality of it. When the low pulsing beat began, he didn't know at first what was happening, but as his failing heart picked up the rhythm, he felt her glowing, azure blue, shot with gold. Her spectrum flickered turquoise, as his breathing steadied and as it changed, no longer sighing towards death, the rich soprano lifted and he was bathed in the power that she summoned. He had a brief image of blue flybys, flowers and other symbols glowing soft and lambent and then as another voice blended greenly with Jalni's in melodic counterpoint, he felt himself being firmly but inexorably steered towards sleep. As he let go, spinning towards oblivion, he heard Lallee whisper sorrowfully, "I'm afraid that I may have broken it Terris.", and caught a glimpse of a sand-glass, brutally disassembled, lying on his wash-stand and realised with weary humour that someone had placed a spoonful of sand, Opal sand, on his naked navel. He smiled and slept.

Chapter 30 - The Heart of Selesh

Jalni lay, quietly listening to the sound of steady breathing from Daro's bed. She only needed to check him every two sectors of the sand-glass, but was satisfied with the evidence of his recovery so far.

In the two days since the last episode, she had watched him exercising weakened muscles under Marran's tutelage, accepting that with regular sleep, a total withdrawal from magic and the simplest of foods he was ready to rejoin the company. She had only restrained his adventuring this long by pointing out that finding his Seguidor was secondary to his survival, at which he had given in with astonishingly good grace and she privately suspected that he had been sufficiently frightened to see her point.

She waited in the dark, slowly relaxing into a light doze, from which the slightest movement would rouse her and had been gently "sifting the Source", sorting out her impressions of Daro's spectacular collapse, when she recognised the signature of another empowered being nearby.

Lying quite still, she turned her eyes towards Daro's sleeping form and saw the old man she had seen listening to Daro three nights past.

He bent over the bed, observing Daro calmly and Jalni waited with bated breath. He didn't attempt to rouse the sleeping man, but held his hand out over Daro's head moving it down to his throat, back to his face and then the other hand was brought into play. As Jalni watched, the old man seemed to be "polishing the air", above Daro's head.

Fascinated, she watched, absorbed by what seemed to be an advanced Healing technique, albeit something she had never seen practised. The visitor paused, placing one hand over Daro's throat, finger and thumb extended, then nodded to himself, seeming satisfied and Jalni was wondering what would come next, when Daro shifted, rolling on to his side, discarding the light blanket to curl naked like a child. She slid out of her own blankets and ignoring Daro's visitor, covered him again, stroking her hand tenderly over his hair as she settled his pillows, then turning, looked the old man in the face.

"I can see you, as I did before.", she said conversationally and this time, he looked her straight in the eye and said quietly, "I know, but you shouldn't be able to. Jalni isn't it?".

She nodded, shivering in her thin nightshirt and he said kindly, "Get into bed child. I simply can't have any more of you getting ill.", and she meekly obeyed thinking that he would be gone when she looked up, but he came and sat in the chair and spoke, his face grave, voice serious.

"You'll have to harvest any Opal Sand you find in his clothing, shoes, or pouch until we find a missing artefact.", and Jalni found herself nodding agreement.

"I know.", she said simply and the old man raised an imperative eyebrow and she added, "He seeks a Seguidor, someone called Feydora told me that he strays into danger without it.".

She ignored the astounded look on the visitors face and continued steadily, "I found Opal Sand on Ichspeller Selunsanni's person the night he collapsed,", she retold the stripping of Daro's body, in order to massage tonic oils into his skin, how she had been startled by finding grains of sand around his navel and blushed confessing, "I don't know if I did wrong, but the strongest response I could sense was around this sand and I remembered him meditating over a handful of Opal Sand he kept in his pouch earlier.".

There was a quiver in her voice as she reminisced. "Marran looked in his pouch, but it was empty, so knowing that all sand-glass makers use Opal Sand, I got Lallee to fetch the sand-glass Terris used for cooking and we took the Sand inside and placed it where the other had appeared. I don't know why, but it seemed to be the right thing to do!", she finished in a rush and the old man looked at her steadily and said slowly, "In so doing young woman, you undoubtedly saved his life. You really are a most intuitive Healer, worthy of your calling.", and Jalni glowed with mixed pride and relief.

"I don't suppose you know anything about his belt?", he mused and Jalni believing that she was about to hear something that Daro needed to know, lowered her eyes humbly and said,

"No. I only know that it came back to him by a circuitous route, having been lost somehow and returned to him in thanks for some act of healing that he performed for a simple boy back in Selesh.".

Her visitor's eyes sharpened.

"He missed telling me about that.", he commented and sighed. "Well young woman, I had better tell you my name and about Daro's belt clasp. He will need to know this and as you act as his body-servant, guide and Healer, so you should know also.".

"I am the Star-Weaver Sentinel.", he made a low courtly bow and Jalni giggled quietly, then said softly,

"What is a Star-Weaver?", and he clapped a hand to his head in horror. "Of course, you don't know, no-one knows anymore!", and he seemed so stricken that Jalni said comfortingly,

"Well, don't worry about that, you can explain all that when Daro is awake. Just tell me the belt bit if that is easier.", and the old man rallied.

"Aah, dear me yes!", he muttered, then drawing himself up said hopefully, "Is the belt anywhere to hand?", and Jalni pointed mutely to Daro's backpack, where she had rolled his cleaned ceremonials and Sentinel crooked a finger and the belt materialised in his hand. Jalni stared, as he flipped the belt over on its wrong side and then watched open mouthed as he removed the gleaming circular fob from his own belt laying it on the clasp of Daro's belt. The fob and clasp met with a tiny "snick" and the clasp (which had dulled noticeably), started to glow as Sentinels Seguidor began to spin lazily. Jalni watched in awe, seeing tiny tendrils of radiance shooting out from the fob as it rotated and then the Opal sand which she had collected into a small dish suddenly glowed, pulsed and vanished as Sentinels Seguidor slowed, stopped and disengaged.

"What did you do?", she whispered and Sentinel said gently,

"The Anduigor, which you know as a belt clasp, is made of Opal Sand, which is why it appears as an Opal on the Singers person. It too has a part to play in helping him maximise his power and it is what gave up the Sand that he could take strength from it.".

Jalni stared, as Daro's Anduigor pulsed once and then the entire belt, clasp and all dematerialised and Sentinel laughed gently at her expression.

"He only needs to hold the clasp to contact the Sands, but this belt and the Sand it contained were too old to support his need. Now we have replenished the sand, all he needs is his own Seguidor and then you must leave.", and Jalni's heart ached at the loneliness in Sentinels voice.

He stroked his beard contemplatively, "I only tell you this my child, to keep him safe. I think you are remarkably perceptive and you should understand that the continuance of your whole world depends on Daro's survival. He cannot channel the power of the Sands without his Seguidor, but he does! That boy is remarkable. He is using his own will-power most of the time, but even that phenomenal resolve has to give sometime!".

The deep voice dropped to an awed whisper, "His own power! I seriously doubt that there has ever been another like him, but you must get your sleep, for I have plans for tomorrow.", he added anxiously, "and the weather is changing, you must leave soon.", he nodded briefly and vanished. Jalni laid down on her mattress and despite her best efforts, slipped off to sleep, a smile curving her lips.

From the moment she woke, the morning after that strange interview, Jalni saw the change in Daro. She watched breathlessly, as he worked with Marran and his "Nightlingbys", falling quite naturally into the rhythms of S'chang , a meditation that involved gentle exercises. That morning he walked among the children, a smile on his lips and a new confidence, bolstered by the use of his long slim Staff.

The children thought this was a wonderful departure and once they had stopped running around and understood that Daro could use the Staff to find his way about, they all relaxed and Daro stopped feeling so self-conscious.

Terris was happy too. In the search for food, she had discovered another cupboard full, more than enough to see them through the necessary few days extension to their stay that Jalni had prescribed and the young Healer mentally applauded Sentinel's skill, while keeping up the illusion that she knew nothing about Daro's strange mentor.

She had watched Daro ward and unward the door with an easy "click" of his fingers and realised that the power ran very strong in his veins and even though his physical strength was depleted, she knew that he would get stronger. He had become calmer, just a little remote from her, but Jalni decided for herself, that she could live with that and didn't miss the flickering fire of sexual attraction, glad that she felt balanced, whole and in command of herself again.

Marran and his crew, put time to good use. Amid howls of laughter, the Nightlingbys had built a kind of sledge, intending it to hold their packs for some of the journey and Daro had examined it, running his hands over it and making nods of approbation, slapping this one and that on the shoulder and with a pang, Jalni saw what a good father he would make and wondered if he would ever get the chance. She wondered what they would do this afternoon, for Marran and Terris had quietly informed her, that this would be their last in the Lookout. Here their supplies were nearly expended and tomorrow they would return to the Home Cave, sleep the afternoon away and leave in the cool of the evening, to take the first part of the long way home.

Even as those plans ran through her mind, another search party was gathering to investigate the higher caves above the Lookout. She rose to join them and the Sandsingers door abruptly thrust open and Daro appeared, dressed in work wear, looking eagerly to join them. He walked independently, using his Staff and so with the occasional word of caution from Jalni, or Brus, insinuated himself into their midst and went to the ancestral halls of the Singers of Scharatel.

As they climbed to the higher level the passageways widened and here and there a remnant of the past remained. A coloured thread hanging where once a tapestry had been, bookshelves, bare now, but still standing sturdily. Ahead of them a child cried out suddenly and Marran ran forward, to see that part of the way was now impassable, a yawning chasm opened up in front of them. Nearly eighty spans below, lost in the dark, they could hear the sound of running water beneath. Jalni pressed her way through the group ahead, until she stood with Marran on the brink of the void and gasped, for on the other side, she could clearly see through a rough-hewn arch, great doors, one slightly ajar.

They stood staring until Daro caught up with them, the children respectfully drawing to one side as he approached the gaping hole. Marran shot out an arm, blocking the blind Sandsinger's path, amusing Daro, who said mildly,

"Jalni, shall you move this barrier or shall I?", and without another word he strode forward and Marran was forced to one side, as the Opal aura sprang up around the Sandsinger with an audible rush of power.

Jalni, knowing that Daro was empowered in a way that she had never previously seen, watched, heart in mouth as the Sandsinger stepped out into thin air. As he strode forward confidently, there was a pulsing sensation, almost from the air itself. At his feet part of a stone stair appeared and as he took another step and another, audible tomes pulsed upward along the scale and the steps appeared just as he was about to put his foot down. As he reached the other side of the chasm, Daro turned and swiftly holding up a hand, called back to them.

"This is a place that you cannot enter. Stay there, all of you. You will find other rooms where you will be safe to the right, behind the blue curtain.".

Never was a truer word spoken, for as the feet of the Sandsinger left the hidden stairway, it completely disappeared again. Daro continued command in every line of his body, "Marran, Jalni, take the children and go and look along the passageway, but do not attempt to cross, I have warded your side for safety. I am quite safe and won't be long.", he passed through the door, disappearing from view.

Marran looked around the party of seniors that he had mustered and said shortly, "You all heard that. We are going to stay together, so fall into line.", and taking Jalni's arm, he ordered cheerily, "Come on, lets go see what we can find.". He pulled her gently along and mute but unresisting, she followed his example.

As glows sprang to life around them, they wandered entranced, into opulence the like of which had long passed from Pelshar. Marran was the first to express their feelings. His eyes standing out on stalks, he gazed at the hangings, the soft pillows piled on the floor, the ornate bed, the carved tables and elaborate chairs. He looked round and his lips pursed.

"Woo Hoo!", The sound of the Nightlingby filled the room and his crew came running and stopped dead in their tracks, staring in amazement.

Brus quavered into life. "Who lived here Jalni?", his voice expressive, as he spun on his heels, crying out, "I'll bet it was a Sandsinger!", as silenced by wonder, the others nodded agreement.

Jalni, fascinated by a string of blue beads that lay unattended on a table, picked them up, running her hand down them, watching them shine against her skin. The bed was turned down as though waiting for the occupant of this room to return. Jalni looked round slowly, drinking in every detail, trying to picture the long dead possessor of such luxury. There was a portrait of a man on the wall and she walked to it, studying the imperious tilt to the head, the sparkle in the eyes, the gleam of dark hair, the smiling mouth, but it sparked no chord within her, so she moved on.

Picking up a curio here, a scarf there, she worked her way round the room, replacing items quickly overcome by the thought that the owner might suddenly return. With no such inhibitions, Quaryn was first to pull open a drawer, looking for usable items. Marran, seeing Jalni's disapproval, called out:

"Nightlingbys! Remember what Solana told us. Touch nothing that we don't need, this is salvage not pillage!", and the search for Daro's Seguidor went on. Jalni reminded herself sternly that no-one living would object if she joined in and ignoring the faintest tinkle of wind chimes, pulled open a drawer in a dresser made in Torrenwood.

Inside, there was a box made in costly Chanite. She hesitated, but eventually gave in to the compulsion and raised the lid. Perhaps her sudden stillness gave the others some indication that she had found something, for suddenly they flocked to her, staring down over her shoulder at the largest Opal that she had ever seen. It lay there, a long, slim spear of a stone, night fire Opal, darkly gleaming at her and immediately she thought of Daro's eyes. The group closed around her, all trying to get a glimpse of her find and lost in the glow she didn't see how he arrived, but she knew that the Sandsinger was there, for the stone she was staring at, woke.

They all felt it flare, as Jalni rose and made a deep bow to him and the group parted, allowing him to tap his Staff, gently probing his way to the stone, which restlessly shifting in its box, seemed to stream a dark path of fire towards him. He stood poised as if listening and then he took a breath and sang a single note.

Within Jalni's grasp the great opal rose with a whisper of sound and smoothly, without hesitation it sought the Voice and the Staff. With a delicate "snick" it locked into place and flared into life!

Jalni was the only one to remain on her feet. She looked at Daro and saw his head lift, his shoulders square, saw the flicker of pride at his lips and knew in her heart that now, now and in her presence, he had fully come into his power and she found herself bathed in the glow from his Staff, bathed in the glow from his eyes and knelt, longing to know what was in his heart.

Daro felt the torrent of power strike the Staff as the great stone slid into place and braced himself mentally and physically. His last few days had been indescribable, filled with the understanding of his own mortality, he had studied with Sentinel, at first unable to visualise the immensity of the power he had craved. He learned with mounting horror that his world was dying, but could be saved if he concentrated on collecting objects of power together, but without his Seguidor, he couldn't focus the major powers, or complete his task.

With no time for orderly study Sentinel placed his old hands to each side of Daro's head and sang the history to him. Images poured in, faster than Daro could process and were stored for future use and unaware that in the glow of the Star Weavers Seguidor, time passed the door of his room. Together, they covered almost a Rotation's worth of tuition, in two days. Through mind-linking, he had learned while asleep and now with the finding of his power stone he felt complete.

As he learned about the great Staff of Tirjhinar, it had never occurred to him that he would hold it and yet it was his already. The Staff he had shaped to his needs in his hands welcomed the power stone like an old friend, pulsing restlessly. He could feel a connection. As if Seleus itself was gathered in its glowing heart and Jalni saw him smile, then as the magic faded he spoke softly.

"Never forget that you were there when the Heart of Selesh beat once more. Never forget that you were there when the Staff of Tirjhinar assembled in the hands of the Opal Singer, this you must never forget.", and as he turned towards the door he said slowly, "Never forget that you heard me say that if it were not for the sacrifice of those who went before, none of us would be here to celebrate the Opal ascendant.".

His guides flanked him, but he walked alone, only remarking in silent speech, "If all goes well, we travel at Sunfall tomorrow.".

Later that night, Marran gathered all the children together, excluding the tinies, who were already sleeping. Daro sat, while they gathered on blankets at his feet and he took his Staff and entranced them, by extending his aura about them, in a warming protective circle of light.

His voice rang with power, though Jalni hadn't noticed the usual effort that it took to engage it, although the Heart of Selesh pulsed gently atop the Staff as he said slowly:

"You, within this circle are part of the greater plan. The Children of Scartel will return, when you are grown and can build your own future. It will be the home of your children and your children's children.".

His voice lifted, certain, sure and the children sighed as he continued. "For now, you are in my charge and I command your loyalties, but one day soon, you will have your own Sandsinger.".

He paused as a hiss ran round the group, smiling and saying gently, "It is not time yet and so you must accept my help until I summon she who is to come.".

As the teens took in what Daro had said, a few of the boys groaned and Torvin was heard to mutter in disgust

"Hadda's balls. Trust us to get a girlie one!", but he was hastily hushed by Nimah's elbow. Marran reached out a long arm and restrained any retaliation and in the spirit of letting youngsters have their heads, Daro continued,

"One day quite soon Torvin, you will discover that girls have their uses.", and Torvin blushed as Terris remarked icily.

"Like tomorrow, when we leave and I forget to bake your bread my lad.", and chuckling to herself, Jalni led the Sandsinger back to their room to sleep.

Chapter 31 - Myth or Legend?

Jalni was only too glad to lie on her pallet, mentally checking their packs, aware that there could be no turning back for mislaid items. The night was incredibly hot and sticky and uncomfortably aware of this, she lay under one thin cover, glad that Daro had gone to sleep without his nightly indulgence in study. The slim book had been packed away in his pocket for the morning, it being, (she considered) "another drain on his stamina.".

As she drifted towards sleep, she was listing her weird experiences silently, "I've met Sandsingers, Mystcats, Rangers, Star Weavers. Seen Power-stones Anduigors, Seguidors…", trailing off as her sleepy mind grappled with the complex nature of Sentinel. Mumbling, "Myth or legend? Legend or Myth?", she finally slept, waking much later to a touch on her arm.

Not sure if she was sleep-drunk, or ensorcelled, she stumbled to her feet and followed Sentinel, knuckling her eyes as she went. Daro had gone already, his bed stood empty, pillows on the floor and the Staff of Tirjhinar had gone with him.

She wrapped her blanket round her like a cloak and hurried in Sentinels wake, as he turned out of the ante - room near the Lookout and ducked through a narrow exit, on to the corona of peaks surmounting the crater of Scartel. She followed as the old man climbed and found herself high above the desert, in the heart of a lightening storm.

"This must be some song-vision.", she decided and strangely unafraid of the ferocious cracks of lightening, sat on a rock to watch. Daro stood, a little to her left and below her. Feet planted firmly apart, his arms uplifted to the raging sky and as the clouds above the mountain boiled and the air turned molten, Jalni witnessed a Sandsinger dancing with a storm.

She felt his delight, as braced on the Staff, he swung giddily, lifting his feet clear of the ground, floating so that his cloak swirled around him. He was singing to himself and the rhythm of the storm was somehow part of that song and as his *othervoice* dictated, so ran the tempo of the night.

Huddled in the blanket, she watched entranced, as Daro sent great bolts of lightening flickering along the Heights of Scartel, laughing joyously as a roll of thunder enveloped them and Jalni saw the mage was riding the wave of power the storm had generated. His eyes gleamed fire opal bright, reflecting in the Heart of Selesh which pulsed, until a low pounding beat thrummed an accompaniment. Out of that turmoil, in every shade of billowing cloud the single horned storm horses materialised. Nimble of foot, wild of eye, unseen since Cataclysm, a whole herd of long legged, silken skinned Zephryn filled the skies, whickering a descant to the storm as it rolled away eastward. Daro stood amongst them, his hands outstretched, an expression of childlike wonder on his face.

It was as if they knew that he couldn't see. One at a time they approached, delicately picking their way, until they could place their long nosed faces in his hands. Jalni gasped as the last one appeared, for she was completely silver. A mere baby in comparison to the others and as Daro reached out for her, placing his hand on the small horn centred in her forehead, it glowed, reflecting in his eyes.

As she nuzzled his hands, Daro stood cradling her head and Jalni heard his *othervoice*, choked with emotion.

"O, there you are.", he said tenderly and the Zephryn foal snickered, then came directly to Jalni and knelt. The foal let out a gusty sigh of blossom-scented breath, laying her head in the startled Healers lap as Daro, one hand tangled in its mane spoke.

"Her name is Araneus.", and quite suddenly Jalni remembered Ikella's scroll-weight and smiled up at him, mentally adding "Zephryn", to her tally of magical experiences, as the foal raised her head and whickered enquiringly.

Jalni "heard" Daro's inner voice say reluctantly, "If you must," and understood instantly, that the herd couldn't stay, must leave with the returning storm. She watched Daro, as one by one, they tossed their manes and leaping skyward, streamed into the cloud above. The last to leave was Araneus. She nuzzled the Sandsingers hands urgently, until he laughed and caught the animal's head, turning it until he could rub his face against one velvet cheek. Araneus dipped her head, thrusting her horn into Daro's hands until the Sandsinger realised that something had been twisted around it and delicately unwound whatever it was, holding it in his palm hidden from Jalni. Then he hugged the foal once and let her go. Araneus tossed her mane, whickered regretfully and joined the herd, leaping skyward gracefully mane and tail streaming as she became one with the storm cloud above.

Daro stood hand outstretched, face turned skyward, as overcome with pity at the desolation on his face, Jalni looked at the lonely path he must follow and went to his aid.

He took the proffered arm, but said softly, "She will come whenever I call her and Jalni, save your pity for those who need it. I had a choice and I took it. If I don't regret it, neither should you. Perhaps one day soon, you'll understand.", and he held up his free hand for her to see.

She stared at it blankly, then saw that around his fingers he had woven a chain and hanging from it, lying on the back of his hand was the missing Seguidor! Jalni raised her eyes to his face and he smiled. Dumbstruck, she pressed his hand gently and thought about how relieved he must feel, now that he was safe to Sing. As they approached the tricky entrance into the caverns below, Daro paused for an instant his face turned as if he would look at her and said simply, "I was the one who offered anything, including my life for this. Now I must live with that bargain. Jalni there are so many dimensions to life besides sight. Just think of the few we've encountered together.", and as Jalni's list flashed into her mind, Daro's inner voice took up the refrain.

"Sandsingers, Mystcats, Star Weavers, Zephryn...", as they walked on, unaware of Sentinel as they went back to their beds.

In the morning, Jalni expected Daro to be exhausted, but to her relief he looked supremely rested. He grinned at her engagingly and held out a hand on which lay the mysterious Seguidor. She stared at it and he patted his bed, his *othervoice* lazy in her mind.

"After all the fuss over this you can bring yourself up here and take a look at it.", he invited, at which she scrambled on to the bed and Daro extended the hand that held his Seguidor to her saying, "I don't suggest you touch it, but take a good look. Is it anything like the object you saw at Selesh?".

She studied his Seguidor closely. As Sentinel had described, it was a good thumb length across and circular in shape and she exclaimed involuntarily, "Oh, its beautiful, but isn't it like a wheel?", and bent her head to examine it minutely. Around a central hub made of silver metal , were nine sections each filled with a kind of sand-paste containing all the Colours of the Sands. These sections were girdled by an infill of Opal, which flowed from its own segment, surrounding and dominating every section. The silver circlet that held it all together gleamed oddly and Jalni had the strangest feeling that it was coated with something , but couldn't put a name to it and so she stared into the Seguidor and didn't notice that Daro had shifted his grasp, so that his fingers held the Azure segment.

She heard a voice whispering, "Remember for me where you saw the Seguidor back in Selesh little one.", and into her mind sprang the image of a drawer full of scrolls and a determined novice. Daro chuckled when he realised that it lay completely unrecognised in his mother's scroll table, if Beneva hadn't rescued it by the time he got home and touched the Seguidor, calculating.

"Ah well.", he smiled at her indulgently. "I don't think it matters right now.", and with that enigmatic comment Jalni had to be content. They ate their last breakfast in the privacy of the small room and Jalni was glad of this time of respite. all too soon she considered glumly, they would be amongst the children night and day and they wouldn't be able to get away from the noise and bustle. She didn't see the considering look on Daro's face, but looked up as he lifted her into his embrace and his mouth descended on hers.

She swayed against him, overwhelmed by the sensuality of his mouth and locked in this torrid embrace, she was unaware when Marran, unaccountably decided to chivvy them along.

The young Ranger, talking over his shoulder to Terris, put one foot inside, then seeing what was going on, gulped, coloured and withdrew discreetly. No sooner had the door closed, when Daro lifted his head and said with deep satisfaction.

"That's our privacy ensured wherever possible, now lets just check through everything and we can join the others.", He touched the Seguidor which now hung on its chain around his neck, raised a hand, into which his Staff flew and Jalni, still reeling from the surge of desire that he had provoked, glared at him as his backpack materialised on to one shoulder and he was ready.

She slung her scrip to her belt, hoisted her own pack and caught up both her own and Daro's cloaks, disposing those to Brus and Calar, who as usual were locked in friendly rivalry as they gathered ready to leave.

Already, the great outer cavern had assumed the air of lifeless, long deserted places. The hearth and oven had grown cold overnight. The bedding rolls, ration packs and walking canes gathered in mute testimony to their occupation and as the pile dwindled with every patrol preparing, the desolation grew. One or two of the children were crying, Lallee walked the perimeter of the great cavern looking distressed and Torvin argued loudly with Quaryn over the way that they would carry the torches ahead of the company. Marran let out a piercing whistle as they entered and miraculously the assembly hushed, formed ranks and then Daro said mildly,

"Marran my friend, I have a gift for you. Last night a messenger brought my Seguidor to me and now I can make the transition to Home Cave easier for everyone. I think that the stress of this entire day might be improved with my help. Will you allow me to walk ahead of the group with you? Terris and Jalni with Nimah's help and Lallee as runner can bring up the rear.", and smiling mysteriously he turned towards the entrance and they filed out behind him.

The hushed company moved down into the passages that led down through the ancient cavern system and then as Jalni stepped forward, there was a subtle shift, a feeling that the walls around them flowed like liquid basalt and ahead of them excited children were bounding out, into Home Cave.

"That was weird!", Calar was saying to a bemused Jalni, "I felt as if the walls were doing the travelling.", and Brus agreed, saying as he threw himself down to rest:

"Wow! Flying through rock.", and he demonstrated a cross between swimming and flying, until Terris poked him with a walking staff and told him to settle down and gradually the children began their pre-journey rest, as the sun drew on through the hottest part of the day.

By common consent the seniors left the teens in charge and withdrew to Solana's workroom, where Terris lit the little brazier to make warm drinks and Jalni headed for the Sandsinger's remedy box. She was leafing through the medicines, when an amused voice tickled her ear.

"Jalni mio, I don't think we'll need all that do you?", and she stared in consternation at the growing pile under her hand. She gulped and said in a bewildered voice, "I don't know where they came from! I didn't think there were that many in the box. How very odd.".

She felt a little light-headed and Terris, handing her a mug of Stemmis said comfortably, "Oh many's the time Solana and I swore we'd run out of something only to find another bag, box or barrel round the corner, tucked out of sight.", and Lallee, hanging in the background whispered,

"Grandfather!", rolling her eyes. However, Daro had caught the flare of Azure as Jalni's tattoos glowed with transient power and he said comfortably,

"Well, I suggest we pack some extra's and put the rest back in the box.", and automatically Jalni complied.

Marran drew Daro away shortly thereafter, leaving Lallee with Terris and making sure that none of the children could hear, spoke softly.

"Solana told me that I should take my short bow and an arrow soaked in pitch, to fire the village before we leave. She was determined that her warding would hold until then, but we must make sure Daro! I couldn't bear others to stray unaware to their deaths.".

Daro said quietly, "You are right my friend. I have held the warding since you learned my secret, but even I can't maintain it once we leave. Solana's weave will hold until tonight, but I hear what you say. This last task is yours, but I will ensure that your family's funeral pyre is effective. I can also leave the children with an experience that will draw them back, when the time is right.".

He didn't elaborate, but sat, comfortably established in Solana's big chair and told Lallee stories of his childhood in Selesh. The scent of drying herbs, the calm bubble of the brazier heated water and the increasing warmth, eventually sent all but Jalni, Daro and Lallee in search of their blankets and then Sentinel appeared.

He simply materialised in the doorway and Daro touched Lallee gently to rouse her, but laid a finger on his lips, to ensure her silence as he warded the room. Jalni looked up and rose from the bench where she had been sitting and said quietly:

"My lord Sentinel.", and dipped a little curtsey to the old man, who remained where he stood, plainly at ease in this company. Daro felt the child's intense interest sharpen and touching the Malachite segment of his Seguidor whispered in Lallee's ear.

"Shush! She doesn't know yet. She has been quieted by her training as a Healer, but I think she is rising Azure. I have no idea when she will come to her power and I cannot call you, until she has. Not all of us know who we are until quite late on, so make the most of understanding your place and work hard at your studies.".

Lallee observed,

"I bet she gave them hell at Selesh!", gruffly sympathetic and then at his nod, slipped from his lap and went to Sentinel, reaching up to hold his hand quite naturally. Jalni stared, her head on one side and then said slowly,

"Does that mean what I think it does?", and the laughter lines on Sentinels face deepened as he said briskly:

"Yes indeed it does.", and then to Daro's consternation, Sentinel said in a businesslike manner, "and you too can see me.".

For a moment Jalni mutely considered this and then she said harshly, "Do I have any choice?", and Sentinel sighed.

"If you mean to ask a question, be precise my girl. That you can see me? No, it is indicative of the direction your power will take. Do you have choice over becoming Sandsinger? Of course you have choice, but until another with greater potential rises, your bonded Lord cannot undertake the task he must perform.".

To Jalni this pronouncement sounded like a death - sentence and her pale face and mutinous eyes showed how she felt more clearly than any words. The old man continued affably:

"Now, there is no need to get in a taking over that. You simply have more potential to become Sandsinger at this time than any other. That is the way of it, none of us can change it, but no destiny is inevitable, so relax, forget it, let it go and get on with your life.".

Jalni's appalled expression dissolved suddenly as she shook her head in bewilderment and said blankly, "I'm sorry everyone. What were you saying Daro, I seem to have lost my place?", She rose and went to the door saying in a weary voice:

"I must lie down before I fall down!", and oblivious of Sentinel, made her way to Daro's blanket roll, spread her bed to one side, lay down and went dreamlessly to sleep.

Lallee stared after her reprovingly, "Grandfather, she walked right past you and didn't do you honour. She ignores Ichspeller Selunsanni a lot too and I don't think she wants to be Sandsinger either. She is very mixed up!", and Sentinel chuckled.

"My fault child, I don't want her fighting the call, so I have removed the memory of my presence. Can you work with that Selunsanni?", and Daro grinned.

"I will do my best.", He sobered suddenly asking,

"Will I see you again?", and Sentinel said easily, "Many times my boy. You can summon me when you need help, wherever you care.", and his hand strayed to Lallee's pale hair, which he ruffled as he said slowly:

"As I am mentor to the Opal, so will he mentor you from now. I am here for emergencies as well, but Daro must take the lead. Soon you will be in Selesh and fostered with kind people. Daro will ensure that you have access to him at all times and we shall meet again, but for now sweeting, you too must forget.".

The old man's hands caught up his Seguidor and a surge of crystal bloomed, sparking reflexions across Lallee's eyes, as she sighed, slumping against Daro, instantly asleep. Sentinel passed a weary hand over his own face, sighing hugely before commenting, "Ah well. They'll both remember at the right time!".

Daro stood and clasped forearms with Sentinel, leaving the sleeping child in his chair.

"How can I mentor a child who knows more than I do?", he asked ruefully and Sentinel said sympathetically, "You will learn faster because you are Opal, because you are grown and do not have the normal learning of childhood to slow you down. You can be a big brother to a parentless child. She can't wake her Sands until puberty, by which time, Sandsingers will be old news and her rise to power will be easier for that.".

He reached out and Daro caught in a rising tide of power said helplessly, "Don't make me forget Grandfather, please!", and Sentinel said softly,

"Never. As Star Weaver to your Sandsinger, I am but one of your own three Guardians. You will learn more when the time comes. I simply wanted to give you my blessing boy!", and Daro felt a gentle touch on his forehead, then Sentinel was gone.

He stood bereft for a moment, then he unwarded the room and carrying the sleeping child on one shoulder, allowed his Staff to guide him back to Home Cave, where he tucked Lallee into Jalmi's bed, found his own and slept.

The evening fell, clear but cool and for a while the activity in Home Cave warmed and encouraged the children, but after a hurried supper, preparations to depart dampened the mood. Even Brus and Calar became quiet and then Marran stood and walked to the entrance and turned.

"Nightlingbys.", he called and the patrols started to form up, until every child was ranged in a group made up so that for every seventh child, there were a pair of patrol "parents". They waited until Marran had inspected them, checking that they all had water flasks, carried spare stoppers and knew who to report to along the way. Terris issued backpacks and blankets, Jalni counted heads and then they were ready and Daro joined them. He squatted to examine the peculiar sledge that the seniors had made and then said quietly. "One or two adjustments I think.", and touched his Staff to the runners, which glowed, lengthened and then floated the sledge a finger-span above the ground. The boys who drew the short straws and had to drag the sledge whooped with excitement and they streamed out of Home Cave and turned towards the moonlit ramp down into the crater. Daro drew on the strength of the Sands, holding a hand clasped loosely around his Seguidor, he moved off with Marran ready to guide him, allowing Jalni to follow and noting her strange reluctance to leave Scartel.

Even the children had fallen silent as they reached the point closest to the dark huddle in the centre of the crater, where they paused to linger, staring at the warded village. Daro waited quietly while Marran made his preparations and then at the low voiced, "Ready!", he stepped forward, fully empowered as a gentle lament came to him. He had never heard his *othervoice* achieve such authority and instinctively knowing that this memory would sustain them through many Rotations, he allowed his own memories of Scartel to guide the melody. A sighing wind gentled hair, blowing soft kisses on tear stained faces. A ghostly threnody of voices filled the air with farewells and in the rapt darkness a voice said quietly in Marran's ear.

"Now!", as Daro's *othervoice* soared, into the night.

Marran felt the flash as the pitch soaked arrow ignited. Ignoring the temptation to let loose, he leant his head into his shoulder remembering Daro's instructions to visualise his target and thought of his Grandfather's hawking loft. It stood high and central to a run of wooden houses that lined the main street. He drew a steadying breath, whispered his Grandfather's name and the arrow rose in a glimmering streak and Daro "followed" it. The fire blossomed, fuelled by the inexorable energy of the Source, it grew, pulsing in waves which devoured all that lay in its path. The good, the bad, the polluted and the dead themselves were cleansed in fire, passing beyond the call of man into the annals of history. Then, from the glowing embers of the village something else grew, drawing all eyes.

Framed in the crater, there was a ghostly city. Towers and turrets, domes and arched bridges and suddenly Jalni saw that the strange ruin they called Gateway, had once been the arch of a far greater bridge. Some disaster had precipitated it into the place that it now occupied, bringing with it other buildings. Once, great piles of salvage had been used to build the village, to construct ordinary homes. Her eyes widened, as pure as the flowing tones of the melody, sprang waterfalls and fountains and the dark stained and empty wasteland of the great crater was filled with the sound of happy laughter, warbling fly-bys and the chiming of tiny bells, echoing in the streets of the ghostly city. Daro imprinted the melody in his memory and the images in the minds of the fascinated children, determined to show Beneva these echoes of the past, then the great city faded, back to the Rotations of sleep it had enjoyed since it had last been seen by man.

As the echoes from the great ring of mountains died away, Jalni already held a separate flask containing restorative and Terris swiftly helped him step back into their previous formation, eyes and Staff alight with Opal fire. He turned to the silent children and said quietly,

"Now do you see what you have to come back for? You will be the builders, you will prepare the way. You have been saved for a purpose and that purpose is to rebuild Shjaratel, to the glory of she who will rule here, that other shade of Mystery, the Sandsinger of the Azure Sands.".

As his *othervoice* died away, leaving a reflection of the glory they had seen on every face, Marran, grandson of the last Ranger of Scartel, lifted a hand, eyes gleaming and said firmly,

"I'll drink to that!", and turning without a backward glance, led his people into the Azure Sands and a brave new future.

Epilogue

By the hand of Carolus. In much confusion and pain.

When in the twentieth Rotation of his life, the Opal Sandsinger turned his feet from othersands and started his long way home, I had recently received a summons from Beneva, Guardian of Knowledge, resident at Selesh.

"Come home Carolus!", she begged, "There is much afoot and Daro has need of your wisdom.".

I watched her reflection in my scrying dish and saw her colour faintly and couldn't resist teasing her a little.

"Don't tell me that he has taken a wife?", I remember saying and she gave me a very strange look and said gently,

"No, worse than that, he has taken Jalni across to Scartel. Haven't you noticed that the sun shines once more?",

I could hardly tell her where I was, but she saw my good friend Olneth over my shoulder and said softly, "Aah.", then, "I assume you gentlemen know what you are doing? Keep safe.", and the glass cleared.

Olneth stared at me. "Recall?", was all he said and though I hated to frustrate his search for his son, I nodded. We rose silently and stealthily made our way to the cavern where Olneth had found a way to breach the barrier that surrounds these Sands. Swiftly disposing of disguises, we departed, careful to remove all trace of our passage.

It was night in the Opal and bitter cold. Heading, as always, to the crossing at Tearchan, where my Zeglurs were turned out in pasture, we took our riding beasts and a couple of pack animals and headed back to Selesh, at a spanking pace arriving just before dawn.

That was a sight to behold. As we approached Selesh, the grey light streaked the sky, then came a glorious harmony of sound from the crystal bearing rocks around us. We shaded our eyes as Seleus rose and watched in wonder as the colours bloomed in the Sand and then we were being taken off our mounts, surrounded by our friends, all anxious to tell us what had occurred during my long absence and then the torrent of news died away and she was there.

Ikella, my Sorceress, my friend, stood staring at me and I thought that she somehow looked different. Older suddenly, sad definitely and my heart sank as I asked:

"What news of my Songchild then?".

I was shocked to see tears on her face, but she shook her head, stubbornly ignoring them and said softly, "It would take a lifetime to tell all of it Carolus. Save that Daro returned and we have made our peace.".

Her voice was level, with no hint of what she was about to say, when she raised brimming eyes and said flatly, "He was right. All those Rotations of fighting an instinctive knowledge, wasted Rotations in exile have only led him to disaster. O yes, he is Sandsinger, but what use is magic to a blind man? What use was that power when Ahnell died in its pursuit?".

I had hardly taken in these words, when the same eyes blazed angrily green and she said,

"I always wondered who gave him his strange ideas and now I am sure. I blame you Carolus! I blame you!".

Now I wait in Selesh Minoria and listen to the tales about Ichspeller Selunsanni. Tonight I drink with Lown, First of the Sandsworn and I mourn the loss of my quarters , my position of trust and I grieve for what might have been and wonder what I have done to my Songchild. My Ichspeller Selunsanni, knowing that only time will tell.".

END

Now read on...

"Excerpt from Song of Sorcery".

When tragedy overcame them, it didn't come gently. There was no gradual failing wrought upon them by fatigue, or the manifestation of the dreaded plague that haunted their every footstep as they wended their way west towards the Drekken Pass and safety in Selesh. No, tragedy had struck savagely, silencing even the most cheerful childish chatter, piercing them all with the single terrorised scream as the path collapsed under the feet of Daro's guide. There was a roar of coruscating stones, a chorus of horrified shrieks, a sickening thud, then a pathetic whimper from below.

The Sandsinger cried out, his very protest empowering the protective aura that he cast around the others teetering on the edge of the crumbling track. It formed, a blossom of opalescence, locking them in mid –stride, a man's span from the edge that had launched Brus, down, down to crash into the rocks below the mountain track and held so, the wail of the distraught and disorientated party mocked the Sandsinger for his temerity in thinking that he could protect them.

As soon as Daro recovered his own feet, freeing the adults to bring his charges over the gap that had appeared in the track, they formed a weeping huddle, in which Terris, the would be Apothecary moved solicitously, bending over a child here and there, calming, comforting, reassuring, leaving Jalni Daro's healer and young Marran, to contrive the retrieval of Brus's body, for there was no doubt in any mind that he must have perished.

Jalni stood steadily, grim-faced as she payed out the rope that Marran had silently hitched around her body, slowly guiding it for Daro, who took the physical strain of supporting the Ranger who swung perilously off the over-hang below. There was a sheen on Daro's skin, his half open eyes revealed a whorl of fire opal burning in their blind depths, as the muscles stood out on his chest and arms. She trembled, her own hands clawing painfully as she guided the rope, aware that his breath had shortened to tortured gasps. An increasingly panicky mantra had begun to chatter through her mind, "O, how can I help him? What can I do?", when she thankfully felt the light touch of Lladro's hand, as he took up the loose end of the rope, adding himself as anchorman in this silent tug of life and death.

Daro's neck braced backward as a new strain was placed on the ominously creaking rope. His teeth gritted as Marran began an uncertain ascent , then Jalni was transfixed as Daro employed both the ancient powers within his belt clasp and fob, which blazed a line of fire through the hand plaited rope. She heard a hiss of amazement from Lladro as he too felt the whisper of some otherstrength reinforcing their grip, then was caught fast in the gleam of Daro's slowly opening eyes, as the power took him.

Those Opal fired orbs sought her soul and her will fled, subjugated by the hypnotic flicker of iced fire as his compelling othervoice commanded her obedience.

"Bind your strength to my purpose, subject your will to mine, strength to strength, soul to soul, surrender and know only that you are Opal-sworn, bondswoman mine.".

Aware of a gasp of wonder behind her and a whisper of awe from the children, she concentrated, channelling her own not inconsiderable strength into his grip, empowering his tautening sinews, lifting his chest to help him breathe and thus reinforced, Daro doubled his efforts, drawing Marran over the edge of the pathway and into the willing hands awaiting both him and the tiny, limp and broken shape he shouldered.

There was no time to waste here, no room to manoeuvre, yet Marran cradled the child's body protectively and in the fading of the day the Rangers face (white beneath the tan) looked shocked as he said gruffly.

"He still breathes, we have to make for Sholtan's Gap if he is to stand any chance…"

Coming in 2011

"Song of Sorcery."

Returning from Scartel to safety, Daro and Jalni are shaken by the death of a child. As Daro questions his faith in magic, Jalni decides that if he can face the past of a world, she can face her own and slips away unseen.

En route to Jerritol, followed by an old friend, she encounters Orto and decides to help him find the Tapestry of Tten. At the Temple of the Winds there's no trace of the relic, but the Oracle predicts, Jalni will become, "Mother to the Tenth Wind.".

Frightened by this concept, Jalni retreats to Darnesh, but when the Sorceress Tirjella is poisoned, she usurps Sandsinger powers and saves her. Returning to Selesh, Jalni can predict Ikella's reaction, but Daro's she couldn't have foreseen in a thousand Rotations!

Empathise with Jalni's struggle to control her own destiny. Watch Daro confront the limitations of his power and smile as Jalni finds love. Does it last? Read the sequel, "Sword of Honour" to find out.

"The Tapestry of Tten", a gripping series of Fantasy Fiction novels by Julia Caesar is published by arima Publishing. To order, please visit our website, http://www.arimapublishing.co.uk , or write to us at,

arima publishing
ASK House
Northgate Avenue
Bury St Edmunds
Suffolk
IP32 6BB
UK

"Sword of Honour."

Gravely shaken by her experiences in Darnesh, Jalni has retreated to seek Daro's protection once more and for once her happiness is complete, but her past reaches out again, luring her back to Scartel as the eldest survivors demand to return. Already unsettled by Daro's frequent "absences", as he journeys about with his Ranger, Jalni contemplates returning to Scartel permanently, but her Healing skills appear to have deserted her and she seeks Beneva's advice with devastating consequences.

Her reactions and her determination to follow her own destiny take her into the Ashgenar wilderness once more under the protection of Marran, who becomes guardian of her secrets in spite of bearing the Opal Sandsinger's Sword of Honour. What Jalni will find in this remote and deserted wilderness will ensure the survival of her kind, but she must sacrifice her most precious possession in order to find her way.

The reader must bear Jalni's pain and disappointment. Watch her find her purpose and endure the Rangers vigil before they go looking for "The Shadow of the Singer".

"The Tapestry of Tten", a gripping series of Fantasy Fiction novels by Julia Caesar is published by arima Publishing. To order, please visit our website, http://www.arimapublishing.co.uk , or write to us at,

arima publishing
ASK House
Northgate Avenue
Bury St Edmunds
Suffolk
IP32 6BB
UK

RNIB Talking Books - A message from the Author.

A proportion of the purchase price of this book, is being donated by the author to RNIB, The Royal National Institute for Blind and Partially Sighted People and will be directed to their National Library Service which runs the Talking Book Service and the Learning and Skills Library. These provide visually Impaired people with an accessible source of entertainment and education, through the conversion of books into an audio format, known as DAISY (Digitally Accessible Information System). This is a unique system that allows navigation of audio books.

The resulting CD's dropping through the letterbox are a powerful tool in the battle for equality, giving blind and partially sighted people access to thousands of books which were previously not available. This lifeline service is invaluable to some tens of thousands of people across the UK.

"You have already supported this significant service simply by buying my book, but if you want to help further the aim of making it possible for all books to become accessible to Visually Impaired Readers, or need information about the RNIB Please call their helpline on

0303 123 9999 or visit www.rnib.org.uk

Thank you for your support,

Julia Cæsar

Where can you find out more about the Tapestry of Tten and get regular updates about forthcoming books?

Why not visit
www.sandsingers.co.uk

The official home of The Tapestry of Tten and find out more about the fascinating world of Pelshar. Get a feel for this troubled planet, find out about the Clans, the culture and the ideas that drove Julia to write the series. Find out about the parallels between our world and theirs, follow the characters, study the maps and see where they lead.

Website designed and maintained by our friends at
Red Dragon I.T. Ltd

+44 1303 723456   www.rdit.co.uk